USA TODAY bestselling author **Kat Cantrell** read her first Mills & Boon novel in third grade and has been scribbling in notebooks since she learned to spell. She's a So You Think You Can Write winner and a Romance Writers of America Golden Heart® Award finalist. Kat, her husband and their two boys live in north Texas.

In Name Only

KAT CANTRELL

MILLS & BOON

® and ™ are trademarks owned and used by the trademark owner and/or its licensee. Trademarks marked with ® are registered with the United Kingdom Patent Office and/or the Office for Harmonisation in the Internal Market and in other countries.

First Published in Great Britain 2019
by Mills & Boon, an imprint of HarperCollins*Publishers*
1 London Bridge Street, London, SE1 9GF

IN NAME ONLY © 2019 Harlequin Books S. A.

Best Friend Bride © 2017 Kat Cantrell
One Night Stand Bride © 2017 Kat Cantrell
Contract Bride © 2018 Kat Cantrell

ISBN: 978-0-263-27483-7

0419

BEST FRIEND BRIDE

KAT CANTRELL

One

Jonas Kim would typically describe himself as humble, but even he was impressed with the plan he'd conceived to outwit the smartest man he knew—his grandfather. Instead of marrying Sun, the nice woman from a prominent Korean family, a bride Grandfather had picked out, Jonas had proposed to Viviana Dawson. She was nice, too, but also his friend and, more importantly, someone he could trust not to contest the annulment when it came time to file it.

Not only was Viv amazing for agreeing to this ridiculous idea, she made excellent cupcakes. It was a win all the way around. Though he could have done without the bachelor party. So not his thing.

At least no strippers had shown up. Yet.

He and his two best buddies had flown to Vegas this morning and though Jonas had never been to the city of sin before, he was pretty sure it wouldn't take much to have naked women draped all over the suite. He could think of little he'd like less. Except for marrying Sun. That he would hate, and not only because she'd been selected on his behalf. Sun was a disaster waiting to happen that would happen to someone else because Jonas was marrying Viv tomorrow in what would go down as the greatest favor one friend had ever done for another.

"Sure you wanna do this?" Warren asked as he popped open the bottle of champagne.

Also a bachelor party staple that Jonas could have done without, but his friends would just laugh and make jokes about how Jonas needed to loosen up, despite being well aware that he had been raised in an ultra-conservative family. Grandfather had a lot of traditional ideas about how a CEO should act, and Jonas hadn't landed that job, not yet. Besides, there was nothing wrong with having a sense of propriety.

"Which part?" Jonas shot back. "The bachelor party or inviting you morons along?"

Hendrix, the other moron, grinned and took his glass of champagne from Warren. "You can't get married without a bachelor party. That would be sad."

"It's not a real wedding. Therefore, one would assume that the traditions don't really have to be observed."

Warren shook his head. "It is a real wedding. You're going to marry this woman simply to get out of having a different bride. Hence my question. Are you sure this is the only way? I don't get why you can't just tell your grandfather thanks but no thanks. Don't let him push you around."

They'd literally been having the exact same argument for two weeks. Grandfather still held the reins of the Kim empire closely to his chest. In Korea. If Jonas had any hope of Grandfather passing those reins to him so he could move the entire operation to North Carolina, he had to watch his step. Marrying a Korean woman from a powerful family would only solidify Jonas's ties to a country that he did not consider his home.

"I respect my elders," Jonas reminded Warren mildly. "And I also respect that Sun's grandfather and my grandfather are lifelong friends. I can't expose her or it might disrupt everything."

Sun had been thrilled with the idea of marrying Jonas; she had a secret—and highly unsuitable—lover she didn't want anyone to find out about and she'd pounced on the idea of a husband to mask her affair. Meanwhile, their grandfathers were cackling over their proposed business merger once the two families were united in marriage.

Jonas wanted no part of any of that. Better to solve the problem on his own terms. If he was already married, no one could expect him to honor his grandfather's agreement. And once the merger had gone through, he and Viv could annul their marriage and go on with Jonas's integrity intact.

It was brilliant. Viv was the most awesome person on the planet for saving his butt from being burned in this deal. Tomorrow, they'd say some words, sign a piece of paper and poof. No more problems.

"Can you guys just be happy that you got a trip to Vegas out of this and shut up?" Jonas asked, and clinked glasses with the two men he'd bonded with freshman year at Duke University.

Jonas Kim, Hendrix Harris and Warren Garinger had

become instant friends when they'd been assigned to the same project group along with Marcus Powell. The four teenagers had raised a lot of hell together—most of which Jonas had watched from the sidelines—and propped each other up through everything the college experience could throw at them. Until Marcus had fallen head over heels for a cheerleader who didn't return his love. The aftermath of that still affected the surviving three members of their quartet to this day.

"Can't. You said no strippers," Hendrix grumbled, and downed his champagne in one practiced swallow. "Really don't see the point of a bachelor party in Las Vegas if you're not going to take full advantage of what's readily available."

Jonas rolled his eyes. "Like you don't have a wide array of women back in Raleigh who would get naked for you on demand."

"Yeah, but I've already seen them," he argued with a wink. "There are thousands of women whose breasts I've yet to ogle and I've been on my best behavior at home. What happens in Vegas doesn't affect my mom's campaign, right?"

Hendrix's mom was running for governor of North Carolina and had made him swear on a stack of Bibles that he would not do anything to jeopardize her chances. For Hendrix, that meant a complete overhaul of his social life, and he was feeling the pinch. So far, his uncanny ability to get photographed with scantily clad women hadn't surfaced, but he'd just begun his vow of chastity, so there was plenty of opportunity to cause a scandal if he really put his mind to it.

"Maybe we could focus on the matter at hand?" Warren suggested, and ran his fingers through his wavy brown hair as he plopped down on the love seat near the floor-to-ceiling glass wall of the Sky Suite they'd booked at the Aria. The dizzying lights of Vegas spread out in a panoramic view sixty stories below.

"Which is?"

Warren pointed his glass at Jonas. "You're getting married. Despite the pact."

The pact.

After the cheerleader had thoroughly eviscerated Marcus, he'd faded further and further away until eventually, he'd opted to end his pain permanently. In the aftermath of his death, the three friends had sworn to never let love destroy them as it had Marcus. The reminder sobered them all.

"Hey, man. The pact is sacred," Jonas said with a scowl. "But we never vowed to remain single the rest of our lives. Just that we'd never let a woman take us down like that. Love is the problem, not marriage."

Once a year, the three of them dropped whatever they were doing and spent the evening honoring the memory of their late friend. It was part homage, part reiteration of the pact. The profoundly painful incident had affected them in different ways, but no one would argue that Warren had taken his roommate's suicide harder than anyone save Marcus's mother.

That was the only reason Jonas gave him a pass for the insult. Jonas had followed the pact to the letter, which was easier than he'd ever let on. First of all, a promise meant something to him.

Second, Jonas never got near a woman he could envision falling in love with. That kind of loss of control... the concept made his skin crawl. Jonas had too much to lose to let a woman destroy everything he'd worked for.

Warren didn't look convinced. "Marriage is the gateway, my friend. You can't put a ring on a woman's finger and expect that she won't start dreaming of romantic garbage."

"Ah, but I can," Jonas corrected as he let Hendrix top off his champagne. "That's why this plan is so great. Viv knows the score. We talked about exactly what was going to happen. She's got her cupcake business and has no room for a boyfriend, let alone a permanent husband. I wouldn't have asked her to do this for me if she wasn't a good friend."

A friend who wasn't interested in taking things deeper. That was the key and the only reason Jonas had continued their friendship for so long. If there was even a possibility of getting emotional about her, he'd have axed their association immediately, just like he had with every other woman who posed a threat to the tight rein he held on his heart.

Hendrix drank straight from the champagne bottle to get the last few drops, his nearly colorless hazel eyes narrowed in contemplation as he set the empty bottle on the coffee table. "If she's such a good friend, how come we haven't met her?"

"Really? It's confusing to you why I'd want to keep her away from the man voted most likely to corrupt a nun four years in a row?"

With a grin, Hendrix jerked his head at Warren. "So Straight and Narrow over there should get the thumbs-up. Yet she's not allowed to meet him either?"

Jonas shrugged. "I'll introduce you at the ceremony tomorrow."

When it would be unavoidable. How was he supposed to explain that Viv was special to a couple of knuckleheads like his friends? From the first moment he'd met her, he'd been drawn to her sunny smile and generosity.

The little bakery near the Kim Building called Cupcaked had come highly recommended by Jonas's admin, so he'd stopped in to pick up a thank-you for his staff. As he'd stood in the surprisingly long line to place his order, a pretty brown-haired woman had exited from the back. She'd have captured his interest regardless, but when she'd stepped outside to slip a cupcake to a kid on the street who'd been standing nose pressed to her window for the better part of fifteen minutes, Jonas couldn't resist talking to her.

He'd been dropping in to get her amazing lemon cupcakes for almost a year now. Sometimes Viv let him take her for coffee to someplace where she didn't have to jump behind the counter on the fly, and occasionally she dropped by the Kim Building to take Jonas to lunch.

It was an easy, no-pressure friendship that he valued because there was no danger of him falling in too deep when she so clearly wasn't interested in more. They weren't sleeping together, and that kind of relationship wouldn't compute to his friends.

Didn't matter. He was happy with the status quo. Viv was doing him a favor and in return, he'd make it up to her with free business consulting advice for the rest of her life. After all, Jonas had singlehandedly launched Kim Electronics in the American market and had grown revenue to the tune of $4.7 billion last year. She could do worse than to have his undivided attention on her balance sheet whenever she asked, which he'd gladly make time for.

All he had to do was get her name on a marriage

certificate and lie low until his grandfather's merger went through. Then Viv could go back to her single cupcake-baker status and Jonas could celebrate dodging the bullet.

Warren's point about marriage giving a girl ideas about love and romance was pure baloney. Jonas wasn't worried about sticking to the pact. Honor was his moral compass, as it was his grandfather's. Love represented a loss of control that other men might fall prey to, but not Jonas. He would never betray his friends or the memory of the one they'd lost.

All he had to do was marry a woman who had no romantic feelings for him.

Viviana Dawson had dreamed about her wedding day a bunch of times and not once had she imagined the swirl in her gut, which could only be described as a cocktail of nerves and *holy crap*.

Jonas was going to be her husband in a few short minutes and the anticipation of *what if* was killing her.

Jonas Kim had asked her to marry him. *Jonas.* The man who had kept Viv dateless for almost a year because who could measure up to perfection? Nobody.

Oh, sure, he'd framed it all as a favor and she'd accepted under the premise that they'd be filing for annulment ASAP. But still. She'd be Mrs. Kim for as long as it lasted.

Which might be short indeed if he figured out she had a huge crush on him.

He wasn't going to figure it out. Because *oh, my God.* If he did find out...

Well, he couldn't. It would ruin their friendship for one. And also? She had no business getting into a serious relationship, not until she figured out how to do and be whatever the opposite was of what she'd been doing and being with men thus far in her adult dating life.

Her sisters called it clingy. She called it committed. Men called it quits.

Jonas was the antidote to all that.

The cheesy chapel wasn't anything close to the venue of her fantasies, but she'd have married Jonas in a wastewater treatment plant if he'd asked her to. She pushed open the door, alone and not too happy about it. In retrospect, she should have insisted one of her sisters come to Vegas with her. Maybe to act as her maid of honor.

She could really use a hand to hold right about now, but no. She hadn't told any of her sisters she was getting married, not even Grace, who was closest to her in age and had always been her confidante. Well, until Grace had disappeared into her own family in much the same fashion as their other two sisters had done.

Viv was the cute pony in the Dawson family stable of Thoroughbreds. Which was the whole reason Viv hadn't mentioned her quickie Vegas wedding to a man who'd never so much as kissed her.

She squared her shoulders. A fake marriage was exactly what she wanted. Mostly.

Well, of course she wanted a real marriage eventually. But this one would get her into the secret club that the rest of the married Dawson sisters already belonged to. Plus, Jonas needed her. Total win across the board.

The chapel was hushed and far more sacrosanct than she'd have expected in what was essentially the drive-through lane of weddings. The quiet scuttled across her skin, turning it clammy. She was really doing this. It had all been conceptual before. Now it was real.

Could you have a nervous breakdown and recover in less than two minutes? She didn't want to miss a second of her wedding. But she might need to sit down first.

And then everything fell away as she saw Jonas in a slim-fitting dark suit that showcased his wiry frame. His energy swept out and engulfed her, as it always had from that first time she'd turned to see him standing outside her shop, his attention firmly on her instead of the sweet treats in the window.

Quick with a smile, quicker with a laugh, Jonas Kim's beautiful angular face had laced Viv's dreams many a night. He had a pretty rocking body, too. He kept in great shape playing racquetball with his friends, and she'd spent hours picturing him shirtless, his chest glistening as he swung a racket. In short, he was a truly gorgeous individual who she could never study long enough to sate herself.

Jonas's dark, expressive eyes lit up as he caught sight of her and he crossed the small vestibule to sweep her into a hug. Her arms came up around his waist automatically. How, she had no idea, when this was literally the first time he'd ever touched her.

He even smelled gorgeous.

And now would be a great time to unstick her tongue from the roof of her mouth. "Hey."

Wonderful. They'd had spirited debates on everything from the travesty of pairing red wine with fish to the merits of the beach over the mountains. Shakespeare, *The Simpsons*. But put her in the arms of the man she'd been salivating over for months and the power of speech deserted her.

He stepped back. Didn't help. And now she was cold.

"I'm so glad you're here," he said, his smooth voice

ruffling all her nerve endings in the most delicious way. Despite being born in North Carolina, he had almost no accent. Good thing. He was already devastating enough.

"Can't have a wedding with no bride," she informed him. Oh, thank God, she could still talk, Captain Obvious moment aside. "Am I dressed okay for a fake marriage?"

His intense eyes honed in on her. "You look amazing. I love that you bought a new dress for this."

Yeah, that was why she passed up the idiots who hit on her with lame lines like "Give me your number and I'll frost your cupcakes for you." Jonas paid attention to her and actually noticed things like what she wore. She'd picked out this yellow dress because he'd mentioned once that he liked the color.

Which made it all the more strange that he'd never clued in that she had a huge thing for him. She was either better at hiding it than she'd had a right to hope for, or he knew and mercifully hadn't mentioned it.

Her pulse sped out of control. He didn't know, she repeated silently. Maybe a little desperately.

There was no way he could know. He'd never have asked her to do this marriage favor otherwise.

She'd been faking it this long. No reason to panic.

"I wanted to look good," she told him. *For you.* "For the pictures."

He smiled. "Mission accomplished. I want you to meet Warren."

Jonas turned, absently putting his arm around her and oh, that was nice. They were a unit already, and it had seemed to come so naturally. Did he feel it, too?

That's when she realized there was another man in the vestibule. Funny, she hadn't even noticed him, though she supposed women must fawn all over him, with those cheekbones and that expensive haircut. She held out her hand to the friend Jonas had talked endlessly about. "Nice to meet you. Jonas speaks very highly of you."

"Likewise," Warren said with a cryptic glance at Jonas. "And I'm sure whatever he's told you is embellished."

Doubtful when she didn't need Jonas's help to know that the energy drink company his friend ran did very well. You couldn't escape the logo for Flying Squirrel no matter where you looked.

Jonas waved that off with a smirk. "Whatever, man. Where's Hendrix?"

"Not my turn to babysit him." Warren shrugged, pulling out his phone. "I'll text him. He'll be here."

Somehow, Jonas seemed to have forgotten his arm was still around Viv's waist and she wasn't about to remind him. But then he guided her toward the open double doors that led to the interior of the chapel with firm fingers. Well, if this almost-intimacy was part of the wedding package, she'd take it.

"I'm not waiting on his sorry ass," Jonas called over his shoulder. "There are a thousand more couples in line behind us and I'm not losing my spot."

Warren nodded and waved, still buried in his phone.

"Some friends," Jonas murmured to her with a laugh, his head bent close. He was still taller than her even when she wore heels, but it had never been as apparent as it was today, since she was still tucked against his side as if he never meant to let go. "This is an important day in my life and you see how they are."

"I'm here." For as long as he needed her.

Especially if he planned to put his arm around her a whole bunch more. His warm palm on her waist had oddly settled her nerves. And put a whole different kind of butterfly south of her stomach.

Wow, was it hot in here or what? She resisted the urge to fan herself as the spark zipped around in places that *could not* be so affected by this man's touch.

His smile widened. "Yes, you are. Have I mentioned lately how much I appreciate that? The slot for very best friend in the whole world has just become yours, since clearly you're the only one who deserves it."

As reminders went, it was both brutal and necessary. This was a favor. Not an excuse for a man to get handsy with her.

Fine. Good. She and Jonas were friends, which was perfect. She had a habit of pouring entirely too much of herself into a man who didn't return her level of commitment. Mark had stuck it out slightly longer than Zachary, and she didn't like to think about how quickly she'd shed Gary and Judd. A sad commentary on her twenties that she'd had fewer boyfriends than fingers on one hand.

A favor marriage was the best kind because she knew exactly how it would end. It was like reading the last page of the book ahead of time, and for someone who loved surprise flowers but hated surprise discussions that started with "we have to talk," the whole thing sounded really great.

No pressure. No reason to get clingy and drive Jonas away with her neediness. She could be independent and witty and build her confidence with this marriage. It was a practice run with all the best benefits. He'd already asked her to move into his penthouse on Boylan

Avenue. As long as she didn't mess up and let on how much she wanted to cling to every last inch of the man, it was all good.

Back on track, she smiled at the friend she was about to marry. They were friends with benefits that had nothing to do with sex. A point she definitely needed to keep in the forefront of her brain.

A lady in a puke-green suit approached them and verified they were the happy couple, then ran down the order of the ceremony. If this had been a real marriage, Viv might be a little disappointed in the lack of fanfare. In less than a minute, traditional organ music piped through the overhead speakers and the lady shoved a drooping bouquet at Viv. She clutched it to her chest, wondering if she'd get to keep it. One flower was enough. She'd press it into a book as a reminder of her wedding to a great man who treated her with nothing but kindness and respect.

Jonas walked her down the aisle, completely unruffled. Of course. Why would he be nervous? This was all his show and he'd always had a supreme amount of confidence no matter the situation.

His friend Warren stood next to an elderly man holding a Bible. Jonas halted where they'd been told to stand and glanced at her with a reassuring smile.

"Dearly beloved," the man began and was immediately interrupted by a commotion at the back. Viv and Jonas both turned to see green-suit lady grappling with the door as someone tried to get into the room.

"Sir, the ceremony has already started," she called out to no avail as the man who must be Hendrix Harris easily shoved his way inside and joined them at the front.

Yep. He looked just like the many, many pictures she'd seen of him strewn across the media, and not just because his mother was running for governor. Usually he had a gorgeous woman glued to his side and they were doing something overly sensual, like kissing as if no one was watching.

"Sorry," he muttered to Jonas. His eyes were bloodshot and he looked like he'd slept in his expensively tailored shirt and pants.

"Figured you'd find a way to make my wedding memorable," Jonas said without malice, because that's the kind of man he was. She'd have a hard time being so generous with someone who couldn't be bothered to show up on time.

The officiant started over, and in a few minutes, she and Jonas exchanged vows. All fake, she chanted to herself as she promised to love and cherish.

"You may kiss the bride," the officiant said with so little inflection that it took a minute for it to sink in that he meant *Jonas* could kiss *her*. Her pulse hit the roof.

Somehow, they hadn't established what would happen here. She glanced at Jonas and raised a brow. Jonas hesitated.

"This is the part where you kiss her, idiot," Hendrix muttered with a salacious grin.

This was her one chance, the only time she had every right to put her lips on this man, and she wasn't missing the opportunity. The other people in the room vanished as she flattened her palms on Jonas's lapels. He leaned in and put one hand on her jaw, guiding it upward. His warmth bled through her skin, enlivening it, and then her brain ceased to function as his mouth touched hers.

Instantly, that wasn't enough and she pressed forward, seeking more of him. The kiss deepened as his lips aligned properly and oh, yes, that was it.

Her crush exploded into a million little pieces as she tasted what it was like to kiss Jonas. That nice, safe attraction she had been so sure she could hide gained teeth, slicing through her midsection with sharp heat. The dimensions of sensation opened around her, giving her a tantalizing glimpse of how truly spectacular it would feel if he didn't stop.

But he did stop, stepping back so quickly that she almost toppled over. He caught her forearms and held her steady…though he looked none too steady himself, his gaze enigmatic and heated in a way she'd never witnessed before.

Clearly that experience had knocked them both for a loop. What did you say to someone you'd just kissed and who you wanted to kiss again, but really, that hadn't been part of the deal?

"That was nice," Jonas murmured. "Thanks."

Nice was not the word on her mind. So they were going to pretend that hadn't just happened, apparently.

Good. That was exactly what they should do. Treat it like a part of the ceremony and move on.

Except her lips still tingled, and how in the world was Jonas just standing there holding her hand like nothing momentous had occurred? She needed to learn the answer to that, stat. Especially if they were going to be under the same roof. Otherwise, their friendship—and this marriage—would be toast the second he clued in to how hot and bothered he got her. He'd specifically told her that he could trust her because they were *friends* and he needed her to be one.

"I now pronounce you husband and wife," the officiant intoned, completely oblivious to how the earth had just swelled beneath Viv's feet.

Jonas turned and led her back up the aisle, where they signed the marriage license. They ended up in the same vestibule they'd been in minutes before, but now they were married.

Her signature underneath Jonas's neat script made it official, but as she'd expected, it was just a piece of paper. The kiss, on the other hand? That had shaken her to the core.

How was she going to stop herself from angling for another one?

"Well," Hendrix said brightly. "I'd say this calls for a drink. I'll buy."

Two

Jonas had never thought of his six-thousand-square-foot penthouse condo as small. Until today. It was full of Viviana Dawson. Er, *Kim*. Viviana Kim. She'd officially changed her name at the Department of Motor Vehicles, and soon, she'd have a new driver's license that said she had the legal right to call herself that. By design. His sense of honor wouldn't permit him to outright lie about his relationship with Viv; therefore, she was Mrs. Kim in every sense of the word.

Except one.

The concept was surreal. As surreal as the idea that she was his wife and he could introduce her as such to anyone who asked.

Except for himself apparently because he was having a hard time thinking of her that way no matter how many times he repeated the word *wife* when he glimpsed her through the archway leading to the kitchen. Boxes upon boxes covered every inch of the granite countertops, and though she'd been working on unpacking them for an hour, it looked like she'd barely made a dent.

He should quit skulking around and get in there to help. But he hadn't because he couldn't figure out how to manage the weird vibe that had sprung up between them.

That *kiss*.

It had opened up a Pandora's box that he didn't know how to close. Before, he'd had a sort of objective understanding that Viv was a beautiful woman whose company he enjoyed.

Ever since the ceremony, no more. There was a thin veil of awareness that he couldn't shake. But he needed to. They were living together as *friends* because she'd agreed to a favor that didn't include backing her up against the counter so he could explore her lush mouth.

He liked Viv. Add a previously undiscovered attraction and she was exactly the kind of woman he'd studiously avoided for nearly a decade. The kind he could easily envision taking him deeper and deeper until he was emotionally overwhelmed enough to give up everything.

The problem of course being that he couldn't stop calling her, like he usually did with women who threatened his vow. He'd married this one.

He was being ridiculous. What was he, seventeen? He could handle a little spark between friends, right? Best way to manage that was to ignore it. And definitely not let on that he'd felt something other than friendly ever since kissing her.

All he and Viv had to do was live together until he could convince his grandfather to go through with the merger anyway. Once the two companies signed agreements, neither would back out and Jonas was home free. Since he was covering Viv's rent until then, she could move back into her apartment at that point.

This plan would work, and soon enough, he could look back on it smugly and pinpoint the exact moment when he'd outsmarted his grandfather.

Casually, he leaned on the exposed-brick column between the dining room and the kitchen and crossed his arms like everything was cool between them. It *would* be cool. "What can I do?"

Viv jerked and spun around to face him, eyes wide. "You scared me. Obviously."

Her nervous laugh ruffled his spine. So they were both feeling the weirdness, but it was clearly different weirdness on her side than on his. She was jumpy and nervous, not hot and bothered. He had not seen that coming. That was…not good. "Sorry. I didn't mean to. We've both been living alone for so long that I guess we have to get through an adjustment period."

Which was the opposite of what he'd expected. They'd always been so relaxed with each other. How could they get back to that?

She nodded. "Yes, that's what I've been telling myself."

Was it that bad? Her forlorn voice tripped something inside him and it was not okay that she was uncomfortable around him now. "Best way to adjust is to spend time together. Let me help you put away these…" He grabbed a square glass dish from the counter. "Pans?"

"Pyrex." She smiled and it seemed like it came easier. "I can't imagine you care anything about where I put my bakeware."

He waggled his brows. "That depends on whether that's something you use to make cupcakes or not."

Her cupcakes weren't like the store-bought ones in the hard plastic clamshells. Those tasted like sugared flour with oily frosting. Viv's lemon cupcakes—a flavor he'd never have said he'd like—had a clean, bright taste like she'd captured lemonade in cake form.

"It's not. Casseroles."

"Not a fan of those." He made a face before he thought better of it.

Maybe she loved casseroles and he was insulting her taste. And her cooking skills. But he'd never said one word about her whipping up dinner for him each night, nor did he expect her to. She knew that. Right?

They had so much to learn about each other, especially if they were going to make this marriage seem as real as possible to everyone, except select few people they could trust, like Warren and Hendrix. If word got back to his grandfather that something wasn't kosher, the charade would be over.

And he'd invested way too much in this marriage to let it fail now.

His phone beeped from his pocket, and since the CEO never slept, he handed over the glass dish to check the message.

Grandfather. At 6:00 a.m. Seoul time. Jonas tapped the message. All the blood drained from his head.

"Jonas, what's wrong?" Viv's palm came to rest on his forearm and he appreciated the small bit of comfort even as it stirred things it shouldn't.

"My grandfather. My dad told him that we got married." Because Jonas had asked him to. The whole point had been to circumvent his grandfather's arranged-marriage plan. But this—

"Oh, no. He's upset, isn't he?" Viv worried her lip with her teeth, distracting him for a moment.

"On the contrary," Jonas spit out hoarsely. "He's thrilled. He's so excited to meet you, he got on a plane last night. He's here. In Raleigh. Best part? He talked my dad into having a house party to welcome you into the family. This weekend."

It was a totally unforeseen move. Wily. He didn't believe for a second that his grandfather was thrilled with Jonas's quick marriage or that the CEO of one of the largest conglomerates in Korea had willingly walked away from his board meetings to fly seven thousand miles to meet his new granddaughter-in-law.

This was something else. A test. An "I'll believe it when I see it." Maybe Grandfather scented a whiff of the truth and all it would take was one slipup before he'd pounce. If pressed, Jonas would feel honor bound to be truthful about Viv's role. The marriage could be history before dark.

A healthy amount of caution leaped into Viv's expression. "This weekend? As in we have two days to figure out how to act like a married couple?"

"Now you're starting to see why my face looks like this." He swirled an index finger near his nose, unbelievably grateful that she had instantly realized the problem. "Viv, I'm sorry. I had no idea he was going to do this."

The logistics alone… How could he tell his mom to give them separate bedrooms when they were essentially still supposed to be in the honeymoon phase? He couldn't. It was ludicrous to even think in that direction when what he should be doing was making a list of all the ways this whole plan was about to fall apart. So he could mitigate each and every one.

"Hey."

Jonas glanced up as Viv laced her fingers with his as if she'd done it many times, when in fact she hadn't. She shouldn't. He liked it too much.

"I'm here," she said, an echo of her sentiment at the wedding ceremony. "I'm not going anywhere. My comment wasn't supposed to be taken as a 'holy cow how are we going to do this.' It was an 'oh, so we've got two days to figure this out.' We will."

There was literally no way to express how crappy that made him feel. Viv was such a trouper, diving into this marriage without any thought to herself and her own sense of comfort and propriety. He already owed her so much. He couldn't ask her to fake intimacy on top of everything else.

Neither did he like the instant heat that crowded into his belly at the thought of potential intimate details. *He* couldn't fake intimacy either. It would feel too much like lying.

The only way he could fathom acting like he and Viv were lovers would be if they were.

"You don't know my grandfather. He's probably already suspicious. This house party is intended to sniff out the truth."

"So?" She shrugged that off far too easily. "Let him sniff. What's he going to find out, that we're really legally married?"

"That the marriage is in name only."

To drive the point home, he reached out to cup Viv's

jaw and brought her head up until her gaze clashed with his, her mouth mere centimeters away from his in an almost-kiss that would be a real one with the slightest movement. She nearly jumped out of her skin and stumbled back a good foot until she hit the counter. And then she tried to keep going, eyes wide with…something.

"See?" he said. "I can't even touch you without all sorts of alarms going off. How are we going to survive a whole weekend?"

"Sorry. I wasn't—" She swallowed. "I wasn't expecting you to do that. So clearly the answer is that we need to practice."

"Practice what?" And then her meaning sank in. "Touching?"

"Kissing, too." Her chest rose and fell unevenly as if she couldn't quite catch her breath. "You said we would best get through the adjustment period by spending time together. Maybe we should do that the old-fashioned way. Take me on a date, Jonas."

Speechless, he stared at her, looking for the punch line, but her warm brown eyes held nothing but sincerity. The idea unwound in his gut with a long, liquid pull of anticipation that he didn't need any help interpreting.

A date with his wife. No, with Viv. And the whole goal would be to get her comfortable with his hands on her, to kiss her at random intervals until it was so natural, neither of them thought anything of it.

Crazy. And brilliant. Not to mention impossible.

"Will you wear a new dress?" That should not have been the next thing out of his mouth. *No* would be more advisable when he'd already identified a great big zone of danger surrounding his wife. But *yes* was the only answer if he wanted to pull off this plan.

She nodded, a smile stealing over her face. "The only caveat is no work. For either of us. Which means I get dessert that's not cupcakes."

Oddly, a date with Viv where kissing was expected felt like enough of a reward that he didn't mind that addendum so much, though giving up cupcakes seemed like a pretty big sacrifice. But as her brown eyes seared him thoroughly, the real sacrifice was going to be his sanity. Because he could get her comfortable with his hands on her, but there was no way to get *him* there.

The date would be nothing but torture—and an opportunity to practice making sure no one else realized that, an opportunity he could not pass up. Having an overdeveloped sense of ethics was very inconvenient sometimes.

"It's a deal. Pick you up at eight?"

That made her laugh for some reason. "My bedroom is next door to yours, silly. Are we going to have a secret knock?"

"Maybe." The vibe between them had loosened gradually to where they were almost back to normal, at least as far as she was concerned. Strange that the concept of taking Viv on a date should be the thing to do it. "What should it be?"

Rapping out a short-short-pause-short pattern, she raised her brows. "That means we're leaving in five minutes so get your butt in gear."

"And then that's my cue to hang out in the living room with a sporting event on TV because you're going to take an extra twenty?"

Tossing her head, she grinned. "You catch on fast. Now, I have to go get ready, which means you get to unload the rest of these boxes."

Though he groaned good-naturedly as she scampered out of the kitchen, he didn't mind taking over the chore. Actually, she should be sitting on the couch with a drink and a book while he slaved for hours to get the house exactly the way she liked it. He would have, too, simply because he owed her for this, but she'd insisted that she wanted to do it in order to learn where everything was. Looked like a date was enough to trump that concept.

As the faint sound of running water drifted through the walls, he found spots in his cavernous kitchen for the various pieces Viv had brought with her to this new, temporary life. Unpacking her boxes ended up being a more intimate task than he'd anticipated. She had an odd collection of things. He couldn't fathom the purpose of many of them, but they told him fascinating things about the woman he'd married. She made cupcakes for her business but she didn't have so much as one cupcake pan in her personal stash. Not only that, each item had a well-used sheen, random scrapes, dents, bent handles.

Either she'd spent hours in her kitchen trying to figure out what she liked to bake the most or she'd cleaned out an estate sale in one fell swoop. He couldn't wait to find out, because what better topic to broach on a date with a woman he needed to know inside and out before Friday night?

As he worked, he couldn't help but think of Viv on the other side of the walls, taking a shower. The ensuing images that slammed through his mind were not conducive to the task at hand and it got a little hard to breathe. He should not be picturing her "getting ready" when, in all honesty, he had no idea what that entailed. Odds were good she didn't lather herself up and spend extra time stroking the foam over her body like his brain seemed bent on imagining.

What was his *problem*? He never sat around and fantasized about a woman. He'd never felt strongly enough about one to do so. When was the last time he'd even gone on a date? He might stick Warren with the workaholic label but that could easily be turned back on Jonas. Running the entire American arm of a global company wasn't for wimps, and he had something to prove on top of that. Didn't leave a lot of room for dating, especially when the pact was first and foremost in his mind.

Of course the women he dated always made noises about not looking for anything serious and keeping their options open. And Jonas was always completely honest, but it didn't seem to matter if he flat-out said he wasn't ever going to fall in love. Mostly they took it as a challenge, and things got sticky fast, especially when said woman figured out he wasn't kidding.

Jonas was a champion at untangling himself before things went too far. Before *he* went too far. There were always warning signs that he was starting to like a woman too much. That's when he bailed.

So he had a lot of one-night stands that he'd never intended to be such. It made for stretches of lonely nights, which was perhaps the best side benefit of marriage. He didn't hate the idea of having someone to watch a movie with on a random Tuesday night, or drinking coffee with Viv in the morning before work. He hoped she liked that part of their marriage, too.

Especially since that was all they could ever have between them. It would be devastating to lose her friendship, which would surely happen if they took things to the next level. Once she found out about the pact, either she'd view it as a challenge or she'd immediately shut down. The latter was more likely. He'd hate either one.

At seven forty he stacked the empty boxes near the door so he could take them to the recycling center in the basement of the building later, then went to his room to change clothes for his date.

He rapped on Viv's door with the prescribed knock, grinning as he pictured her on the other side deliberately waiting for as long as she could to answer because they'd made a joke out of this new ritual. But she didn't follow the script and opened the door almost immediately.

Everything fled his mind but her as she filled the doorway, her fresh beauty heightened by the colors of her dress. She'd arranged her hair up on her head, leaving her neck bare. It was such a different look that he couldn't stop drinking her in, frozen by the small smile playing around her mouth.

"I didn't see much point in making you wait when I'm already ready," she commented. "Is it okay to tell you I'm a little nervous?"

He nodded, shocked his muscles still worked. "Yes. It's okay to tell me that. Not okay to be that way."

"I can't help it. I haven't been on a date in…" She bit her lip. "Well, it's been a little while. The shop is my life."

For some reason, that pleased him enormously. Though he shouldn't be so happy that they were cut from the same workaholic cloth. "For me, too. We'll be nervous together."

But then he already knew she had a lack in her social life since she'd readily agreed to this sham marriage, telling him she was too busy to date. Maybe together,

they could find ways to work less. To put finer pleasures first, just for the interim while they were living
together. That could definitely be one of the benefits
of their friendship.

She rolled her eyes. "You're not nervous. But you're
sweet to say so."

Maybe not nervous. But something.

His palms itched and he knew good and well the
only way to cure that was to put them on her bare arms
so he could test out the feel of her skin. It looked soft.

Wasn't the point of the date to touch her? He had
every reason to do exactly that. The urge to reach out
grew bigger and rawer with each passing second.

"Maybe we could start the date right now?" she suggested, and all at once, the hallway outside her room
got very small as she stepped closer, engulfing him in
lavender that could only be her soap.

His body reacted accordingly, treating him to some
more made-up images of her in the shower, and now
that he had a scent to associate with it, the spike through
his gut was that much more powerful. And that much
more of a huge warning sign that things were spiraling
out of control. He just couldn't see a good way to stop.

"Yeah?" he murmured, his throat raw with unfulfilled need. "Which part?"

There was no mistaking what she had in mind when
she reached out to graze her fingertips across his cheek.
Nerve endings fired under her touch and he leaned into
her palm, craving more of her.

"The only part that matters," she whispered back.
"The part where you don't even think twice about getting close to me. Where it's no big thing if you put your
arm around my waist or steal a kiss as I walk by."

If that was the goal, he was failing miserably because it was a big thing. A huge thing. And getting bigger as she leaned in, apparently oblivious to the way her lithe body brushed against his. His control snapped.

Before he came up with reasons why he shouldn't, he pulled her into his arms. Her mouth rose to meet his and, when it did, dropped them both into a long kiss. More than a kiss. An exploration.

With no witnesses this time, he had free rein to delve far deeper into the wonders of his wife than he had at the wedding ceremony.

Her enthusiastic response was killing him. *His* response was even worse. How had they been friends for so long without ever crossing this line? Well, he knew how—because if they had, he would have run in the other direction.

He groaned as her fingers threaded through his hair, sensitizing everything she touched. Then she iced that cake with a tentative push of her tongue that nearly put him on his knees. So unexpected and so very hot. Eagerly, he matched her sweet thrust with his own. Deeper and deeper they spiraled until he couldn't have said which way was up. Who was doing the giving and who was greedily lapping it up.

He wanted more and took it, easing her head back with firm fingers until he found the right angle to get more of her against his tongue. And now he wanted more of her against his body.

He slid a hand down the curve of her spine until he hit a spot that his palm fit into and pressed until her hips nestled against his erection. Amazing. Perfect.

The opposite of friendly.

That was enough to get his brain in gear again. This

was not how it should be between them, with all this raw need that he couldn't control.

He ended the kiss through some force of will he'd never understand and pulled back, but she tried to follow, nearly knocking herself off balance. Like she had at the ceremony. And in a similar fashion, he gripped her arms to keep her off the floor. It was dizzying how caught up she seemed to get. A rush he could get used to and shouldn't.

"Sorry," he said gruffly. "I got a little carried away."

"That's what was supposed to happen," she informed him breathlessly, "if we have any hope of your grandfather believing that we're deliriously happy together."

Yeah, that wasn't the problem he was most worried about at this moment. Viv's kiss-swollen lips were the color of raspberries and twice as tempting. All for show. He'd gotten caught up in the playacting far too easily, which wasn't fair to her. Or to his Viv-starved body that had suddenly found something it liked better than her cupcakes.

"I don't think anyone would question whether we spark, Viv," he muttered.

The real issue was that he needed to kill that spark and was pretty certain that would be impossible now.

Especially given the way she was gazing up at him with something a whole lot hotter than warmth in her brown eyes. She'd liked kissing him as much as he'd liked it. She might even be on board with taking things a step further. But they couldn't consummate this marriage or he could forget the annulment. Neither did he want to lead her on, which left him between a rock and an extremely hard place that felt like it would never be anything but hard for the rest of his life.

"In fact," he continued, "we should really keep things platonic behind closed doors. That's better for our friendship, don't you think?"

He'd kissed his wife and put his hands on her body because she'd told him to. And he was very much afraid he'd do it again whether it was for show or not unless he had some boundaries. Walking away from Viv wasn't an option. He had to do something that guaranteed he never got so sucked into a woman that she had power over his emotional center.

Thankfully, she nodded. "Whatever works best for you, Jonas. This is your fake marriage."

And how messed up was it that he was more than a little disappointed she'd agreed so readily?

Three

Viv hummed as she pulled the twenty-four-count pan from the oven and stuck the next batch of Confetti Surprise in its place. Customers thronged the showroom beyond the swinging door, but she kept an eye on things via the closed-circuit camera she'd had installed when she first started turning a profit.

Couldn't be too careful and besides, it made her happy to watch Camilla and Josie interact with the cupcake buyers while Viv did the dirty work in the back. She'd gotten so lucky to find the two college-aged girls who worked for her part-time. Both of them were eager students, and soon Viv would teach them the back-office stuff like bookkeeping and ordering. For now, it was great to have them running the register so Viv could focus on product.

Not that she was doing much focusing. Her mind

wandered constantly to the man who'd kissed her so passionately last night.

Jonas had been so into the moment, so into her, and it had been heady indeed. Score one for Viv to have landed in his arms due to her casual suggestion that they needed to "practice." Hopefully he'd never clue in that she jumped when he touched her because he zapped a shock of heat and awareness straight to her core every dang time, no matter how much she tried to control it.

Of course, he'd shut it all down, rightfully so. They were friends. If he'd been interested in more, he would have made a move long before now.

Didn't stop her from wishing for a repeat.

A stone settled into her stomach as three dressed-to-the-nines women breezed through the door of her shop. On the monitor, she watched her sisters approach the counter and speak to Josie, oblivious to the line of customers they'd just cut in front of. Likely they were cheerfully requesting to speak with Viv despite being told countless times that this wasn't a hobby. She ran a business, which meant she didn't have time to dash off with them for tea, something the three housewives she shared parentage with but little else didn't seem to fully grasp.

Except she couldn't avoid the conversation they were almost certainly here for. She'd finally broken down and called her mother to admit she'd gotten married without inviting anyone to the wedding. Of course that news had taken all of five minutes to blast its way to her sisters' ears.

Dusting off her hands, Viv set a timer on her phone and dropped it into her pocket. Those cupcakes in the oven would provide a handy out if things got a little intense, and knowing Hope, Joy and Grace, that was likely. She pushed open the swinging door and pasted a smile on her face.

"My favorite ladies," she called with a wave and crossed the room to hug first Grace, her next-oldest sister, then Joy and Hope last. More than a few heads turned to check out the additions to the showroom. Individually, they were beautiful women, but as a group, her sisters were impressive indeed, with style and elegance galore.

Viv had been a late-life accident, but her parents tried hard not to make her feel like one. Though it was obvious they'd expected to have three children when they couldn't come up with a fourth virtue to name their youngest daughter. She'd spent her childhood trying to fit in to her own family and nothing had changed.

Until today. Finally, Viviana Kim had a new last name and a husband. Thanks to Jonas and his fake marriage deal, she was part of the club that had excluded her thus far. Just one of many reasons she'd agreed.

"Mom told us," Hope murmured, her social polish in full force. She was nothing if not always mindful of propriety, and Viv appreciated it for once, as the roomful of customers didn't need to hear about Viv's love life. "She's hurt that you ran off to Vegas without telling anyone."

"Are you happy?" Grace butted in. She'd gotten married to the love of her life less than a year ago and saw hearts and flowers everywhere. "That's the important thing."

"Mom said you married Jonas Kim," Joy threw in before Viv could answer, not that she'd intended to interrupt before everyone had their say. That was a rookie mistake she'd learned to avoid years ago. "Surely his family would have been willing to make a discreet contribution to the ceremony. You could have had the wedding of the year."

Which was the real crime in Joy's mind—why spend *less* money when you could spend more, particularly when it belonged to someone else? Joy's own wedding had garnered a photo spread in *Bride* magazine five years ago, a feat no other Raleigh bride had scored since.

It had been a beautiful wedding and Joy had been a gorgeous bride. Of course, because she'd been so happy. All three of her sisters were married to handsome, successful men who treated them like royalty, which was great if you could find that. Viv had made do with what had been offered to her, but they didn't have to know that. In fact, she'd do everything in her power not to tip off her sisters that her marriage was anything but amazing. Was it so wrong to want them to believe she'd ended up exactly where she'd yearned to be for so long?

"Also, he's Korean," Hope added as if this might be news to Viv. "Mom is very concerned about how you'll handle the cultural differences. Have you discussed this with him?"

That was crossing a line. For several reasons. And Viv had had enough. "Jonas is American. He was born in the same hospital as you, so I'm pretty sure the cultural differences are minimal. Can you just be happy for me and stop with the third degree?"

All three women stared at her agape, even Grace, and Viv was ashamed at how good the speech had made her feel. She rarely stood up to the steamroller of her sisters, mostly because she really did love them. But she was married now, just like they were, and her choices deserved respect.

"Jonas does make me happy," she continued, shooting Grace a smile. "But there's nothing to be concerned about. We've known each other for about a year and our relationship recently grew closer. That's all there is to it."

Despite the fact that it was absolute truth, prickles swept across her cheeks at the memory of how *close* they'd gotten last night.

An unconvinced expression stole over Hope's face. As the oldest, she took her role as the protector seriously. "We still don't understand why the secrecy. None of us even remember you so much as mentioning his name before."

"Of course we know who he *is*," Joy clarified. "Everyone in Raleigh appreciates that he's brought a global company to this area. But we had no idea you'd caught his eye."

Viv could read between those lines easily enough. She didn't wear nine-thousand-dollar Alexander McQueen suits to brunch and attend the opera with a priceless antique diamond necklace decorating her cleavage. "He's been coming in to buy cupcakes for quite some time. We go to lunch. It's not that big of a mystery."

Did it seem like a mystery to others? A lick of panic curled through her stomach. She couldn't ruin this for Jonas. If other people got suspicious because she wasn't the type of woman a billionaire CEO should want to marry, then everything might fall apart.

Breathe. He'd made that decision. Not her. He'd picked Viv and anyone who thought she wasn't good enough for him could jump in a lake.

"But he married you." Grace clapped her hands, eyes twinkling. "Tell us how he proposed, what you wore at the wedding. Ooooh, show us pictures."

Since his proposal had begun with the line "This is going to sound crazy, but hear me out," Viv avoided that subject by holding out her left hand to dazzle her sisters with the huge diamond and then grabbing her phone to thumb up the shots Warren had taken at Jonas's request. The yellow of her dress popped next to Jonas's dark suit and they made an incredibly striking couple if she did say so herself. Mostly because she had the best-looking husband on the planet, so no one even noticed her.

"Is that Hendrix Harris in the shot?" Hope sniffed and the disapproval on her face spoke volumes against the man whose picture graced local gossip rags on a regular basis.

"Jonas and Hendrix are friends," Viv said mildly as she flipped through a few more pictures that mercifully did not include North Carolina's biggest scandalmonger. "They went to Duke together. I'll try not to let him corrupt me if we socialize."

As far as she could tell, Hendrix had scarcely noticed her at the wedding, and he'd seemed preoccupied at the cocktail lounge where they'd gone to have drinks after the ceremony. The man was pretty harmless.

"Just be careful," Hope implored her, smoothing an invisible wrinkle from her skirt. "You married Jonas so quickly and it appears as if he may have some unsavory associations. I say this with love, but you haven't demonstrated a great track record when it comes to the men you fall for."

That shouldn't have cut so deeply. It was true. But still.

"What Hope means is that you tend to leap before you look, Viv," Grace corrected, her eyes rolling in their sister's direction, but only Viv could see the show of support. It soothed the ragged places inside that Hope's comment had made. A little.

"It's not a crime to be passionate about someone." Hands on her hips, Viv surveyed the three women, none of whom seemed to remember what it was like to be single and alone. "But for your information, Jonas and I were friends first. We share common interests. He gives me advice about my business. We have a solid foundation to build on."

"Oh." Hope processed that. "I didn't realize you were being so practical about this. I'm impressed that you managed to marry a man without stars in your eyes. That's a relief."

Great. She'd gotten the seal of approval from Hope solely because she'd skirted the truth with a bland recitation of unromantic facts about her marriage. Her heart clenched. That was the opposite of what she wanted. But this was the marriage she had, the one she could handle. For now. Tomorrow, Jonas would take her to his father's house to meet his grandfather and she hoped to "practice" being married a whole lot more.

Thankfully, she'd kept Jonas in the dark about her feelings. If he could kiss her like he had last night and not figure out that she'd been this close to melting into a little puddle, she could easily snow his family with a few public displays of affection.

It was behind closed doors that she was worried about. That's where she feared she might forget that

her marriage was fake. And as she'd just been uncere-
moniously reminded, she had a tendency to get serious
way too fast, which in her experience was a stellar way
to get a man to start looking for the exit.

That was the part that hurt the most. She wanted to
care about someone, to let him know he was her whole
world and have him say that in return. It wasn't neediness. She wasn't being clingy. That's what love looked
like to her and she refused to believe otherwise.

But she'd yet to find a man who agreed with her,
and Jonas was no exception. They had a deal and she
would stick to it.

The house Jonas had grown up in lay on the outskirts
of Raleigh in an upscale neighborhood that was homey
and unpretentious. Jonas's father, who had changed his
name to Brian when he became a legal US citizen upon
marrying his American wife, hadn't gone into the family business, choosing to become a professor at Duke
University instead.

That had left a hole in the Kim empire, one Jonas
had gladly filled. He and Grandfather got along well,
likely because they were so similar. They both had a
drive to succeed, a natural professionalism and a sense
of honor that harbored trust in others who did business
with Kim Electronics.

Though they corresponded nearly every day in some
electronic form, the time difference prevented them
from speaking often, and an in-person visit was even
rarer. The last time Jonas had seen Grandfather had
been during a trip to Seoul for a board meeting about
eighteen months ago. He'd invited his parents to come
with him, as they hadn't visited Korea in several years.

"Are you nervous?" Jonas glanced over at Viv, who had clutched her hands together in her lap the second the car had hit Glenwood Avenue. Her knuckles couldn't get any whiter.

"Oh, God. You can tell," she wailed. "I was trying so hard to be cool."

He bit back a grin and passed a slow-moving minivan. "Viv, they're just people. I promise they will like you."

"I'm not worried about that. Everyone likes me, especially after I give them cupcakes," she informed him loftily.

There was a waxed paper box at her feet on the floorboard that she'd treated as carefully as a newborn baby. When he'd reached for it, she'd nearly taken his hand off at the wrist, telling him in no uncertain terms the cupcakes were for her new family. Jonas was welcome to come by Cupcaked next week and pick out whatever he wanted, but the contents of that box were off-limits.

He kind of liked Bossy Viv. Of course he liked Sweet Viv, Uncertain Viv, Eager-to-Help Viv. He'd seen plenty of new facets in the last week since they'd moved in together, more than he'd have expected given that they'd known each other so long. It was fascinating.

"What are you worried about then?" he asked.

"You know good and well." Without warning, she slid a hand over his thigh and squeezed. Fire rocketed up his leg and scored his groin, nearly doubling him over with the sudden and unexpected need.

Only his superior reflexes kept the Mercedes on the road. But he couldn't stop the curse that flew from his mouth.

"Sorry," he muttered but she didn't seem bothered by his language.

"See, you're just as bad as me." Her tone was laced with irony. "All that practice and we're even jumpier than we were before."

Because the practice had ended before he started peeling off her clothes. Ironic how his marriage of convenience meant his wife was right there in his house—conveniently located in the bedroom next to his. He could hear her moving around between the walls and sometimes, he lay awake at night listening for the slightest movement to indicate she was likewise awake, aching to try one of those kisses with a lot less fabric in the way.

That kind of need was so foreign to him that he wasn't handling it well.

"I'm not jumpy," he lied. "I'm just…"

Frustrated.

There was no good way to finish that sentence without opening up a conversation about changing their relationship into something that it wasn't supposed to be. An annulment was so much less sticky than a divorce, though he'd finally accepted that he was using that as an excuse.

The last thing he could afford to do was give in to the simmering awareness between them. Jonas had convinced himself it was easy to honor the pact because he really didn't feel much when it came to relationships. Sure, he enjoyed sex, but it had always been easy to walk away when the woman pushed for more.

With Viv, the spiral of heat and need was dizzyingly strong. He felt too much, and Marcus's experience was like a big neon sign, reminding him that it was better never to go down that path. What was he supposed to do, stop being friends with Viv if things went haywire between them? Neither was there a good way to end their relationship before the merger.

So he was stuck. He couldn't act on his sudden and fierce longing to pull this car over into a shadowy bower of oak trees and find out if all of Viv tasted like sugar and spice and everything nice.

"Maybe we shouldn't touch each other," he suggested.

That was a good solution. Except for the part where they were married. Married people touched each other. He bit back the nasty word that had sprung to his lips. Barely.

"Oh." She nodded. "If you think that won't cause problems, sure."

Of course it was going to cause problems. He nearly groaned. But the problems had nothing to do with what she assumed. "Stop being so reasonable. I'm pulling you away from your life with very little compensation in return. You should be demanding and difficult."

Brilliant. He'd managed to make it sound like touching her was one of the compensation methods. He really needed to get out of this car now that he had a hyperawareness of how easily she could—and would—reach out to slide a hand full of questing fingers into his lap.

Viv grinned and crossed her arms, removing that possibility. "In that case, I'm feeling very bereft in the jewelry department, Mr. Kim. As your wife, I should be draped in gems, don't you think?"

"Absolutely." What did it say about how messed up he was that the way *Mr. Kim* rolled off her tongue turned him on? "Total oversight on my part. Which I will rectify immediately."

The fourteen-carat diamond on her finger was on loan from a guy Jonas knew in the business, though the hefty fee he'd paid to procure it could have bought enough bling to blind her. Regardless, if Viv wanted jewelry, that's what she'd get.

They drove into his parents' neighborhood right on time and he parked in the long drive that led to the house. "Ready?"

She nodded. "All that talk about jewelry got me over my nerves. Thanks."

That made one of them.

His mom opened the door before they'd even hit the stone steps at the entryway, likely because she'd been watching for the car. But instead of engulfing Jonas in the first of what would be many hugs, she ignored her only child in favor of her new daughter-in-law.

"You must be Viviana," his mother gushed, and swept Viv up in an embrace that was part friendly and part *Thank you, God, I finally have a daughter.* "I'm so happy to meet you."

Viv took it in stride. "Hi, Mrs. Kim. I'm happy to meet you, too. Please call me Viv."

Of course she wasn't ruffled. There was so little that seemed to trip her up—except when Jonas touched her. All practicing had done was create surprisingly acute sexual tension that even a casual observer would recognize as smoldering awareness.

He was currently pretending it didn't exist. Because that would make it not so, right?

"Hi, Mom," he threw in blithely since she hadn't even glanced in his direction.

"Your grandfather is inside. He'd like to talk to you while I get to know Viviana. Tell me everything," she said to her new daughter-in-law as she accepted the box of cupcakes with a smile. "Have you started thinking about kids yet?"

Jonas barely bit back another curse. "Mom, please. We just got here. Viv doesn't need the third degree about personal stuff."

Right out of the gate with the baby questions? Really? He'd expected a little decorum from his mom. In vain, obviously, and a mistake because he hadn't had a chance to go over that with Viv. Should they say they didn't want children? That she couldn't have any?

He and Viv clearly should have spent less time "practicing" and more in deep conversation about all aspects of potential questions that might come up this weekend. Which they'd have to rectify tonight before going to bed. In the same room.

His mother shot him a glare. "Grandchildren are not personal. The hope of one day getting some is the only reason I keep you around, after all."

That made Viv laugh, which delighted his mother, so really, there was nothing left to do but throw up his hands and go seek out Grandfather for his own version of the third degree.

Grandfather held court in the Kim living room, talking to his son. The older Jonas's dad got, the more he resembled Grandfather, but the similarities ended there. Where Brian Kim had adopted an American name to match his new homeland, Kim Jung-Su wore his Korean heritage like the badge of honor it was.

Kim Electronics had been born after the war, during a boom in Korean capitalism that only a select few had wisely taken advantage of. Jonas loved his dad, but Grandfather had been his mentor, his partner as Jonas had taken what Jung-Su had built and expanded it into the critical US market. They'd created a chaebol, a family-run conglomerate, where none had existed, and they'd done it together.

And he was about to lie to his grandfather's face solely to avoid marrying a disaster of a woman who might cause the Kim family shame.

It was a terrible paradox and not for the first time he heard Warren's voice of reason in his head asking why he couldn't just tell Grandfather the truth. But then he remembered that Sun's grandfather and Jonas's grandfather had fought in the war together and were closer than brothers. Jonas refused to out Sun and her unsuitable lover strictly for his own benefit. No, this way was easier.

And it wasn't a lie. He and Viv were married. That was all anyone needed to know.

Grandfather greeted Jonas in Korean and then switched to English as a courtesy since he was in an English-speaking house. "You are looking well."

"As are you." Jonas bowed to show his respect and then hugged his dad, settling in next to him on the couch. "It's a pleasure to see you."

Grandfather arched a thick brow. "An unexpected pleasure I assume? I wanted to meet your new wife personally. To welcome her into the family."

"She is very honored. Mom waylaid her or she'd be here to meet you, as well."

"I asked your mother to. I wanted to speak with you privately."

As if it had been some prearranged signal, Jonas's

dad excused himself and the laser sights of Jung-Su had zero distractions. The temperature of the room shot up about a thousand degrees. One misstep and the whole plan would come crashing down. And Jonas suddenly hated the idea of losing this tenuous link with Viv, no matter how precarious that link was.

"Now, then." Grandfather steepled his hands together and smiled. "I'm very pleased you have decided to marry. It is a big step that will bring you many years of happiness. Belated congratulations."

Jonas swallowed his surprise. What was the wily old man up to? He'd expected a cross-examination designed to uncover the plot that Grandfather surely suspected. "Thank you. Your approval means a lot to me."

"As a wedding gift, I'd like to give you the Kim ancestral home."

"What? I mean, that's a very generous gesture, Grandfather." And crafty, as the property in question lay outside of Seoul, seven thousand miles away from North Carolina. Jonas couldn't refuse or Grandfather would be insulted. But there was an angle here that Jonas couldn't quite work out.

"Of course I'd hoped you'd live in it with Sun Park, but I understand that you cannot curb the impulses of the heart."

Jonas stared at his grandfather as if he'd suddenly started speaking Klingon. The impulses of the heart? That was the exact opposite of the impression he'd wanted to convey. Sure, he'd hoped to convince everyone that they were a couple, but only so that no one's suspicions were aroused. Solid and unbreakable would be more to his liking when describing his marriage, not *impulsive* and certainly not because he'd fallen madly in love.

This was the worst sort of twist. Never would he have thought he'd be expected to sell his marriage as a love match. Was that something that he and Viv were going to have to practice, too? His stomach twisted itself inside out. How the hell was he supposed to know what love looked like?

Regardless of the curveball, it was the confirmation Jonas had been looking for. Grandfather was on board with Viv, and Jonas had cleared the first hurdle after receiving that ominous text message the other day. "I'm glad you understand. I've been seeing Viv for almost a year and I simply couldn't imagine marrying anyone else."

That much at least was true, albeit a careful hedge about the nature of his intentions toward Viv during that year. And thankfully they'd become good enough friends that he felt comfortable asking her to help him avoid exactly what he'd suspected Grandfather had in mind. Apparently throwing Sun in his path *had* been an attempt to get Jonas to Korea more often, if not permanently. It was counter to Jonas's long-term strategy, the one he still hadn't brought to Grandfather because the merger hadn't happened yet. Once Park Industries and Kim Electronics became one, they could leverage the foothold Jonas had already built in America by moving the headquarters to North Carolina, yet keep manufacturing in Korea under the Park branch.

It was also the opportune time to pass the reins, naming Jonas the CEO of the entire operation. The dominoes were in much better position now, thanks to the huge bullet Viv had helped him dodge without upsetting anyone. It was…everything.

Grandfather chatted for a few more minutes about his plans while in the US, including a request for a tour of the Kim Building, and then asked Jonas to introduce him to Viv.

He found her in the kitchen writing down her cupcake recipe for his mother.

"You got her secret recipe already, Mom?" Jonas asked with a laugh. "I guess I don't have to ask whether everyone is getting along."

His mother patted his arm. "You obviously underestimate how much your wife cares for you. I didn't even have to ask twice."

Viv blushed and it was so pretty on her, he couldn't tear his gaze from her face all at once, even though he was speaking to his mom. "On the contrary, I'm quite aware of how incredibly lucky I am that Viv married me."

"You didn't have to ask me *that* twice either," Viv pointed out. "Apparently I lack the ability to say no to anyone with the name Kim."

An excellent point that he really wished she hadn't brought up on the heels of his discovery of how much he enjoyed it when she called him Mr. Kim. All at once, a dozen suggestions designed to get her to say yes over and over sprang to his lips. But with his mom's keen-eyed gaze cutting between the two of them, he needed to get himself under control immediately.

"Come and say hi to my grandfather," he said instead, and she nodded eagerly.

She was far too good to him. For the first time, it bothered him. What was she getting out of this farce?

Some advice about how to run her business? That had seemed inadequate before they'd gotten married. Now? It was nearly insulting how little he was doing for her.

She had to have another reason for being here. And all at once, he wanted to know what it was.

Four

Ten minutes into dinner, Jonas figured out his grandfather's angle. The wily old man was trying to drive him insane with doubt about pulling off this ruse, especially now that he had *impulses of the heart* echoing through his head. Jonas was almost dizzy from trying to track all the verbal land mines that might or might not be strewn through random conversational openers.

Even "pass the butter" had implications. Grandfather hated butter.

And if Grandfather failed at putting Jonas in the loony bin, Viv was doing her part to finish the job, sitting next to him looking fresh and beautiful as she reminded him on a second-by-second basis that she was well within touching distance. Not just easily accessible. But *available* to be touched. It was *expected*. Would a loving husband sling his arm across the back of her chair? Seemed reasonable.

But the moment he did it as he waited for his mom to serve the kimchi stew she'd made in honor of Grandfather's visit, Viv settled into the crook of his elbow, which had not been his intent at all. She fit so well, he couldn't help but let his arm relax so that it fully embraced her and somehow his fingers ended up doing this little dance down her bare arm, testing whether the silkiness felt as good all the way down as it did near her shoulder.

It did.

"...don't you think, Jonas?"

Blinking, Jonas tore his attention away from his wife's skin and focused on his dad. "Sure. I definitely think so."

"That's great," Brian said with a nod and a wink. "It wasn't a stretch to think you'd be on board."

Fantastic. What in the world had he just agreed to that had his father winking, of all things? Jonas pulled his arm from around Viv's shoulders. At this point, it seemed like everyone was convinced they were a couple and all the touching had done nothing but distract him.

Viv leaned in, her hand resting on his thigh. It was dangerously close to being in his lap. One small shift would do it, and his muscles strained to repeat the experience. But before he could sort her intention, she murmured in his ear, "We're playing Uno later. As a team. You'll have to teach me."

Card games with a hard-on. That sounded like the opposite of fun. But at least he knew what he'd absently agreed to, and shot Viv a grateful smile. Her return smile did all sorts of things that it shouldn't have, not the least of which was give him the sense that they were coconspirators. They were in this farce together and he appreciated that more than he could say. At least they could laugh about this later. Or something.

Grandfather was watching him closely as he spooned up a bite of stew, and Jonas braced for the next round of insanity. Sure enough, Grandfather cleared his throat.

"Will you and your bride be starting a family soon?"

Not this again and from his grandfather, too? Obviously Jonas's mother had a vested interest in the answer strictly because she wanted babies to spoil, but Grandfather wasn't asking for anything close to that reason. It was all part of the test.

"Not soon," he hedged because family was important to the Kims. It was a source of frustration for both his parents and his grandparents that they'd only had one child apiece, and Jonas imagined they'd all be thrilled if he said Viv wanted a dozen. "Viv owns a bakery and it's doing very well. She'd like to focus on her career for a while."

Yes. That was the reason they weren't having kids right away. Why had he been racking his brain over that? Except now he was thinking about the conversation where he had to tell everyone that while he cared about Viv, they were better as friends, so the marriage was over. While it soothed his sense of honor that it was the truth, he'd never considered that the annulment would upset his family.

"We're having her cupcakes for dessert," his mother threw in with a beaming smile. "They look scrumptious."

Perfect segue and took some heat off a subject that Jonas suddenly did not want to contemplate. "The lemon are my favorite. One bite and that was when I decided I couldn't let Viv get away."

The adoring glance she shot him thumped him in the gut. The little secret smile playing about her lips worked in tandem, spreading tendrils of heat through him in ways that should be uncomfortable at a table full of Kims who were all watching him closely. But the sensation was too enjoyable to squelch.

"Honestly, that was when I knew he was special," Viv admitted, and Jonas nearly did a double take at the wistful note in her voice. "He appreciates my cupcakes in a way regular customers don't. A lot goes into the recipes and I don't just mean my time. It's a labor of love, born out of a desire to make people happy, and I can see on his face that I've done that. Most customers just devour the thing without stopping to breathe, but Jonas always takes one bite and immediately stops to savor it. Then he tells me how great it is before taking another bite."

Well, yeah, because he could taste the sunshine in it, as if she'd somehow condensed a few rays and woven them through the ingredients. How could he not take his time to fully appreciate the unique experience of a Viviana Dawson cupcake?

Jonas blinked, dragging his lids down over his suddenly dry eyes. He didn't do that *every* time, not the way she was describing it, as if a cupcake held all that meaning.

He glanced at his mom, who looked a little misty.

"That sounds like a magical courtship," she said.

"Oh, it was," Viv agreed enthusiastically. "It was like one of those movies where the hero pretends he only wants the cupcakes when he comes into the shop, but it's really to see the baker. But I always knew from the first that the way to his heart was through my frosting."

His mother laughed and Jonas checked his eye roll because the whole point was to sell this nonsense. Everyone was eating it up, no pun intended, so why mess with the ridiculous story Viv was spinning?

Except the whole thing made him uncomfortable.

Surely his grandfather wouldn't appreciate hearing his successor described with such romanticism. If anything, Viv could help Jonas's case by telling everyone how hard he worked and how difficult it was to pry him away from his cell phone when they went to lunch.

He sighed. She couldn't say that. It would be a big, fat lie. When he did anything with Viv, he always switched his phone to do not disturb. He loved listening to stories about her sisters, or a new recipe she was working through. But it didn't mean he was gaga over her like a besotted fool.

Yet…that's what he needed his grandfather to buy, as difficult as it was to envision. Grandfather hadn't accepted Jonas's marriage to Viv because she'd helped him increase profits or created an advantageous business alliance. Viv was an *impulse of the heart*.

How had he gotten caught in the middle of trying to prove to his grandfather that Jonas was a committed, solid CEO candidate, while also attempting to convince him that he and Viv had fallen in love? And Jonas had no illusions about the necessity of maintaining the current vibe, not after his grandfather smiled over Viv's enthusiastic retelling of what would probably forever be called the Cupcake Courtship. It was madness.

"Will you bring your wife to Seoul to visit the Kim ancestral home?" Grandfather asked in the lull. "It's yours now. Perhaps you'll want to redecorate?"

Jonas nearly groaned. He hadn't had four seconds

to mention the gift to Viv. Her eyebrows lifted in silent question and he blessed her discretion.

"We're actually looking for a house together in Raleigh," Jonas improvised much more smoothly than he would have guessed he could. Viv's eyebrows did another reach-for-the-sky move as he rushed on. "So probably we won't make it to Korea anytime soon. But we do both appreciate the gift."

Nothing like a good reminder that Jonas's home was in America. The future of the company lay here, not in Seoul. The more he could root himself in North Carolina, the better. Of course the answer was to buy a property here. With Viv. A new ancestral home in North Carolina. Then his statement to his grandfather wouldn't be a lie.

"Yes, thank you so much, Mr. Kim," Viv said sweetly. "We'll discuss our work schedules and find a mutual time we can travel. I would be honored to see your ancestral home. Mrs. Kim, perhaps you'd advise me on whether the decor needs refurbishing?"

Jonas's mom smiled so widely that it was a wonder she didn't crack her face. "That's a lovely idea. I would be thrilled to go to lunch and discuss the house, as I've always loved the locale."

Speechless, Jonas watched the exchange with a very real sense of his life sliding out of control and no way to put on the brakes. In the last two minutes, he'd managed to rope himself into shopping for a house in Raleigh, then traveling to Korea so Viv could visit Seoul with the express intent of redecorating a house neither of them wanted…with his mom. What next?

"While you're in Korea," Grandfather said, and his tone was so leading that everyone's head turned toward him, "we should discuss taking next steps toward increasing your responsibilities at Kim Electronics. The board will look very favorably on how you've matured, Jonas. Your accomplishments with the American market are impressive. I would be happy to recommend you as the next CEO when I retire."

The crazy train screeched to a halt in the dead center of Are You Kidding Me Station. *Say something. Tell him you're honored.*

But Jonas's throat froze as his brain tried to sort through his grandfather's loaded statements.

Everything he'd worked for had just been handed to him on a silver platter—that Viv was holding in her delicate fingers. The implications were staggering. Grandfather liked that Jonas was married. It was a huge wrinkle he had never seen coming.

Now he couldn't annul the marriage or he'd risk losing Grandfather's approval with the board. How was he supposed to tell Viv that the favor he'd asked of her had just been extended by about a year?

And what did it mean that his insides were doing a secret dance of happiness at getting to keep Viv longer than planned?

The spare bedroom lay at the end of a quiet hall and had its own en suite bathroom. Nice. Viv wasn't too keen on the idea of wandering around in her bathrobe. At least not outside the bedroom. Inside was another story.

Because Jonas was on this side of the closed door. Time to ramp it up.

If she hoped to build her confidence with a man, there was no better scenario to play that out than this one, especially since she already knew they were attracted to each other And headed for a divorce. None of this was real, so she could practice without fear.

She shivered as her gorgeous husband loosened his tie and threw himself onto the bed with a groan. *Shivered.* What was that but a commentary on this whole situation?

"Bad day, sweetie?" she deadpanned, carefully keeping her voice light. But holy cow, Jonas was so sexy with his shirtsleeves rolled up and his bare feet crossed at the ankle as he tossed an elbow over his eyes.

"That was one of the most difficult dinners I've ever endured," he confessed, as if there was nothing odd about being in a bedroom together with the door closed, while he lounged on the bed looking like a commercial for something sensual and expensive.

"Your family is great." She eased onto the bed because she wanted to and she could. It wasn't like there were a ton of other seats in the cute little bedroom. Well, except for the matching chairs near the bay window that flanked an inlaid end table. But she didn't want to sit way over there when the centerpiece of the room lay on the bed.

As the mattress shifted under her weight, he peeked out from beneath his elbow, his dark eyes seeking hers. "You're only saying that to be nice. You should stage a fight and go home. It would serve me right to have to stay here and field questions about the stability of our marriage."

As if she'd ever do that when the best part of this fake marriage had just started. She was sharing a bedroom with Jonas Kim and he was her husband and the night was rife with possibilities.

There came the shiver again and it was delicious.
Careful.

This was the part where she always messed up with men by seeming too eager. Messing up with Jonas was not happening. There was no do-over.

Of course, scoring with Jonas had its issues, too. Like the fact that she couldn't keep him. This was just practice, she reminded herself. That was the only way she could get it together.

"I'm not staging a fight." She shook her head and risked reaching out to stroke Jonas's hair in a totally casual gesture meant to soothe him, because after all, he did seem pretty stressed. "What would we fight about? Money?"

"I don't know. No." The elbow came off his face and he let his eyes drift closed as she ran her fingers over his temples. "That feels nice. You don't have to do that."

Oh, yes. She did. This was her chance to touch Jonas in a totally innocuous way and study her husband's body while he wasn't aware.

"It's possible for me to do something because I want to instead of out of a sense of obligation, you know."

He chuckled. "Point taken. I'm entirely too sensitive to how big a favor this is and how difficult navigating my family can be."

Stroking his hair might go down as one of the greatest pleasures of her life. It was soft and silky and thick. The inky strands slid across her fingertips as she buried them deep and rubbed lightly against his scalp, which earned her a groan that was amazingly sexy.

"Relax," she murmured, and was only half talking to herself as her insides contracted. "I don't find your family difficult. Your mom is great and I don't know if you know this or not, but your grandfather does not in fact breathe fire."

"He gave us a house." His eyes popped open and he glanced over at her, shrinking the slight distance between them. "There are all sorts of underlying expectations associated with that, not the least of which is how upset he's going to be when I have to give it back."

She shrugged, pretending like it wasn't difficult to get air into her lungs when he focused on her so intently. "Don't give it back. Keep it and we'll go visit, like we promised."

"Viv." He sat up, taking his beautiful body out of reach, which was a shame. "You're being entirely too accommodating. Were you not listening to the conversation at dinner? This is only going to get more complicated the longer we drag it out. And we *are* going to be dragging it out apparently."

Normally, this would be where she threw herself prostrate at a man's feet and wept with joy over the fact that he wasn't calling things off. But she wasn't clingy anymore. Newly Minted Independent Viv needed to play this a whole different way if she wanted to get to a place where she had a man slavishly devoted to her. And she would not apologize for wishing for a man who loved her so much that he would never dream of calling the duration of their marriage "dragging it out."

"You say that like being married to me is a chore," she scolded lightly. "I was listening at dinner. I heard the words *CEO* and *Jonas* in the same sentence. Did you? Because that sounded good to me."

"It is good. For me. Not you. I'm now essentially in the position of using you to further my career goals for an extended period of time. Not just until the merger happens. But until my grandfather retires and fully transitions the role of CEO to me. That could take months. A year."

Oh, God. A whole year of living with Jonas in his amazing loft and being his wife? That was a lot of practicing for something that would never be real. How could she possibly hide her feelings for Jonas that long? Worse, they'd probably grow stronger the longer she stayed in his orbit. How fair was it to keep torturing herself like this?

On the flip side, she'd promised to do this for Jonas as a favor. As a *friend*. He wasn't interested in more or he'd have told her. Practice was all she could reasonably expect from this experience. It had to be enough.

"That's a significant development, no doubt. But I don't feel used. And I'm not going anywhere."

Jonas scowled instead of overflowing with gratitude. "I can't figure out what you're getting out of this. It was already a huge sacrifice, even when it was only for a few weeks until my grandfather got his deal going with Park. Now this. Are you dying of cancer or something?"

She forced a laugh but there was nothing funny about his assumptions. Or the fact that she didn't have a good answer for why she didn't hate the idea of sticking around as long as Jonas would have her. Maybe there was something wrong with that, but it was her business, not his. "What, like I'm trying to check off everything on my bucket list before I die and being married to Jonas Kim was in the top three? That's a little arrogant, don't you think?"

When he flinched, she almost took it back, but that's how Newly Minted Viv rolled. The last thing he needed to hear was that being married to him occupied the top spot on all her lists. And on that note, it was definitely time to put a few more logs on the pile before she set it on fire.

"Running a cupcake business is hard," she told him firmly. "You've built Kim Electronics from the ground up. You should know how it is. You work seventy hours a week and barely make a dent. Who has time for a relationship? But I get lonely, same as anyone. This deal is perfect for me because we can hang out with no pressure. I like you. Is that so hard to believe?"

Good. Deflect. Give him just enough truth to make it plausible.

His face relaxed into an easy grin. "Only a little. I owe you so much. Not sure my scintillating personality makes up for being stuck sharing a bedroom with me."

"Yeah, that part sucks, all right," she murmured, and let her gaze trail down his body. What better way to "practice" being less clingy than to get good and needy and then force herself to walk away? "We should use this opportunity to get a little more comfortable with each other."

The atmosphere got intense as his expression darkened, and she could tell the idea intrigued him.

"What? Why? We've already sold the coupledom story to my family. It's a done deal and went way better than I was expecting. We don't have to do the thing where we touch each other anymore."

Well, that stung. She'd had the distinct impression he liked touching her.

"Oh, I wish that was true." She stuck an extra tinge of dismay into her tone, just to be sure it was really clear that she wasn't panting after him. Even though she was lying through her teeth. "But we still have all of tomorrow with your family. And you're planning to meet mine, right? We have to sell that we're hopelessly in love all over again. I'm really concerned about tongues wagging. After all, Joy's husband knows everyone who's anyone. The business world is small."

Jonas's eyes went a little wide. "We just have to sell being married. No one said anything about love."

"But that's why people get married, Jonas." Something flickered through his expression that looked a lot like panic. And it set a bunch of gears in motion in her head. Maybe they should be using this time to get matters straight instead of doing a lot of touching. Because all at once, she was really curious about an important aspect of this deal that she'd thus far failed to question. "Don't you think so?"

"That people should only get married if they're in love? I don't know." But he shifted his gaze away so quickly that it was obvious he had something going on inside. "I've never been married before."

That was a careful way to answer the question. Did that mean he had been in love but not enough to marry the girl? Or he'd never been in love? Maybe he was nursing a serious broken heart and it was too painful to discuss. "Your parents are married. Aren't they in love?"

"Sure. It's just not something I've given a lot of thought to."

"So think about it." She was pushing him, plain and simple, but this was important compatibility stuff that she'd never questioned. Everyone believed in love. Right? "I'm just wondering now why you needed a fake wife. Maybe you should have been looking for someone to fall in love with this whole time instead of taking me to lunch for a year."

He hadn't been dating anyone, this she knew for a fact because she'd asked. Multiple times. Her curiosity on the matter might even be described as morbid.

"Viv." His voice had gone quiet and she liked the way he said her name with so much texture. "If I'd wanted to spend time with someone other than you over the last year, I would have. I like you. Is that so hard to believe?"

Her mouth curved up before she could catch it. But why should she? Jonas made her smile, even when he was deflecting her question. Probably because he didn't think about her "that way" no matter how hot the kiss outside her bedroom had been. One-sided then. They were friends. Period. And she should definitely not be sad about that. He was a wonderful, kind man who made not thinking wicked thoughts impossible the longer they sat on a bed together behind closed doors.

Yeah, she could pretend she was practicing for a relationship with some other man all she wanted. Didn't change the fact that deep in her heart Viv wished she could be the person Jonas would fall madly in love with.

But she knew she couldn't keep Jonas. At least she was in the right place to fix her relationship pitfalls.

Now, how did one go about seducing a man while giving him the distinct impression she could take him or leave him?

Five

The bed in Jonas's mother's guest room must have razor blades sewn into the comforter. It was the only explanation for why his skin felt like it was on fire as he forced himself to lie there chatting with Viv as if they really were a real married couple having a debrief after his family's third degree.

They *were* a real married couple having a chat.

If only she hadn't brought up the *L* word. The one concept he had zero desire to talk about when it came to marriage. Surely Viv knew real married couples who didn't love each other. It couldn't be that huge of a departure, otherwise the divorce rate would be a lot lower.

But they were a married couple, albeit not a traditional one behind closed doors. If they were a traditional married couple, Jonas would be sliding his fingers across the mattress and taking hold of Viv's thigh so he could brace her for the exploration to come. His lips would fit so well in the hollow near her throat. So far, she hadn't seemed to clue in that every muscle beneath his skin strained toward her, and he had no idea how she wasn't as affected by the sizzling awareness as he was.

They were on a bed. They were married. The door was closed. What did that equal? Easy math—and it was killing him that they were getting it so wrong. Why wasn't he rolling his wife beneath him and getting frisky with breathless anticipation as they shushed each other before someone heard them through the walls?

"Since we like each other so much, maybe we should talk about the actual sleeping arrangements," she suggested. "There's not really a good way to avoid sharing the bed and we're keeping things platonic when no one's around."

Oh, right, because this was an exercise in insanity, just like dinner. He really shouldn't be picturing Viv sliding between cool sheets, naked of course, and peeking up at him from under her lashes as she clutched the pale blue fabric to her breasts.

"I can sleep on the floor," he croaked. She cocked a brow, eyeing him as if she could see right through his zipper to the hard-on he wasn't hiding very well. "I insist. You're doing me a favor. It's the least I can do."

"I wasn't expecting anyone to sleep on the floor. We're friends. We can sleep in the same bed and keep our hands off each other. Right?" Then she blinked and something happened to her eyes. Her gaze deepened, elongating the moment, and heat teased along the edges of his nerve endings. "Unless you think it would be too much of a temptation."

He swallowed. Was she a mind reader now? How had she figured out that he had less than pure thoughts about sharing a bed with his wife? How easy it would be to reach out in the middle of the night, half-asleep, and pull her closer for a midnight kiss that wouldn't have any daylight consequences because nothing counted in the dark.

Except everything with Viv counted. That was the problem. They had a friendship he didn't want to lose and he had taken a vow with Warren and Hendrix that he couldn't violate.

"No, of course not," he blurted out without checking his emphatic delivery. "I mean, definitely it'll be hard—" *Dear God.* "Nothing will be hard! Everything will be…" *Not easy. Don't say easy.* "I have to go check on…something."

Before he could fully internalize how much of an ass he was making of himself, he bolted from the bed and fled the room, calling over his shoulder, "Feel free to use the bathroom. I'll wait my turn."

Which was a shame because what he really needed was a cold shower. Prowling around the house like a cat burglar because he didn't want to alert anyone he'd just kicked himself out of his own newlywed bedroom, Jonas poked around in his dad's study but felt like he was intruding in the hallowed halls of academia.

He and his dad were night and day. They loved each other, but Brian Kim wasn't a businessman in any way, shape or form. It was like the entrepreneurial gene had skipped a generation. Put Brian in a lecture hall and he was in his element. In truth, the only reason Jonas had gone to Duke was because his father was on faculty and his parents had gotten a discount on tuition. They'd refused to take a dime of Grandfather's money since Brian hadn't filled a position at Kim Electronics.

If his dad had taken a job at any other university, Jonas never would have met Warren, Hendrix and Marcus. His friendship with those guys had shaped his twenties, more so than he'd ever realized, until now.

The funeral had been brutal. So hard to believe his friend was inside that casket. His mom had held his hand the entire time and even as a twenty-one-year-old junior in college who desperately wanted to be hip, he hadn't let go once. Marcus had been down in the dumps for weeks, but they'd all shrugged it off. Typical male pride and bruised feelings. Who hadn't been the victim of a woman's fickle tastes?

But Marcus had been spiraling down and none of them had seen it. That was the problem with love. It made you do crazy, out-of-character things. Like suicide.

Jonas slid into his dad's chair and swiveled it to face the window, letting the memory claw through his gut as he stared blindly at the koi pond outside in the garden. There was no shame in having missed the signs. Everyone had. But that reassurance rang as hollow today as it had ten years ago. What could he have done? Talked sense into the guy? Obviously the pain had been too great, and the lesson for Jonas was clear: don't let a woman get her hooks into you.

That was why he couldn't touch Viv anymore. The temptation wasn't just too much. It was deadly. Besides, she was his friend. He'd already crossed a bunch of lines in the name of ensuring his family bought into the marriage, but it was all just an excuse to have his cake and eat Viv, too.

Bad, bad thing to be thinking about. There was a part of him that couldn't believe Viv would be dangerous to his mental state. But the risks were too great, especially to their friendship. They'd gone a whole year without being tempted. What was different now? Proximity? Awareness? The fact that he'd already kissed her and couldn't undo the effect on his body every time he got within touching distance of her?

That one.

Sleeping with her in the bed was going to be torture. He really didn't know if he had it in him. Probably the best thing to do was sleep on the couch in the living room and set an alarm for something ridiculous like 5:00 a.m. Then he could go for a jog and come back like he'd slept in Viv's bed all night long. Of course he'd never jogged in his life...but he could start. Might burn off some of the awareness he couldn't shake.

That was the best plan. He headed back to the bedroom they shared to tell her.

But when he eased open the door and slipped inside, she was still in the bathroom. He settled onto the bed to wait, next to her open suitcase. There was literally no reason for him to glance inside other than it was right there. Open. With a frothy bunch of racy lingerie laid out across the other clothes.

Holy crap. Jonas's eyes burned the longer he stared at the thin straps and drapes of lace. Was that the *top*? Viv's breasts were supposed to be covered by that? Something that skimpy should be illegal. And red. But the lace was lemon yellow, the color of the frosting Viv slathered all over the cupcakes she always brought him when they had lunch. His mouth watered at the thought of tasting Viv through all that lace. It would be easy. The pattern would show 90 percent of her skin.

The little panties lay innocuously to the side as if

an afterthought. Probably because there wasn't enough lace making up the bottom half of the outfit to rightfully call them panties. He could picture them perfectly on his wife's body and he could envision slowly stripping them off even more vividly.

Wait. What was Viv doing with such smoking-hot lingerie?

Was she planning to wear it for *him*? His brain had no ability to make sense of this revelation. She'd brought lingerie. To wear. Of course the only man in the vicinity was Jonas. Who else would she be wearing it for?

That was totally against the rules.

And totally against what he was capable of giving her in this marriage. She might as well drape herself in hearts and flowers. Viv clearly thought love was a recipe for marriage. Stir well and live happily ever after. He wasn't the right ingredient for that mix.

The sound of running water being shut off rattled through the walls. Viv had just emerged from the shower. He should get the hell out of that bedroom right now. But before he could stand, she walked out of the bathroom holding a towel loosely around her body. Her *naked* body. She was still wet. His gaze traced the line of one drop as it slid down her shoulder and disappeared behind the towel.

"Oh. I didn't know you'd come back," she announced unnecessarily as he was reasonably certain she wouldn't have waltzed into the room mostly naked if she'd known he was sitting on the bed.

"Sorry," he muttered, and meant to avert his eyes but the towel had slipped a little, which she'd done nothing to correct.

Maybe she wanted him to catch a glimpse of her perfect breasts. Not that he knew for sure that they were perfect. But the little half-moon slices peeking above the towel flashed at him more brightly than a neon sign, and his whole body went up in flames.

Anything that powerful at only a quarter strength had to be perfect in its entirety.

"Did you want to take a turn in the bathroom?" she asked casually. Still standing there. Wet. In a towel. Naked.

"Uh, sure." He didn't stand. He should cross the room and barricade himself in the bathroom, where it wouldn't matter if she'd used all the hot water because the shower needed to be glacial.

"Okay. Can you give me two minutes? I need to dry my hair." And then she laughed with a little peal that punched him the gut. "Normally I would wrap it up in the towel but there are only two and I didn't want to hog them all."

Then she pulled on the edge of the towel, loosening it from the column it formed around her body and lifted the tail end to the ends of her dripping hair. A long slice of skin peeked through the opening she'd unwittingly created and the answering flash of heat that exploded in his groin would have put him on his knees if he'd been standing. Good thing he hadn't moved.

"You should get dressed," he suggested, but she didn't hear him because his voice wasn't working. Besides, *dressed* could have a lot of different meanings, and the frothy yellow concoction in her suitcase appeared to be the next outfit of choice. If she hadn't been planning to slip it on, it wouldn't be on top, laid out so carefully.

Oh, man. Would she have been wearing it when he got into bed later? No warning, just bam!

He should pretend he hadn't seen the yellow concoction. How else could he find out if that had been her plan? That had to be her plan. Please, God, let it be her plan.

He was so hard, it was a wonder his erection hadn't busted out of his zipper.

Clearing his throat, he tested out speaking again. "I can come back."

That, she heard. "Oh, you don't have to. Really, I've taken way too long already. We're sharing and I'm not used to that. The shower was lovely and I couldn't help standing there under the spray, just letting my mind drift."

Great. Now his mind was drifting—into the shower with her as she stood there. Naked. Letting the water sluice down her body, eyes closed with a small, rapturous smile gracing her face.

He groaned. What was he doing to himself?

"Are you okay?" Her attention honed in on him and she apparently forgot she wasn't wearing anything but a damp towel because she immediately crossed the room to loom over him, her expression laced with concern.

It would take less than a second to reach out and snag her by the waist, pulling her down into his lap. That towel would fall, revealing her perfect breasts, and they'd be right there, ripe and available to taste. No yellow concoction needed. But that would be criminal. She should get to wear her newlywed lingerie if she wanted.

"Oh." Viv blushed all at once, the pink stain spreading across her cheeks, and Jonas could not tear his eyes off her face. But she was staring at the open suitcase. "You didn't see that ridiculous thing Grace gave me, did you?"

She picked up the yellow lacy top and held it up to her body, draping it over the towel one-handed, which had the immediate consequence of smooshing her breasts higher. "Can you imagine me wearing this?"

With absolute, brilliant clarity.

"I don't know what she was thinking," Viv continued as if his entire body wasn't poised to explode. "'Open this with Jonas,' she says with a sly wink. I thought it was going to be a joke, like a gravy boat, and besides, this isn't a real marriage, so I didn't think you'd actually want to help open gifts. Sorry I didn't wait for you."

She rolled her eyes with another laugh that did not help things down below.

"That's okay. Next time." What was he saying? *Sure, I'll help open future gifts full of shockingly transparent clothing that would make a porn star blush?* "Your sister meant well. She doesn't know we're not sleeping together."

Or rather they weren't yet. In a scant few minutes, they'd be in the bed. Together. Maybe some sleeping would occur but it wasn't looking too likely unless he got his body cooled down to something well below its current thermonuclear state.

"Well, true. But obviously she expects us to be hot and heavy, right? I mean, this is the kind of stuff a woman wears for a man who can't keep his hands off her." Suddenly, she swept him with a glance that held a glittery sort of challenge. "We should probably practice that, don't you think?"

"What?" he squawked. "You want me to practice not being able to keep my hands off you?"

Actually, he needed to practice self-control, not the other way around. Restraint was the name of the game. Perfect. He could focus on that instead of the fact that the lingerie had been a gift, not a carefully crafted plan to drive him over the brink.

It was a testament to how messed up he was that he couldn't squelch his disappointment.

She nodded. "My sister just got married not too long ago and she's pretty open with me about how hot the sex is. I think she envisions all newlyweds being like that."

"That doesn't mean she expects us to strip down in your parents' foyer," he countered a little too forcefully. Mostly because he was envisioning how hot *this* newlywed couple could be. They could give Grace and her husband a run for her money, all right.

No. No, they could not.

Viv was not wearing the yellow lacy gateway to heaven for him tonight or any night. She wasn't challenging him to out-sex her sister's marriage. There was no sex at all in their future because Viv had a career she cared about and really didn't have time for a man's inconvenient attraction. Even if the man was her husband. Especially if the man was her husband who had promised to keep things platonic.

Of course he'd done that largely for himself. He'd never experienced such a strong physical pull before and he wasn't giving in to it no matter how badly he wanted to. There was a slippery edge between keeping himself out of trouble so he could honor his promise to his late friend and maintaining his integrity with Viv and his family about the nature of his marriage.

On that note, he needed to change the subject really fast. And get his rampant need under control before he lost everything.

Viv couldn't quite catch her breath. Her lungs ached to expand but the towel was in a precarious spot. If she breathed any deeper, it would slip completely from her nerveless fingers.

Though based on how long it was taking Jonas to clue in that this was a seduction scene, maybe throwing her boobs in his face would get the point across.

God, she sucked at this. Obviously. The girls on TV made it look so simple. She'd bet a million dollars that if this scene had happened on *Scandal*, the seductress would already be in the middle of her third orgasm.

Maybe she *should* have opened the wedding gift with Jonas instead of laying it out so he could find it. For some reason, she'd thought it would give him ideas. That he'd maybe take the lead and they could get something going while they had the perfect setup to indulge in the sparks that only burned hotter the longer they didn't consummate their marriage.

How was she supposed to prove she could be the opposite of clingy with a man she wanted more than oxygen if he wouldn't take her up on the invitation she'd been dangling in his face?

"Instead of practicing anything physical," Jonas said, "we should get our stories straight. We're not going to be hanging out with your family anytime soon but mine is just on the other side of the door. I don't want any missteps like the one at dinner where we didn't plan our responses ahead of time and somehow ended up promising to go to Korea."

"I don't mind going to Korea, Jonas. I would love to see it."

He shook his head with bemusement. "It's a sixteen-hour trip and that's only if there's a not a horribly long line in customs, which even a Kim cannot cut through. Trust me, I'm doing you a favor by not taking you."

How had they shifted from talking about hot sex to visiting his grandfather? That was not how this was supposed to go.

"Well, we have plenty of time to talk about our stories, too," she said brightly. "And the good news is that my hair is almost dry so the bathroom is yours. I like to read before going to sleep so I'll just be here whenever you're ready."

"Oh. Um…" Jonas glanced at the bed and back at her. "Okay. I was thinking about sleeping on the couch and setting an alarm—"

"You can't do that," she cut him off in a rush. That would ruin everything. "What if someone gets up for a midnight snack? Also, the couch would be so uncomfortable. Sleep here. I insist."

She shooed him toward the bathroom and the moment he shut the door, she dragged air into her lungs in deep gulps as she dropped the towel and twisted her hair into a modified updo at her crown, spilling tendrils down her cheeks. Then she slithered into the shameless yellow teddy and panties set that she'd picked out with Grace yesterday. Strictly so she could rub it in that she had a hot husband to wear it for, of course. And then she'd had Grace gift wrap it. The sly wink had been all her sister's idea, so she really hadn't fibbed much when she'd related the story to Jonas.

The lace chafed at her bare nipples, sending ripples

of heat through her core. The panties rode high and tight, the strings threading between her cheeks. Not a place she was used to having pressure and friction, but it was oddly exciting.

No wonder women wore this stuff. She felt sexy and more than a little turned on just by virtue of getting dressed. Who knew?

The sound of running water drifted through the walls as Jonas went through his nightly routine. She dove into bed and pulled up the covers until they were tight around her shoulders. Wait. That wasn't going to work. Experimentally, she draped the sheet across her chest like a toga, and threw her shoulders back. Huh. The one breast looked spectacular in the low-cut lace teddy, but the other one was covered up, which didn't seem like the point. Inching the sheet down, she settled into place against the pillow until she was happy with how she looked.

That was a lot of skin on *display*. Much more than she was used to. The lace left little to the imagination.

Surely this would be enough to entice Jonas into making the most of this opportunity to share a bedroom.

Light. She leaped up and slammed down the switch, leaving only the bedside lamp illuminated and leaped back under the covers. The doorknob to the bathroom rattled and she lost her nerve, yanking the sheet back up to cover the yellow lace until X-ray vision would be the only way Jonas could tell what she was wearing. He strode into the room.

Oh, God. Was a more delicious man ever created in the history of time? He'd untucked his button-down and the tail hung casually below his waist. Plenty of access for a woman to slide her hands underneath. There was a gaping hole where his tie had been. A V framed a slice of his chest and he'd rolled his sleeves up to midforearm. It was the most undressed she'd ever seen him and her pulse quickened the closer he came.

This gorgeous creature was about to strip all that off and *get into bed*. With her. This was such a bad idea. Alluring and aloof was not in her wheelhouse and at that moment, she wanted Jonas with a full body ache that felt completely foreign and completely right at the same time.

"I thought you were going to be reading," he said, and stopped in the middle of the room as if he'd hit an invisible wall.

So close. And yet so far.

She shook her head, scrambling for a plausible excuse when she'd just said that was what she planned to do. Couldn't hold an e-reader and pretend you weren't wearing sexy lingerie that screamed *put your hands on me* at the same time.

In retrospect, that might have been a nice scene. She could have been reading with the tablet propped up on her stomach, which would have left her torso completely bare without making it look like she'd set up the scene that way. Dang it. Too late now.

"I couldn't find anything that held my attention."

"Oh. Okay."

And then the entire world fell away along with most of her senses as Jonas started unbuttoning his shirt. It was a slow, torturous event as he slipped the buttons free and each one revealed more of his beautiful body.

Thank God she hadn't stuck a book in front of her face. Otherwise she'd have missed the Jonas Striptease.

She glanced up to see his dark eyes on hers. Their

gazes connected and she had the distinct impression he hadn't expected her to be watching him undress. But he didn't seem terribly unhappy about the audience, since he kept going. She didn't look away either.

He let the shirt fall, revealing first one shoulder, then the other. It shouldn't have been such a shock to see the indentations of muscles in his biceps as his arms worked off the shirt. She knew he hit the gym on a regular basis. They'd been friends for a year and talked about all manner of subjects. Sometimes he told her about his workout routine or mentioned that he'd switched it up and his arms were sore. Little had she realized what a visual panorama had been in store for her as a result.

"I feel like I should be wearing something sparkly underneath my pants," Jonas said with wry amusement. "Would it be possible for you to not watch me?"

"Oh. Um…sure." Cheeks on fire, she flipped over and faced the wall, careful to keep the sheet up around her neck. With the motion, it stretched tight. More mummy than Marilyn Monroe, but this was her first seduction. Surely even a woman like Marilyn had a few practice runs before she got it right. This one was Viv's.

And she needed a lot of practice, clearly, since she'd been caught staring and made Jonas uncomfortable at the same time. The whisper of fabric hitting the carpet made her doubly sorry she hadn't been facedown in a book when he came out of the bathroom because she could easily have pretended to be reading while watching the slow reveal out of the corner of her eye.

The bed creaked and the mattress shifted with Jonas's weight. "Still think this is a good idea?"

"I never said it was a good idea," she shot back over her shoulder. "I said our friendship could take it."

Which wasn't a given now that he was so close and so male and so much the subject of her fantasies that started and ended in a bed very much like this one. And she'd been forced to miss half of it due to Jonas's inconvenient sense of propriety. Well, he was done undressing now, right? This was her seduction and she wanted to face him. Except just as she rolled, he snapped off the bedside lamp, plunging the room into darkness.

"Good night," Jonas said, his voice sinfully rich in the dark.

The covers pulled a little as he turned over and settled into position. To go to sleep.

As mood killers went, that was a big one. She'd totally botched this.

Okay. Not totally. This was just a minor setback, most likely because she was trying to play hard to get, which was not as easy as it sounded, and frankly, not her typical method of operation. Plus? This was not a typical relationship. Jonas needed to keep her around, so by default this wasn't going to go like it had with her ex-boyfriends.

She had to approach this like a new recipe that hadn't quite turned out because she'd gone against her instincts and added an ingredient that she didn't like. And if she didn't like it, what was the point?

This was her cupcake to bake. Being the opposite of clingy and needy had only gotten her a disinterested husband—and rightfully so. How was he even supposed to know she wished he'd roll back over and explore the lingerie-clad body she'd hidden under the covers like a blushing virgin bride? Viv wasn't the kind of woman to inspire a man to slavish passion or it would have happened already.

She had to be smart if she couldn't be a femme fatale.

She blinked against the dark and tried not to focus on how the sound of Jonas breathing fluttered against her skin in a very distracting way. Somehow she was going to have to announce her interest in taking things to the next level in big bold letters without also giving him the impression she couldn't live without him. Though perhaps that last part wouldn't be too difficult; after all, she'd already been pretending for a year.

Six

After the weekend of torture, Jonas went to work on Monday with renewed determination to get his grandfather moving on the Park Industries merger. The sooner the ink was dry on that deal, the better. Then Jonas could get over his irritation that his marriage to Viv was what had tipped the scales toward his grandfather's decision to retire.

Grandfather recognized Jonas's accomplishments with Kim Electronics. Deep down, he knew that. But it rankled that the conversation about naming Jonas as the next CEO had come about *after* Grandfather had met Viv.

Didn't matter. The subject had come up. That was enough. And Jonas intended to make sure the subject didn't get dropped, because if he was forced to stay married to Viv, he should get something out of it. An Academy Award wouldn't be out of line after the stellar performance he'd turned in at his parents' house. How he'd acted like he'd been sleeping all night while lying next to his wife was still a mystery to him and he was the one who'd pulled it off.

Her scent still haunted him at odd moments. Like now. This conference call he'd supposedly been participating in had gotten maybe a quarter of his attention. Which was not a good way to prove he deserved the position of CEO.

But it was a perfect way to indulge in the memory of the sweet way she'd curled up next to him, her even breathing oddly arousing and lulling at the same time. He'd expected it to be weird the next morning, like maybe they wouldn't look each other in the eye, but Viv had awoken refreshed and beautiful, as if she'd gotten a great night's sleep. He pretended the same and they settled into an easy camaraderie around his parents that hadn't raised a single brow.

At least that part was over. Viv's mom and dad had invited them for dinner on Friday and he was plenty nervous about that experience. It would probably be fine. As long as he didn't have to act like he couldn't keep his hands off Viv. Or act like he didn't want to touch her. Actually, he'd lost track of *what* he was supposed to be doing. Hence the reason he hated lying. The truth was so much easier.

But when he got home that evening after a long day that had included a two-hour debrief with Legal regarding the merger proposal, Viv was sitting on the couch with two glasses of wine. She smiled at him and he felt entirely incapable of faking anything. Especially if it came down to pretending he didn't want to be with her.

His answering smile broadened hers and that set off

all sorts of fireworks inside that should have been a big fat warning to back off, but he was tired and there was absolutely nothing wrong with having a glass of wine with his friend Viv after work. That was his story and he was sticking to it.

"Are we celebrating something?" he asked as he hung his work bag on the hook near the refrigerator.

"Yes, that I can in fact open a bottle of wine all by myself." She laughed with that little peal he'd never noticed before he'd married her, but seemed to be a common occurrence lately. Or had she always laughed like that and he'd been too stuck in his own head to notice how warm it was?

"Was that in question?" He took the long-stemmed glass from her outstretched fingers and eased onto the couch next to her. Instantly, that turned into a big mistake as her scent wrapped around him. It slammed through his gut and his arm jerked, nearly spilling the wine.

For God's sake. This ridiculousness had to stop, especially before Friday or the second family trial by fire would end in a blaze.

"I'm just not talented in the cork-pulling arena," she answered casually as if she hadn't noticed his idiocy. "My skills start and end with baking."

Yes. Baking. They could talk about cupcakes while he got back on track. "Speaking of which, I wasn't expecting you home. Doesn't the shop stay open until seven on Mondays?"

She smiled. "You've been memorizing my work schedule? That's sweet. Josie is closing up for me. I wanted to be here when you got home."

"You did? Why?"

Because I couldn't stay away, Jonas. You're so much more interesting to me than cupcakes, Jonas. I want to strip you naked and have my wicked way with you, Jonas.

There came her gorgeous laugh again. He couldn't hear it enough, especially when he was in the middle of being such a doofus. If she was laughing, that was a good thing. Otherwise, he'd owe her an apology. Not that she could read his thoughts, thank God.

"I wanted to see you. We're still friends, right?"

Oh, yeah. "Right."

"Also, I wasn't kidding when I said my sisters are going to have an eagle eye on our relationship this Friday." Viv sipped her wine, her gaze on his over the rim. "We're still a little jumpy around each other. I'm not sure why, but sharing a bed didn't seem to help."

Huge mystery there. Maybe because his awareness level had shot up into the stratosphere since he'd woken up with a woman whom he hadn't touched one single time. Or it could be because he'd been kicking himself over his regret ever since. He shouldn't regret not touching her. It was the right move.

"No, it didn't help," he muttered. "That wasn't ever going to be the result of sleeping together platonically."

She nodded sagely. "Yes, I realized that sometime between then and now. Don't worry. I have a new plan."

"I wasn't worried. What is it?"

"We're trying too hard. We need to dial it back and spend time as friends. We were comfortable around each other then. It can totally be that way again."

That sounded really great to him. And also like there was a catch he couldn't quite see. Cautiously he eyed her. "What, like I take you to lunch and we just talk about stuff?"

"Sure." She shrugged and reached out to lace her fingers through his free hand. "See, we can hold hands and it doesn't mean anything. I'm just hanging out with my friend Jonas, whom I like. Hey, Jonas, guess what?"

He had to grin. This was not the worst plan he'd ever heard. In fact, it was pretty great. He'd missed their easy camaraderie and the lack of pretension. Never had she made him feel like he should be anything other than himself when they hung out. "Hey, Viv. What?"

"I made reservations at this new restaurant in Cary that sounds fab. It's Thai."

"That's my favorite." Which she well knew. It was hers, too. He took the first deep breath in what seemed like hours. They were friends. He could dang well act like one and stop nosing around Viv like a hormonal teenager.

"Drink your wine and then we'll go. My treat."

"No way. You opened the bottle of wine. The least I can do is spring for dinner."

"Well, it was a major accomplishment," she allowed, and clinked her glass to his as he held out the stemware. "I'm thrilled to have it recognized as such."

And the evening only got better from there. Jonas drove Viv to the restaurant and they chattered all the way about everything and nothing, which he'd have called a major accomplishment, too, since he managed to concentrate on the conversation and not on the expanse of Viv's bare leg mere inches from his hand resting on the gearshift. The food was good and the service exceptional.

As they walked in the door of the condo later, Jonas paused and helped Viv take off her jacket, then turned to hang it up for her in the foyer coat closet.

"I have to say," he called over his shoulder as he slid the hanger into place. "Dinner was a great idea."

He shut the door and Viv was still standing there in the foyer with a small smile.

"It's the best date I've been on in a long time," she said. "And seems like the plan worked. Neither of us is acting weird or jumpy."

"True." He'd relaxed a while back and didn't miss the edginess that had plagued him since the wedding ceremony. He and Viv were friends and that was never going to change. That was the whole reason he'd come up with this idea in the first place. "We may not set off the fire alarms when we visit with your family on Friday, but we can certainly pull off the fact that we like each other, which is not something all married couples can say."

That was fine with him. Better that way anyway. His reaction to the pull between him and Viv was ridiculous. So unlike him. He had little experience with something so strong that it dug under his skin, and he'd handled it badly.

Fortunately, he hadn't done anything irreversible that would have ruined their friendship. Though there'd been more than a handful of moments in that bed at his parents' that he'd been really afraid it was going to go the other way.

But then she stepped a little closer to him in the foyer, waltzing into his space without hesitation. The foyer was just a small area at the entrance of the condo with a coat closet and nothing more to recommend it. So there was little else to take his attention off the woman who'd suddenly filled it with her presence.

"We've been friends a long time," she said, and it was such a strange, unnecessary comment, but he nodded anyway because something had shifted in the atmosphere.

He couldn't put his finger on it. The relaxed, easy vibe from the restaurant had morphed into something else—a quickened sense of anticipation that he couldn't explain, but didn't hate. As if this really was a date and they'd moved on to the second part of the evening's activities.

"We've done a lot of firsts in the last little while," she continued, also unnecessarily because he was well aware that he'd shifted the dynamic of their relationship by marrying her.

"Yeah. Tonight went a long way toward getting us back to normal. To being friends without all the weirdness that sprang up when I kissed you."

That was probably the dumbest thing he could have said. He'd thrown that down between them and it was like opening the electrical panel of a television, where all the live components were exposed, and all it would take was one wrong move to fry the delicate circuitry.

Better to keep the thing covered.

But it was too late. Her gaze landed square on his mouth as if she was reliving the kiss, too. Not the nice and unexpectedly sweet kiss at the wedding ceremony. But the hot, tongue-on-tongue kiss outside her bedroom when they'd been practicing being a couple. The necessity of that practice had waned since his family had bought the marriage hook, line and sinker. Sure, they still had to get through her family, but he wasn't worried about it, racy lingerie gifts aside.

Now the only reason to ever kiss Viv again would be because he couldn't stop himself.

Which was the worst reason he could think of. And keep thinking about, over and over again.

"I don't think it was weirdness, Jonas," she murmured.

Instantly, he wished there was still some circumstance that required her to call him Mr. Kim. Why that was such a turn-on remained a mystery to him. But really, everything about Viv was a turn-on. Her laugh. Her cupcakes. The way her hair lay so shiny and soft against her shoulders.

"Trust me, it was weird," he muttered. "I gave myself entirely too many inappropriate thoughts with that kiss."

And that was the danger of being lulled back into a false sense of security with the sociable, uneventful dinner. He'd fallen into friendship mode, where he could say anything on his mind without consequence.

The admission that had just come out of his mouth was going to have consequences.

Her smile went from zero to sixty in less than a second and all at once, he wasn't sure the consequences were going to be anything close to what he'd envisioned. She waltzed even closer and reached up to adjust his tie in a provocative move that shouldn't have been as affecting as it was.

The tie hadn't needed adjusting. The knot was precisely where he'd placed it hours ago when he'd gotten dressed for work. It slid down a few centimeters and then a few more as she loosened it.

Loosened it. As if she intended to take it off.

But she stopped short of committing, which was good. Really…good. He swallowed as she speared him with her contemplative gaze, her hands still at his collar in an intimate touch. She was so close he could pull her into his arms if he wanted to.

He wanted to. Always.

Dinner hadn't changed that.

"The thing is, Jonas," she said. "I've had some thoughts, too. And if yours are the same as mine, I'm trying to figure out why they're inappropriate."

She flattened her hands on his lapels. The pressure sang through him and it would feel even better if he didn't have a whole suit jacket and two shirts between her palms and his skin.

The direction of this conversation floored him. And if she kept it up, the floor was exactly where they were going to end up.

"What are you saying, Viv?" he asked hoarsely, scrambling to understand. "That you lie awake at night and think about that kiss, aching to do it again?"

She nodded and something so powerful swept through his body that he could hardly breathe. This was the opposite of what should be happening. She should be backing off and citing her inability to focus on a man and her career at the same time. She was too busy, too involved in her business to date. This was the absolute he'd banked on for long agonizing hours, the thing that was keeping him from indulging in the forbidden draw between them.

Because if he gave in, he'd have no control over what happened next. That certainty had already been proven with what little they'd experimented so far. More would be catastrophic.

And so, so fantastically amazing.

"After tonight, I'm convinced we're missing an opportunity here," she said, her voice dripping with something sensual that he'd never have expected from his sunny friend Viviana Dawson. *Kim.*

Viv wasn't his friend. She was his wife. He'd been ignoring that fact for an entire day, but it roared back to the forefront with an implication he couldn't ignore. Except he didn't know what it meant to him, not really. Not just a means to an end, though it was an inescapable fact that she'd married him as a favor.

And he wanted to exploit that favor to get her naked and under him? It was improper, ridiculous. So very illicit that his body tightened with thick anticipation.

"What opportunity is that?" he murmured, letting his gaze flick over her face, searching for some sign that the answer about to come out of her mouth *was not* a green light to get naked.

Because he'd have a very difficult time saying no. In fact, he couldn't quite remember why he should say no. He shouldn't say no. If nothing else, taking this next step meant he wasn't lying to anyone about their marriage.

Her limpid brown eyes locked on to his. "We're both too busy to date. And even if we weren't, I have a feeling that 'oh, by the way, I'm married' isn't a great pickup line. You said it yourself. We spark. If our friendship can take a kiss, maybe it can take more. We should find out."

More. He liked the word *more* a lot. Especially if her dictionary defined it as lots and lots of sex while maintaining their friendship. If things got too intense, he could back off with no harm, no foul. It was like the absolute best of all worlds.

Unless that wasn't what she meant.

Clarification would be in order, just to be sure they were speaking the same language. "More?"

"Come on, Jonas." She laughed a little breathlessly and it trilled through him. "Are you going to make me spell it out?"

"Yes, I absolutely am," he growled, because the whole concept of Viv talking dirty to him was doing things to his insides that he was enjoying the hell out of. If he'd known dinner was *this* kind of date, he'd have skipped dessert. "I want to be crystal clear about what's on the table here."

Instead of suggesting things Jonas could do to her— all of which he'd immediately commit to memory so he didn't miss a single one—she watched him as she hooked the neckline of her dress and pulled it to the side. A flash of yellow seared his vision as his entire body tensed in recognition.

"I'm wearing my sister's gift," she murmured, and that admission was as much of a turn-on as any dirty talk. Maybe more so because he'd been fantasizing about that scrap of yellow lace for a million years.

"I bet it looks amazing on you."

"Only one way to find out," she shot back and curled her fingers around his lapels to yank him forward.

He met her mouth in a searing kiss without hesitation. All of his reservations melted in an instant as he sank into her, shaping her lips with his as he consumed her heat, letting it spread deep inside.

Why had he resisted this? Viv didn't want anything from him, didn't expect an emotional outpouring or even anything permanent. This was all going to end at some point and thus didn't count. No chance for romantic nonsense. No declarations of love would ever be forthcoming—on either side. Jonas's sense of honor would be intact, as would his sworn vow to Warren and Hendrix.

Instead of two friends pretending to be a married couple having sex, they were going to be married friends who *were* having sex. Living the truth appealed to him enormously. Desire swept through him as he got great handfuls of Viv's skin under his palms and everything but his wife drained from his mind.

Viv would have sworn on a truckload of Bibles that the kiss outside her bedroom last week had been the hottest one she'd ever participate in.

She'd have been wrong.

That kiss had been startling in its perfection. Unexpected in its heat. It had gotten her motor humming pretty fast. She'd been angling for another one just like that. Thank God she hadn't gotten her wish.

This kiss exploded in her core like a cannon. Desire crackled through the air as Jonas backed her up against the wall, crowding her against it with his hard body, demanding that her every curve conform to him. Her flesh rapidly obeyed. She nearly wept with the glory of Jonas pressed against her exactly as she'd fantasized hundreds of times.

He angled her jaw with his strong fingers until he got her situated the way he apparently wanted and then plunged in with the wickedest of caresses. His tongue slicked across hers so sensuously that she moaned against it, would have sagged if he hadn't had her pinned to the wall.

His hands nipped at her waist, skimmed upward and

hooked both sides of the neckline. The fabric tore at the seams as he separated it from her shoulders, and she gasped.

"I need to see you," he murmured fiercely. "I'll buy you two to make up for this one."

And with that, the dress came apart in his hands. He peeled it from between them, following the line of the reveal with his hot mouth, laving at her exposed flesh until he caught the silk strap of the yellow teddy in his teeth, scraping the sensitive hollow of her shoulder.

The sensation shot through her center with tight, heated pulls. *Oh, my.* His fingers tangled in the strap, binding his palm to her shoulder as he explored the skin beneath the yellow lace with his tongue, dipping and diving into the holes of the pattern. Then his lips closed around her nipple through the fabric and her whole body jerked. Hot, wet heat dampened the scrap between her legs. The awareness that Jonas had drenched her panties so quickly only excited her more.

What had happened to the kind, generous man she'd been so intent on seducing? He'd become a hungry, untamed creature who wanted to devour her. She loved every second. His tongue flicked out to tease her nipple, wetting the lace, and it was wickedly effective. Moans poured from her throat as her head thunked back against the wall.

All at once, he sank to his knees and trailed his lips across the gap between the top and the bottom of her sexy lingerie set, murmuring her full name. *Viviana.* The sound of it rang in her ears as he worshipped her stomach with his mouth, and it was poetry.

Her thighs pressed together, seeking relief from the ache his touch had created, and she arched into his lips, his hands, crying out as his fingers worked under the hem of her soaked panties. The gorgeous man she'd married glanced up at her from his supine position, his gaze so wickedly hot that she experienced a small quake at that alone, but then he slid one finger along her crease, teasing her core until she opened wider, begging him to fill her.

He did. Oh, how he did, one quick motion, then back out again. The exquisite friction burned through her core a second time and she cried out.

"Please, Jonas" dripped from her mouth with little gasping sighs and she whimpered as she pleaded with him for whatever he planned to give her next.

She didn't know she could be this wanton, that the man she'd married could drive her to neediness so easily. It was so hot that she felt the gathering of her release before she was ready for the exquisite torture to end. No way to hold back. She crested the peak and came with hard ripples against Jonas's fingers. The orgasm drained her of everything but him.

Falling apart at his hands was better than what she'd dreamed of, hoped for, imagined—and then some. And it still wasn't over.

He nipped at her lace-covered sex and swept her up in his arms, still quaking, to carry her to his bedroom. Blindly, she tried to clear her senses long enough to gain some semblance of control. Why, she wasn't sure, but being wound up in Jonas's arms wearing nothing but wet lace while he was still fully dressed felt a lot like she'd surrendered more than she'd intended to.

But he wasn't finished with the revelations.

He laid her out on the comforter and watched her as he stripped out of his suit jacket and tie. She shivered long and hard as he began unbuttoning his shirt, but she didn't dare blink for fear of missing the greatest show on earth—the sight of her husband shedding his clothes. For her. Because she'd finally gotten him to see reason.

They were friends. What better foundation was there to get naked with someone than because you liked each other? It was sheer brilliance, if she did say so herself. The fact that she'd been racking her brain over how to best get to this place when the answer had been staring her in the face for a year? She'd rather not dwell on that.

Good thing she had plenty else to occupy her mind. That beautiful torso of his came into sight, still covered by a white undershirt that clung to his biceps and lean waist, and she wanted to touch him so badly her fingers tingled. But then his hands moved to his belt and she didn't move. Couldn't. Her lungs rattled with the need to expand. Slowly, the belt loosened and he pulled it from the loops. After an eternity, it dropped to the floor, followed shortly by the pants, and then came the pièce de résistance. Jonas stripped off his undershirt and worked off his boxers in the most spectacular reveal of all. Better than Christmas, her birthday and flipping the sign in Cupcaked's window to Open for the first time.

Her husband's body was gorgeous, long, lean. Vibrating with need that hungrily sniffed out hers as he crawled onto the bed and onto her, easily knocking her back to the mattress, covering her body with his.

And then she wasn't so coherent after that. His arms encircled her as easily as his dominant presence did. His kiss claimed her lips irrevocably, imprinting them with his particular brand of possession, the likes of which she'd never known. Never understood could exist.

The sensuous haze he dropped her into was delicious

and she soaked it in, content to let him take his time as he explored her body with his hands more thoroughly than she'd have imagined possible when she still wore the yellow lace. She was so lost in him that it took her a minute to remember that she could indulge herself, too, if she wished.

Viv flattened her palms to his chest, memorizing the peaks and valleys of his body, reveling in the heat under her fingertips. She slid downward to cup his buttocks, shifting to align their hips because the ache at her core had only been awakened, not sated, and he had precisely what she needed.

He groaned deep in his throat as she circled against his thick, gorgeous erection, grinding her hips for maximum impact. The answering tilt of his hips enflamed her. As did the quickening of his breath.

"I need to be inside you," he murmured. "Before I lose my mind."

Rolling with her in his arms, he reached one hand out to sling open the bedside table and extracted a box of condoms with ruthless precision. In seconds, he'd sheathed himself and rolled back into place against her.

His thumb slid into the indentation in her chin, levering her head up to lock his hot-eyed gaze onto her as he notched himself at her entrance.

The tip of his shaft tormented her, sensitizing everything it touched as he paused in the worst sort of tease.

"Jonas," she gasped.

"Right here, sweetheart. Tell me what you want."

"Everything." And she couldn't take it back, no matter how much of a mistake it was to admit that she wasn't the kind of woman who could be in the midst of such passion and hold back.

Except she wasn't entirely sure he meant for her to as he gripped her hip with his strong fingers, lifted and pushed in with a groan, spreading her wide as he filled her. The luscious solid length of him stretched her tight, and before she could question it, one tear slipped from the corner of her eye. It was a testament to the perfection of how he felt moving inside her, how wholly encompassing the sensations were that washed over her as Jonas made love to her.

And she was ten kinds of a fool if she thought she could keep pretending this was practice for her next relationship.

"Amazing. Beautiful. Mine." Words rained down on her from Jonas's mouth as he increased the tempo. "I can't believe how this feels…you're so wet, so silky. I can't stop. Can't hold back."

For a woman who had never incited much more than mild interest in a man, to be treated to this kind of evidence that she was more than he could take—it was everything. "Give it all to me."

Unbelievably, there *was* more and he gave it to her, driving her to a soaring crescendo that made her feel more alive than anything in her memory. No longer was this bed a proving ground to show she could be with a man and not pour all of herself into him. He demanded her participation, wrung every drop of her essence out of her body.

She gladly surrendered it. Jonas was it for her, the man she'd married, the man she'd wanted for so very long.

As they both roared toward a climax, she had half a second to capture his face in her palms and kiss him with all the passion she could muster before they both shattered. She swallowed his groan and took the shudders of his body, absorbing them into hers even as she rippled through her own release. Everything was so much bigger, stronger, crisper than she'd have ever imagined and his mouth under hers curved into a blissful smile that her soul echoed.

And as he nestled her into his arms for a few badly needed moments of recovery time, she bit her lip against the wash of emotions that threatened to spill out all over their friendship.

She'd told him their relationship could take this. Now she had to stick to her promise. How in the world she was going to keep him from figuring out that she was in love with him?

Seven

For the second day in a row, Jonas struggled to maintain his composure at work. It was for an entirely different reason today than it had been yesterday. But still. His wife swirled at the center of it and he wasn't sure what to do with that.

Last night had been legendary. Off the charts. Far more explosive than he would have ever guessed—and he'd spent a lot of time contemplating exactly how hot things with Viv could be.

She'd surpassed everything he'd ever experienced. Even here in his somewhat sterile office that had all the hallmarks of a CEO who ran a billion-dollar global company, his loins tightened the second he let his thoughts stray. She'd made him thoroughly question what he knew about how it could be between a man and a woman. How it could be between Jonas and Viv, more importantly, because he had a feeling they weren't done.

How could they be done? He'd barely peeled back the first layer of possibilities, and he was nothing if not ravenous to get started on the second and third layers. Hot Viv. Sensual Viv. The list could be endless.

Instead of drooling like an idiot over the woman he'd married, Jonas squared his shoulders and pushed the erotic images from his mind. The merger with Park was still just a nebulous concept and no one had signed anything. This was the deal of the century, and Jonas had to get it done before anyone thought twice about marriage alliances. Sun Park's grandfather could still pull the plug if he'd had his heart set on a much more intimate merger. Thus far, Jonas had done little but meet with Legal on it.

Four hours later, he had sketched out a proposed hierarchy for the business entities, worked through the human resources tangle of potential duplicate positions and then run the numbers on whether the Kim Building could support the influx of new people. His grandfather would be coming by soon to take a tour and this was exactly the data Jonas needed at his fingertips. Data that would solidify his place as the rightful CEO of Kim Electronics, with or without an *impulse of the heart* on his résumé.

So that was still a sore spot apparently. Jonas tried to shrug it off and prepare for his grandfather's arrival, but wasn't at all surprised that Jung-Su showed up twenty minutes early. Probably a deliberate move to see if Jonas was prepared.

He was nothing if not ready, willing and able to prove

that he was the right choice. He'd been preparing to be his grandfather's successor since college.

He strolled to the reception area, where his admin had made Grandfather comfortable. Technically Jung-Su was the boss of everyone in this building, but he hadn't visited America in several years. Jonas held the helm here and he appreciated that Grandfather didn't throw his weight around. They had professional, mutual respect for each other, which Jonas had to believe would ultimately hold sway.

Jung-Su glanced up as Jonas came forward, his weathered face breaking into a polite smile. Grandfather stood and they shook hands.

"Please follow me," Jonas said, and indicated the direction. "I'd like to show you the executive offices."

Jung-Su nodded and inclined his head, but instead of following Jonas, he drew abreast and walked in lockstep toward the elevator. Over the weekend, they'd done a lot of sitting down and Jonas hadn't noticed how much his grandfather had shrunk. Jonas had always been taller and more slender to his grandfather's stocky build, but more so now, and it was a visual cue that his grandfather had aged. As much as Jonas had focused on getting his grandfather comfortable with passing the mantel, he'd given little thought to the idea that becoming the next CEO of the global company meant his mentorship with Jung-Su would be over.

"Tell me," Grandfather said as they reached the elevator. "How is your lovely wife?"

"She's…" *A vixen in disguise.* Not the kind of information his grandfather was looking for with the innocuous question. "Great. Her shop is constantly busy."

And Viv had ducked out early to take him on the ride

of his life last night. For the first time, he wondered if she'd planned the evening to end as it had or if it had been as spontaneous on her part as it had been on his. Maybe she'd been thinking about getting naked since the weekend of torture, too. If so, he liked that she'd been similarly affected.

They rode two floors up to the executive level. As they exited, Jonas and Jung-Su nodded to the various employees going about the business of electronics in a beehive of activity.

"You've mentioned your wife's business frequently," his grandfather commented just outside the boardroom where Jonas conducted the majority of his virtual meetings. "Doesn't she have other interests?"

The disapproval in his grandfather's voice was faint. "You don't understand. Her bakery is much more than just a business. It's an extension of her."

Cupcakes had been a mechanism to fit in among her older, more accomplished sisters, as she'd told him on numerous occasions. But it had morphed from there into a business that she could be proud of. Hell, it was a venture *he* was proud of.

"Anyone can pull a package of cupcake mix off the shelf at the grocery store," Jonas continued, infusing as much sincerity into his speech as he could. His grandfather had no call to be throwing shade at his wife's profession. "That's easy. Viv spends hours in her kitchen doing something special to hers that customers can't get enough of."

"It seems as if you are smitten by her cupcakes, as well," Grandfather commented with a tinge of amusement.

Jonas forced a return smile that hopefully didn't look

as pained as he suspected it did. *Smitten*. He wasn't smitten with Viv and it rankled that he'd managed to convince his grandfather that he was. Cupcakes, on the other hand—no pretending needed there. "Of course I am. That's what first drew me to her."

Like it was yesterday, he recalled how many times he'd found excuses to drop by Cupcaked to get a glimpse of Viv in those first few weeks after meeting her. Often she was in the back but if she saw him, she popped out for a quick hi, ready with a smile no matter what she had going on in the kitchen. That alone had kept him coming back. There was always someone in the office with a birthday or anniversary, and cupcakes always made an occasion more festive.

"Ah, yes, I recall that conversation at dinner where she mentioned you pretended to go there for her cupcakes but were really there to see her."

"It was both," he corrected easily since it was true. He could own that he liked Viv. They were friends.

Who'd seen each other naked.

Before he could stop it, images of Viv spilled through his mind.

The rush of heat to his body smacked him, sizzling across his skin so fast he had little chance of reeling it back. But he had to. This was the most inappropriate time to be thinking about his wife wearing that see-through yellow lacy concoction strictly for his benefit.

"Pardon me for a moment," Jonas croaked, and ducked into the executive washroom to get himself under control. Or as close to it as he could with an enormous erection that showed no signed of abating.

And while he stood in front of the mirror concentrating on his breathing and doing absolutely nothing constructive, he pulled out his phone to set a reminder to drop by the jewelry store on the way home. Viv had expressly asked for jewels as compensation for the favor she was doing him. She needed something pretty and ridiculously expensive.

Thinking of her draped in jewelry he'd bought wasn't helping.

After the longest five minutes of his life, Jonas finally got the tenting mostly under control. No one had noticed. Or at least that's what he tried to tell himself. His staff didn't walk around with their eyes on his crotch.

The biggest hit was to Jonas's psyche. How had he let Viv get under his skin like that? It was unacceptable. If nothing else, he needed to maintain his professionalism during this period when his grandfather's support meant everything. There were other contenders for Jung-Su's job, such as vice presidents who lived in Korea and had worked alongside the CEO for thirty years. Some of Mr. Park's staff could rise to the top as worthy heads of a global company, and those under the Park umbrella arguably had more experience running the factories that would come into play with the merger.

Jonas had to reel it back with Viv. Way back. There was no excuse for falling prey to baser urges and he definitely didn't want to find out what happened next if he kept going down this path. That was one absolute he trusted—the less he let a woman get tangled up in his emotions, the better.

Resolute, Jonas returned to find his grandfather in deep discussion with Jonas's chief financial officer, a man without whom Kim Electronics would suffer in the American market.

Perfect. This was an opportunity to guide the discussion to Jonas's accomplishments as well as those of his staff, who were a reflection of his ability to run the Americas branch. Back on track, Jonas smiled at the two men and jumped into the conversation as if he hadn't just had a minor freak-out over an incontrollable urge to drive straight home and bury himself in his wife.

That wasn't happening. Boundaries needed to happen. Jonas didn't have the luxury of letting his wife dig further under his skin. But when he got home later that night, it was to an empty house, and boundaries didn't seem like such a fun plan.

More disappointed than he had a right to be, Jonas prowled around the enormous condo to be sure Viv hadn't tucked herself away in a corner to read or watch TV. *Nada.* He glanced at his watch. It was well after seven. She must have gotten caught up at the shop. Totally her right to work late. They didn't answer to each other.

For a half second, he contemplated walking the four blocks to Cupcaked. Strictly so he could give Viv her gift, of course. But that smacked of eagerness to see her that he had no intention of admitting to. So instead, he flopped on the couch and scrolled through his never-ending inbox on his phone, desperate for something to take his mind off the resounding silence in the condo. Wow, was it quiet. Why had he never noticed that before? The high ceilings and exposed beams usually created an echo that reminded him of a museum, but he'd have to be making noise for that echo to happen.

Viv had made a lot of noise last night, but he hadn't been paying a whole lot of attention to whether the sounds of her gasps and sighs had filled the cavernous part of the loft. And now he was back to thinking about his wife, her gorgeous body and why she wasn't currently naked in his lap.

He scowled. They'd done zero to establish how their relationship would progress after last night. They should have. *He* should have. Probably the smartest thing would have been to establish that last night was a onetime thing. He couldn't keep having meltdowns at work or moon around over whether Viv planned to hang out with him at night.

He should find something else to do. Like… He glanced around the condo, suddenly at a loss. Prior to getting married, what had he done on a random Tuesday when he was bored?

Nothing. Because he was rarely bored. Usually he had work and other stuff to occupy him. *Friends.* Of course the answer was to ping his friends. But Warren didn't respond to his text message and Hendrix was in New York on a business trip.

Viv's key rattled in the lock. Finally. He vaulted off the couch to greet her, totally not okay with how his pulse quickened at the prospect of seeing her and completely unsure how to stop it.

As she came through the door, her smile widened as she spied Jonas standing in the hall, arms crossed, hip casually cocked out against the wall.

"Hi," she said, halting just short of invading his space. "Were you waiting for me?"

No sprang to his lips before he thought better of it. Well, he couldn't really deny that, now, could he? If he'd stayed sprawled on the couch and given her a casual "what's up?" as she strolled through the door, he might have had a leg to stand on. Too late.

"Yeah," he admitted, and held up the shiny blue foil bag clutched in his fingers. "I have something for you."

Her eyes widened as she held out her hand to accept the bag. The most delicious smell wafted between them, a vanilla and Viv combo that made him think of frosting and sex and about a million other things that shouldn't go together but did—like marriage and friendship.

Why couldn't he greet his wife at the door if he felt like it? It wasn't a crime. It didn't mean anything.

The anticipation that graced her smile shouldn't have pleased him so much. But he couldn't deny that it whacked him inside in a wholly different way than the sultry smile she'd laid on him last night, right before she informed him that she had on yellow lingerie under her clothes.

Which was not up for a repeat tonight. Boundaries should be the first order of business. Viv had sucked him down a rabbit hole that he didn't like. Well, he *liked* it. It just didn't sit well with how unbelievably tempting she was. If she could tempt him into letting go of his professionalism, what other barriers could she knock down? The risk was not worth it.

But then she opened the box, and her startled gasp put heat in places that he should be able to control a hell of lot better.

"Jonas, this is too much," she protested with a laugh and held out the box like she expected him to take it back or something.

"Not hardly. It's exactly right." Before she got ideas in her head about refusing the gift that had taken him thirty minutes to pick out, he plucked the diamond necklace from its velvet housing and undid the clasp so he could draw it around her neck. "Hush, and turn around."

She did and that put him entirely too close to her sweet flesh. That curve where her shoulder flared out called to him. Except it was covered by her dress. That was a shame.

Dragging her hair out of the way, she waited for him to position the chain. He let the catch of the necklace go and the ten-carat diamond dropped to rest against her chest, just above the swell of her breasts. Which were also covered, but he knew precisely where they began.

His lips ached to taste that swell again. Among other things. Palms flat across her back, he smoothed the chain into place, but that was really just an excuse to touch her.

"If you're sure," she murmured, and she relaxed, letting her body sink backward until it met his and heat flared between them.

"Oh, I'm sure." She'd meant about the diamond. Probably. But his mouth had already hit the bare spot she'd revealed when she'd swept her long brown hair aside and the taste of Viv exploded under his tongue.

Groaning, he let his hands skim down her waist until he found purchase and pulled until their bodies nested together tighter than spoons in a drawer. The soft flesh of her rear cradled the iron shaft in his pants, thickening his erection to the point of pain. He needed a repeat of last night. Now.

He licked the hollow of her collarbone, loving the texture under his tongue. More Viv needed. Her answering gasp encouraged him to keep going.

Gathering handfuls of her dress, he yanked it from between them and bunched it at her waist, pressing harder into the heat of her backside the moment he bared it. His clothes and a pair of thin panties lay between him and paradise, and he wanted all that extraneous fabric gone.

She arched against him as his fingers cruised along the hem of her drenched underwear and he took that as agreement, stripping them off in one motion. Then he nudged her legs wider, opening her sex, and indulged them both by running a fingertip down the length of her crease. Her hands flew out and smacked the wall and she used it to brace as she ground her pelvis into his.

Fire tore through his center and he needed to be inside her with an uncontrollable urge, but the condoms were clear across the cavernous living area in his bedside table. He couldn't wait. Viv cried out his name as he plunged one then two fingers into her center, groaning at the slick, damp heat that greeted him. She was so wet, so perfect.

As he fingered her, she shuddered, circling her hips in a frenzied, friction-induced madness that pushed him to the brink. Her hot channel squeezed his fingers and that was nearly all she wrote. Did she have a clue how much he wanted to yank his zipper down, impale her and empty himself? Every muscle in his body fought him and his will crumbled away rapidly. Reaching between them, he eased open his belt.

But then she came apart in his arms, huffing out little noises that drove him insane as she climaxed. His own release roared to the forefront and all it would take was one tiny push to put him over the edge. Hell, he might not even need a push. Shutting his eyes against the strain, he drew out her release with long strokes that made her whimper.

She collapsed in his arms as she finished and he

held her upright, murmuring nonsense to her as she caught her breath.

"Let me take you to bed," he said, and she nodded, but it was more of a nuzzle as she turned her cheek into his.

To hell with boundaries.

He hustled her to his room, shed his clothes and hers without ripping anything this time—because he was in control—and finally she was naked. Sultry smile in place, she crawled onto the bed and rolled into a provocative position that begged him to get between her legs immediately and hammer after his own release. But despite being positive the only thing he could possibly do next was get inside her as fast as humanly possible, he paused, struck immobile all at once.

That was *his wife* decked out on the bed.

The sight bled through him, warming up places inside dangerously fast. Places that weren't what he'd call normal erogenous zones. And that's when he realized his gaze was on her smile. Not her body.

What was wrong with him? A naked woman was on display for his viewing pleasure. He forced his gaze to her breasts, gratified when the pert tips pebbled under his watchfulness. That was more like it. This was about sex and how good two people could make each other feel.

With a growl, he knelt on the bed and kissed his way up her thigh. He could absolutely keep his hands off her if he wanted to. He had total control over his desires, his emotions. There was nothing this woman could do to drive him to the point of desperation, not in bed and certainly not out of it. To prove it, he pushed her thighs open and buried his face between them.

She parted for him easily, her throaty cry washing over him as he plunged his tongue into her slickness. That wet heat was *his*. He'd done that to her and he lapped at it, groaning as her musky scent flooded his senses. The ache in his groin intensified into something so strong it was otherworldly. He needed to feel her tight, slick walls close around him, to watch her face as it happened. He needed it, but denied himself because she didn't own his pleasure. He owned hers.

Her hips rolled and bucked. He shoved his mouth deeper into her center as she silently sought more, and he gave it to her. Over and over he worked his lips and tongue against her swollen flesh until she bowed up with a release that tensed her whole body. And then she collapsed against the mattress, spilling breathy, satisfied sighs all over him. Only then did he permit his own needs to surge to the surface.

Fingering on a condom that he'd retrieved from the drawer, he settled over her and indulged his intense desire to kiss her. She eagerly took his tongue, sucking it into her hot mouth, and he groaned as he transferred her own taste back to her. Their hips came together, legs tangling, and before he could fully register her intent, she gathered him up in her tight fist and guided him into the paradise at her core.

A strong urge to fill her swelled. But he held on by the scrabbly edge of his fingertips, refusing to slam into her as he ached to do. Slowly, so slowly that he nearly came apart, he pushed. Her slickness accepted him easily, wringing the most amazing bliss from a place he scarcely recognized. The deeper he sank, the better it felt.

Her gaze captured his and he fell into her depths.

She filled him, not the other way around. How was that physically possible? He couldn't fathom it, but neither could he deny it. Or halt the rush of Viviana through his veins as she streamed straight to his heart in a kill shot that flooded all four chambers at once.

And then there was nothing but her and the unbelievable feel of her skin against his, her desire soaking through his pores in an overwhelming deluge. He meant to hold back, determined to prove something that escaped him as she changed the angle. Somehow that allowed him to go deeper, push harder. Her cries spurred him on, and unbelievably, she took it higher, sucking him under into a maelstrom of sensation and heightened pleasure.

When her hips began pistoning in countermeasure to his, it nearly tore him in two. Delirious with the need to come, he grabbed one of her legs and pushed at the knee, opening her wider so he had plenty of room to finger her at the source of her pleasure. Two circular strokes and she climaxed, squeezing him so tight that it tripped the wire on his own release.

Bright pinpoints of light streamed behind his eyes as he came so hard that he would have easily believed he'd crossed over into an alternate dimension. In this new dimension, he could let all the things crowding through his chest spill out of his mouth. But those things shouldn't exist in any universe.

If he didn't acknowledge them, they didn't exist. Then he wouldn't be breaking his word.

As his vision cleared and his muscles relaxed, rendering him boneless, he collapsed to the mattress, rolling Viv into his arms.

The heavy diamond swung down from the chain he'd

latched around her neck, whacking him on the shoulder. He fingered it back into place silently, weighing out whether he could actually speak or if that spectacular orgasm had in fact stolen his voice.

"I get the sense you've been saving up," Viv commented huskily, her lips moving against his chest, where her face had landed after he'd nestled her close. Probably he shouldn't have done that, but he liked coming down from a post-lovemaking high with her in his arms.

"It's been a while," he allowed. "I mean, other than last night, obviously."

Her mouth curved up in a smile. "Both times were amazing. I could get used to this."

He could, too. That was enough to get the panic really rolling. "We should probably talk about that."

To soften the blow, he threaded some of her pretty, silky hair through his fingers. That felt so nice, he kept going, running all the way down her head to her neck and back again.

"Mmm," she purred, pressing into his fingers, which were somehow massaging her with little strokes that she clearly liked. "I'm listening."

"We're still friends, right?" Pathetic. That hadn't been what he'd intended to say at all, but now that it was out there…it was exactly what he wanted to know. He wanted to hear her say that having an amazing encounter that he'd felt to his soul hadn't really affected her all that much. Then he could keep lying to himself about it and have zero qualms.

"Sure."

She kissed his chest right above his nipple and then flicked her tongue across the flat disk. Flames erupted under his skin, fanning outward to engulf his whole body, including his brain, because he suddenly couldn't recall what he'd been so convinced he needed to establish.

Then she slung a leg over his, nestling her thigh against the semi-erection that grew a lot less semi much faster than he would have credited, considering how empty he'd have sworn he was already.

"Geez, Viv." He bit back the curse word that had sprung to his lips. "You're insatiable."

Not that he was complaining. Though he should be saying something that sounded a lot like "Let's dial it back about one hundred and eighty degrees."

"You make me that way," she said throatily. "I've been celibate for like a billion years and that was totally okay, but all of a sudden, you kiss me and I can't think. I just want to be naked with you 24/7."

"Yeah?" he growled. That pretty much mirrored his thoughts perfectly. "That can be arranged."

No. No, it could not.

He had a merger to manage. Reins to pick up from his grandfather. What was he talking about, letting Viv coerce him into a day-and-night screw fest? That sounded like a recipe for disaster, especially given how strong his reactions to her were. They needed to cool it off.

"We can't." She sighed. "I've got a mountain of paperwork and Josie requested the rest of the week off so she can study for final exams. As nice as this is, we should probably back off for a while. Don't you think?"

"Absolutely not." Wrong answer. *Open your mouth and take it back.* "We're doing fine winging it. Aren't we? There's no pressure. If you come home from work hot and needy and want to strip down in the foyer to let me take care of you, I'm perfectly fine with that."

In fact, he'd gladly etch that date on his planner with a diamond drill bit. Mental note: buy Viv more jewelry and more racy lingerie. If he really tried, he could space out the gifts, one a night for oh, at least two weeks.

She arched a brow. "Really? This isn't feeling a little too real?"

His mood deflated. And now he was caught in a trap of his own making. He couldn't lie to Viv, but neither could he admit that it had been feeling too real since the ceremony. The same one he'd tried to sell to Warren and Hendrix as a fake wedding when Warren had clued in immediately that there was nothing fake about any of this.

This was what he got for not nodding his head the second the words *back off* came out of her mouth.

"See, the thing is," he began and would have sworn he'd been about to say that being friends with no benefits worked better for him. But that's not what happened. "I need this to be real. I don't have to pretend that I'm hot for you, because I am. We don't have to sell that we're burning up the sheets when we have dinner with your family on Friday. Why not keep going? The reasons we started this are still true. Unless I've dissatisfied you in some way?"

"Oh, God. No!" Her hand flew to her mouth. "Not in the slightest. You're the hottest lover I've ever had, bar none."

That pleased him enormously. "Then stop talking about easing off. We can be casual about it. Sometimes you sleep in my bed. Sometimes you don't. No rules. We're just friends who're having really great sex."

"That sounds like a plan."

She shrugged like she could take it or leave it, which raked across his spine with a sharpness that he didn't like. She obviously wasn't feeling any of the same things he was. She'd been a half second from calling it quits. Would have if he hadn't stopped her.

"Great." And somehow he'd managed to appease his sense of honor while agreeing to continue sleeping with his wife in what was shaping up to be the hottest affair he'd ever had.

It was madness. And he couldn't wipe the grin off his face.

Eight

If there was a way to quit Jonas, Viv didn't want to know about it.

She should be looking for the exit, not congratulating herself on the finest plea for remaining in a man's bed that had ever been created in the history of time. She couldn't help it. The scene after the most explosive sexual encounter of her life had been almost as epic. Jonas had no idea how much it had killed her to act so nonchalant about ending things. He'd been shocked she'd suggested backing off. It had been written all over his face.

That kept her feeling smug well into the dawn hours the next morning. She rolled toward the middle of the bed, hoping to get a few minutes of snuggle time before work. Cold sheets met her questing fingers. Blinking an eye open, she sought the man she'd gone to sleep with.

Empty. Jonas had gotten out of bed already. The

condo was quiet. Even when she was in her bedroom, she could hear the shower running through the pipes in the ceiling—a treat she normally enjoyed, as she envisioned the man taking a shower in all his naked glory.

Today, she didn't get that luxury, as Jonas was clearly already gone. Profoundly disappointed that he hadn't kissed her goodbye, said goodbye or thought about her at all, she climbed out from under the sheets and gathered up her clothes for the return trek to her bedroom.

It was fine. They'd established last night that there were no rules. No pressure. When he'd gotten on board with convincing her that they could keep sleeping together—which she still couldn't quite believe she'd orchestrated so well—she'd thought that meant they were going to spend a lot of time together. Be goofy and flirty with each other. Grow closer and closer until he looked up one day and realized that friendship plus marriage plus sex equaled something wonderful, lasting and permanent. Obviously she'd thought wrong.

The whole point had been to give him the impression she wasn't clingy. That Independence was her middle name and she breezed through life just fine, thanks, whether she had a man or not. Apparently he'd bought it. *Go me.*

The sour taste wouldn't quite wash from her mouth no matter how much mouthwash she used. After a long shower to care for her well-used muscles, Viv wandered to the kitchen barefoot to fight with Jonas's espresso machine. She had a machine at Cupcaked but Jonas's was a futuristic prototype that he'd brought home from work to test. There were more buttons and gizmos than on a spaceship. Plus, it hated her. He'd used it a couple of times and made it seem so easy, but he had a natural affinity with things that plugged in, and the machine had his name on it, after all. Finally, she got a passably decent latte out of the monstrosity.

She stood at the granite countertop to drink it, staring at the small, discreet Kim Electronics logo in the lower right-hand corner of the espresso machine. Jonas's name had been emblazoned on her, too, and not just via the marriage license and subsequent trip to the DMV to get a new driver's license. He'd etched his name across her soul well before they'd started sleeping together. Maybe about the third or fourth time they'd had lunch.

Strange then that she could be so successful with snowing him about her feelings. It had never worked with any man before. Of course, she'd never tried so hard to be cool about it. Because it had never mattered so much.

But now she wasn't sure what her goal here really was. Or what it should be. Jonas had "talked" her into keeping sex on the menu of their relationship. She'd convinced him their friendship could withstand it. Really, the path was pretty clear. They were married friends with benefits. If she didn't like that, too bad.

She didn't like it.

This wasn't practice for another relationship and neither was it fake, not for her. Which left her without a lot of options, since it was fake to Jonas.

Of course, she always had the choice to end things. But why in the world would she want to do that? Her husband was the most amazing lover on the planet, whose beautiful body she could not get enough of. He bought her diamonds and complimented her cupcakes. To top it all off, Viv was *married*. She'd been after that holy grail for ages and it had felt really nice to flash her ring at her sisters when they'd come to the shop last week. It was the best possible outcome of agreeing to do this favor for Jonas.

Convinced that she should be happy with that, she walked the four blocks to Cupcaked and buried herself in the kitchen, determined to find a new cupcake flavor to commemorate her marriage. That was how she'd always done things. When something eventful occurred, she baked. It was a way of celebrating in cake form, because wasn't that the whole point of cake? And then she had a cupcake flavor that reminded her of a wonderful event.

The watermelon recipe she'd been dying to try didn't turn out. The red food coloring was supposed to be tasteless but she couldn't help thinking that it had added something to the flavor that made the cupcake taste vaguely like oil. But without it, the batter wasn't the color of watermelon.

Frustrated, she trashed the whole batch and went in search of a different food coloring vendor. Fruitless. All her regular suppliers required an industrial sized order and she couldn't commit to a new brand without testing it first.

She ended up walking to the market and buying three different kinds off the shelf. For no reason, apparently, as all three new batches she made didn't turn out either. Maybe watermelon wasn't a good cupcake flavor. More to the point, maybe she shouldn't be commemorating a fake marriage that was real to her but still not going to last. That was the problem. She was trying to capture something fleeting that shouldn't be immortalized.

After the cupcake failure, her mood slid into the dumps. She threw her apron on the counter and stayed out of the kitchen until lunch, when she opened for business to the public. On the plus side, every display case had been cleaned and polished, and the plate-glass window between Cupcaked and the world had not one smudge on it. Camilla wouldn't be in until after school, so Viv was by herself for the lunch rush, which ended up being a blessing in disguise.

Wednesday wasn't normally a busy day, but the line stretched nearly out the door for over an hour. Which was good. Kept her mind off the man she'd married. Josie had the rest of the week off, and Viv had approved it thinking she and Camilla could handle things, but if this kind of crowd was even close to a new normal, she might have to see about adding another part-time employee. That was a huge decision, but a good sign. If she couldn't have Jonas, she could have her cupcakes. Just like she'd always told him.

After locking the bakery's door, tired but happy with the day's profits, she headed home. On the way, she sternly lectured herself about her expectations. Jonas might be waiting in the hall for her to come in the door like he had been last night. Or he might not. Her stomach fluttered the entire four blocks regardless. Her husband had just been so sexy standing there against the wall with a hot expression on his face as if he planned to devour her whole before she completely shut the door.

And then he pretty much had, going down on her in the most erotic of encounters. She shuddered clear to her core as she recalled the feel of that first hot lick of his tongue.

Oh, who was she kidding? She couldn't stop hoping he'd be waiting for her again tonight. Her steps quickened as she let herself anticipate seeing Jonas in a few minutes.

But he wasn't in the hall. Or at home. That sucked.

Instead of moping, she fished out her phone and called Grace. It took ten minutes, but eventually her sister agreed to have dinner with Viv.

They met at an Italian place on Glenwood that had great outdoor seating that allowed for people watching. The maître d' showed them to a table and Grace gave Viv a whole three seconds before she folded her hands and rested her chin on them.

"Okay, spill," she instructed. "I wasn't expecting to see you before Friday. Is Jonas in the doghouse already?"

"What? No." Viv scowled. Why did something have to be wrong for her to ask her sister to dinner? Besides, that was none of Grace's business anyway. Viv pounced on the flash of green fire on her sister's wrist in a desperate subject change. "Ooooh, new bracelet? Let me see."

The distraction worked. Grace extended her arm dutifully, her smile widening as she twisted her wrist to let the emeralds twinkle in the outdoor lighting. "Alan gave it to me. It's an anniversary present."

"You got married in April," Viv said.

"Not a wedding anniversary. It's a...different kind of anniversary."

Judging by the dreamy smile that accompanied that admission, she meant the first time she and Alan had slept together, and clearly the act had been worthy of commemorating.

Viv could hardly hide her glee. It was going to be one of *those* discussions and she *finally* got to participate. "Turns out Jonas is big on memorializing spectacular sex, too."

"Well, don't hold back. Show and tell." Grace waggled her brows.

Because she wanted to and she could, Viv fished the diamond drop necklace from beneath her dress and let it hang from her fingers. Not to put too fine a point on it, but hers was a flawless white diamond in a simple, elegant setting. Extremely appropriate for the wife of a billionaire. And he'd put it around her neck and then given her the orgasm of her life.

The baubles she could do without and had only mentioned jewelry in the car on the way to Jonas's parents' house because he'd pushed her to name something he could do for her. She hadn't really been serious. But all at once, she loved that Jonas had unwittingly allowed her to stand shoulder to shoulder with her sister when it came to talking about whose marriage was hotter.

"Your husband is giving you jewelry already?" Grace asked, and her tone was colored with something that sounded a lot like she was impressed. "Things must be going awfully well."

"Oh, yeah, of course," Viv commented airily and waved her hand like she imagined a true lady of the manor would. "We didn't even make it out of the foyer where he gave it to me before his hands were all over me."

Shameless. This was the raciest conversation she'd ever had with anyone except maybe Jonas, but that didn't count. She should be blushing. Or something. Instead she was downright giddy.

"That's the best." Grace's dreamy smile curved back into place. "When you have a man who loves you so much that he can't wait. I'm thrilled you finally have that."

Yeah, not so much. Her mood crashed and burned as reality surfaced. Viv nodded with a frozen expression that she hoped passed for agreement.

Obviously Grace knew what it felt like to have a man dote on her and give her jewelry because he cared, not because they were faking a relationship. Grace could let all her feelings hang out as much as she wanted and Alan would eat it up. Because they were in love.

Something that felt a lot like jealousy reared its ugly head in the pit of Viv's stomach. Which was unfair and petty, but recognizing it as such didn't make it go away.

"Jonas was worth waiting for," she said truthfully, though it rankled that the statement was the best she could do. While Viv's husband might rival her sister's in the attentive lover department, when it came to matters of the heart, Grace and Alan had Viv and Jonas beat, hands down.

"I'm glad. You had a rough patch for a while. I started to worry that you weren't going to figure out how stop putting a man's emotional needs ahead of yours. It's good to see that you found a relationship that's on equal footing."

Somehow, Viv managed to keep the surprise off her face, but how, she'd never know. "I never did that. What does that even mean?"

"Hon, you're so bad at putting yourself first." Grace waved the waiter over as he breezed by and waited until he refilled both their wineglasses before continuing. "You let everyone else dictate how the relationship is going to go. That last guy you dated? Mark? He wanted to keep things casual, see other people, and even though that's not what you wanted, you agreed. Why did you do that?"

Eyebrows hunched together, Viv gulped from her newly filled wineglass to wet her suddenly parched throat. "Because when I told him that I wanted to be exclusive, he said I was being too possessive. What was I supposed to do, demand that he give me what I want?"

"Uh, *yeah*." Grace clucked. "You should have told him to take a hike instead of waiting around for him to do it for you."

"It really didn't take that long," she muttered, but not very loud, because Grace was still off on her tangent.

Her sister was right. Viv should have broken up with Mark during that exact conversation. But on the heels of being told she was "clingy," "controlling" and "moving too fast" by Zachary, Gary and Judd respectively, she hadn't wanted to rock the boat.

Why was it such a big deal to want to spend time with a man she was dating? It wasn't clingy. Maybe it was the wine talking, but Grace's point wasn't lost on Viv—she shouldn't be practicing her independence but finding a different kind of man. One who couldn't stand being apart from her. One who texted her hearts and smiley faces just to let her know he was thinking of her. One who was in love with her.

In other words—not Jonas.

The thought pushed her mood way out of the realm of fit for company. Dinner with Grace was a mistake. Marrying Jonas had been a mistake. Viv had no idea what she was doing with her life or how she was going to survive a fake marriage she wished was real.

"I just remembered," she mumbled. "I have to…do a thing."

Pushing back from the table, Viv stood so fast that her head spun. She'd planned to walk home but maybe a cab would be a better idea.

"What?" Grace scowled. "You called me. I canceled drinks with the ladies from my auxiliary group. How could you forget that you had something else?"

Because Viv wasn't perfect like Grace with the perfect husband who loved her, and frankly, she was sick of not getting what she wanted. "Jonas has scrambled my wits."

Let her sister make what she would out of that. Viv apologized and exited the restaurant as quickly as she could before she started crying. After not seeing Jonas this morning and the watermelon-slash-red-food-coloring disaster and the incredibly busy day at the store and then realizing that she had not in fact gotten to join the club her sisters were in, crying was definitely imminent.

The icing on the cake happened when she got home and Jonas was sprawled on the couch watching TV, wearing jeans with a faded Duke T-shirt that clung to his torso like a second skin.

His smile as he glanced up at her was instant and brilliant and that was all it took to unleash the waterworks.

With tears streaming down her face, Viv stood in the foyer of the condo she shared with Jonas until whatever point in the future he decided to pull the plug on their marriage and it was all suddenly not okay.

"Hey, now. None of that." Jonas flicked off the TV and vaulted to his feet, crossing the ocean of open space between the living room and the foyer in about four strides.

He didn't hesitate to gather Viv in his strong arms, cradling her against his chest, and dang it, that T-shirt was really soft against her face. It was a testament to how mixed-up she was that she let him guide her to the leather couch and tuck her in against his side as he held her while softly crooning in his baritone that she'd heard in her sleep for aeons.

What was wrong with her that she was exactly where she wanted to be—in his arms? She should be pushing away and disappearing into her bedroom. No pressure, no love, no nothing.

"What's wrong, sweetheart?" he asked softly into her hair. "Bad day at work?"

"I wasn't at work," she shot back inanely, sniffling oh so attractively against his shoulder.

"Oh. Well, I wondered where you were when you weren't here."

"You weren't here either," she reminded him crossly. "So I went to dinner with Grace."

He pulled back, the expression on his face both confused and slightly alarmed. "Did we have plans that I forgot about or something? Because if so, I'm sorry. I didn't have anything on my calendar and my grandfather asked me to take him to the airport. I texted you."

He had? And how desperate would it appear to pull out her phone to check? Which was totally dumb anyway. It was obvious he was telling her the truth, which he didn't even have to do. God, she was such a mess. But after he'd disappeared this morning and then she'd come home to an empty house and…so what? He was here now, wasn't he? She was making a mountain out of a molehill.

"It's okay, we didn't have plans. You called it. Bad

day at work," she said a bit more brightly as she latched on to his excuse that wasn't even a lie. Sales had been good, sure, but Cupcaked meant more to her than just profits. "I tried out a new recipe and it was a complete failure."

All smiles again, Jonas stroked her hair and then laid a sweet kiss on her temple. "I hate days like that. What can I do to fix it?"

About a hundred suggestions sprang to her mind all at once, and every last one could easily be considered X-rated. But she couldn't bear to shift the current vibe into something more physical when Jonas was meeting a different kind of need, one she'd only nebulously identified at dinner. This was it in a nutshell—she wanted someone to be there for her, hold her and support her through the trials of life.

Why had she gotten so upset? Because Jonas hadn't fallen prostrate at her feet with declarations of undying love? They were essentially still in the early stages of their relationship, regardless of the label on it. Being married didn't automatically mean they were where Grace and her husband were. Maybe Viv and Jonas were taking a different route to get to the same destination and she was trying too hard.

Also known as the reason her last few relationships hadn't worked out.

"You're already fixing it," she murmured as his fingers drifted to her neck and lightly massaged.

Oh, God, that was a gloriously unfulfilled need, too. After a long day on her feet, just sitting here with Jonas as he worked her tired muscles counted as one of the highest points of pleasure she'd experienced at his hands. Her eyelids drifted closed and she floated.

"Did I wake you up this morning?" he asked after a few minutes of bliss.

"No. I was actually surprised to find that you were gone." Thank God he'd lulled her into a near coma. That admission had actually sounded a lot more casual than she would have expected, given how his absence had been lodged under skin like a saddle burr all day.

"That's good." He seemed a lot more relieved than the question warranted. "I'm not used to sleeping with someone and I was really worried that I'd mess with your schedule."

What schedule? "We slept in the same bed at your parents' house."

"Yeah, but that was over the weekend when no one had to get up and go to work. This is different. It's real life and I'm nothing if not conscious that you're here solely because I asked you to be. You deserve to sleep well."

Warmth gushed through her heart and made her feel entirely too sappy. What a thoroughly unexpected man she had married. "I did sleep well. Thank you for being concerned. But I think I slept so well because of how you treated me before I went to sleep. Not because you tiptoed well while getting dressed."

He did treat her like a queen. That was the thing she'd apparently forgotten. They were friends who cared about each other. Maybe he might eventually fall in love with her, but he certainly wouldn't if she kept being obsessive and reading into his every move.

Jonas chuckled. "Last night was pretty amazing. I wasn't sure you thought so. I have to be honest and tell you that I was concerned I'd done something to make you angry and that's why you weren't here when I got home after taking my grandfather to the airport. I could have called him a car."

"No!" Horrified, she swiveled around to face him, even though it meant his wonderful hands slipped from her shoulders. "We just talked about no pressure and I was—well, I just thought because you weren't here…"

Ugh. How in the world was she supposed to explain that she'd gone out to dinner with Grace because of a hissy fit over something so ridiculous as Jonas not being here because he'd taken his grandfather to the airport? Maybe instead of using the excuse that she'd missed his text messages, she should tell him how she felt. Just flat out say, *Jonas, I'm in love with you.*

"We did talk about no pressure," Jonas threw out in a rush. "And I'm definitely not trying to add any. I like our relationship where it is. I like *you*. It's what makes the extra stuff so much better."

Extra stuff. She absorbed that for a second. Extra stuff like deeper feelings he didn't know he was going to uncover? Extra stuff like being there for each other?

"I value our friendship," she said cautiously, weighing out how honest she could be. How honest she wanted to be given how she managed to screw up even the simplest of relationship interactions.

And just as she was about to open her mouth and confess that she appreciated the extra stuff, too, maybe even tell him that she had a plethora of extra stuff that she could hardly hold inside, he smoothed a hand over her hair and grinned. "I know. I'm being all touchy-feely and that's not what we signed up for. Instead, let's talk about Cupcaked."

"Um…okay?" He'd literally switched gears so fast, she could scarcely keep up.

That was him being touchy-feely? Jonas wasn't one to be gushy about his feelings and usually erred on the side of being reserved; she knew that from the year of lunches and coffee. Clearly, he was uncomfortable with the direction of the discussion. She definitely should not add a level of weirdness, not on top of her storming in here and having a minor meltdown.

This was her relationship to make or break. All at once, it became so obvious what she should be focusing on here.

No, this wasn't practice for the next man she dated. She was practicing for *this* one. If she hoped to get to a point where they were both comfortable with declarations of love, she had to tread carefully. While she didn't think Jonas was going to divorce her if she moved too fast, neither did she have a good handle on how to be less intense.

She needed to back off. Way off. Otherwise, she was going to freak him out. And suddenly she could not fathom giving up this marriage under any circumstances.

"I'd love to talk about Cupcaked," she said with a smile. "Seems like you owe me some advice."

"Yes, exactly." His return smile bordered on relieved. "You've been so patient and I'm a selfish jerk for not focusing on your career when that's the one thing you're getting out of this deal."

"The sex is nice, too," she teased. Look at that. She could be cool.

Jonas shot her a wicked once-over. "That's what makes you so perfect. We can hang out as friends, but if I wanted to, say, slip my hand under your dress, you'd gladly climb in my lap for a little one-on-one time. It's the best."

She shrugged to cover how his compliment had thrilled her to the marrow. "I promised it wouldn't make things weird."

Now she'd stick to that. At the end of the day, Cupcaked *was* important to her. She'd just have to make sure that eventually Jonas realized that he was important to her, as well.

Jonas ducked out of a meeting on Friday with a guilty conscience. While he knew Viv would understand if he put off a thorough analysis of her business plan, he wasn't okay with ignoring his promise. Unfortunately, Park had come through with some amendments to the merger agreement Jonas had drafted, which had taken his time and attention for the whole of the week.

The moment he stepped outside the Kim Building, the sunshine raised his spirits. He was on his way to see his wife at Cupcaked, which oddly would mark the first time he'd graced the store since they'd gotten married. Before the wedding, he found excuses to drop by on a frequent basis. But now he didn't have to. The cupcake baker slept in his bed and if he wanted to see her, all he had to do was turn his head.

It was pretty great. Or at least that's what he'd been telling himself. In reality, the look on Viv's face when she'd told him she valued their friendship had been like a big fat wake-up call. Basically, she was telling him no pressure worked for her regardless of how hot he could get her with nothing more than a well-placed caress.

Well, that *was* great. He didn't have any desire to pressure her into anything. But he couldn't deny that he might like to put more structure around things. Would she think it was weird if he expected her to be his plus-one for events? His admin was planning a big party for the whole company to commemorate the anniversary of opening the Kim Americas branch. He wanted Viv by his side. But it was yet another favor. If they were dating instead of married he wouldn't think twice about asking her.

Everything was backward and weird and had been since that no-pressure discussion, which he'd initiated because he needed the boundaries. For no reason apparently. Viv so clearly wasn't charging over the imaginary lines he'd drawn in the sand. In fact, she'd drawn a few lines of her own. Yet how could he change those lines when Viv had gotten so prickly about the subject? In fact, she'd already tried to call off the intimate aspects of their relationship once. He needed to tread very carefully with her before he got in too deep for them both.

When he got to Cupcaked, the door was locked. Not open yet. He texted Viv that he was outside and within thirty seconds, she'd popped out of the kitchen and hurried to the plate-glass door with a cute smile.

"I didn't know you were coming by," she commented unnecessarily since he was well aware it was a surprise. After she let him in, she locked the door and turned, her brown hair shining in the sunlight that streamed through the glass.

Something was wrong with his lungs. He couldn't breathe. Or think. All he could do was soak in the most beautiful woman he'd ever seen in his life. And all of his good intentions designed to help her with her business flew out the window in a snap.

Without hesitation, he pulled her into his arms and kissed her. She softened instantly and the scent of vanilla and Viv wound through his senses, robbing him of the ability to reason, because the only thing he could think about was getting more of her against him.

Almost as if she'd read his mind, she opened under his mouth, eagerly deepening the kiss, welcoming the broad stroke of his tongue with her own brand of heat. Slowly she licked into his mouth in kind, teasing him with little flutters of her fingers against his back.

That was not going to work. He wanted to feel her fingers against his flesh, not through the forty-seven layers of clothing between them.

Walking her backward, he half kissed, half maneuvered her until they reached the kitchen, and then he spun her through the swinging door to the more private area, where the entire city of Raleigh couldn't see them.

Her mouth was back on his without missing a beat, and he pushed her up against the metal counter, trapping her body with his. Her sweet little curves nestled into the planes of his body and he wasn't sure if he could stand how long it was taking to get her naked.

The zipper of her dress took three tries to find and then slid down easily, allowing him to actually push the fabric from her shoulders instead of ripping it, a near miracle. There was something about her that drove him to a place he didn't recognize, and it bothered him to be this crazy over her. But then her dress slipped off, puddling to the floor, and he forgot about everything but her as she unhooked her bra, throwing it to the ground on top of her dress.

Groaning, he looked his fill of her gorgeous breasts, scarcely able to believe how hard and pointy they were from nothing other than his gaze. Bending to capture one, he swirled his tongue around the perfection of her nipple and the sound she made shot through his erection like an arrow of heat.

"Hurry," she gasped. "I'm about to come apart."

Oh, well, that was something he'd very much like to witness. In a flash, he pushed her panties to her ankles and boosted her up on the counter. Spreading her legs wide, he brushed a thumb through her crease and, yes, she was so ready for him.

She bucked and rolled against his fingers, her eyes darkening with the pleasure he was giving her, and he wanted her more than anything he could recall. As much as he'd like to do any number of things to bring her to climax, there was one clear winner. Ripping out of his own clothes in record time, he stepped back between her thighs and hissed as she nipped at his shoulder.

"Tell me you have a condom," she commanded, and then smiled as he held it up between his fingers.

He'd stashed a couple in his wallet and he really didn't want to examine that particular foresight right now. Instead, he wanted to examine the wonders of Viv and sheathed himself as fast as humanly possible, notching himself at the slick entrance to her channel. Her wet heat welcomed him, begged him to come inside, but he paused to kiss her because that was one of his favorite parts.

Their tongues tangled and he got a little lost in the kiss. She didn't. She wrapped her legs around him, heels firm against his butt, and pushed him forward, gasping as he slammed into her. So that's how she wanted it. Two could play that game.

He engulfed her in his arms and braced her for a demanding rhythm, then gave it to her. She took each and every thrust eagerly, her mouth working the flesh at his throat, his ear, nipping sensuously. *He* was the one about to come apart.

Viv flew through his soul, winging her essence into every diameter of his body. Wiggling a hand between their slick bodies, he fingered her at the source of her pleasure, gratified when she cried out. Her release crashed against his, shocking him with both the speed and intensity.

She slumped against him, still quaking as she held on. He was busy losing the entire contents of his body as everything inside rushed out in a flash to fill her. Fanciful to be sure since there was a barrier preventing anything of the sort. But she'd wrung him out, taken everything and more, and he couldn't have stopped the train as it barreled down the track, even if he wanted to. Why would he want to?

He turned his head, seeking her lips, and there they were, molding to his instantly. Viv was amazing, a woman he liked, cared for deeply even, and they had the most spectacular chemistry. He could hardly fathom how much he still wanted her four seconds after having her. It was everything he said he wanted.

Except the warmth in his chest that had nothing to do with sex wasn't supposed to be there. He wasn't an idiot. He knew what was happening. He'd let her in, pretending that being friends gave him a measure of protection against falling for her. Instead, he'd managed to do the one thing he'd sworn he'd never do—develop feelings for someone who didn't return them.

This was a huge problem, one he didn't have a good solution for. One he could never let her know he was facing because he'd promised not to pressure her.

Best thing would be to ignore it. It wasn't happening if he didn't acknowledge it. And then he wouldn't be lying to her or dishonoring the pact he'd made with his friends, neither of which could ever happen. If he didn't nurture these fledging tendrils of disaster that wound through his chest, he could kill them before they ruined everything.

Actually, the best thing would be to stop being around Viv so much. *Without* letting on to her that he was deliberately creating distance.

The thought hurt. But it was necessary for his sanity.

Nine

Jonas helped Viv off the metal countertop that she'd have to bleach within an inch of its life and pray the fourteen different health-code violations never came to light.

It had been worth it. Whenever Jonas got like that, so into her and excited and feverish as if he'd die if he didn't have her that instant…that was the best part of this fake marriage. Men were never that gaga over her. Except this one. And she secretly loved it. She couldn't tell him. What would she say?

Slow and steady wins the race, she reminded herself. Not-Clingy was her new middle name and she was going to own it. Even if it killed her not to blubber all over him about how it was so beautiful it hurt when he was inside her.

They spent a few minutes setting their clothes back

to rights, no small feat without a mirror. She gladly helped Jonas locate his missing tie and then buttoned his suit jacket for him when he forgot.

"Gorgeous," she commented after slipping the last button into its slot and perusing the final product of her husband in his power suit that she immediately wanted to strip him out of again.

He grinned. "Yes, you are."

Great, now she was blushing, judging by the prickles in her cheeks. Dead giveaway about the things going on inside that she'd rather keep a secret.

"Now, stop distracting me," he continued. "I'm here to get started on my promise to review your books. Lead me to them."

Oh. For some reason, she'd thought he'd come by strictly to have an explosive sexual encounter in her bakery. But in reality, he was here for business reasons. That took a little of the wind from her sails though it shouldn't have. Of course he'd honor his promise to help her, despite absolutely no prompting on her part. "Sure, my office is in the back. We can squeeze in there."

She led him to the tiny hole in the wall where she paid bills and ordered inventory. It wasn't much, not like the Kim Building, where Jonas had an entire office suite expressly designed for the CEO. But she wasn't running a billion-dollar electronics company here, and they both knew that.

He didn't complain about the lack of comfort and space, easily sliding into the folding chair she pulled from behind the door and focusing on her with his dark eyes. "Let me see your balance sheet."

Dutifully, she keyed up her accounting software and ran the report, then pushed the monitor of her ancient computer toward him so he could see it. His gaze slid down the columns and back up again. Within a moment, he'd reviewed the entire thing and then launched into a dizzying speech about how her asset column was blah blah and her inventory was blah blah something else. After five minutes of nodding and understanding almost nothing of what he said, she held up a hand.

"Jonas, while I appreciate your attention on this, you lost me back around 'leveraging your cash.' Can we take a step back and focus on the goal of this?"

She knew what her goal was. Spend time with Jonas. But clearly he'd taken the idea of helping her seriously.

"Sure, sorry." He looked chagrined and adorable as he ran a hand through his hair. "I shouldn't have gone so deep into financial strategy that quickly. Maybe I should ask you what *your* goal is since your career is the most important thing to you. What do you want to see happen with Cupcaked?"

Oh, yeah, right. Her career. The thing she'd sold to him as the reason she didn't date. "I haven't really thought about it."

Should she be thinking about it? She wasn't rich by any stretch, but she made enough and got to bake cupcakes for a living. What else was there?

"Okay." His smile broadened. "I hear you saying that you need help coming up with a five-year plan. Part of that should include a robust marketing strategy and expansion."

Expansion? Her eyebrows lifted almost by themselves. "Are you suggesting I could become a chain?"

The idea seemed so far-fetched. She just made cupcakes and had no ambitions beyond being able to recognize regular customers. But she didn't hate the idea of seeing more Cupcaked signs around Raleigh. Maybe even in Chapel Hill or by the university. The thought of owning a mini-cupcake empire made her smile. Poor substitute for Jonas. But not a terrible one.

"I'm not suggesting it. I'm flat out saying if that's what you want, I will make it happen for you. Sky's the limit, Mrs. Kim." He waggled his brows. "You should take as much advantage of me as you possibly can. Ask for anything."

Mrs. Kim. What if she told him that she'd like to ask him to call her that for the rest of her life? What would he say?

Before she could open her mouth, he launched into another long litany of things to consider for her shop and his gleeful tone told her he was having fun helping her think through the items that might appear on her five-year plan. They talked about any number of ideas from branded cupcake mix to be sold in grocery stores to licensing her flavors to other cupcake bakeries.

Frankly, the discussion was fun for her, too. Partially because she was having it with Jonas and she loved watching his mind churn through the possibilities. But she couldn't deny a certain anticipation regarding the leaps and bounds Cupcaked could take through the doors her husband might open for her.

Camilla popped in to say hi and make sure Viv was okay with her opening the bakery to customers. Viv nodded her assent and dove back into the fascinating concept of franchising, of which Jonas admitted having only a rudimentary knowledge, but he knew way more than she did. She wanted to know more.

His phone rang and he lifted a finger in the universal "one minute" gesture, jabbering away to the caller with a bunch of terms that sounded vaguely legal. Eventually, he ended the call and stood.

"I'm so sorry, but I have to get back to the world of electronics."

She waved off his apology. "You've been here for two hours. I know you're busy. I should give Camilla a hand anyway. If today is anything like the rest of the week, she'll need the help."

Jonas laid a scorching kiss on her and left. Dazed and more than a little hot and bothered, she lost herself in cupcakes until the day got away from her. As planned, she and Jonas went to dinner at her parents' house that night. Given that he shot her smoking-hot glances when he thought no one was watching, and her sisters were nothing if not eagle-eyed when it came to potential gossip, she didn't think they had anything to worry about when it came to revelations about the nature of their marriage.

Or rather, the revelations weren't going to be publicized to the rest of the world. Just to Jonas. As soon as she figured out when she could start clueing him in to the idea that friendship wasn't the only thing happening between them, of course. This was the problem with playing it cool. She wasn't sure when to bring up concepts like *love*, *forever* and *no divorce*.

She bided her time and didn't utter a peep when Jonas carried her to his bed after the successful dinner with her parents. He spent extra time pleasuring her, claiming that tomorrow was Saturday so she had plenty of opportunity to sleep later. Not that she was complaining about his attention. Or anything else, for that matter. Her life was almost perfect.

On Monday, she learned exactly how many people in

the business world jumped when her husband said jump. By nine o'clock, she had appointments lined up every day for the entire week with accounting people, retail space experts and a pastry chef who had ties with the Food Network. A marketing consultant arrived shortly thereafter and introduced herself as Franca, then parked herself in Viv's office, apparently now a permanent part of her staff, as she'd informed Mrs. Kim, courtesy of Mr. Kim.

Franca lived to talk, as best Viv could work out between marathon strategy sessions that filled nearly every waking hour of the day. And some of the hours Viv would have normally said were for sleeping. At midnight, Franca sent a detailed list of the short-term and long-term goals that they'd discussed and asked Viv to vet it thoroughly because once she approved, the list would form the basis of Cupcaked's new five-year plan. Which would apparently be carved in stone.

By Friday, Viv hadn't spent more than five minutes with Jonas. They slept in the same bed, but sometimes he climbed into it well after she had, which was quite a feat since she hadn't hit the sheets until 1:00 a.m. most nights. He'd claimed her busyness came at a great time for him because he was able to focus on the merger with Park Industries without feeling guilty for ignoring her. The hours bled into days and she'd never been so exhausted in her life.

It sucked. Except for the part where sometimes Jonas texted her funny memes about ships passing in the night or had a dozen tulips delivered to the shop to commemorate their one-month anniversary. Once he popped up with Chinese takeout for dinner as a "forced" break for them both. He gave her his fortune cookie and told her a story about how one of the ladies in his procure-ment department had gone into labor during a meeting. Those stolen moments meant the world to her because she could almost believe that he missed her as much as she missed him.

The pièce de résistance came when the pastry chef she'd met with a couple of weeks ago contacted her via Franca to let her know that he'd loved her cupcakes and gotten her a spot on one of the cupcake shows on the Food Network. Agape, Viv stared at Franca as the tire-less woman reeled off the travel plans she'd made for Viv to fly to Los Angeles.

"I can't go to Los Angeles," Viv insisted with a head shake. "I have a business to run."

Franca tapped her phone on Viv's new desk. "Which will become nationally known once you appear on the show."

She'd had Viv's office completely redone and ex-panded at Jonas's expense and the top-of-the-line computer that had replaced the old one now recessed underneath the surface of the desk with the click of a button. It was very slick and gave them a lot more work-ing space, which Franca used frequently, as she spread brochures and promo items galore across the top of it at least twice a week.

"How long would I be gone?" Viv asked. Josie and Camilla had never run the bakery by themselves for a whole day, let alone several. They needed her. Or did they? She was often in the back strategizing with Franca anyway. They had four or five irons in the fire at any given time and the woman was indefatigable when it came to details. There was literally nothing she couldn't organize or plan and often took on more of a personal assistant role for Viv.

"Depends on whether you make the first cut." Franca shrugged and flipped her ponytail behind her back, a move she made when she was about to get serious. "It's a competition. You lose the first round, you come home. You win, you stay. I would advise you to win."

Viv made a face. "You're talking days."

"Sure. I hope so anyway. We're going to launch the new website with online ordering at the same time. It'll be an amazing kick start to the virtual storefront."

Sagging a little, Viv gave herself about four seconds to pretend she was going to refuse when in reality, she couldn't pass up the opportunity. It really didn't matter if she won or not because it was free advertising and all it would cost her was some time away from Jonas. Whom she rarely saw awake anyway.

"When do I leave?"

Franca grinned like she'd known the direction Viv would end up going the whole time. "I'll get the rest of the arrangements settled and let you know."

With a nod, Viv texted the news to Jonas, who instantly responded with at least four exclamation marks and a *congrats* in all caps. Funny, they were basically back to being friends with no benefits, thanks to her stupid career. She had all the success she'd lied to Jonas about wanting and none of the happiness that she'd pretended would come along with it.

Worse, if she hadn't been so busy, she'd be sitting around the condo by herself as Jonas worked his own fingers to the bone. This was really, really not the marriage she'd signed up for.

Or rather it was absolutely the one she'd agreed to but not the one she wanted.

The day before she was supposed to fly to Los Angeles for the taping, Viv came home early to pack. Shockingly, Jonas was sitting on the couch still decked out in his gorgeous suit but on the phone, as he nearly always was anytime she'd been in the same room with him lately.

For half a second, she watched him, soaking in his pretty mouth as it formed words. Shuddered as she recalled what that mouth could do to her when he put his mind to it. God, she missed him. In the short amount of time they'd been married, they'd gone from zero to sixty to zero again. She'd prefer a hundred and twenty.

She waved, loath to interrupt him, but before she could skirt past him to her bedroom, where her clothes still were since she'd never really "moved in" to Jonas's room, he snagged her by the hips and settled her on the couch near him as he wrapped up his phone call.

Tossing his phone on the glass-and-steel conglomeration that he called a coffee table, he contemplated her with the sort of attention she hadn't experienced in a long while. It was delicious.

"You're going to LA in the morning?" he said by way of greeting, and picked up her hand to hold it in his, brushing his thumb across her knuckles.

"Yeah. I don't know for how long. Franca left the plane ticket open-ended." The little strokes of his thumb stirred something inside that had been dormant for a million years. He'd been so distant lately. Dare she hope that they might be coming back together?

No reason she had to let him be the instigator. She lifted his hand to her mouth and kissed it, but he pulled away and sat back on the couch. "That sounds like fun. I hope you have a good time."

Cautiously, she eyed him. Why had he caught her before she left the room if he hadn't been after spending time with her? "Is everything okay? I wasn't expecting you to be here."

"I...came home on purpose. To see you," he admitted. "Before you left."

Her heart did a funny a little dance. But then why all the weird hot and cold? He obviously cared about her—but how much? Enough? She had no idea because they never talked about what was really going on here.

It was high time they had it out. She was leaving for LA in the morning and they rarely saw each other. She had to make this small opportunity work.

"I'm glad. I missed you." There. It was out in the open.

But he just smiled without a hint of anything. "I miss hanging out with you, too. We haven't had coffee in ages."

Or sex. The distinction between the two was legion and she didn't think for a minute that he'd misspoken or forgotten that they'd been intimate. It was a deliberate choice of words. "We haven't had a coffee relationship in ages."

His expression didn't change. "I know. It's been crazy. We're both so busy."

"By design, feels like."

That got a reaction, but why, she couldn't fathom. She watched as unease filtered through his gaze and he shifted positions on the couch, casually folding one leg over the other but also moving away from her. "We're both workaholics, that's for sure."

"I'm not," she corrected. "Not normally. But I've been dropped into an alternate reality where Franca drives me fourteen hours a day to reach these lofty goals that don't represent what I really want out of life."

Jonas frowned, his gaze sweeping over her in assessment. "You're finally getting your career off the ground. She's been keeping me apprised and I've been pleased with the direction she's taking you. But if you're not, we should discuss it. I can hire a different marketing expert, one that's more in line—"

"It's not the direction of the marketing," she broke in before he called in yet another career savant who would be brilliant at taking her away from her husband. "It's that I was happier when Cupcaked was a little bakery on Jones Street and we had sex in the foyer."

Something flitted through his gaze that she wished felt more like an invitation. Because she would have stripped down right here, right now if that had gotten the reaction she'd hoped for. Instead, his expression had a huge heaping dose of caution. "We agreed that we'd take that part as it came. No pressure. You're focusing on your career, just like I am. If Franca's not guiding you toward the right next level, then what do you want her to do?"

"I want her to go away!" Viv burst out. "She's exhausting and so chipper and can do more from 10:00 p.m. to midnight than a general, two single moms and the president combined. I want to have dinner with you, and lie in bed on a Saturday morning and watch cartoons with my head on your shoulder. I want you to rip my dress at the seams because you're so eager to get me naked. Most of all, I don't want to think about cupcakes."

But he was shaking his head. "That's not me. I'm not the kind of guy who rips a woman's dress off."

"But you are. You did," she argued inanely because what a stupid thing to say. He was totally that man and she loved it when he was like that. "I don't understand why we were so hot and heavy and then you backed off."

There came another shadow through his gaze that darkened his whole demeanor. "Because we're friends and I'm nothing if not interested in preserving that relationship."

"I am, too," she shot back a little desperately. This conversation was sliding away from her at an alarming pace, turning into something it shouldn't be, and she wasn't sure how that had happened. Or how to fix it. "But I'm also not happy just being friends. I love the text messages and I'm thrilled with what you've done for my business. But it's not enough."

"What are you saying?" he asked cautiously, his expression blank.

"That I want a real marriage. A family. I want more than just cupcakes."

Jonas let the phrase soak through him. Everything inside shifted, rolling over. In six words, Viv had reshaped the entire dynamic between them, and the effects might be more destructive than a nuclear bomb.

His chest certainly felt like one had gone off inside. While he'd been fighting to keep from treating Viv to a repeat of the dress-ripping incident, she'd been quietly planning to cut him off at the knees. Apparently he'd been creating distance for no reason.

Viv's gorgeous face froze when he didn't immediately respond. But what was he supposed to say?

Oh, that's right. *What the hell?*

"Viv, I've known you for over a year. We've been married for almost five weeks. For pretty much the entire length of our acquaintance, you've told me how important your career is to you. I have never once heard you mention that you wanted a family. Can you possibly expand on that statement?"

The weird vibe went even more haywire and he had the impression she regretted what she'd said. Then, she dropped her head into her hands, covering her eyes for a long beat. The longer she hid from him, the more alarmed he got. What was she afraid he'd see?

"Not much to expand on," she mumbled to her palms. "I like cupcakes, but I want a husband and a family, too."

Which was pretty much what she'd just said, only rephrased in such a way as to still not make any sense. "Let me ask this a different way. Why have you never told me this? I thought we were friends."

Yeah, that was a little bitterness fighting to get free.

How well did he really know the woman he'd married if this was just now coming out after all this time? After all the intimacies that they'd shared?

The lick of temper uncurling inside was completely foreign. He'd asked her to marry him strictly because he'd been sure—*positive* even—that she wasn't the slightest bit interested in having a long-term relationship.

Otherwise, he never would have asked her to do this favor. Never would have let himself start to care more than he should have.

His anger fizzled. He could have been more forthcoming with his own truths but hadn't for reasons that he didn't feel that self-righteous about all at once.

"I never told you because it...never came up." Guilt flickered in her tone and when she lifted her face from her hands, it was there in her expression, too. "I'm only telling you now because you asked."

Actually, he hadn't. He'd been sorting through her comments about the marketing consultant he'd hired, desperately trying to figure out if Viv and Franca just didn't get along or if the references he'd received regarding the consultant's brilliance had been embellished. Instead, she'd dropped a whole different issue in his lap. One that was knifing through his chest like a dull machete.

Viv wanted a real husband. A family. This fake marriage was in her way. *Jonas* was in her way. It was shattering. Far more than he would have said.

He didn't want to lose her. But neither could he keep her, not at the expense of giving her what she really wanted. Obviously he should have given more weight to the conversation they'd had at his parents' house about love being a good basis for marriage. Clearly that was what she wanted from a husband.

And he couldn't give her that, nor was she asking him to. He'd made a promise that he'd never let a woman have enough sway to affect his emotions. Judging by the swirl of confusion beneath his breastbone, it was already too late for that.

If she just hadn't said anything. He could have kept pretending that the solution to all his problems was to keep her busy until he figured out how to make all his inappropriate feelings go away.

But this…he couldn't ignore what he knew was the right thing to do.

"Viv." Vising his forehead between his fingers, he tried like hell to figure out how they'd gotten so off track. "You've been telling me for over a year that your career sucked up all your time and that's why you didn't date. How were you planning to meet said husband?"

"I don't know," she shot back defensively. "And cupcakes are important to me. It's just not the only thing, and this marathon of business-plan goals kind of solidified that fact for me. I love the idea of sharing my recipes with a bigger block of customers. But not at the expense of the kind of marriage I think would make me happy. I want—need—to back off."

Back off. From him, she meant. Jonas blinked as something wrenched loose in his chest, and it felt an awful lot like she'd gripped his heart in her fingers, then twisted until it fell out. "I understand. You deserve to have the kind of marriage you want and I can't give that to you."

Her face froze, going so glacial all at once he scarcely recognized her.

"You've never thought about having a real marriage?" she asked in a whisper.

Not once. Until now. And now it was all he could think about. What was a real marriage to her? Love, honor and cherish for the rest of her days? He could do two out of three. Would she accept that? Then he could keep her friendship, keep this marriage and… how crappy was that, to even contemplate how far he could take this without breaking his word to anyone? It was ridiculous. They should have hashed out this stuff long ago. Like before they got married. And he would have if she'd told him that she harbored secret dreams of hearts and googly eyes. Too bad that kind of stuff led to emotional evisceration when everything went south.

Like now.

"Viv." She shifted to look at him, apparently clueing in that he had something serious to say. "I married you specifically because I have no intention of having a real marriage. It was deliberate."

Something that looked a lot like pain flashed through her gaze. "Because I'm not real marriage material?"

A sound gurgled in his throat as he got caught between a vehement denial and an explanation that hopefully didn't make him sound like an ass.

"Not because you're unlovable or something." God, what was wrong with him? He was hurting her with his thoughtlessness. She'd spilled her guts to him, obviously because she trusted him with the truth, and the best he could do was smash her dreams? "I care about you. That's why we're having this conversation, which we should have had a long time ago. I never told you about Marcus."

Eyes wide, she shook her head but stayed silent as he spit out the tale of his friend who had loved and lost and then never recovered. When he wound it up with the tragedy and subsequent pact, she blinked away a sheen of tears that he had no idea what to do with.

"So you, Warren and Hendrix are all part of this... club?" she asked. "The Never Going to Fall in Love club?"

It sounded silly when she said it like that. "It's not a club. We swore solemn vows and I take that seriously."

She nodded once, but confusion completely screwed up her beautiful face. "I see. Instead of having something wonderful with a life partner, you intend to stick to a promise you made under duress a decade ago."

"No," he countered quietly. "I intend to stand by a promise I made, period. Because that's who I am. It's a measure of my ethical standards. A testament to the kind of man I want to be."

"Alone? That's the kind of man you want to be?"

"That's not fair." Why was she so concerned about his emotional state all at once? "I don't want to be alone. That's why I like being married to you so much. We have fun together. Eat dinner. Watch TV."

"Not lately," she said pointedly, and it was an arrow through his heart. If he was going to throw around his ethics like a blunt instrument, then he couldn't very well pretend he didn't know what she meant.

"Not lately," he agreed. "I'd like to say it's because we've both been busy. But that's not the whole truth. I…started to get a little too attached to you. Distance was necessary."

The sheen was back over her eyes. "Because of the pact. You've been pulling back on purpose."

He nodded. The look on her face was killing him, and he'd like nothing more than to yank her into his arms and tell her to forget that nonsense. Because he wanted his friend back. His lover. His everything.

But he couldn't. In the most unfair turnabout, he'd told her about the pact and instead of her running in the other direction like a lot of women, *he* was the one shutting down. "It was the only way I could keep you as my wife and honor the promises I made to myself and to my friends. And to you. I said no pressure. I meant to keep it that way. Which still stands, by the way."

She laughed, but he didn't think it was because she

found any of this funny. "I think this is about the lowest-pressure marriage on the planet."

"You misunderstand. I'm saying no pressure to stay married."

Her gaze cut to him and he took the quick, hard punch to the gut in stride without letting on to her how difficult it had been to utter those words.

Take them back. Right now.

But he couldn't.

"Jonas, we can't get divorced. You'd lose your grandfather's support to take over his role."

The fact that she'd even consider that put the whole conversation in perspective. They were friends who cared about each other. Which meant he had to let her go, no matter how hard it was. "I know. But it's not fair to you to stay in this marriage given that you want something different."

"I do want something different," she agreed quietly. "I have to go to LA. I can't think about any of this right now."

He let her fingers slip from his, and when she shut herself in her bedroom, the quiet click of the door burst through his chest like a gunshot to the heart. He wished he felt like congratulating himself on his fine upstanding character, but all he felt like doing was crawling into bed and throwing a blanket over his head. The absence of Viv left a cold, dark place inside that even a million blankets couldn't warm.

Ten

The trip to LA was a disaster. Oh, the cooking show was fine. She won the first round. But Viv hated having to fake smile, hated pretending her marriage wasn't fake, hated the fakeness of baking on camera with a script full of fake dialogue.

There was nothing real about her, apparently. And it had been slowly sapping her happiness away until she couldn't stand it if one more person called her Mrs. Kim. Why had she changed her name? Even that was temporary until some ambiguous point in the future.

Well, there was one thing that was real. The way she felt about Jonas, as evidenced by the numbness inside that she carried 24/7. Finally, she had someone to care about and *he* cared about *her*. Yay. He cared so much that he was willing to let her out of the favor of being married to him so she could *find someone else*.

How ironic that she'd ended up exactly where she'd intended to be. All practiced up for her next relationship, except she didn't want to move on. She wanted Jonas, just like she had for over a year, and she wanted him to feel the same about her.

The cooking show, or rather the more correctly labeled entertainment venue disguised as a cupcake battle, wrapped up the next day. Viv won the final round and Franca cheered from the sidelines, pointing to her phone, where she was presumably checking out the stats on Cupcaked's new digital storefront. Every time the show's camera zoomed in on Viv's face, they put a graphic overlay on the screen with her name and the name of her cupcake bakery. Whatever results that had produced made Franca giddy, apparently.

It was all too overwhelming. None of this was what she wanted. Instead of cooking shows, Viv should have been spending fourteen hours a day working on her marriage. The what-ifs were all she could think about.

On the plane ride home, Franca jabbered about things like click-through rates, branding and production schedules. They'd already decided to outsource the baking for the digital storefront because Viv's current setup couldn't handle the anticipated volume. Judging by the numbers Franca was throwing out, it had been a good decision.

Except for the part where none of this was what Viv wanted. And it was high time she fixed that.

When she got home, she drafted a letter to Franca thanking her for all of her hard work on Viv's behalf but explaining that her career was not in fact the most important thing in her life, so Franca's services were no longer needed. The improvements to Cupcaked were great and Viv intended to use the strategies that they'd both developed. But she couldn't continue to invest so much energy into her business, not if she hoped to fix whatever was broken in Jonas's head that made him think that saying a few words a decade ago could ever compare with the joy of having the kind of marriage she'd watched her sisters experience. Viv had been shuffled to the side once again and she wasn't okay with that.

Jonas came home late. No surprise there. That seemed to be the norm. But she was not prepared to see the lines of fatigue around his eyes. Or the slight shock flickering through his expression when he caught sight of her sitting on the couch.

"Hey," he called. "Didn't know you were back."

"Surprise." Served him right. "Sit down so we can talk."

Caution drenched his demeanor and he took his time slinging his leather bag over the back of a chair. "Can it wait? I have a presentation to the board tomorrow and I'd like to go over—"

"You're prepared," she told him and patted the cushion next to her. "I've known you for a long time and I would bet every last cupcake pan I own that you've been working on that PowerPoint every spare second for days. You're going to kill it. Sit."

It was a huge kick that he obeyed, and she nearly swooned when the masculine scent of her husband washed over her. He was too far away to touch, but she could rectify that easily. When it was time. She was flying a little blind here, but she did know one thing—she was starting over from scratch. No familiar ingredients. No beloved pan. The oven wasn't even heated up yet.

But she had her apron on and the battle lines drawn. Somehow, she needed to bake a marriage until it came out the way she liked.

"What's up? How was the show?" he asked conversationally, but strictly to change the subject, she was pretty sure.

"Fine. I won. It was fabulous. I fired Franca."

That got his attention. "What? Why would you do that?"

"Because she's too good for me. She needs to go help someone run an empire." She smiled as she gave Jonas a once-over. "You should hire her, in fact."

"Maybe I will." His dark eyes had a flat, guarded quality that she didn't like. While she knew academically that she had to take a whole different track with him, it was another thing entirely to be this close but yet so far.

"Jonas, we have to finish our conversation. The one from the other day."

"I wasn't confused about which one you meant." A brief lift of his lips encouraged her to continue, but then the shield between them snapped back into place. "You've decided to go."

"No. I'm not going anywhere." Crossing her arms so she couldn't reach out to him ranked as one of the hardest things she'd done. But it was necessary to be clear about this without adding a bunch of other stuff into the mix. "I said I was going to do you this favor and as strongly as you believe in keeping your word, it inspires me to do the same. I'm here for the duration."

Confusion replaced the guardedness and she wasn't sure which one she liked less. "You're staying? As my wife?"

"And your friend." She shrugged. "Nothing you said changed anything for me. I still want the marriage I envision and I definitely won't get that if I divorce you."

Jonas flinched and a million different things sprang into the atmosphere between them. "You're not thinking clearly. You'll never meet someone who can give you what you want if you stay married to me."

"For a smart man, you're being slow to catch on." The little noise of disgust sounded in her chest before she could check it. But *men*. So dense. "I want a real marriage with *you*, not some random guy off the street. What do you think we've been doing here but building this into something amazing? I know you want to honor your word to your friends—"

"Viv." The quiet reverberation of her name stopped her cold and she glanced at him. He'd gone so still that her pulse tumbled. "It's not just a promise I made to my friends. I have no room in my life for a real marriage. The pact was easy for me to make. It's not that I swore to never fall in love. It's that I refuse to. It's a destructive emotion that leads to more destruction. That's not something I'm willing to chance."

Her mouth unhinged and she literally couldn't make a sound to save her life. Something cold swept along her skin as she absorbed his sincerity.

"Am I making sense?" he asked after a long pause.

That she could answer easily. "None. Absolutely no sense."

His mouth firmed into a long line and he nodded. "It's a hard concept for someone like you who wants to put your faith and trust in someone else. I don't. I can't. I've built something from nothing, expanded Kim Electronics into a billion-dollar enterprise in the American market, and I'm poised to take that to the next level. I cannot let a woman nor the emotions one might introduce ruin everything."

She'd only thought nothing could make her colder than his opening statement. But the ice forming from this last round of crazy made her shiver. "You're lumping *me* in that category? *I'm* this nebulous entity known as 'woman' who might go Helen of Troy on your business? I don't even know what to say to that."

Grimly, he shook his head. "There's nothing to say. Consider this from my perspective. I didn't even know you wanted anything beyond your career until a couple of days ago. What else don't I know? I can't take that risk. Not with you."

"What?" Her voice cracked. "You're saying you don't trust me because I didn't blather on about hearts and flowers from the first moment I met you?"

Pathetic. Not-clingy hadn't worked. In fact, it might have backfired. If she'd just told him how she felt from the beginning, she could have used the last five weeks to combat his stupid pact.

Something white-hot and angry rose up in her throat. Seriously, this was so unfair. She couldn't be herself with *anyone*. Instead there were all these rules and games and potholes and loopholes, none of which she understood or cared about.

"Viv." He reached out and then jerked his hand back before touching her, as if he'd only just realized that they weren't in a place where that was okay. "It's not a matter of trust. It's…me. I can't manage how insane you make me."

She eyed him, sniffling back a tsunami of tears. "So

now I make you crazy? Listen, buster, I'm not the one talking crazy here—"

A strangled sound stopped her rant. Jonas shook his head, clearly bemused. "Not crazy. Give me a break. I was expecting you to walk out the door, not grill me on things I don't know how to explain. Just stop for a second."

His head dropped into his hands and he massaged his temples.

"Insane and crazy are the same thing."

"I mean how much I want you!" he burst out. "All the time. You make me insane with wanting to touch you, and roll into you in the middle of the night to hold you. Kiss you until you can't breathe. So, yeah, I'll give you that. It makes me crazy. In this case, it does mean the same thing."

Reeling, she stared at him, dumbstruck, numb, so off balance she couldn't figure out how to make her brain work. What in the world was wrong with *any* of that?

"I don't understand what you're telling me, Jonas."

"It's already way too much." He threw up his hands. "How much worse will it get? I refuse to let my emotions control me like that."

This was awful. He was consciously rejecting the concept of allowing anything deeper to grow between them. Period. No questions asked. She let that reality seep into her soul as her nails dug into her palms with little pinpricks of pain that somehow centered her. If this was his decision, she had to find a way to live with it.

"So, what happens next?" she whispered. "I don't want a divorce. Do you?"

At that, he visibly crumpled, folding in on himself as if everything hurt. She knew the feeling.

"I can't even answer that." His voice dipped so low that she could scarcely make it out. "My grandfather asked me to come to Korea as soon as possible. He got some bad news from his doctor and he's retiring earlier than expected."

"Oh, no." Viv's hand flew to her mouth as she took in the devastation flitting through Jonas's expression. "Is he going to be okay?"

"I don't know. He wants you to come. How can I ask that of you?" His gaze held a world of pain and indecision and a million other things that her own expression probably mirrored. "It's not fair to you."

This was where the rubber met the road. He wasn't asking her to go, nor would he. He was simply stating facts and giving the choice to her. If she wanted to claim a real marriage for herself, she had to stand by her husband through thick and thin, sickness and health, vows of honor and family emergencies.

This was the ultimate test. Did she love Jonas enough to ignore her own needs in order to fulfill his? If nothing else, it was her sole opportunity to do and be whatever she wanted in a relationship. Her marriage, her rules. If she had a mind to cling like Saran Wrap to Jonas, it was her right.

In what was probably the easiest move of the entire conversation, she reached out to lace her fingers with his and held on tight. "If you strip everything else away, I'm still your wife. Your grandfather could still pass his support to someone else if he suspects something isn't right between us. If you want me to go, I'll go."

Clearly equal parts shocked and grateful, he stared at her. "Why would you do that for me?"

She squared her shoulders. "Because I said I would." No matter how hard it would be.

Jonas kept sneaking glances at Viv as she slept in the reclined leather seat opposite his. She'd smiled for nearly ten minutes after claiming a spot aboard the Kim private jet that Grandfather had sent to Raleigh to fetch them. It was fun to watch her navigate the spacious fuselage and interact with the attentive staff, who treated her like royalty. Obviously his grandfather had prepped them in advance.

But after the initial round of post-takeoff champagne, Viv had slipped back into the morose silence that cloaked them both since their conversation. He'd done everything in his power to drive her away so he didn't hurt her and what had she done? Repacked the suitcase that she'd just pulled off a conveyor belt at the airport hours before and announced she was coming with him to Korea. No hesitation.

What was he going to do with her?

Not much, apparently. The distance between them was nearly palpable. Viv normally had this vibe of openness about her as if she'd never met a stranger and he could talk to her about anything. Which he had, many times. Since he'd laid down the law about what kind of marriage they could have in that desperate bid to stop the inevitable, there might as well have been an impenetrable steel wall between them.

Good. That was perfect. Exactly what he'd hoped for. He hated it.

This purgatory was exactly what he deserved, though. If Viv wasn't being her beautiful, kind, amazing self, there was no chance of his emotions engaging.

Or rather, engaging further. He was pretty sure there was a little something already stirring around inside. Okay a lot of something, but if he could hold on to that last 50 percent, he could still look Warren and Hendrix in the eye next time they were in the same room.

If he could just cast aside his honor, all of this would be so much easier.

Seoul's Incheon Airport spread out beneath them in all its dazzling silvery glory, welcoming him back to Korea. He appreciated the birthplace of his father and the homeland of his grandfather. Seoul was a vibrant city rich in history with friendly people who chattered in the streets as they passed. It was cosmopolitan in a way that Raleigh could never be, but Jonas preferred the more laid-back feel of his own homeland.

"It's beautiful," Viv commented quietly as the limo Grandfather had sent wound through the streets thronged with people and vehicles.

"I'll take you a few places while we're here," he offered. "You shouldn't miss Gyeongbokgung Palace."

They could walk through Insa-dong, the historic neighborhood that sold art and food, then maybe breeze by the Seoul Tower. He could perfectly envision the delighted smile on her face as she discovered the treasures of the Eastern world that comprised a portion of his lineage. Maybe he'd even find an opportunity to take her hand as they strolled, and he could pretend everything was fine between them.

But Viv was already shaking her head. "You don't have to do that. I don't need souvenirs. You're here for your grandfather and I'm here for you."

That made him feel like crap. But it was an inescapable fact that she'd come because he needed her.

Warmth crowded into his chest as he gazed at her, the beauty of Seoul rushing past the limousine window beyond the glass.

"Why?" he asked simply, too overcome to be more articulate.

Her gaze sought his, and for a brief moment, her normal expressiveness spilled onto her face. Just as quickly, she whisked it away. "No matter what, you're still my friend."

The sentiment caught in his throat. Her sacrifice and the unbelievable willingness to be there for him would have put him on his knees if he wasn't already sitting down. Still might. It didn't make any sense for her to be so unselfish with her time, her body, her cupcakes even without some gain other than the righteous promise of *friendship*. "I don't believe that's the whole reason."

A tiny frown marred her gorgeous mouth and he wished he could kiss it away. But he didn't move. This was something he should have questioned before they got on the plane.

"Is this another conversation about how you don't trust me?" she asked in a small voice.

Deserved that. He shook his head. "This is not a trust issue. It's that I don't understand what you're getting out of all of this. I've always wondered. I promised you that I would help you with your business since you claimed that as your passion. Then you politely declined all the success my efforts have produced. I give you the option to leave and you don't take it. Friendship doesn't seem like enough of a motivator."

Guilt crowded through her gaze. What was that all about? But she looked away before he got confirmation that it was indeed guilt, and he had a burning need to understand all at once.

The vows he'd taken with Warren and Hendrix after Marcus's death seemed like a pinky swear on the playground in comparison to Viv's friendship standards, yet he'd based his adult life on that vow. If there was something to learn from her about the bonds of friendship, he'd be an instant student.

Hooking her chin with his finger, he guided her face back toward his, feathering a thumb across her cheek before he'd barely gotten purchase. God, she felt so good. It was all he could do to keep from spreading his entire palm across her cheek, lifting her lips into a kiss that would resolve nothing other than the constant ache under his skin.

He'd enjoy every minute of the forbidden, though.

Since she still hadn't answered, he prompted her. "What's your real reason, Viv? Tell me why you'd do this for me after all I've said and done."

She blinked. "I agreed to this deal. You of all people should know that keeping your word is a choice. Anyone can break a promise but mine to you means something."

That wasn't it, or rather it wasn't the full extent. He could tell. While he appreciated her conviction, she was hedging. He hadn't expanded Kim Electronics into the American market and grown profits into the ten-figure range by missing signs that the person on the other side of the table wasn't being entirely forthcoming. But she wasn't a factory owner looking to make an extra million or two or a parts distributor with shady sources.

She was his wife. Why couldn't he take what she said at face value and leave it at that?

Because she hadn't told him about wanting a real

marriage, that was why. It stuck under his rib cage, begging him to do something with that knowledge, and the answer wasn't pulling her into his arms like he wanted to. He should be cutting her free by his choice, not hers.

Yet Viv was quietly showing him how to be a real friend regardless of the cost. It was humbling, and as the limo snaked through the crowded streets of Seoul toward his grandfather's house, his chest got so tight and full of that constant ache he got whenever he looked at Viv that he could hardly breathe.

Caught in the trap of his own making, he let his hand drop away from her face. He had a wife he couldn't let himself love and two friends he couldn't let himself disappoint. At what point did Jonas get what he wanted? And when had his desire for something more shifted so far away from what he had?

There was no good answer to that. The limo paused by his grandfather's gates as they opened and then the driver pulled onto the hushed property draped with trees and beautiful gardens. The ancestral home that Grandfather had given Jonas and Viv lay a kilometer down the road up on a hill. Both properties were palatial, befitting a businessman who entertained people from all over the world, as Jung-Su did. As Jonas would be expected to do when he stepped into Grandfather's shoes. He'd need a wife to help navigate the social aspects of being the CEO of a global company.

But the painful truth was that he couldn't imagine anyone other than Viv by his side. He needed *her*, not a wife, and for far more reasons than because it might or might not secure the promotion he'd been working toward. At the same time, as much as he'd denied that his questions were about trust, he was caught in a horrible catch-22. Trust *was* at the root of it.

Also a trap of his own making. He was predisposed to believe that a woman would string him along until she got tired of him and then she'd break his heart. So he looked for signs of that and pounced the moment he found evidence, when in reality, he'd have to actually give his heart to a woman before it could be broken. And that was what he was struggling to avoid.

Grandfather's *jibsa* ushered them into the house and showed them to their rooms. A different member of the staff discreetly saw to their needs and eventually guided Jonas and Viv to where his grandfather sat in the garden outside, enjoying the sunshine. The garden had been started by Jonas's grandmother, lovingly overseen until her death several years ago. Her essence still flitted among the mugunghwa blooms and bellflowers, and he liked remembering her out here.

His grandfather looked well, considering he'd recently been diagnosed with some precursors to heart disease and had begun rounds of medication to reverse the potential for a heart attack.

"Jonas. Miss Viviana." Grandfather smiled at them each in turn and Viv bent to kiss his cheek, which made the old man positively beam. "I'm pleased to see you looking well after your flight. It is not an easy one."

Viv waved that off and took a seat next to Jung-Su on the long stone bench. His grandfather sat on a cushion that was easier on his bones but Viv didn't seem to notice that she was seated directly on the cold rock ledge. Discreetly, Jonas flicked his fingers at one of the many uniformed servants in his grandfather's employ, and true to form, the man returned quickly with another cushion for her.

She took it with a smile and resituated herself, still chatting with Grandfather about the flight and her impressions of Korea thus far. Grandfather's gaze never left her face and Jonas didn't blame him. She was mesmerizing. Surrounded by the lush tropical beauty of the garden and animated by a subject that clearly intrigued her, she was downright breathtaking. Of course, Jonas was biased. Especially since he hadn't been able to take a deep breath pretty much since the moment he'd said *I do* to this woman.

"Jonas. Don't hover." Grandfather's brows came together as he shot a scowl over the head of his new grand-daughter-in-law. "Sit with us. Your lovely wife was just telling me about baking cupcakes on the American television show."

"Yes, she was brilliant," Jonas acknowledged. But he didn't sit on the bench. The only open spot was next to Viv and it was entirely too much temptation for his starving body to be that near her.

"Jonas is too kind." Viv's nose wrinkled as she shook her head. "The show hasn't even aired yet."

"So? I don't have to see it to know that you killed it." Plus, she'd told him she'd won, like it was no big deal, when in fact, it was. Though the result was hardly shocking. "*Brilliant* is an understatement."

Viv ducked her head but not before he caught the pleased gleam in her eye. He should have told her that already and more than once. Instead, he'd been caught up in his own misery. She deserved to hear how wonderful she was on a continual basis.

"It's true," he continued. "She does something special with her recipes. No one else can touch her talent when it comes to baking."

Grandfather watched them both, his gaze traveling back and forth between them as if taking in a fascinating tennis match. "It's very telling that you are your wife's biggest fan."

Well, maybe so. But what it told, Jonas had no idea. He shrugged. "That's not a secret."

"It's a sign of maturity that I appreciate," his grandfather said. "For years I have watched you do nothing but work and I worried that you would never have a personal life. Now I see you are truly committed to your wife and I like seeing you happy. It only solidifies my decision to retire early."

Yeah. *Committed* described Jonas to a T. Committed to honor. Committed to making himself insane. Committed to the asylum might well be next, especially since his grandfather was so off the mark with his observation. But what was he supposed to do, correct him?

"It's only fair," Viv murmured before Jonas could formulate a response. "I'm his biggest fan, as well."

"Yes, I can see that, too," Jung-Su said with a laugh.

He could? Jonas glanced at Viv out of the corner of his eye in case there was some kind of sign emanating from her that he'd managed to miss. Except she had her sights firmly fixed on him and caught him eyeing her. Their gazes locked and he couldn't look away.

"You're a fan of workaholic, absentee husbands?" he asked with a wry smile of his own. Might as well own his faults in front of God and everyone.

"I'm a fan of your commitment, just like your grandfather said. You do everything with your heart. It's what I first noticed about you. You came into the shop to get cupcakes for your staff, and every time, I'd ask you 'What's the occasion today?' and you always knew the smallest details. 'It's Mrs. Nguyen's fiftieth birthday' or 'Today marks my admin's fourth anniversary working for me.' None of my other customers pay attention to stuff like that."

He shifted uncomfortably. Of course he knew those things. They'd been carefully researched excuses to buy cupcakes so he could see Viv without admitting he was there to see her. Granted, she'd already figured that out and blathered on about it to his parents during their first official married-couple dinner. Why bring that up again now?

"That's why he'll make the best CEO of Kim Global," she said to his grandfather as an aside. "Because he cares about people and cares about doing the right thing. He always keeps his word. His character is above reproach and honestly, that's why I fell for him."

That was laying it on a bit thick, but his grandfather just nodded. "Jonas is an honorable man. I'm pleased he's found a woman who loves him for the right reasons."

Except it was all fake. Jonas did a double take as Viv nodded, her eyes bright with something that looked a lot like unshed tears. "He's an easy man to love. My feelings for him have only grown now that we're married."

Jonas started to interrupt because…come on. There was playacting and there was outright lying to his grandfather for the sake of supporting Jonas's bid to become the next CEO. But as one tear slipped from her left eye, she glanced at him and whatever he'd been about to say vanished from his vocabulary. She wasn't lying.

He swallowed. Viv was in love with him? A band

tightened around his lungs as he stared at her, soaking in the admission. It shouldn't be such a shock. She looked at him like that all the time. But not seconds after saying something so shocking, so provocative *out loud*. She couldn't take it back. It was out there, pinging around inside him like an arrow looking for a target.

A servant interrupted them, capturing Grandfather's attention, and everything fell apart as it became apparent that they were being called for dinner. Jonas took Viv's hand to help her to her feet as he'd done a hundred times before but her hand in his felt different, heavier somehow as if weighted with implications. She squeezed his hand as if she knew he needed her calming touch.

It was anything but calming. She was in love with him. The revelation bled through him. It was yet another thing that she'd held back from him that changed everything. He worked it over in his mind during dinner, longing to grab her and carry her out of this public room so he could ask her a few pointed questions. But Grandfather talked and talked and talked, and he'd invited a few business associates over as well, men Jonas couldn't ignore, given that the whole reason he was in Korea was to work through the transition as his grandfather stepped down.

Finally all the obstacles were out of the way and he cornered his wife in their room. She glanced up as he shut the door, leaning against it as he zeroed in on the woman sitting on the bed.

"That went well," she commented, her gaze cutting away from his. "Your grandfather seems like he's in good spirits after his diagnosis."

"I don't want to talk about that." He loved his grandfather, but they'd talked about his illness at length before Jonas had left the States, and he was satisfied he knew everything necessary about Jung-Su's health. Jonas's wife, on the other hand, needed to do a whole lot more talking and he needed a whole lot more understanding. "Why did you tell my grandfather that you're in love with me?"

"It just kind of…came out," she said. "But don't worry, I'm pretty sure he bought it."

"I bought it," he bit out. "It wasn't just something you said. You meant it. How long have you been in love with me?"

She shrugged. "It's not a big deal."

"It is a big deal!" Frustrated with the lack of headway, he crossed the room and stopped short of lifting her face so he could read for himself what she was feeling. But he didn't touch her, because he wanted her to own up to what was really going on inside. For once. "That's why you married me. Why you came to Korea. Why you're still here even though I told you about the pact."

That's when she met his gaze, steady and true. "Yes."

Something wonderful and beautiful and strong burst through his heart. It all made a lot more sense now. What he'd been calling friendship was something else entirely.

Now would be a *really* good time to sit down. So he did. "Why didn't you tell me? That's information that I should have had a long time ago."

"No, Jonas, it's not." She jammed her hands on her hips. "What does it change? Nothing. You're determined to keep your vow to your friends and I can't stop being in love with you. So we're both stuck."

Yes. *Stuck.* He'd been between a rock and a hard place for an eternity because he couldn't stop being in love with her either.

He'd tried. He'd pretended that he wasn't, called it friendship, pushed her away, stayed away himself, thrown his honor down between them. But none of it had worked because he'd been falling for her since the first cupcake.

Maybe it was time to try something else.

"Viv." He stood and waited until he had her full attention. But then when she locked gazes with him, her expressive eyes held a world of possibilities. Not pain. Not destruction. None of the things that he'd tried to guard against.

That was the reason she should leave. Instead of feeling stuck, she should divorce him simply because he was a moron. The character she'd spoken of to his grandfather didn't include being courageous. He was a coward, refusing to acknowledge that avoiding love hadn't saved him any heartache. In fact, it had caused him a lot more than he'd credited. Had caused Viv a lot, too.

Worse, he'd avoided the wonderful parts, and ensured that he'd be lonely to boot. And what had he robbed himself of thus far? Lots of sex with his wife, a chance to have a real marriage and many, many moments where she looked at him like she was looking at him right now. As if he really was worthy of her devotion, despite his stupidity.

He'd had plenty of pain already. Avoiding the truth hadn't stopped that. The lesson here? No more pretending.

"Tell me," he commanded. "No more hiding how you really feel. I want to hear it from you, no holds barred."

"Why are you doing this?" Another tear slipped down her face and she brushed it away before he could, which seemed to be a common theme. She had things inside that she didn't trust him with and he didn't blame her.

"Because we haven't been honest with each other. In fact, I'd say my behavior thus far in our marriage hasn't been anything close to honorable, and it's time to end that. You know what? I should go first then." He captured her hand and held it between his. "Viv. You're my friend, my lover, my wife, my everything. When I made a vow to never fall in love, it was from a place of ignorance. Because I thought love was a bad thing. Something to be avoided. You taught me differently. And I ignored the fact that I took vows with you. Vows that totally overshadow the promise I made to Warren and Hendrix before I fully understood what I was agreeing to give up. I'm not okay with that anymore. Not okay with pretending. What I'm trying to say, and not doing a very good job at, is that I love you, too."

Like magic, all of his fear vanished simply by virtue of saying it out loud. At last, he could breathe. The clearest sense of happiness radiated from somewhere deep inside and he truly couldn't fathom why it had taken him so long to get to this place.

Viv eyed him suspiciously instead of falling into his waiting arms. "What?"

He laughed but it didn't change her expression. "I love you. I wouldn't blame you if you needed to hear it a hundred more times to believe me."

Her lips quirked. "I was actually questioning the part where you said you weren't doing a good job explaining. Because it seemed pretty adequate to me."

That seemed like as good an invitation as any to sweep her into his arms. In a tangle, they fell back against the mattress, and before he could blink, she was kissing him, her mouth shaping his with demanding little pulls, as if she wanted everything inside him. He didn't mind. It all belonged to her anyway.

Just as he finally got his hands under her dress, nearly groaning at the hot expanse of skin that he couldn't wait to taste, she broke the kiss and rolled him under her.

That totally worked for him. But she didn't dive back in like his body screamed for her to. Instead, she let him drown in her warm brown eyes as she smiled. "What's going to happen when we get home and you have to explain to Warren and Hendrix that you broke your word to them?"

"Nothing. Because that's not what I'm going to say." He smoothed back a lock of her hair that had fallen into her face, and shifted until her body fell into the grooves of his perfectly. This position was his new favorite. "We made that pact because we didn't want to lose each other. Our friendship isn't threatened because I finally figured out that I'm in love with you. I'll help them realize that."

"Good. I don't want to be the woman who came between you and your friends."

"You couldn't possibly. Because you're the woman who *is* my friend. I never want that to change."

And then there was no more talking as Viv made short work of getting them both undressed, which was only fair since she was on top. He liked Take Charge Viv almost as much as he liked In Love with Him Viv.

She was everything he never expected when he fell in love with his best friend.

Epilogue

Jonas walked into the bar where he'd asked Warren and Hendrix to meet him. He'd tried to get Viv to come with him, but she'd declined with a laugh, arguing that the last person who should be present at the discussion of how Jonas had broken the pact was the woman he'd fallen in love with.

While he agreed, he still wasn't looking forward to it. Despite what he'd told Viv, he didn't think Warren and Hendrix were going to take his admission lightly.

His friends were already seated in a high-backed booth, which Jonas appreciated given the private nature of what he intended to discuss. They'd already taken the liberty of ordering, and three beers sat on the table. But when he slid into the booth across from Warren, Hendrix cleared his throat.

"I'm glad you called," Hendrix threw out before

Jonas could open his mouth. "I have something really important to ask you both."

Thrilled to have an out, Jonas folded his hands and toyed with his wedding band, which he did anytime he thought about Viv. He did it so often, the metal had worn a raw place on his finger. "I'm all ears, man."

Warren set his phone down, but no less than five notifications blinked from the screen. "Talk fast. I have a crisis at work."

Hendrix rolled his eyes. "You always have a crisis. It's usually that you're not there. Whatever it is can wait five minutes." He let out a breath with a very un-Hendrix-like moan. "I need you guys to do me a favor and I need you to promise not to give me any grief over it."

"That's pretty much a guarantee that we will," Warren advised him with cocked eyebrow. "So spill before I drag it out of you."

"I'm getting married."

Jonas nearly spit out the beer he'd just sipped. "To one woman?"

"Yes, to one woman." Hendrix shot him a withering glare. "It's not that shocking."

"The hell you say." Warren hit the side of his head with the flat of his palm. Twice. "I think my brain is scrambled. Because I'd swear you just said you were getting married."

"I did, jerkoff." Hendrix shifted his scowl to Warren. "It's going to be very good for me."

"Did you steal that speech from your mom?" Warren jeered, his phone completely forgotten in favor of the real-life drama happening in their booth. "Because it sounds like you're talking about eating your veggies, not holy matrimony."

"You didn't give Jonas this much crap when he got married," Hendrix reminded him as Warren grinned.

"Um, whatever." Jonas held up a finger as he zeroed in on the small downturn of Hendrix's mouth. "That is completely false, first of all. You have a short memory. And second, if this is like my marriage, you're doing it for a reason, one you're not entirely happy about. What's this really about?"

Hendrix shrugged, wiping his expression clear. "I'm marrying Rosalind Carpenter. That should pretty much answer all of your questions."

It *so* did not. Warren and Jonas stared at him, but Warren beat him to the punch. "Whoa, dude. That's epic. Is she as much a knockout in person as she is in all those men's magazines?"

He got an elbow in his ribs for his trouble, but it wasn't Warren's fault that there were so many sexy pictures of Rosalind Carpenter to consider.

"Shut up. That's my fiancée you're talking about."

Jonas pounded on the table to get their attention. "On that note…if the question is will we be in the wedding party, of course we will." They had plenty of time to get the full story. After Jonas steered them back to the reason why he'd called them with an invitation for drinks. "Get back to us when you've made plans. Now chill out while we talk about my thing."

"Which is?" Warren gave him the side-eye while checking his messages.

"I broke the pact."

The phone slipped out of Warren's hand and thunked against the leather seat. "You did what? With Viv?"

Jonas nodded and kept his mouth shut as his friends lambasted him with their best shots at his character, the depths of his betrayal and the shallowness of his definition of the word *vow*. He took it all with grace because he didn't blame them for their anger. They just needed to experience the wonders of the right woman for themselves and then they'd get it.

When they were mostly done maligning him, Jonas put his palms flat on the table and leaned forward. "No one is more surprised by this than me. But it's the truth. I love her and I broke the pact. But it's not like it was with Marcus. She loves me back and we're happy. I hope you can be happy for us, too. Because we're going to be married and in love for a long time."

At least that was his plan. And by some miracle, it was Viv's, too.

"I can't believe you're doing this to us," Warren shot back as if he hadn't heard a word Jonas said. "Does keeping your word mean nothing to you?"

"Integrity is important to me," he told them without blinking. "That's why I'm telling you the truth. Lying about it would dishonor my relationship with Viv. And I can't stop loving her just to stick to a pact we made. I tried and it made us both miserable."

"Seems appropriate for a guy who turns on his buddies," Hendrix grumbled.

"Yeah, we'll see how you feel after you get married," Jonas told him mildly. Hendrix would come around. They both would eventually. They'd been friends for too long to let something like a lifetime of happiness come between them, strictly over principle.

Warren griped about the pact for another solid five minutes and then blew out a breath. "I've said my piece and now I have to go deal with a distribution nightmare. This is not over."

With that ominous threat, Warren shoved out of the booth and stormed from the restaurant.

Hendrix, on the other hand, just grinned. "I know you didn't mean to break the pact. It's cool. Things happen. Thank God that'll never be me, but I'm happy that you're happy."

"Thanks, man." They shook on it and drank to a decade of friendship.

When Jonas got home, Viv was waiting in the foyer. His favorite. He flashed her the thumbs-up so she would know everything was okay between him and his friends—which it would be once Warren calmed down—then wrapped Viv in his arms and let her warmth infuse him. "I have another favor to ask."

"Anything."

No hesitation. That might be his favorite quality of hers. She was all in no matter what he asked of her— because she loved him. How had he gotten so lucky? "You're not even going to ask what it is?"

She shrugged. "If it's anything like the last favor, which landed me the hottest husband on the planet, by the way, why would I say no? Your favors are really a huge win for me so…"

Laughing, he kissed her and that made her giggle, too. His heart was so full, he worried for a moment that it might burst. "Well, I'm not sure this qualifies as a win. I was just going to ask you to never stop loving me."

"Oh, you're right. I get nothing out of that," she

teased. "It's torture. You make me happier than I would have ever dreamed. Guess I can find a way to put up with that for the rest of my life."

"Good answer," he murmured, and kissed his wife, his lover, his friend. His everything.

* * * * *

ONE NIGHT STAND BRIDE

KAT CANTRELL

One

The Las Vegas tourism department needed to change their slogan because what happened in Vegas did *not* stay there. In fact, what had happened in Vegas followed Hendrix Harris home to North Carolina and landed above the fold on every media outlet known to man.

He wanted his money refunded, a spell to wipe the memories of an entire city and an aspirin.

Though even he had to admit the photographer had perfectly captured the faces of Hendrix and Rosalind Carpenter. The picture was erotic without being pornographic—a trick and a half since it was abundantly clear they were both buck naked, yet somehow, all the naughty bits were strategically covered. A miracle that had allowed the picture to be print-worthy. It was a one-in-a-million shot. You could even see the steam rising from the hot tub.

And thanks to that photographer being in the right place at the wrong time, Hendrix's luck had run out.

He'd fully expected his mother to have a heart attack when she saw her son naked with the daughter of the wealthiest man in North Carolina. Especially since Hendrix's mother had warned him to keep his clothes on once she launched her gubernatorial campaign.

Joke was on Hendrix. No heart attacks. Instead, his mother was thrilled. *Thrilled* that he'd gotten chummy with Paul Carpenter's daughter. So thrilled that somehow she'd gotten Hendrix to agree that marrying Rosalind would fix everything.

Really, this whole scandal was his fault, and it was on him to make amends, or so he'd been told. The Carpenter family had old money and lots of influence, which provided a nice balance to the Harris new money.

Grumbling in his head because he loved and respected his mother too much to do it out loud, Hendrix threw himself into the task of figuring out how to contact Roz. Their naked Vegas romp had been most definitely of the one-night stand variety. Now he would have to convince her that she loved his mother's plan.

Hendrix didn't hate the idea of marriage, per se, not when it solved more than one problem. So it was now his goal to make sure a big fat yes was Roz's response to the question *Will you marry me?*

The only problem being that he hadn't actually spoken to her since that night and they'd expressly agreed they wouldn't see each other again. Minor detail. When he put his mind to something, rare was the obstacle that didn't get the hell out of his way.

Luck crept back onto his side. Roz hadn't blocked

all the web crawlers that posted her address to one of those seamy "find anyone for a price" sites. Hendrix had no qualms about throwing money at this problem.

Hendrix drove himself to the building Rosalind Carpenter lived in on Fayetteville Street instead of taking a car. Arriving with fanfare before he'd gotten this done didn't fit his idea of a good plan. After she said yes, of course there'd be lots of sanctioned pictures of the happy couple. And they'd be dressed.

His mother hadn't properly appreciated just how hard her son had worked to get his abs to look so centerfold-worthy. It was a shame that such a great shot of what had been a truly spectacular night with the hottest woman he'd ever met had done so much damage to Ms. Harris's family values campaign.

He charmed his way past the security desk because everyone liked him instantly, a fact of life he traded on frequently. Then he waited patiently until someone with the right access to Roz's floor who was also willing to listen to his tale of woe got on the elevator. Within fifteen minutes, he knocked on Ms. Carpenter's door.

To her credit, when she answered, she didn't even blink.

He did.

Holy hell. How could he have forgotten what she did to him?

Her sensuality leaped from her like a tidal wave, crashing over him until he scarcely knew which way was up, but he didn't care because surfacing was the last thing on his mind. He gasped for air in the wake of so much sensation as she tucked a lock of dark hair behind her ear. She pursed those lush lips and surveyed him with cool amusement.

"You don't follow instructions well," she fairly purred, leaning on the door, kicking one foot to the side and drawing attention to the sexy slice of leg peeking out from her long flowy skirt.

"Your memory is faulty," he returned easily, a smile sliding across his face in spite of the reason for his visit. "I recall being an instant slave to your instructions. 'Faster, harder, take me from behind.' I can't think of a single thing you told me to do that I didn't follow to the letter."

One dark brow rose. "Other than the one where I said Vegas was a onetime thing?" she reminded him with a wry twist of her lips. "That there were reasons we shouldn't hook up at home and you agreed."

Hendrix waved that off with a grin. "Well, if you're going to get into specifics. Sure. That was the only one, though."

"Then I guess the only thing left to do is ask to what do I owe the pleasure?" That's when she blinked. "Perhaps I should rephrase the question since I have the distinct impression this is not a social call."

No point in dragging it out when they were both to blame for the scandal and they both had a vested interest in fixing the problem. But he did take a moment to appreciate how savvy she was. Contrary to what the majority of women in the Raleigh-Durham-Cary area would argue, Hendrix did notice when a woman had assets outside of the obvious ones.

Roz's brain turned him on. She saw things—layers—that normal people took at face value. It was captivating. He still wasn't sure why it had taken a trip to

Vegas for them to hook up when they'd known each other peripherally for years.

"You saw the picture," he said.

"Along with half of the eastern seaboard. But it's been circulating for a week." She slid a once-over down his body, lingering along the way like she'd found something worth noting. "Not sure why that would suddenly cause you to seek me out now."

The region under her hot gaze woke up in a hurry, galvanized into action by the quick, sharp memories of this woman under his mouth as he'd kissed, licked and tasted his way over every inch of her luscious body.

"We're definitely going to have to do something about your defective memory," he growled as he returned her heat with a pointed glance of his own. "If you can look at that photograph and not want to immediately repeat the experience."

She crossed her arms over her filmy top that did little to curb his appetite. "Nothing wrong with my memory and I have no problem admitting that your reputation is well-founded. What's not going to happen is a repeat. Vegas was my last hurrah. I told you that."

Yeah, she had. Repeatedly. While they'd been naked in her bed. And maybe once in the shower. It had been an all-night romp that had nearly caused him to miss his friend Jonas's wedding the next morning. But Hendrix had left behind his delectable companion and made it to the chapel on time, assuming he'd never see her again, as instructed.

His mother, Helene Harris, presumptive future Governor of North Carolina, had reset his thinking. It had taken a week to work through the ramifications and about that long to get him on board with the idea of a wedding as the antidote. But he was all in at this point. And he needed Roz to be all in, too.

"Here's the thing. The picture never should have happened. But it did. So we need to mitigate the damage. My mother's people think that's best accomplished by the two of us getting married. Just until the election. Then her people have agreed that we can get a quiet divorce."

Roz laughed and the silky sound tightened all the places that she'd affected so easily by sheer virtue of standing there looking lush and gorgeous.

"Your mom's people, Hendrix? That's so precious."

"Like your dad doesn't have people?" Carpenter Furniture ranked as one of the top-grossing businesses in the world. Her father had been the CEO since its inception thirty years ago. He had people.

The mirth left her face in a snap. "My dad's people aren't spewing nonsense like a *marriage* to fix a nonexistent problem. This conversation is boring me and I have things to do, so if you'll excuse me."

"Not so fast." Hendrix stuck a foot in the door before Roz could slam it in his face. Time to change tactics. "Let me buy you a drink so we can discuss this like rational adults."

"Yeah. You and alcohol creates a rational atmosphere."

Sarcasm dripped from her tone and it was so cute, he couldn't help but grin.

"Aww. That was very nearly an admission of how crazy I can make you."

"And I'm done with this." She nearly took off his foot with the force of the door closing but he didn't yank it free, despite the pinch in his arch.

"Wait, Roz." He dropped his tone into the *you can't resist me even if you try* realm. "Please give me five minutes. Then you can sever my toes all you want."

"Is the word marriage going to come out of your mouth again?"

He hesitated. Without that, there was no reason for him to be here. But he needed her more than she needed him. The trick was to make sure she never realized that.

"Is it really so much of a stretch to contemplate a merger between our families that could benefit us all? Especially in light of the photograph."

Her face didn't relax, but he could tell he had her attention. Pushing on their mutual attraction wasn't the ticket, then. Noted. So he went with logic.

"Can you honestly say you've had no fallout from our…liaison?" he asked. "Because I have or I wouldn't be standing on your doorstep. I know we agreed no contact. I know the reasons why. Things changed."

But not the reasons why. The reasons for no contact were for pure self-preservation.

He and Roz were like kindling dropped into a forest fire together. They'd gone up in flames and frankly, he'd done more dirty things in one night with Rosalind Carpenter than with the last ten women he'd dated. But by the time the sun rose, they were done. He had a strict one-time-only rule that he never broke and not just because of the pact he'd made his senior year at Duke. He'd vowed to never fall in love—because he'd been rejected enough in life and the best way to avoid all that noise was to avoid intimacy.

Sex he liked. Sex worked for him. But intimacy was off the table. He guaranteed it with no repeats.

Only at his mother's insistence would he consider making Roz his onetime exception.

"So this marriage idea. That's supposed to fix the fallout? From where I'm sitting, you're the reason for the scandal. Where's the plus for me?"

Like she hadn't been the one to come on to him on the dance floor of the Calypso Room, with her smoky eyes undressing him, the conclusion of their evening foregone the second their bodies touched.

At least she hadn't denied that the photograph had caused her some difficulty. If she had, he'd remind her that somewhere around 2:00 a.m. that night, she'd confessed that she was looking to change her reputation as the scandalous Carpenter daughter. The photograph couldn't have helped. A respectable marriage would.

That fact was still part of his strategy. "Helene's your plus. You'll be the daughter-in-law of the next governor of North Carolina. I'm confused why you're struggling with this."

"You would be." She jerked her head toward him. "I'm morbidly curious. What's in this for you?"

Legitimacy. Something hard to come by in his world. His family's chain of tobacco shops wasn't a respected industry and he was the bastard son of a man who had never claimed him.

But what he said was, "Sex."

She rolled her eyes. "You're such a liar. The last thing you need to bargain for is a woman willing to get naked with you."

"That sounded like a compliment." He waggled his brows to hide how his insides suddenly felt wobbly and precarious. How had she seen through that flippant answer?

That was what he got with a smart woman, apparently.

"It wasn't. Seduction is less of an art when you're already starting out with the deck stacked."

He had to laugh, though he wasn't quite sure if he was supposed to say thank you for the backhanded nod to his skill set. "I'm not leaving here without an answer. Marry me and the scandal goes away."

She shook her head, a sly smile spreading over her face. "Over my dead body."

And with that, she pushed his foot from the gap and shut the door with a quiet click.

Dumbfounded, Hendrix stared at the fine-grain wood. Rosalind Carpenter had just rejected his proposal. For deliberately not putting anything emotional on the line, the rejection sure stung.

Roz leaned on the shut door and closed her eyes.

Marriage. To Hendrix Harris. If she hadn't understood perfectly why he'd come up with such a ridiculous idea, she'd call the cops to come cart away the crazy man on her doorstep.

But he wasn't crazy. Just desperate to fix a problem. She was, too.

The big difference was that her father wasn't working with his "people" to help her. Instead, he was sitting up in his ivory tower continuing to be disappointed in her. Well, sometimes she screwed up. Vegas had been one of those times. Fixing it lay solely at her feet and she planned to. Just not by marrying the person who had caused the scandal in the first place.

Like marriage was the solution to anything, especially marriage to Hendrix Harris, who indeed had a reputation when it came to his exploits with the opposite sex. Hell, half of her interest back on that wild night had been insatiable curiosity about whether he could be as much trouble as everyone said.

She should have run the moment she recognized him. But no. She'd bought him a drink. She was nothing if not skilled at getting into trouble.

And what trouble she'd found.

He was of the hot, wicked and oh-so-sinful variety—the kind she had a weakness for, the kind she couldn't resist. The real question was how she'd shut the door in his face a moment ago instead of inviting him in for a repeat.

That would be a bad idea. Vegas had marked the end of an era for her.

She'd jetted off with her friend Lora to let loose in a place famed for allowing such behavior without ramifications. One last hurrah, as Roz had informed him. Make it memorable, she'd insisted. *Help me go out with a bang*, had been her exact words. Upon her return to the real world, she'd planned to make her father proud for once.

Instead, she'd found exactly the trouble she'd been looking for and then some.

It was a problem she needed to fix. She'd needed to fix it before she'd ever let Hendrix put his beautiful, talented mouth on her. And now memories of his special brand of trouble put a slow burn in her core that she couldn't shake. Even now, five minutes after telling him to shove off. Still burning. She cursed her weakness for gorgeous bad boys and went to change clothes so she could dig into her "make Dad proud" plan on her terms.

Marriage. Rosalind Carpenter. These two things did not go together under any circumstances, especially not as a way to make her father proud of her.

After watching her father cope with Roz's mother's extended bout with cancer, no thank you. That kind of pain didn't appeal to her. Till death do you part wasn't a joke, nor did she take a vow like that lightly. Best way to avoid testing it was to never make a vow like that in the first place.

Roz shed the flirty, fun outfit she'd worn to brunch with Lora and donned a severe black pencil skirt coupled with a pale blue long-sleeved blouse that screamed "serious banker." She twisted her long hair into a chignon, fought with the few escaped strands and finally left them because Hendrix had already put her behind for the day. Her afternoon was booked solid with the endless tasks associated with the new charity she'd founded.

She arrived at the small storefront her father's admin had helped her rent, evaluating the layout for the fourteenth time. There was no sign yet. That was one of the many details she needed to work through this week as she got Clown-Around off the ground. It was an endeavor of the heart. And maybe a form of therapy.

Clowns still scared her, not that she'd admit to having formed a phobia during the long hours she'd sat at her mother's hospital bedside, and honestly, she didn't have to explain herself to anyone, so she didn't. The curious only needed to know that Rosalind Carpenter had started a charity that trained clowns to work in children's hospitals. Period.

The desk she'd had delivered dwarfed her, but she'd taken a page from her father's book and procured the largest piece she could find in the Carpenter ware-house near the airport. He'd always said to buy furniture for the circumstances you want, not the ones you have. Buy quality so it will last until you make your dreams a reality. It was a philosophy that had served Carpenter Furniture well and she liked the sentiment. So she'd bought a desk that made her feel like the head of a successful charity.

She attacked the mountain of paperwork with gusto, cheerfully filling out forms and ordering supplies. There was an enormous amount of overhead that went along with running a charity and when you had zero income to use in hiring help, there was only one person to do the work—the founder.

Before she'd barely dug into the task, the lady from the first hospital Roz had called her back.

"Ms. Smith, so happy to speak with you," Roz began smoothly. "I'd like to see what your requirements are for getting Clown-Around on the approved list of organizations available to work with the children at your hospital."

"I could have saved you some time, Ms. Carpenter," the liaison replied and her tone could only be described as frosty. "We already have an approved group we work with. No need for any additional ones."

That threw Roz for a loop. "Oh. Well, we'd be happy to go on the backup list. You know, in case the other group cancels unexpectedly."

"That's okay," she cut in quickly. "That almost never happens and it's not like we have scheduled times. The clowns come in on a pretty casual basis."

This was not a good conversation. Unease prickled at the back of Roz's neck and she did not like the feeling. "I'm having a hard time believing that you can't use extra cheer in the children's ward. We're talking about sick kids who don't want to be in the hospital. Surely if your current clowns come and go at will, you can add some of mine to the rotation. A clown is a clown, right?"

The long pause boded badly. Roz braced for the next part.

"To be frank, Ms. Carpenter, the hospital board would not appreciate any association with a charity you helm," Ms. Smith stated bluntly. "We are required to disclose any contact a patient has with outside parties, particularly when the patients are minors. The clowns must have accreditation and thorough vetting to ensure we're not exposing patients to…unseemly influences."

Roz went hot and then cold as the woman's meaning flashed through her. The reputation of the charity's founder preceded her apparently. "I take it I qualify as an unseemly influence. Then may I be as frank and ask why you bothered to call me back?"

"Strictly in deference to your father. One of his vice presidents is on the board, if you're not aware," she replied tightly. "If we've reached an understanding…"

"We have. Thank you for your candor." Roz stabbed the end call button and let her cell phone drop to the desk of a successful charity head. Too bad that wasn't who was sitting at it.

Wow. Her hands were shaking.

And because her day hadn't been crappy enough, the door she'd forgotten to lock behind her opened to the street and Hendrix Harris walked into her nightmare.

"What are you doing here?" she snapped, too off-kilter to find some manners when she'd already told him to step off once today. "This is private property. How did you find me?"

Not one perfect brown hair out of place, the man waltzed right in and glanced around her bare-bones operation with unabashed curiosity. "I followed you, naturally. But I didn't want to interrupt your phone call, so I waited."

"Bless your heart," she shot back and snatched up her phone to call the cops. "You have two seconds to vacate or I'm going to lodge a trespassing complaint."

Instead of hightailing it out the door—which was what he should have done—Hendrix didn't hesitate to round the desk, crowd into her space without even a cursory nod to boundaries and pluck the phone from her hand. "Now, why would you do a thing like that? We're all friends here."

Something that felt perilously close to tears pricked beneath her lashes. "We're not friends."

Tears. In front of Hendrix. It was inexcusable.

"We could be friends," he announced quietly, without an ounce of flirt. Somehow that was exactly the right tone to burn off the moisture. "Friends who help each other. You didn't give me much of a chance to tell you how earlier."

Help. That was something she needed. Not that *he* needed to know that, or how grateful she was that he'd found a way to put her back on even footing. She didn't for an instant believe he'd missed her brief flash of vulnerability and his deft handling of it made all the difference.

The attitude of the hospital lady still chilled her. But she wasn't in danger of falling apart any longer, thank God.

"Because I have a zone of crazy around me." She nodded to the floor, near his feet. "There's the perimeter and you're four feet over the line."

Problem being that she liked him where he was—one lean hip cocked against her desk and all his good stuff at eye level. Naked, the man rivaled mythical gods in the perfection department. She could stare at his bare body for hours and never get tired of finding new ways to appreciate his deliciousness.

And dang it, he must have clued in on the direction of her thoughts. He didn't move. But the temperature of the room rose a few sweat-inducing degrees. Or maybe that was just her body catching fire as he treated her to the full force of his lethal appeal.

His hot perusal did not help matters when it came to the temperature. What was it about his pale hazel eyes that dug into her so deeply? All he had to do was look at her and sharp little tugs danced through her core.

It pissed her off. Why couldn't he be ugly, with a hunchback and gnarled feet?

Which was a stupid thing to wish for because if that was the case, she wouldn't be in this position. She'd never have hooked up with him in Vegas because yes, she was that shallow and a naked romp with a man built like Hendrix had righted her world—for a night.

Now she'd pay the price for that moment of hedonism. The final cost had yet to be determined, though.

Hendrix set her phone down on the desk, correctly guessing he had her attention and the threat of expulsion had waned. For now. She could easily send him packing if the need struck. Or she could roll the chair back a few inches and move the man into a better position to negotiate something of the more carnal variety. This was a solid desk. Would be a shame not to fully test its strength.

No. She shook her head. This was the danger of putting herself in the same room with him. She forgot common sense and propriety.

"Since I'm already in the zone of crazy," he commented in his North Carolina–textured twang, "you should definitely hear me out. For real this time. I don't know what you think I'm proposing, but odds are good you didn't get that it starts and ends with a partnership."

That had *not* come across. Whatever he had in mind, she'd envisioned a lot of sex taking center stage. And that she'd have to do without because she'd turned over a new leaf.

A partnership, on the other hand, had interesting possibilities.

As coolly as she could under the circumstances, she crossed her arms. Mostly as a way to keep her hands to herself. "Talk fast. You've got my attention for about another five minutes."

Two

Hendrix had been right to follow Rosalind. This bare storefront had a story behind it and he had every intention of learning her secrets. Whatever leverage he could dig up might come in handy, especially since he'd botched the first round of this negotiation.

And the hard cross of Roz's arms told him it was indeed a negotiation, one he shouldn't expect to win easily. That had been his mistake on the first go-round. He'd thought their chemistry would be good trading currency, but she'd divested him of that notion quickly. So round two would need a completely different approach.

"What is this place?" he asked and his genuine curiosity leaked through. He had a vision in his head of Rosalind Carpenter as a party girl, one who posed for men's magazines and danced like a fantasy come to life. Instead of tracking her down during an afternoon shopping spree, he'd stumbled over her *working*.

It didn't fit his perception of her and he'd like to get the right one before charging ahead.

"I started a charity," she informed him with a slight catch in her voice that struck him strangely.

She expected him to laugh. Or say something flippant. So he didn't. "That's fantastic. And hard. Good for you."

That bobbled her composure and he wouldn't apologize for enjoying it. This marriage plan should have been a lot easier to sell and he couldn't put his finger on why he'd faltered so badly thus far. She'd been easy in Vegas—likable, open, adventurous. All things he'd assumed he'd work with today, but none of those qualities seemed to be a part of her at-home personality. Plus, he wasn't trying to get her into bed. Well, technically, he *was*. But semi-permanently, and he didn't have a lot of experience at persuading a woman to still be there in the morning.

No problem. Winging it was how he did his best work. He hadn't pushed Harris Family Tobacco Lounge so close to the half-billion mark in revenue without taking a few risks.

"What does your charity do?" he asked, envisioning an evening dress resale shop or Save the Kittens. Might as well know what kind of fundraiser he'd have to attend as her husband.

"Clowns," she said so succinctly that he did a double take to be sure he hadn't misheard her. He hadn't. And it wasn't a joke, judging by the hard set of her mouth.

"Like finding new homes for orphan clowns?" he

guessed cautiously, only half kidding. Clown charity was a new one for him.

"You're such a moron." She rolled her eyes, but they had a determined glint now that he liked a lot better than the raw vulnerability she'd let slip a few minutes ago. "My charity trains clowns to work with children at hospitals. Sick kids need to be cheered up, you know?"

"That's admirable." And he wasn't even blowing smoke. It sounded like it meant something to her and thus it meant something to him—as leverage. He glanced around, taking in the bare walls, the massive and oddly masculine dark-stained desk and the rolling leather chair under her very fine backside. Not much to her operation yet, which worked heavily in his favor. "How can I help?"

Suspicion tightened her lush mouth, which only made him want to kiss it away. They were going to have to fix this attraction or he'd spend all his time adjusting her attitude in a very physical way.

On second thought, he couldn't figure out a downside to that approach.

"I thought you were trying to talk me into marrying you," she said with a fair amount of sarcasm.

"One and the same, sweetheart." He gave it a second and the instant his meaning registered, her lips curved into a crafty smile.

"I'm starting to see the light."

Oh yes, *now* they were ready to throw down. Juices flowing, he slid a little closer to her and she didn't roll away, just coolly stared up at him without an ounce of give. What was wrong with him that he was suddenly more turned on in that instant than he had been at any point today?

"Talk to me. What can I do in exchange for your name on a marriage certificate?"

Her smile gained a lot of teeth. "Tell me why it's so important to you."

He bit back the curse. Should have seen that one coming. As a testament to her skill in maneuvering him into giving up personal information, he opted to throw her a bone. "I told you. I've had some fallout. My mother is pretty unhappy with me and I don't like her to be unhappy."

"Mama's boy?"

"Absolutely." He grinned. Who didn't see the value in a man who loved and respected his mama? "There's no shame in that. We grew up together. I'm sure you've heard the story. She was an unwed teenage mother, yadda, yadda?"

"I've heard. So this is all one hundred percent about keeping your mom happy, is it?"

Something clued him in that she wasn't buying it, which called for some serious deflection. The last thing he wanted to have a conversation about was his own reasons for pursuing Roz for the first and only Mrs. Hendrix Harris.

He liked being reminded of his own vulnerabilities even less than he liked being exposed to hers. The less intimate this thing grew, the better. "Yeah. If she wasn't in the middle of an election cycle, we wouldn't be having this conversation. But she is and I messed up. I'm willing to do whatever it takes to get this deal done. Name your price."

"Get your mom to agree to be a clown for me and I'll consider it."

That was what she wanted? His gaze narrowed as

they stared at each other. "That's easy. Too easy. You must not want me to figure out that you're really panting to get back into my bed."

Her long silky laugh lodged in his chest and spread south. She could turn that sentiment back on him with no trouble at all.

Which was precisely what she did. "Sounds like a guilty conscience talking to me. Sure you're not the one using this ploy to get me naked without being forced to let on how bad you want it?"

"I'm offended." But he let a smile contradict the statement. "I'll tell you all day long how much I want you if that floats your boat. But this is a business proposition. Strictly for nonsexual benefits."

Any that came along with this marriage could be considered a bonus.

She snorted. "Are you trying to tell me you'd give up other women while we're married? I don't think you're actually capable of that."

Now, that was just insulting. What kind of a philanderer did she take him for? He'd never slept with more than one woman at a time and never calling one again made that a hundred percent easier.

"Make no mistake, Roz. I am perfectly capable of forgoing other women as long as you're the one I'm coming home to at the end of the day."

All at once, a vision of her greeting him at the door wearing sexy lingerie slammed through his mind and his body reacted with near violent approval. Holy hell. He had no problem going off other women cold turkey if Roz was on offer instead, never mind his stupid rules about never banging the same woman twice. This situation was totally different, with its own set of rules. Or at least it would be as soon as he got his head out of her perfect cleavage and back on how to close this deal.

"Let me get this straight. You're such a dog that the only way you can stay out of another woman's bed is if I'm servicing you regularly?" She wrinkled her nose. "Stop me when I get to the part where I'm benefiting from this arrangement."

Strictly to cover the slight hitch in his lungs that her pointed comment had caused, he slid over until he was perched on the desk directly in front of her. Barely a foot of space separated them and an enormous amount of heat and electricity arced through his groin, draining more of his sense than he would have preferred. All he could think about was yanking her into his arms and reminding her how hot he could get her with nothing more than a well-placed stroke of his tongue.

He let all of that sizzle course through his body as he swept her with a heated once-over. "Sweetheart, you'll benefit, or have you forgotten how well I know your body?"

"Can you even go without sex?" she mused with a lilt, as if she already knew the answer. "Because I bet you can't."

What the hell did that have to do with anything?

"I can do whatever I put my mind to," he growled. "But to do something as insane as go without sex, I'd need a fair bit of incentive. Which I have none of."

Her gaze snapped with challenge. "Other than getting my name on a marriage license you mean?"

The recoil jerked through his shoulders before he could catch it, tipping her off that she'd just knocked him for a loop. That was uncool. Both that she'd realized it and that she'd done it. "What are you proposing, that I go celibate for a period of time in some kind of test?"

"Oh, I hadn't thought of it like that." She pursed her lips into a provocative pout that told him she was flat-out lying because she'd intended it to be exactly that. "That's a great deal. You keep it zipped and I'll show up at the appointed time to say 'I do.'"

His throat went dry. "Really? That's what it's going to take?"

"Yep. Well, that and Helene Harris for Governor in a clown suit. Can't forget the children."

Her smug tone raked at something inside him. "That's ridiculous. I mean, my mom would be happy to do the clown thing. It's great publicity for her, too. But no sex? Not even with you? There is literally no reason for you to lay down such a thing except as cruel and unusual punishment."

"Careful, Hendrix," she crooned. "It's starting to sound like you might have a problem keeping it in your pants. I mean, how long are we talking? A couple of months?"

A couple of *months*? He'd been slightly panicked at the thought of a week or two. It wasn't that he was some kind of pervert like she was making it sound. Sex was a necessary avoidance tactic in his arsenal. A shield against the intimacy that happened in the small moments, when you weren't guarded against it. He kept himself out of such situations on purpose.

If he wasn't having sex with Roz, what would they *do* with each other?

"I think the better question is whether *you* can do it," he countered smoothly. "You're the same woman who was all in for every wicked, dirty escapade I could dream up in Vegas. You're buckling yourself into that chastity belt too, honey."

"Yeah, for a reason." Her eyes glittered with conviction. "The whole point of this is to fix the problems the photograph caused. Do you really think you and I can keep ourselves out of Scandalville if we're sleeping together?" His face must have registered his opinion on that because she nodded. "Exactly. It's a failsafe. No sex—with *anyone*. No scandals. Or no 'I do.'"

The firm press of a rock and a hard place nearly stole his breath. If no sex was important to her, how could he refuse?

"Six weeks," he said hoarsely. "We'll be engaged for six weeks. Once we're married, all bets are off."

"We'll see. I might keep the no sex moratorium. You and I don't make sense together, Hendrix, so don't pretend that we do."

She swallowed that sentence with a squeak as he hauled her out of that chair and into his arms for a lesson on exactly how wrong she was. God, she fit the contours of his body like the ocean against the sand, seeping into him with a rush and shush, dragging pieces of him into her as her lips crashed against his.

Her taste exploded under his mouth as he kissed her senseless. But then it was his own senses sliding through the soles of his feet as Roz sucked him dry with her own sensual onslaught. For a woman who'd just told him they didn't work, she jumped into the kiss with enthusiasm that had him groaning.

The hot, slick slide of her tongue against his dissolved his knees. Only the firm press of that heavy desk against his backside kept him upright. The woman was a wicked kisser, not that he'd forgotten. But just as he slid his hand south to fill his palms with her luscious rear, she wrenched away, taking his composure with her.

"Where are you going?" he growled.

"The other side of the room." Her chest rose and fell as if she'd run a marathon as she backed away. Frankly, his own lungs heaved with the effort to fill with air. "What the hell was that for?"

"You wanted that kiss as much as I did."

"So it was strictly to throw it back in my face that I can't resist you?"

Well, now. That was a tasty admission that she looked like she wished to take back. He surveyed her with renewed interest. Her kiss-reddened lips beckoned him but he didn't chase her down. He wanted to understand this new dynamic before he pressed on. "You said we didn't work. I was simply helping you see the error in that statement."

"I said no such thing. I said we don't make sense together. And that's why. Because we *work* far too well."

"I'm struggling to see the problem with that." They'd definitely worked in Vegas, that was for sure. Now that he'd gotten a second taste, he was not satisfied with having it cut short.

"Because I need to stay off the front page," she reminded him with that funny hitch in her voice that shouldn't be more affecting than her heated once-overs. "There are people walking by the window as we speak, Hendrix. You make me forget all of that. No more kissing until the wedding. Consider it an act of good faith."

The point was painfully clear. She wanted him to prove he could do it.

"So we're doing this. Getting married," he clarified.

"As a partnership. When it stops being beneficial, we get a divorce. No ifs, ands or buts." She caught him in her hot gaze that still screamed her desire. "Right? Do we need to spell it out legally?"

"You can trust me," he grumbled. She was the one who'd thrown down the no-sex rule. What did she think he was going to do, force her to stay married so he could keep being celibate for the rest of his life? "As long as I can trust you."

"I'm good."

He thought about shaking on it but the slightly panicked flair to her expression made him think twice. It didn't matter. The deal was done, as painful as it would ultimately end up being.

It was worth it. He had to make it up to his mom for causing her grief, and this was what she'd asked him to do. And if deep inside, he craved the idea of belonging to such an old-guard, old-money family as the Carpenters, no one would be the wiser.

All he had to do was figure out how to be engaged to Roz without trying to seduce her again and without getting too chummy. Should be a walk in the park.

Being engaged was nothing like Roz imagined. Of course she'd spent zero time daydreaming about such a thing happening to her. But her friend Lora had been engaged for about six months, which had been a whirlwind of invitations and dress fittings. Until the day she'd walked in on her fiancé and a naked barista who was foaming the jackass's latte in Lora's bed. Roz and Lora still didn't hit a coffee place within four blocks of the one where the wedding-wrecker worked.

Roz's own engagement had a lot fewer highs and

lows in the emotion department and a lot less chaos. For about three days. The morning of the fourth day, Hendrix texted her that he was coming by, and since there'd been no question in that statement, she sighed and put on clothes, wishing in vain for a do-over that included not flying to Vegas in the first place. Or maybe she should wish that she and Lora had gone to any other club besides the Calypso Room that night.

Oh, better yet, she could pretend Hendrix didn't do it for her in a hundred scandalous ways.

That was the real reason this engagement/marriage/partnership shouldn't have happened. But how could she turn down Helene Harris in a clown outfit? No hospital would bar the woman from the door and thus Clown-Around would get a much-needed lift, Roz's reputation notwithstanding. It was instant publicity for the gubernatorial candidate and the fledgling charity in one shot, which was a huge win. And she didn't have to actually ask her father to use his influence, which he probably wouldn't do anyway.

Plus, and she'd die before she'd admit this to Hendrix, there had to be something about being in the sphere of Helene Harris that Roz's father would find satisfactory. He was so disappointed about the photographs. If nothing else, marrying the man in them lent a bit of respectability to the situation, right? Now Roz just had to tell her father about the getting married part. But first she had to admit to herself that she'd actually agreed to this insanity.

Thus far it had been easy to stick her head in the sand. But when Hendrix buzzed her to gain access to the elevator, she couldn't play ostrich any longer.

"Well, if it isn't my beloved," he drawled when she opened the door.

God, could the man look like a slouch in *something*? He wore the hell out of a suit regardless of the color or cut. But today he'd opted for a pair of worn jeans that hugged his hips and a soft T-shirt that brazenly advertised the drool-worthy build underneath. He might as well be naked for all that ensemble left to the imagination.

"Your beloved doesn't sit around and wait for you to show up on a Saturday," she informed him grumpily. "What if I had plans?"

"You do have plans," he returned, his grin far too easy. "With me. All of your plans are with me for the next six weeks, because weddings do not magically throw themselves together."

She crossed her arms and leaned against the doorjamb in a blatant message—*you're not coming in and I'm not budging, so...* "They do if you hire a wedding planner. Which you should. I have absolutely no opinion about flowers or venues."

That was no lie. But she wanted to spend time with Hendrix even less than she wanted to pick out flowers. She could literally feel her will dissolving as she stood there soaking in the carnal vibe wafting from him like an invisible aphrodisiac.

"Oh, come on. It'll be fun."

The way his hazel eyes lit up as he coaxed her should be illegal. Or maybe her reaction should be. How did he put such a warm little curl in her core with nothing more than a glance? It was ridiculous. "Your idea of fun and mine are worlds apart."

A slow, lethal smile joined his vibrant gaze and it

pretty much reduced her to a quivering mess of girl parts inside. All the more reason to stay far away from him until the wedding.

"Seems like we had a pretty similar idea of fun one night not too long ago."

Memories crashed through her mind, her body, her soul. The way he'd made her feel, the wicked press of his mouth against every intimate hollow an unprecedented experience. It was too much for a Saturday morning after she'd signed up to become Mrs. Hendrix Harris.

"I asked you not to kiss me again," she reminded him primly but it probably sounded as desperate to him as it did to her.

She could *not* get sucked into his orbit. As it was, she fantasized about that kiss against her desk at odd times—while in the shower, brushing her teeth, eating breakfast, watching TV, walking, breathing. Sure it was prudent to avoid any more scandals but that was just window dressing. This was a partnership she needed to take seriously, and she had no good defenses against Hendrix Harris.

He was temporary. Like all things. She couldn't get invested, emotionally or physically, and one would surely lead to the other. The pain of losing someone she cared about was too much and she would never let that happen again—which was the sole reason she liked sex of the one-night stand variety. What she'd do when that wasn't an option, like after she said I do, she had no clue.

"Wow. Who said anything about kissing?" He waggled his brows. "We were talking about the definition of fun. That kiss must have gotten you going something fierce if you're still hung up on it."

She rolled her eyes to hide the guilt that might or might not be shuffling through her expression. "Why are you here?"

"We're engaged. Engaged people hang out, or didn't you get the memo?"

"We're not people. Nor is our engagement typical. No memos required to get us to the…insert whatever venue we're using to get hitched here. Until then, I don't really feel the need to spend time together." She accompanied that pitiful excuse of his with crooked fingers in air quotes.

"Well, I beg to differ," he drawled, the North Carolina in his voice sliding through her veins like fine brandy. "This partnership needs publicity or there's no point to it. We need to be seen together. A lot. When people think of you, they need to think of me. We're like the peanut butter and jelly of the Raleigh social scene."

"That's a nice analogy," she said with a snort so she didn't laugh or smile. That would only encourage him to keep being adorable. "Which one am I?"

"You choose," he suggested magnanimously and that's when she realized she was having fun. How dare he charm her out of her bad mood?

But it was too late, dang it. That was the problem. She genuinely liked Hendrix or she wouldn't have left the Calypso Room with him.

"I suppose you want to come in." She jerked her head toward the interior of her loft that had been two condos until she bought both and hired a crew of hard hats to meld the space into one. They should probably discuss living arrangements at some point because she was *not* giving up this condo under any circumstances.

"I want you to come out," he countered and caught her hand, tugging on it until she cleared the threshold on the wrong side of the door. "We can't be seen together in your condo and besides, there are no people walking past the window. No photographers in the bushes. I could slip a couple of buttons free on this shirt of yours and explore what I uncover with my tongue and no one would know."

He accompanied that suggestion with a slow slide of his fingertip along the ridge of buttons in question, oh so casually, as if the skin under it hadn't just exploded with goose bumps.

"But you won't," she said breathlessly, cursing her body's reaction even as she cursed him for knowing exactly how to get her hot and ready to burst with so little effort. "Because you promised."

"I did." He nodded with a wink. "And I'm a man of my word."

She'd only reminded him of his promise as a shield against her own weaknesses, but he'd taken it as an affirmation. He would keep his promise because it meant something to him. And his sense of honor was doing funny things to her insides that had nothing to do with desire. Hendrix Harris was a bad boy hedonist of the highest order. Nothing but wicked through and through. Or at least that was the box she'd put him in and she did not like the way he'd just climbed out of it.

She shook her head, but it didn't clear her sudden confusion. Definitely they should not go into her condo and shut the door. Not now or any day. But at that moment, she couldn't recall what bad things might happen as a result. She could only think of many, many very good things that could and would occur if she invited him in for a private rendezvous.

"I think we should visit a florist," he commented casually, completely oblivious to the direction of her thoughts, thank God.

"Yes. We should." That was exactly what she needed. A distraction in the form of flowers.

"Grab your handbag." The instruction made her blink for a second until he laughed. "Or is it a purse? I have no clue what to call the thing you women put your lives into."

Gah, she should have her head examined if a simple conversation with a man had her so flipped upside down. Nodding, she ducked back into the condo, snagged her Marc Jacobs bag from the counter in the kitchen and rejoined Hendrix in the hall before he got any bright ideas about testing his will behind closed doors. Hers sucked. The longer she kept that fact from him, the better.

He ushered her to a low-slung Aston Martin that shouldn't have been as sexy as it was. At best, it should have screamed *I'm trying too hard to be cool*. But when Hendrix slid behind the wheel, he owned the beast under the hood and it purred beneath his masterful hands.

She could watch him drive for hours. Which worked out well since she'd apparently just volunteered to spend the day planning flowers for her wedding with her fiancé. Bizarre. But there it was.

Even she had heard of the florist he drove to. Expensive, exclusive and very visible, Maestro of the Bloom lay in the Roundtree shopping district near downtown.

Hendrix drove around the block two times, apparently searching for a parking place, and she opened her mouth to remind him of the lot across the street when he braked at the front row to wait for a mother and daughter to get into their car. Of course he wanted the parking place directly in front of the door, where everyone could see them emerge from his noteworthy car.

It was a testament to his strategic mind that she appreciated. As was the gallant way he sped around to her side of the car to open the door, then extended his hand to help her from the bucket seat that was so low it nearly scraped the ground. But he didn't let go of her hand, instead lacing their fingers together in a way that shouldn't have felt so natural. Hands nested to his satisfaction, he led her to the door and ushered her inside.

A low hum of conversation cut off abruptly and something like a dozen pairs of eyes swung toward them with varying degrees of recognition—some of which held distaste. These were the people whose approval they both sought. The society who had deemed their Vegas tryst shocking, inappropriate, scandalous, and here the two of them were daring to tread among more decent company.

Roz's fingers tightened involuntarily and dang it, Hendrix squeezed back in a surprising show of solidarity. That shouldn't have felt as natural as it did either, like the two of them were a unit already. Peanut butter and jelly against the world.

Her knees got a little wobbly. She'd never had anything like that. Never wanted to feel like a duo with a man. Why did it mean so much as they braved the social scene together? Especially given that she'd only just realized that turning over a new leaf meant more than fixing her relationship with her father. It was about shifting the tide of public opinion too, or her charity wouldn't benefit much from Helene's participation. Roz would go back to being shunned in polite society the moment she signed the divorce papers.

Against all odds, he'd transformed Roz into a righteous convert to the idea of marriage with one small step inside the florist. What else would he succeed in convincing her of?

With that sobering thought, Roz glanced at Hendrix and murmured, "Let's do this."

Three

As practice for the bigger, splashier engagement party to come, Hendrix talked Roz into an intimate gathering at his house. Just family and close friends. It would be an opportunity to gauge how this marriage would fly. And it was a chance to spend time together as a couple with low pressure.

The scene at the florist had shaken Roz, with the murmurs and dirty looks she'd collected from the patrons. That was not okay. Academically, he knew this marriage deal was important to his mother and her campaign. In reality, he didn't personally have a lot of societal fallout from that photo. No one's gaze cut away from him on the street, but he was a guy. Roz wasn't. It was a double standard that shouldn't exist but it did.

Who would have ever thought he'd be hot to ease Roz's discomfort in social situations? It had not been

on his list of considerations, but it was now. If this
party helped, great. If it didn't, he'd find something
else. The fragile glint in her eye while they'd worked
with the florist to pick out some outrageously priced
flowers had hooked something inside and he'd spent
a considerable amount of time trying to unpierce his
tender flesh, to no avail. So he did what he always did.
Rolled with it.

The catering company had done a great job getting
his house in order to host a shindig of this magnitude.
While the party had been floated as casual, Hendrix
had never entertained before. Unless you counted a
handful of buddies sprawled around his dining room
table with beer and poker chips.

Roz arrived in the car he'd sent for her and he ignored the little voice inside taunting him for hovering
at the front window to watch for her. But it was a sight
to see. Roz spilled from the back of the car, sky-high
stilettos first, then miles of legs and finally the woman
herself in a figure-hugging black cocktail dress designed to drive a man insane.

She'd even swept up her wavy dark hair into a chignon that let a few strands drip down around her face.
It was the sexiest hairstyle he'd ever seen on a woman,
bar none.

He opened the door before she could knock and his
tongue might have gone numb because he couldn't even
speak as she coolly surveyed him from under thick
black eyelashes.

"Thanks for the car. Hard to drive in heels," she
commented, apparently not afflicted by the stupid that
was going around.

He shouldn't be, either. He cleared his throat. "You look delicious."

Amazing might have been a better term. It would make it seem more like he'd seen a beautiful woman before and it was no big thing. But she was *his* beautiful woman. For as long as they both deemed it beneficial.

That seemed like a pretty cold agreement all at once for two people who'd burned so very hot not so long ago.

She smiled with a long slow lift of her pink-stained lips. "I'll take that as a compliment, as weird as it is."

"Really? It's weird to tell my beautiful fiancée that she looks good enough to eat?" he questioned with a heated once-over that she didn't miss.

"You can't say stuff like that," she murmured and glanced away from the sizzling electricity that had just arced between them right there on his doorstep.

"The hell I can't. You said no kissing. At no point did I agree to keep my carnal thoughts to myself, nor will I ever agree to that. If I want to tell you that I'm salivating to slide that dress off your shoulders and watch it fall to the ground as it bares your naked body, I will. I might even tell you that I taste you in my sleep sometimes and I wake up with a boner that I can't get rid of until I fantasize about you in the shower." Her cheeks flushed. From embarrassment at his dirty talk or guilt because she liked it? He couldn't tell. He leaned closer and whispered, "Believe it or not, I can tell you what I want to do to you without acting on it."

A car door slammed behind her and she recoiled as if it had been a gunshot to her torso.

"Invite me in," she muttered with a glance over her shoulder. "This is a party, isn't it?"

Should have been a party for two with a strict dress code—birthday suits only. Why had he agreed to her insane stipulation that they abstain from any kind of physical contact until the wedding? It was a dumb rule that made no sense and if Jonas and his wife, Viv, weren't waltzing up the front walk at that precise moment, Hendrix would be having a completely different conversation about it with his fiancée.

He stepped back and allowed Roz to enter, slipping an arm around her waist as she tried to flounce past him into the living room. "Oh, no you don't, sweetheart. Flip around and greet the guests. We're a couple."

Her smile grew pained as he drew her close. "How could I forget?"

Jonas and Viv hit the welcome mat holding hands. Funny how things worked. Jonas and Viv had gotten married in Vegas during the same trip where Hendrix had hooked up with Roz.

"Hey, guys. This is Roz," Hendrix announced unnecessarily, as he was pretty sure both Jonas and Viv knew who she was. If not from the photo flying around the internet, strictly by virtue of the fact that she was glued to his side.

Viv, bless her, smiled at Roz and shook her hand. "I'm Viv Kim. It's nice to meet you, and not just because I love any opportunity to use my new name."

With an intrigued expression, Roz glanced at the male half of the couple. "Are you newly married?"

Jonas stuck his hand out. "Brand-new. I'm Jonas Kim. My name is still the same."

Hendrix nearly rolled his eyes but checked it in deference to one of his oldest friends. "Thanks for coming.

Roz and I are glad you're here to celebrate our engagement. Come in, please."

He guided them all to the cavernous living area that had been designed with this type of gathering in mind. The ten-thousand-square-foot house in Oakwood had been a purchase born out of a desire to stake his claim. There was a pride in ownership that this house delivered. It was a monument of a previous age, restored lovingly by someone with an eye for detail, and he appreciated the history wafting from its bones.

The house was a legitimate home and it was his.

Curiously, Viv's gaze cut between the two of them as she took a seat next to Jonas on the couch. "Have you set a wedding date?"

"Not yet," Roz answered and at the same time, Hendrix said, "Five weeks."

She shot him a withering look. "We're waiting until we pick a venue, which might dictate the date."

The doorbell rang and his mother arrived with Paul Carpenter right on her heels. Introductions all around went smoothly as nearly everyone knew each other. As the CEO of Kim Electronics, Jonas had met Mr. Carpenter several times at trade shows and various retail functions. Helene frequented Viv's cupcake shop on Jones Street apparently and exclaimed over the baker's wares at length. It was Paul and Helene's first meeting, however.

Hendrix raised a brow at the extra beat included in their hand shake, but forgot about it as Roz's friend Lora showed up with a date. Hendrix's other best friend, Warren Garinger, was flying solo tonight, which was lately his default. He arrived a pointed thirty minutes late.

It wasn't until later that evening that Hendrix had a chance to corner his friend on his tardiness.

"Just the man I was looking for," he said easily as he found Warren in the study examining one of the many watercolors the decorator had insisted went with the spirit of the house.

Warren pocketed his phone, which should have melted from overuse a long time ago. He worked ninety hours a week running the energy drink company his family had founded, but Hendrix didn't think that was what had put the frown on his friend's face. "I had to take a call. Sorry."

"The CEO never gets a day off," Hendrix acknowledged with a nod. "It's cool. I was just making sure you weren't hiding out in protest."

"I'm here, aren't I?" Warren smoothed out his expression before it turned into a full-bore scowl. "You've obviously made your decision to get married despite the pact."

Hendrix bit back a sigh. They'd been over this. Looked like they were going over it again. "The pact means something to me. And to Jonas. We're still tight, no matter what."

Jonas, Warren and Hendrix had met at Duke University, forming a friendship during a group project along with a fourth student, Marcus Powell. They'd had a lot of fun, raised a lot of hell together in the quintessential college experience—until Marcus had gotten his heart tangled up over a woman who didn't deserve his devotion. She'd been a traitorous witch of a cheerleader who liked toying with a man's affections more than she'd liked Marcus. Everyone had seen she was trouble. Except their friend.

He'd grown paler and more wasted away the longer she didn't give him the time of day and eventually, his broken heart had overruled his brain and somehow suicide had become his answer. Shell-shocked and embittered, the three surviving friends had vowed to never let a woman drive them to such lows. They'd formed a pact, refusing to fall in love under any circumstances.

Hell, that had been a given for Hendrix, pact or not. Love wasn't something he even thought much about because he never got close enough to a woman to develop any kind of tender feelings, let alone anything deeper.

But the pact—that was sacred. He'd had little in his life that made him feel like he belonged and his friendship with Jonas and Warren meant everything to him. He'd die before violating the terms of their agreement.

"If the pact is so important, then I don't understand why you'd risk breaking it with marriage," Warren countered and the bitterness lacing his tone sliced at Hendrix far more severely than he'd have expected.

They both glanced up as Jonas joined them, beers in hand. "Thought I'd find you two going at it if I looked hard enough. I'm the one you want to yell at, Warren. Not this joker."

Hendrix took the longneck from his friend's hand and gave Warren a pointed look until the other man sighed, accepting his own beer. No one was confused about the significance. It was a peace offering because Jonas had already broken the pact by falling in love with Viv. Warren had not taken it well. The three of them were still figuring out how to not be bachelor pals any longer, and how to not be at odds over what Warren viewed as Jonas's betrayal.

Hendrix just wanted everything to be on an even keel again so he didn't get a panicky feeling at the back of his throat when he thought of losing the one place where he felt fully accepted no matter what—inside the circle of his friends.

"If it makes you feel better," Hendrix said after a long swallow of his brew, "the odds of me falling in love with Roz are zero. We're not even sleeping together."

Jonas choked on his own beer. "Please. Is this April Fools' Day and I missed it?"

"No, really." Hendrix scowled as both his friends started laughing. "Why is that funny?"

"You've finally met the one woman you can't seduce and you're *marrying* her?" Warren clapped Hendrix on the back, still snickering.

"Shut up," he growled. Why did that have to be the one thing that got his buddy out of his snit? "Besides, I can go without sex."

"Right." Jonas drew the word out to about fourteen syllables, every one of them laden with sarcasm. "And I can pass as Norwegian."

Since Jonas was half-Korean, his point was clear. And Hendrix didn't appreciate his friend's doubt, never mind that he'd been angling for a way to kibosh the no-sex part of his agreement with Roz. "I don't have to explain myself to you guys."

Jonas sipped his beer thoughtfully. "Well, I guess it's a fair point that this is a fake marriage, so maybe you're pretty smart to skip sex in order to avoid confusion. I of all people can understand that."

"This marriage is not fake," Hendrix corrected. "*Your* marriage was fake because you're a moron who thought it was better to live together and just pretend you're hot and heavy. I'm not a moron. Roz and I will have a real marriage, with plenty of unfake hot and heavy."

Especially the honeymoon part. He was already glancing at travel websites for ideas on places he could take his bride where they'd have no interruptions during a weeklong smorgasbord where Roz was the only thing on the menu.

Jonas raised his eyebrows. "You're trying to tell me you're waiting until marriage before you sleep together? That's highly unconventional for anyone, let alone you."

It was on the tip of his tongue to remind Jonas how late Hendrix had been to his wedding. Roz had been the reason, and these yokels were lucky he'd showed up at all. It had been sheer hell to peel himself out of Roz's bed to make it to the chapel before the nuptials were over.

But something held him back from flinging his escapades in his friends' faces. Maybe it had something to do with their assumption that he was a horndog who couldn't keep it in his pants, which had frankly been Roz's assumption, too. Was that all there was to him in everyone's mind? Always on the lookout for the next woman to nail? There was a lot more complexity to his personality than that and he was suddenly not thrilled to learn he'd overshadowed his better qualities with his well-deserved reputation.

"That's me. Unconventional," he agreed easily.

And now he had an ironclad reason to stick to his agreement…to prove to himself that he could stay out of a woman's bed.

* * *

Roz's father had smiled at her tonight more times than he had in the past five years. As much as she'd craved his approval, all this cheer made her nervous. Paul Carpenter ran a billion-dollar furniture enterprise, with manufacturing outlets and retail stores under his command as far away as the Philippines and as close as within walking distance. He rarely smiled, especially not at Roz.

"I've always liked this house," her father commented to her out of the blue as they found themselves at the small minibar at the same time.

"I think Hendrix mentioned it's on the Raleigh Historical Society's list as one of the oldest homes in Oakwood. It's really beautiful."

Small talk with her father about her fiancé's house. It was nearly surreal. They didn't chat often, though that could be because she rarely gave him a chance. After years of conversations laden with her father's heavy sighs and pointed suggestions, she preferred their communication to be on a need-only basis.

Maybe that tide had turned. Hendrix, Jonas and Warren had disappeared, likely having a private no-girls-allowed toast somewhere away from the crowd, so there was no one to interrupt this nice moment.

"You haven't mentioned it, but I'd really like it if you allowed me to walk you down the aisle," her father suggested casually.

Something bright and beautiful bloomed in her chest as she stared at his aged but still handsome face. She'd never even considered having the kind of wedding where such a thing happened, largely because it had never occurred to her that he'd be open to the idea.

They'd never been close, not even after her mother died. The experience of witnessing someone they both loved being eaten alive by cancer should have bonded them. For a long time, she let herself be angry that it hadn't. Then she'd started to wonder if he'd gotten so lost in his grief that he'd forgotten he had a daughter dealing with her own painful sense of loss.

Eventually, she sought to cauterize her grief in other ways, which had led to even further estrangement. Was it possible that she'd erased years of disappointment with the one simple act of agreeing to Hendrix's outrageous proposal?

"Of course." She swallowed a brief and unexpected tide of emotion. "That would be lovely."

Thankfully, her fiancé was already on board with planning an honest-to-God wedding with all the trimmings. She'd have to talk him into a longer engagement if they were going to have the type of wedding with an aisle, because she'd envisioned showing up at the justice of the peace in a Betsey Johnson dress that could support a corsage. The simpler the better.

But that was out the window. She had another agenda to achieve with her wedding now, and it included walking down an aisle on her father's arm. Dare she hope this could be a new beginning to their relationship?

"I wasn't sure you'd like the idea of me marrying Hendrix Harris," she said cautiously, trying to gauge how this new dynamic was supposed to work. She'd left a message to tell him about the party and its purpose, effectively announcing her engagement to her father via voice mail so he couldn't express yet more disappointment in her choices.

"I think it's great," he said with enthusiasm she'd rarely heard in his voice. "I'm happy that you're settling down. It will be good for you."

Keep her out of trouble, more like. It was in the undertone of his words and she chose not to let it sour the moment. She did have some questionable decisions in her rearview mirror or she wouldn't have needed to marry Hendrix in the first place. The fact that her dad liked the move was a plus she hadn't dared put on the list of pros, especially given that she was marrying a man her father and everyone else had seen in the buff.

"I think it will be good for me, too," she said, though her reasons were different than his.

"I did wonder if this wedding wasn't designed to eliminate the negative effects of that unfortunate photograph on Helene Harris's campaign." Her father sipped the scotch in a highball, deliberately creating a pregnant pause that prickled across the back of Roz's neck. "If so, that's a good move. Additionally, there are a lot of benefits to being the governor's daughter-in-law, and I like the idea of being tied to the Harris family through marriage."

That had not been a chance statement. "What, like maybe I could put in a good word for you?"

He nodded thoughtfully, oblivious to her sarcasm. "Something like that. I've had some thoughts about going into politics. This is an interesting development. Lots of opportunities unfolding as we speak."

She shouldn't be so shocked. But her stomach still managed to turn over as she absorbed the idea that her father only liked that she was marrying Hendrix because of how it benefited *him*. Did it not occur to her father that she didn't have any sort of in with Helene Harris yet? Geez. She'd only met the woman for the first time tonight. And Roz might only have a certain number of favor chips to cash in. The first item on her list was Ms. Harris in white face paint with big floppy shoes.

What was going to happen if she couldn't create the opportunity her father was looking for?

Everyone was expecting something from this union. Why that created such a bleak sense of disillusionment, she had no idea. It wasn't like she'd ever done anything else her father liked. It was just that for once, she'd thought they were finally forming a relationship.

Of course that wasn't the case. Fine. She was used to losing things, used to the temporary nature of everything good that had ever happened to her. It was just one more reason to keep everyone at arm's length.

But Hendrix made that vow harder to keep almost immediately, cornering her in the kitchen where she'd gone to lick her wounds.

"Studying up on my pots and pans so you can cook me a proper dinner once you're the little woman?" he asked as he sauntered into the room and skirted the wide marble-topped island that separated the sink from the 12-burner Viking range to join her on the far side.

"Unless you like your balls in your throat, I would refrain from ever referring to me as the little woman again," she informed him frostily, not budging an inch even as the big, solid wall of Hendrix's masculinity overwhelmed her. "Also, this is a private party. See yourself out."

He had some nerve, waltzing into her space without invitation. All it would take was one slight flex of her hips and they'd be touching. Hell, that might even happen if she breathed deeper.

Instead of getting huffy about her command, he just watched her, his eyes darkening. He was too close, smelled too much like a memory of sin and sex.

"What?" she asked testily as a long, sensual thread pulled at her center.

She swallowed a yelp as he snagged a lock of hair, tucking it behind her ear. But the touch was just an excuse to get even closer, of course, because once he had his hand on her, he didn't stop there. His thumb cruised down her jaw, sensitizing her entire face.

In some alternate dimension, there was a Rosalind Carpenter with the will to slap this man's hand away when he took liberties she hadn't invited. In this dimension, her stilettos had been cemented to the floor and she couldn't do anything but stand frozen as he tipped up her chin.

She braced for the crush of his lips on hers. Anticipated it. Leaned into it ever so slightly.

But then he shocked the hell out of her by tilting her head to the side and grazing her cheek as he murmured in her ear, "Wanna tell me what's got you so upset?"

Oh, no he didn't. How dare he make this about something other than sex and be dead on target about her reasons for hiding out at the same time?

"I'm not upset." Her pulse tripped all over itself, scrambling to sort his dominating presence from his uncanny ability to read her. "Maybe I like the kitchen."

And sure enough—with each breathy catch of her lungs—their bodies brushed and the contact sang through her.

"You can't snow the master of winter," he advised

her so softly that she had to lean in a little closer to hear. Or at least that was her excuse and she'd cling to it as long as she could. "So lie to your friends, your dad. Anyone other than me. We're in this together and I need you."

Her knees went a little mushy. *Mushy*. The one person she had zero intention of letting under her skin had just demonstrated a remarkable ability to blaze right past every barrier she'd ever constructed. And it didn't even seem to matter that he hadn't meant those words the way they'd sounded, like he cared about her and had her back.

No. He wanted her to stick to the deal and stop being such a big baby about the fact that her father expected favors from this union. Weren't favors the whole purpose of this marriage? For God knew what reason, the fact that Hendrix had figured out all the subtle nuances of her mood hooked something inside her.

That pissed her off. He wasn't supposed to be good at handling her. He wasn't supposed to be anything but a means to an end.

"Yes," she purred and let her hips roll forward just a touch until she hit the thick, hard length she'd been seeking. "I can feel how much you need me."

"Careful." His lips feathered against her ear, sending shafts of need deep inside *her*. "Or I might think you're trying to entice me into breaking my promise. The Roz I know wouldn't play so dirty. So I'm going to assume it's a distraction from what's really going on with you and roll with it."

Before she could blink, his arm snaked around her waist, shoving her firmly into the cradle of his body, exactly where she wanted to be.

What did it say that he knew that about her too without being told?

"Put some of that sass where it belongs," he said into her ear as their embrace got a whole lot more intimate. He pressed her back against the counter, one leg teasing her thighs like he might push between them but he'd give her a minute to think about it. "Don't let a stray comment cramp your style. Be the life of the party because no one else's opinion matters."

Her eyes burned all at once. Oh, God, he was going to make her cry. What was wrong with her that a couple of compassionate phrases from a player like Hendrix could yank loose *tears*?

Except he wasn't just a creep looking to score. They were engaged, as unbelievable as that was to reconcile, and he needed her to *pull it together*.

"You're right," she admitted. "I'm letting crap that doesn't matter get me down."

What was she doing skulking around in the kitchen when there was a party going on? More importantly, he'd given her the perfect excuse to step out of his arms as everything settled inside.

She didn't move.

"Of course I am," he told her and she could hear the smile in his voice even as she absorbed his heat through her little black dress. "Roz, this is practice for the wider swath of society that we have to wade through an exhausting number of times over the next few weeks. They're not going to be any more forgiving. But I'm here. I'm not going anywhere and I'll be holding your hand the whole time."

"PB&J for the win," she murmured and dang it, her arms fit so well around his waist that she couldn't do anything but leave them there. "Although I have to ask why we couldn't have had this conversation without you wrapping yourself around me like an octopus."

"Oh, we could have." He nuzzled her ear. "This was strictly for me. You're driving me insane in that dress and all I can think about is that I don't get to take it off at the end of the night. I deserve something for my suffering."

That shouldn't have made her laugh. Especially since the whole of his body pressed into hers felt more like the opening act than the finale.

"Also," he continued, "I didn't think you were in the mood for an audience. If anyone came through that door right now, they'd exit pretty quickly for fear of intruding on a moment between lovers."

Did the man ever miss an angle? She did not want to appreciate any of his qualities, let alone the non-sexual variety.

Neither should she be recalling with perfect clarity what he'd said to her on his front porch. He'd never been shy about using his mouth in whatever inventive way came to mind, and he had a really great imagination, especially when it came to talking dirty.

That was enough to jump-start her brain. This wasn't the start of a seduction, never mind how easily it could be. It was a Come to Jesus at the hands of her partner and she was the one who'd taken sex off the table. For a reason. The man made her forget her own name and she needed to keep her wits about her, or she'd never survive this. She had to get Clown-Around off the ground and Hendrix was nothing to her except a ticket to achieving her goals.

"The moment is over," she informed him through sheer force of will.

"I disagree." But he stepped back immediately, taking all his delicious heat with him.

Even in that, he'd read her expertly, extracting himself as soon as he sensed her consent had changed. His gaze burned hot and she had no doubt he'd sweep her back into his arms if she gave the word.

And that put the steel in her spine that had been missing. She had equal power in this partnership. He wasn't going to slip through her fingers when she wasn't looking because they weren't a couple basing their relationship on fleeting feelings. They both had goals, none of which would be accomplished when one of them moped around poking at old bruises.

Hendrix was a smart choice. Obviously. He got her in ways no one ever had and she refused to examine how much she liked that.

"We're a power couple." She held out her hand to him. "Let's go act like one."

Four

Hendrix nursed a Jack Daniel's on the rocks as he hung out near the fireplace on the east end of the house and wished like hell he could blame the whiskey for the burn in his throat. But that pain was pure Roz.

And maybe some leftover crap from the discussion with Jonas and Warren, where his so-called friends had made it known in no uncertain terms how weak they thought he was when it came to women.

He could go without sex. He could. Hadn't he walked away from Roz when she'd said walk? If that wasn't a stellar test of his iron will, he didn't know what was. And he'd passed.

So why was he still so pissed? His skin felt like a hundred ants were crawling over it as he failed yet again at keeping his eyes off his fiancée. She lit up the room as she talked to his mother. So what if anyone caught him staring? He and Roz were engaged and he was allowed to look at her. In fact, he'd say it was expected.

The unexpected part was how…fierce the whole encounter in the kitchen had made him. Someone had upset Roz and he didn't like it. Didn't like how fragile she'd felt in his arms as he did his best to beat back whatever was going on with her internally. But she'd snapped out of it like the champ she was and he'd had a hard time letting her go when what he really wanted to do was explore that lush mouth of hers. That wasn't what she'd needed. Wasn't what he needed, either.

Okay, it was what he *needed* all right. But he also needed to prove to everyone—and maybe to himself—that he had what it took to reel back his sex-soaked lifestyle. If he'd learned to do that when his mother had asked him to, Vegas wouldn't have happened and there'd be no photograph of Hendrix's bare butt plastered all over the internet.

Paul Carpenter loomed in Hendrix's peripheral vision and then the man parked near him with a lift of his glass. "Haven't had a chance to speak to you one-on-one yet."

"No, sir."

Hendrix eyed the older man whose wealth and power in the retail industry eclipsed almost everyone in the world. Certainly a smaller chain like Harris Tobacco Lounge had nothing on Carpenter Furniture, nor did people get vaguely distasteful looks on their faces when talking about the business Roz's father had founded. Tobacco wasn't in vogue any longer, not the way it had been in the late eighties when Helene had partnered with her brother to build a string of shops from the ground up. Hendrix had joined the company almost a year after Uncle Peter died and then worked ninety hours a week to pull miracle after miracle from thin air to increase revenue over the past decade as he gradually took over the reins from his mom.

But Hendrix didn't assume for a moment that a man like Paul Carpenter respected one thin dime of Harris tobacco money, regardless of how hard he and his mom had worked for their fortune.

Mr. Carpenter eyed Hendrix as he swished his own amber liquid around the ice in his highball. "I suppose soon enough you'll be my son-in-law."

"Yes, sir." Why did it feel like he'd been called to the principal's office? He'd bet every last dollar of Harris money that Carpenter didn't think Hendrix was good enough for his daughter. "Roz is pretty important to me."

Uncomfortable didn't begin to describe this conversation. Hendrix shifted his stance. Didn't help.

"She's important to me, too," Paul said with a small smile. "It's just been the two of us since she was eight, you know."

"Yes, she mentioned that her mother had passed away." It was something they had in common—a missing parent. But Carpenter hadn't thrown that tidbit in for anything close to the same reason as Roz had. At the time, they'd been playing truth or dare and doing Jell-O shots off each other's bare stomachs. "I'm sorry for your loss, sir."

The memory of Roz's hot body decked out on the bed with the little circle of raspberry gelatin covering her navel slammed through his senses with far more potency than he'd have expected given that he'd just had the woman in his arms less than fifteen minutes ago.

Problem was that she'd been dressed. And off-limits. And probably even if he'd had permission to boost her up on the counter so he could get underneath that black dress, he'd still want her with a bone-deep ache. That had happened in Vegas, too. He couldn't get enough of her skin, her abandon, the way she was always game for whatever he did next.

And that was a conviction of his crimes as much as anything else. He had few memories of Roz that didn't involve her naked. That was the way he liked it…and lent entirely too much credence to everyone's certainty that he was a walking boner, panting after the next piece of tail he could get his hands on.

God, what was wrong with him? He was having a conversation with his future father-in-law and all he could think about was casting the man's daughter in the dirtiest sex scenario imaginable.

Something that might have been a blush if he'd been a girl prickled across his cheeks. But embarrassment wasn't something he did. Ever. He had nothing to be ashamed of. Except for the handful of scandals he'd managed to fall into over the past few years—Roz had certainly not been the first. She was just the one that had been the most worth it.

He sighed as Paul nodded his thanks over Hendrix's condolences. Maybe if he thought about something else, like cars, he could pretend the hard-on he'd been carrying around since Roz walked through his front door would eventually go away.

"I'm not one to pry," Paul said in that tone people used when they meant the exact opposite of what they'd just claimed. "And it's none of my business. But I wanted you to know that if you're marrying Roz to eliminate the scandal, I approve."

"You, um…what?" Hendrix swallowed. It didn't work. Throat still burned. He gulped enough whiskey to choke a horse, coughed and then had to wipe his watering eyes.

Paul Carpenter *approved* of Hendrix's marriage to Roz. As if Hendrix was someone he might have picked out for his daughter. It was as shocking as it was unbelievable.

For the first time in his life, he'd been automatically accepted by a male of note, one he wasn't related to, whom he admired, one whose approval he would have never sought, save this specific situation. And he'd *never* expected to get it.

"It's high time that Roz take responsibility for the questionable decisions she makes, especially the one that led to so much trouble for you and your mother's campaign. I appreciate that you've been a willing party to the *fix*." Paul accompanied that word with two fingered air quotes.

The elation that had accompanied the man's initial statement fizzled. Fast.

A willing party? As if Roz had somehow seduced him into indulging a one night stand and then orchestrated the photograph? As if Hendrix had been an innocent victim of her stupidity?

Agape and unable to actually close his mouth around the sour taste coating his tongue, Hendrix let Paul's meaning filter through his brain for a good long while. At least until he felt like he could respond without punching Paul in the mouth.

"It takes two to tango. Sir." Hendrix lifted his chin. "Roz and I are partners. I'm making all my own decisions and rest assured, one of them is to treat her like the amazing, wonderful woman that she is."

He stopped short of telling Paul that he should take a lesson.

Figured the one time he'd had a few moments of approval from a man who could have been a father figure would end in the realization that Roz hadn't had a relationship with her surviving parent the way Hendrix had. Hendrix's mother loved him and while his exploits exasperated her, she never judged. Not the way this sanctimonious jerk had just judged Roz.

Roz was Paul's daughter and he should be on her side. If anything, Hendrix had been expecting a talking-to about corrupting the Carpenter daughter with his evil ways, which would have been well-deserved and easy to pretend didn't affect him. Instead, he felt like he needed to take a shower and then tuck Roz away where this man couldn't touch her.

"Well, be that as it may, I for one am quite happy with the development. Marriage will be good for Roz and with any luck, she'll stop the naked romps in hot tubs."

"Sir, I mean this with all due respect, but I sincerely hope not."

Hendrix whirled and left Paul standing by the fireplace with a bemused look on his face. Having an in with Carpenter Furniture wasn't going to pave the way to belonging in the upper echelon of North Carolina businessmen then. But what *would* make Hendrix finally feel like he was legitimate?

He found Roz talking to Lora in his study and took only half a second to gauge Roz's mood. Better. She didn't seem fragile any longer. Good. He grabbed his fiancée's hand, threw an apologetic glance at her friend and dragged Roz from the room.

"What are you doing?" she demanded once they hit the hall.

"You and I are going to go do something together. And we'll be dressed."

Then he'd have a memory of her that had nothing to do with sex. They both needed that.

"Darling, we *are* doing something together. Dressed." And Roz's sarcasm wasn't even as thick as it should be. "We're at our engagement party, remember?"

"Of course I do," he grumbled. A lie. He'd forgotten that he couldn't just leave and take Roz on an honest-to-God date.

Soon. It was an oversight that he'd beat himself up for later. He and Roz would—and *should*—go on lots of dates with each other while they weren't having sex. Spend time together. Get to know each other. Then he could stop thinking about her naked forty-seven times a minute.

But one thing he *couldn't* stop thinking about was the fact that he'd never have realized she was upset earlier if he'd been permitted to turn it into a sexual encounter. What else had he already missed because his interactions with his fiancée started and ended with how best to get into her panties? That question put a hollow feeling in his chest that stayed with him the rest of the night.

* * *

Roz took a long shower when she got home from the engagement party, hoping it would wash the evening from her brain. But nothing could dislodge the surprising things she'd learned about Hendrix in the course of a few hours. The man never did what she expected. But she'd already known *that*.

What she hadn't known was how easily he'd figure out how to bend her to his will. She'd naively assumed that as long as they weren't naked, she'd be good. Wrong. Somehow, he'd gotten her to agree to a date.

A date with Hendrix Harris. That was almost more unbelievable than the fact that she was marrying him. Yeah, their "date" was a public spectacle that he'd dreamed up as a way to push their agenda. Couldn't get society used to the idea that they were a respectable couple if they hid at home. She got that.

But for the love of God… What were they going to talk about? She didn't date. She had a lot of sex with men who knew their way around a woman's body but conversation by candlelight in an intimate booth at a swanky restaurant wasn't in her repertoire—by design. One she could handle; the other she could not. Intimacy born of conversation and dating led to feelings she had no intention of developing, so she avoided all of the above like the plague.

One surefire way to ensure a man never called you again? Sleep with him. Worked every time. Unless his name was Hendrix Harris, apparently. That guy she couldn't figure out how to shake, mentally or physically.

At least the concept of going on a date with her fiancé had pushed the unpleasantness of the encounter with her father to the background. Actually, Hendrix had almost single-handedly done that with his comfort-slash-seduction scene in the kitchen, which she'd appreciated more than she'd ever let on.

The less the man guessed how much he affected her, the better.

The next morning, she rifled through her closet for something appropriate for a date with the man who'd blown through half the female population of Raleigh. All eyes would be on her and not for the normal reasons.

Nothing. How was it possible not to have a thing to wear in an entire eight-hundred-square-foot closet? She'd have to go shopping after she got some work done.

Donning a severe suit that she secretly called her Grown-up Outfit, she twisted her hair into a sleek up-do that made her feel professional and drove to Clown-Around to push some paperwork across her desk.

Her phone rang and she almost didn't answer the call from an unfamiliar number. It was too early and she hadn't had nearly enough coffee to endure more rejection from yet another hospital.

But she was the only one here. There was no one else to do the dirty work. She answered.

"Rosalind?" the female voice said. "This is Helene Harris. How are you?"

Roz nearly dropped the phone but bobbled it just enough to keep it near her face. "Ms. Harris. I'm fine. Thank you. It was lovely to meet you last night."

"Likewise. I hope you don't mind that I asked Hendrix for your number. I'd like to take you to lunch, if you're free."

"I'm free." That had probably come out a little too eagerly. Thank you, Jesus, she'd worn an outfit that even a future mother-in-law would approve of. "And thank you. That would be lovely."

They made plans to meet at a restaurant on Glenwood Avenue, dashing Roz's notion to go shopping for a date dress, but she couldn't think about that because *holy crap*—she was having lunch with her future mother-in-law, who was also running for governor and who had presumably agreed to be a clown. Plus there was a whole mess of other things running through her head and now she was nervous.

By lunchtime, Roz truly thought she might throw up. That would put the cap on her day nicely, wouldn't it? A photo of her yakking all over a gubernatorial candidate would pair well with the one of her *in flagrante delicto* with the woman's son.

Ms. Harris had beaten her to the restaurant and was waiting for Roz near the maître d' stand, looking polished, dignified and every inch a woman who could run a state with one hand tied behind her back. In other words, not someone Roz normally hung around with.

"Am I late?" she asked Ms. Harris by way of greeting. Because that was a great thing to point out if so.

Ms. Harris laughed. "Not at all. I got here early so I didn't have to make you wait."

"Oh. Well, that was nice. Thank you." A little floored, Roz followed the older woman to a table near the window that the maître d' pointed them to.

The murmur of voices went into free fall as the two ladies passed. Heads swiveled. Eyes cut toward them.

But unlike what had happened to Roz the last time she'd braved polite society, the diner's faces didn't then screw up in distaste as they recognized her. Instead, the world kept turning and people went back to eating as if nothing had happened.

Miraculous.

Roz slid into her chair and opened her menu in case she needed something to hide behind. Ms. Harris didn't do the same. She folded her hands on the table and focused on Roz with a sunny smile that reminded her of Hendrix all at once.

"I'm so jealous that you can wear your hair up," Ms. Harris said out of the blue and flicked a hand at her shoulder-length ash-blond hair. "I can't. I look like a Muppet. But you're gorgeous either way."

"Um…thank you," Roz spit out because she had to say something, though it felt like she was repeating herself. "Ms. Harris, if I may be blunt, I need some context for this lunch. Are we here so you can tell me to lie low for the foreseeable future? Because I'm—"

"Helene, please." She held up a hand, palm out in protest, shooting Roz a pained smile. "Ms. Harris is running for governor and I hear that enough all day long. I like to leave her at the office."

"Helene, then." Roz blinked. And now she was all off-kilter. Or rather more so than she'd been since the woman had called earlier that morning. Come to think of it, she'd been upside down and inside out since the moment she'd caught Hendrix's eye at the Calypso Room. Why would lunch with his mother be any different? "I'm sorry. Call me Roz. Rosalind is an old-fashioned name that would be better suited for an eighty-year-old woman who never wears pants and gums her food."

Fortunately, Helene laughed instead of sniffing and finding something fascinating about the tablecloth the way most polished women did when confronted with Roz's offbeat sense of humor. She hadn't grown up going to cotillions and sweet-sixteen balls the way other girls in her class had, and her lack of decorum showed up at the worst times. Her father had been too busy ignoring the fact that he had a daughter to notice that she preferred sneaking out and meeting twenty-year-old boys with motorcycles to dances and finishing school.

"I think it's a beautiful name. But I get that we can't always see our own names objectively. If I had a dime for every person who called me Helen." She made a tsk noise and waved away the waiter who was hovering near her elbow. "And then try to give your own kid an unusual name that no one on the planet can mispronounce and all you get is grief."

In spite of herself, Roz couldn't help but ask. "Hendrix doesn't like his name? Why not?"

Helene shrugged and shook her head, her discreet diamond earrings catching the low light hanging over the table. "He says Hendrix was a hack who would have faded by the time he reached thirty if he hadn't overdosed. Blasphemy. The man was a legend. You'd think your fiancé would appreciate being named after a guitar hero, but no."

"He…he thinks Jimi Hendrix is a *hack*?" Roz clutched her chest, mock-heart-attack style, mostly to play along because she knew who the guitarist was of course, but she had no opinion about his status as a legend. Neither had she been born yesterday. You didn't argue musical taste with the woman who would most likely be sitting in the governor's chair after the election. "I might have to rethink this whole wedding idea."

The other woman grinned wide enough to stick a salad plate in her mouth sideways. "I knew I liked you." Helene evaluated Roz for a moment and then signaled the waiter. "As much as I'd prefer to spend the rest of the afternoon hanging out, duty calls. We should eat."

Since it sounded like a mandate, Roz nodded, trying to relax as Helene ordered a salad and water. This wasn't the Spanish Inquisition that she'd expected, not yet anyway. Maybe that was coming after lunch. She ordered a salad despite loathing them because it was easy to eat and obviously an approved dish since Helene had gotten the same.

And that was the root cause of her nervousness— she wanted Helene to like her but had no clue how to go about that when she had no practice cozying up to a motherly type. Furthermore, the woman had just said she liked her. What more did Roz need in the way of validation, a parade?

She sipped her water and yearned for a glass of wine, which would be highly inappropriate. Wouldn't it?

"Thank you," Helene murmured to her after the waiter disappeared. "For agreeing to this wedding plan that we came up with. It speaks a lot of your character that you'd be willing to do something so unconventional to help me."

"I..." *Have no idea how to respond to that.* Roz sat

back in her chair and resisted the urge to rub at her temples, which would only clue in everybody that she'd fallen completely out of the rhythm of the conversation. "I— You're welcome?"

Smiling, Helene patted Roz's hand, which was currently clenched in a fist on the tablecloth. "Another thing. You're making me nervous, dear. I can't decide if you're about to bolt or dissolve into tears. I asked you to lunch because I want to get to know you. You're the only daughter I've ever had. For as long as I've got you, let's make this a thing, shall we?"

Unexpected tears pricked at Roz's eyelids, dang it. The Harris family shared that gene apparently—Hendrix had that uncanny ability to pull stuff out of her depths, too.

"I don't have a mother," she blurted out. "So this is all new to me."

Helene nodded. "I understand that. I didn't have a good relationship with my mother. Sometimes growing up, I wondered if it would have been easier if she'd disowned me instead of spending every waking second being disappointed in me."

Roz nodded, mortified as she dashed tears away with the white napkin from her lap. This was not the conversation she'd intended to have with her new mother-in-law. She didn't believe for a second that shouting, *I still wonder that about my father!* would be the best way to foster the relationship Helene seemed to be asking for.

But Helene's story so closely mirrored the way Roz felt about her father that it was uncanny. How familiar was she allowed to be on her first one-on-one with Helene? This was uncharted—and so not what she'd expected. If anything, she'd earned an indictment for playing a role in the problems that Helene had just thanked her for helping to solve. There'd been two naked people in that hot tub, after all.

"I'm sorry about the photograph," she said earnestly and only because Helene hadn't called her on the carpet about it. That was why Roz and her father were always at such odds. He always adopted that stern tone when laying out Roz's sins that immediately put her back up.

Accepting the apology with a nod, Helene waited for the server to put their salads on the table and leaned forward. "Trust me when I tell you that we all have questionable exploits in our pasts. You just got lucky enough for yours to be immortalized forever, which frankly wouldn't have happened if you'd been with anyone other than Hendrix."

That was entirely false. Bad luck of the male variety followed her around like a stray dog, waiting to turn its canines on her the moment she tried to feed it. Roz swallowed and ate a tiny bit of salad in order not to seem ungrateful. "I have a tendency to get a little, um, enthusiastic with my exploits unfortunately."

"Which is no one's business but yours. The unfortunate part is that my son forgot that political enemies have long reaches and few scruples. You can only tell the kid so much. He does his own thing." She shrugged good-naturedly, far more so than should have been the case. It was a testament to Helene's grace, which was something Roz had no experience with.

"You're very generous," Roz said with a small frown that she couldn't quite erase. "Most parents aren't so forgiving."

At least that had never been Roz's experience. Parents were harsh, not understanding.

"I'm not most parents. Hendrix is my life and I love him more than I could possibly tell you. He saved me." Helene paused to eat some of her own salad but Roz didn't dare interrupt. "I have a bit of a wild past myself, you know."

Was this the part where Roz was supposed to nod and say, *Why yes, I have heard all the gossip about your rebellious teenage years*? Especially when Roz's own rebellious teenage years had been nothing but practice for her even more defiant twenties, when she'd really tested the limits of her father's patience.

"Getting pregnant at seventeen was a huge wake-up call," Helene recounted in the pause. "Without that baby, I might have continued in a self-destructive cycle that wouldn't have ended well. And now look at me. I created a successful business that Hendrix runs like the maestro of the boardroom that he was born to be and I'm running for governor. *Governor*. Some days, I don't know what I did to earn these blessings."

Roz's own eyes misted in commiseration as Helene dabbed at hers with her napkin. "I honestly wasn't sure what to think when you asked me to lunch. But making each other cry wasn't even on the top ten."

Helene's smile widened. One thing Roz noticed, no matter what, the woman's smile never slipped. It was a trait she'd like to learn because not for one moment did Roz believe that Helene's life was all smooth sailing. No, instead, Helene had some innate quality that allowed her to be happy regardless of the subject or circumstance. Voters must really be drawn to that happiness the same way Roz was.

Of course that apple did not fall far from the tree. Hendrix's bright personality had been a huge turn-on. Still was. He just laced it with pure carnal intentions that he did not mind making her fully aware of, and then followed through like the maestro of the *bedroom* that he was.

Roz shivered and tried like hell to reel back those thoughts because fantasizing about a woman's son while sitting with her in an upscale restaurant felt like bad form.

"I didn't plan to make you cry when I called you," Helene confessed sunnily. "Just happened. But I love that you're a companionable crier. No one wants to cry alone."

No. No one did. But that was some people's lot in life and if they didn't change the subject, there were going to be a lot more tears. The raw place inside was growing a lot bigger the longer she sat here. This wonderful woman had just said she'd be happy having a mother-daughter relationship with Roz for as long as Roz was married to Hendrix. Like that was an invitation Roz got every day and it was no big thing.

It was. And Roz wanted to cling to it, hold it and wrap her arms around it. But like everything—*everything*—in her life, Helene would be gone one day soon. Too soon. Any day was too soon because Roz had just realized that she craved whatever relationship this woman would grant her. Helene could be a...mentor of sorts. A friend. A stand-in mother.

It was overwhelming to contemplate. Overwhelmingly sad to think about having that and then giving it up.

But how could Roz refuse? She didn't *want* to refuse.

Helene was helping her blow away the scandal if nothing else and Roz owed the woman respect and allegiance for that alone.

The rest was all a huge bonus.

Five

Hendrix picked Roz up at the door of her loft for their date because he wanted to and he could. Also? What better way to prove he had all the skill necessary to resist pushing his way inside and having his way with her than not to do it?

But when he knocked on the door, she swung it wide to give him an eyeful of soft, gorgeous skin on display. Being that edible should be a crime. Her cleavage should be framed and hung on the wall of the Louvre.

"What happened to your pants?" he growled hoarsely.

Roz glanced down at the river of bare legs flowing from the hem of the blouse-like thing she had on. "What pants? This is a dress."

"The hell you say." He couldn't take her on a date in that outfit. His will would slide into the toilet in about a microsecond. Surely that would be the easiest dress in the history of time to get his hands under, even if they were someplace normally reserved for hands off, like a high-backed booth in the corner of a dimly lit restaurant.

His will made a nice whooshing sound as it flushed away and all his good intentions crumbled into dust. He might have whimpered.

Do not step over the threshold. Do not. No stepping.

"Let me make this perfectly clear to you," he ground out. "If you wear that dress—and I use that term *very* loosely—I cannot be responsible for what carnal activities may befall you in the course of this evening."

"Please." She waved that off. "You made a promise to keep your hands off me and you will, I have no doubt. What you're really saying is that you'd be embarrassed to be seen with me in this, right? So kiss off. I'm wearing it."

Oh, so it was going to be one of those nights. Not only would he have to contend with the idea that she had absolute faith in him, but she'd also assigned some kind of nefarious intent to his comments.

Her attitude needed to go and fast. "I wasn't embarrassed to be seen with you naked in a photograph. Not embarrassed now. Stop projecting your own crap all over me and get your purse. If you want to wear something that's one stiff breeze away from being illegal, be my guest."

"What's with you?" she called over her shoulder as she did exactly as he'd commanded without seeming to realize it. "You asked me on this date. If you're going to be nasty to me the whole time, then I'd be happy to slam the door in your face and order takeout."

That wasn't happening. He'd been looking forward to this date all day. "Why is it so hard to believe my objection to that dress starts and ends with how spectacular you look in it? You tell me what's with you and I'll tell you what's with me."

She smirked and flounced past him to the building's elevator. "You never had a problem with what I wore in Vegas. What's changed now? Only that we're engaged and you want me to look like a proper Harris bride."

Whatever *that* meant.

"Stop putting words in my mouth." The elevator door closed around them and they were alone in a space that got a whole lot smaller the more of her scent he breathed in. "In Vegas, I didn't care what you wore because I was taking it off you at some point. That's not the situation tonight and if you're really confused about the state of my extreme sexual frustration, the evidence is ready and available for your hands-on examination."

Her gaze flicked to his crotch, which put a little more heat into his already painful erection. Her sweet fingers on it would be legendary indeed but she didn't take him up on the invitation. Shame.

"I— You know what? Never mind." Her lush pink lips clamped together and she looked away.

Not so fast. His beleaguered senses were still working well enough to alert him that there was more here that he didn't know. "Spit it out, sweetheart. Or I'll be forced to kiss it out of you."

"What?" She slid him a sideways glance. "There's no stipulation in the rules that says you're allowed to kiss me to get information."

He shrugged. "How come you get to make all the

rules? If you're not going to be honest with me, I have to make up my own rules."

Her sigh worked its way through his gut and he was a half second away from sweeping her into his arms to show her he always put his money where his mouth was. But then she did as he suggested.

"I am projecting," she admitted.

It was as much of a shock now as it had been in the kitchen during their party—he'd figured out how to make progress with Roz. She was such a mystery, one he'd like to spend many long hours solving. Usually he would do that in bed. But that was off-limits here, so he'd been forced to be more creative. Looked like it was working. "Don't do that. Tell me what's up and then we'll go paint the town."

"Maybe you want a wife more like your mom. Smart and accomplished." She shrugged, her face blank. "That's not who I am. I have to be me, even if I don't look like I'm supposed to be here."

"What does that even mean? Of course you're supposed to be here. What, are you worried how you stack up?" The long, intense silence answered his flippant question in spades. "Are you *kidding* me? That's really something that even crossed your mind?"

Ridiculous. But apparently it wasn't to her. She rolled her shoulders back and her spine went stiff.

"Can we just forget about it?"

That wasn't happening any more than not taking Roz on this date. But first they obviously needed to get a few things straight. The elevator reached the ground floor and he waited until she reached his car.

Instead of opening the door for her, he snagged her by the waist and turned her into his arms, trapping her against the car. Instantly, everything but Roz drained from his mind as her body aligned with his so neatly that he could feel the heat of her core against his leg.

That was some dress.

"I already told you what you wanted to know, Hendrix." She glanced up at him through her lashes and the look was so sexy it put at least an inch on his already impossibly hard erection. "What are you going to do now, kiss me anyway?"

"No need." His hips fit so well into the hollow of her stomach that he swayed into her a little deeper. "This is strictly Exhibit A. B and C will have to wait."

Because he'd given his word. How had that become such a thing? Fine time for something like principles. Before Roz, he'd have said he had none when it came to women. Or rather, women said that on his behalf and he'd never corrected the notion.

"Make no mistake, though. You need kissing," he murmured, ignoring the fact that it was so backward it wasn't even funny. "In the worst way. Anytime you find yourself worried about whether you're the most gorgeous woman in the room, you think about this. Remember what my body feels like against yours and don't you dare question whether you're the woman I want to take home with me."

"I wasn't worried about that," she said and blinked her long sooty lashes coquettishly. "But I do appreciate exhibit A."

Not enough to lift the no-kissing moratorium apparently. She was crushed against his body, wearing a filmy, flirty dress that barely covered her good parts and her lips came together in the sweetest little bow that he wanted to taste so badly he feared for his sanity.

But not enough that he'd lost all decorum. Looked like his will wasn't completely broken because he found the wherewithal to step back. His chest heaved as he met her gaze. It was enigmatic and full of heat.

"Let me know when you're ready for the rest of the exhibit. I can open it up for your viewing pleasure any time."

Why were they torturing themselves like this again?

Due punishment, he reminded himself. His mom deserved to have a campaign free from other people's darts because of her son's actions. He owed it to his mother to fix it, especially after already messing up once because he couldn't resist this woman.

Plus, marrying Roz and introducing something real and legitimate into his life meant something to him, more than he'd ever admit, to her or anyone.

He tucked his fiancée into the car and slid into his own seat. She leaned on the center console instead of settling back against the leather, spilling way too much of her presence into his space.

"This seat has plenty of room for two," he murmured instead of starting the engine like a good boy.

"Don't threaten me unless you plan to follow through," she shot back and tucked her chin into her palm as if she planned to watch him the entire time he drove. "Where are you taking me? Not Randolph Room. That's where your mom took me to lunch."

"You had lunch with my mom?" That was news to him. He frowned.

Had his mother mentioned something about it last night and he'd forgotten in all the hoopla of the engagement party and the disturbing conversation with Paul Carpenter? He distinctly recalled giving Roz's number to his mom, but he'd assumed that was so they could coordinate the clown thing.

His mother usually told him her schedule and it was bothersome that she hadn't given him a heads-up about having lunch with his fiancée. He and Helene were business partners, and Hendrix sometimes offered advice on her campaign. And they were friends, which was often weird to people so he seldom talked about it.

Of course, since the photograph, she'd been a little on edge with him. It stung to find out they weren't totally back to normal.

"Yeah. She called me and asked if I was free. I wasn't going to say no."

"You shouldn't have. What did you talk about?"

"Girl stuff."

That was code for *mind your own business*. Hendrix started the car to give himself something to do that wasn't prying into the social life of his mother and fiancée. Nor did he want to obsess over the reasons why it was bothering him.

At least now he had some context for why Roz had all of a sudden joined the Helene Harris fan club and developed a complex about whether she stacked up against other women.

They drove to the restaurant where he'd made reservations and he cursed the silence that had fallen inside the car. Normally he had no problem finding something to talk about, particularly when it came to Roz, but he didn't want to spend the evening discussing all the ways he planned to have her after the wedding.

Well, he *wanted* to. There was absolutely nothing wrong with a healthy attraction to the woman you were going to marry. But he genuinely didn't think he had it in him to talk dirty to Roz and then not follow through yet again.

"Did you and my mother work out the clown stuff?" That was a safe enough subject.

"No. I mean, she mentioned it, but only to say that she's overcommitted right now and to bug her about it at lunch next week so she can fit it in. She actually said it like that. *Bug* her." Roz laughed. "As if I'd pester Helene like that. 'Mom, Mom, can you be a clown? Pleeeeease?'"

Hendrix did a double take at Roz's cute little girl voice. And the mention of additional lunches. "You're having lunch again?"

"Sure, we decided it was important to have a standing lunch date once a week from now on. Is there a problem with that?"

Yes. A huge problem. He didn't like the idea of his mom getting chummy with Roz. Why? How the hell should he know? He just…didn't. "Of course not. I was making conversation. This is a date. The whole point is to get to know each other, right?"

"That was how you posed it," she reminded him with another laugh that should have had him thinking of all the ways he could get her to do that a lot because it meant she was having fun.

Instead, his back was up and his mood had slid into a place normally reserved for tense board meetings. What was *wrong* with him? Not enough sex lately, most likely.

At the restaurant, they waited in a discreet corner as the maître d' readied their table, both of them ignoring the pointed attention from the other guests. At least Roz hadn't stiffened up like she had at the florist. He'd consider that a win.

Wedding plans. That was a good subject. Surely they could talk about that. He waited until they'd both taken their seats and he'd given the waiter their wine preference.

"So. You're going to hang out with my mom once a week now?"

She lifted a brow. "That's really bothering you, isn't it?"

Apparently. And now it was evident to them both. He bit back a curse.

When was the last time his mom had asked him to lunch? Ages ago. Not since the photograph had hit the news. She'd been really upset. But it had all blown over after he'd agreed to marry Roz—he'd thought.

And look, here he was in a restaurant with Roz. Engaged. That had been a major feat to pull off. People were noticing them together and a waiter had even taken a discreet picture with his phone that would likely make the rounds with some positive press attached. Surely Helene could appreciate all of the steps Hendrix had taken toward legitimizing his relationship with Roz so that his mom's political opponents wouldn't have any fodder to lob at her via the press.

Now would be a great time to stop sulking and get back to the reason he was torturing himself with a stunning companion whom he would not be taking to bed later. They hadn't even scored a dimly lit booth, which was good. And bad.

"This is the part where you're supposed to back me into the kitchen and stick your hands all over my body so I can have something else to focus on besides the stuff in my head," he informed her.

"I would if that would help." She eyed him nonchalantly. "But I'm pretty sure that only works on me. Instead, why don't you tell me why you're so threatened by the idea of me having lunch with your mom?"

Lazily, he sipped his wine to cover the panic that had uncurled in his stomach. The alcohol didn't help. "*Threatened* is a strong word."

And so correct. How dare she be the one to figure that out when he hadn't? The back of his neck flashed hot. That was a big wake-up call.

He'd never in a million years expected that getting married would mean he'd have to share his mother with someone. It had been the two of them for so long, and they'd become even more of a unit as he'd grown into adulthood, made even stronger after Uncle Peter had died. His reaction was pure selfishness and he didn't feel like apologizing for it all at once.

"Then you tell me what would be a better word," she said.

No quarter. If he wasn't already feeling pushed against a wall, her cool insistence would have put him there. *"Curious."*

Her small smile said she had his number and she'd be perfectly within her rights to call him on his complete lie. *Pissed off* and *tense* would be more applicable. Which was dumb. What, was he actually worried that Roz was going to steal his mother from him?

"Curious about why on earth two women who don't know each other and will soon share the same last name could possibly want to have lunch?" She watched him over the rim of her glass as she sipped her own wine.

"You're changing your name?" This evening was full of revelations.

"Yeah. Why not? That's part of the deal here, right? Marrying you is my get-out-of-jail-free card. Might as well go full throttle. Make sure everyone is clear that I'm tied to the governor's office."

"But you're already a Carpenter—" All at once, the conversation with her father slammed through his consciousness. Was he really that dense? Maybe being a Carpenter wasn't all that great for her. After being treated to a glimpse of the judgment levied in her direction, it wasn't so hard to guess why, if so. Maybe she deserved a name change.

Wow. When had he turned into such an ass?

He picked up her hand to hold it in his. Her touch bled through him, convicting him even further since she didn't pull away. "I shouldn't be jumping down your throat about having lunch with my mom. It's fine. I'm glad you're getting along."

She nodded and the mood lightened. The restaurant he'd selected featured a highly rated chef and the meal reflected that. They ate and conversed about innocuous subjects and he relaxed about halfway through dinner.

It wasn't until he escorted Roz to the valet stand that he realized the tension hadn't completely fled on her side. Her back felt stiff under his fingers. Okay, he'd royally screwed up earlier if she was still uptight over the third degree he'd given her. But why had she dropped it like everything was fine? Just like a woman to nurse a grudge and not bother to say anything about it. That wasn't going to fly.

As he pointed the car in the direction of her loft, he

glanced at her from the corner of his eye. "Silent treatment for my crimes?"

She stared out the window. "Don't be ridiculous. I don't play little-girl games with men."

He let that simmer for a few minutes as he put a tight rein on his temper before he did something like comment on big-girl games. Nothing in his experience had prepared him to do this kind of long-term thing with a woman. And they were *getting married*. For the first time, it occurred to him that maybe he wasn't marriage material, that the reason he'd shied away from relationships wasn't solely because of the pact he'd made with Warren and Jonas, but also because he sucked at navigating emotional land mines.

But like the promise he'd made to keep his hands off her, this conversation was just as much a measure of his character. It was worth it to him to figure this out, if for no other reason than to prove he could.

He pulled over into a shadowy parking lot and killed the engine, then turned to face her. "Talk to me, Roz. You're obviously still upset."

"You asked me on a date so we could get to know each other. But then when you had an opportunity to really lay it all out, you didn't. At least have the courtesy to be honest with me. You don't like me being friendly with your mom because I'm just a good-time girl you had to marry because we got caught up in a scandal. I'm not good enough to be a real wife."

He shut his eyes for a blink, as that barb arrowed through his gut nice and deep. He had no excuse for not having seen that coming. Obviously she was playing back things she'd heard from others, and he'd unwittingly stepped right in the center of the land mines.

Yep. Not marriage material. This was why he stuck to sex, which he was good at, and shied away from anything that smacked of intimacy, which he was not good at.

"Roz, look at me." She did, her eyes barely discernible in the dark as he fumbled his way through. "Don't let your father's pigheadedness color your opinion of yourself. No one here is judging you for your sins. The reason I got testy is solely because I'm a jerk who doesn't like to share. My mom has been mine alone for a long time. We're a unit. I didn't want to lose that, or have that diluted somehow if you... Wow, this sounds really bad out loud."

She smiled with the faintest stirrings of tenderness. "No, it sounds honest. Which I like."

"This is me being honest," he agreed. If that was all she was looking for, maybe he didn't have to botch this too badly. "So you have to believe me when I say earlier was a combination of you in that dress and me being territorial. And maybe a bit of foot-in-mouth disease."

Her laugh washed through him, dissolving a lot of the tension, and he had to fight the muscles in his hand so that he didn't reach for her. The reasons he wanted to were totally mixed up and he didn't fully understand this urge to connect himself with that laugh in a way that had nothing to do with sex.

"Honesty is the best policy. So I'll return the favor. I don't remember my mom from when she was healthy. I just remember her sick and in a hospital bed, dying. Today a woman I admire invited me to lunch for the first time in my adult life. The fact that she's your mother didn't even factor into why it meant so much to me. Are you starting to see why I got a little bent out of shape about you getting bent out of shape?"

Her tone walloped him, dredging through his gut with razor-sharp teeth. He'd behaved like a jackass and stabbed at Roz's wounds at the same time. This wasn't a run-of-the-mill fight, like what normal couples might go through. They were surfacing enormously difficult emotions that he shouldn't want any part of.

But he was still here.

"If I say I'm sorry, will that help?"

Her smile widened. "Maybe."

Hell, why was he fighting this insanely strong urge to touch her? He skimmed his fingertips down her jaw and feathered a thumb across her lips. "I'm sorry."

She didn't even blink, just leaned until her lips hit his, and then treated him to the longest, sweetest kiss of his experience. Everything fell away except her and he froze, letting her drive this to whatever completion she wished because this was about feeling her out, learning who she was besides the woman he'd had hot, dirty sex with in Vegas.

God, he'd needed this, needed her in ways he wouldn't have guessed. The anticipation of getting her into his arms just like this flavored it so heavily that kissing her was nearly mind-altering. And this wasn't even close to the kind of kiss he'd envisioned jumping into all night. This was something else.

She pulled back and tilted her forehead to his until they touched. "I'm sorry, too. For being difficult. But not for kissing you. You needed the reminder that *we're* a unit. Peanut butter and jelly."

Yes. *That's* what it was. A solidifying of their union. No longer was this a marriage favor he was doing for his mother. He and Roz were becoming something. What, he wasn't sure yet, but it was so much more real than what he'd envisioned.

No. That wasn't what was happening here. Something lodged in his chest and he couldn't breathe all at once. He *couldn't* care about Roz, not like they were a couple. Not like there was any possibility of something deeper than a surface connection that started and ended with sex.

She didn't think there was something bigger than a marriage of convenience happening here. Did she? Had he messed up her expectations with all the talk of dates and getting to know each other? Had he screwed up his *own* expectations?

Surely not. Maybe some things had gotten a little out of whack, strictly due to the rules she'd laid down. The solution was to marry her and get to the place where he could block all that out with lots of hot sex, obviously. The lack of it was throwing them both off, that was all. He'd been forced into this pseudo-intimacy because of the scandal and now that he'd proven he wasn't a sex addict, it was time to move on to the next level. Once things were on familiar ground, he could fix all their fights with orgasms and then no one had to apologize for anything.

"We've got to get a wedding date on the calendar and you in a dress," he muttered.

The sooner the better.

Six

Somehow, Hendrix pulled off a miracle and got the wedding planned in record time, even down to the last place-setting. Roz wasn't confused about his motivation. She'd thrown down a gauntlet that they couldn't have sex until the wedding and had unwittingly created an environment that meant they'd be tense and irritable around each other.

Frankly, she was a little tired of it, too. They didn't have anything in common other than blind lust and a desire to fix the scandal. She got that. Their one disastrous attempt at a date had ended with solid reminders that her skill set didn't extend to forming connections with people, especially not with men—because she was good at having sex with them, but nothing else. Hendrix was no exception.

After her patient attempt to work through his unexpected freak-out over what should have been a simple announcement that she'd had lunch with Helene, his response? *Let's get you in a wedding dress so I can finally get what I came for.*

Fine. They weren't a real unit. Not like Hendrix and Helene, and the reminder had been brutal. Maybe she'd started to feel a little mushy about the idea of being part of something, but it had been nothing but a mirage.

They were getting married for reasons that had nothing to do with peanut butter and jelly and she'd agreed to that. It was smart. Not romantic, and that was a good thing. Less painful in the long run.

She liked orgasms as much as the next girl, so there was really no downside. Except for the niggling feeling that she and Hendrix had been on the verge of something special in the car and then it had vanished.

Her life was spiraling out of her control faster than she could grab on to it. She combated that by sticking her fingers in her ears and pretending there was no wedding planning going on. Hendrix handled it all, finally getting the message after his fourth attempt to include her in the decisions. Except for the flowers she'd already picked out, she really didn't care.

None of it mattered. They'd be undoing it all in a matter of months. The wedding music would dwindle from everyone's memory the moment the last note faded. Who cared what the piece was called?

The morning of the wedding dawned clear and beautiful, a rare day in Raleigh when the humidity wasn't oppressive. Figured. It was a perfect scenario to wear her hair down, but the pearl-encrusted bodice of her dress required her hair to be up. She dragged herself out of bed and got started on enjoying her wedding day—likely the only one she'd ever get. If nothing else, by the end of it, she and Hendrix would be past the weirdness that had sprung up since their date.

Lora picked her up at nine to take her to the spa, where they'd planned to spend the morning pampering themselves, but Roz couldn't get into the spirit. Hell, what kind of spirit was she supposed to be in on the day of a wedding that was basically an arranged marriage? She'd moved a few things into Hendrix's mansion in Oakwood yesterday and they planned to live together for a few months, at least until the election, at which point they'd agreed to reevaluate. Everything was on track.

The spa did not relax her. The masseur had ham hands, the girl who did Roz's bikini wax burned herself—not badly, but she'd had to find someone else to finish the job—and the facial left Roz's skin feeling raw and slightly dry, so her makeup wouldn't apply correctly. Gah, she'd been putting on foundation for fifteen-plus years. Why did her face suddenly look like the Grand Canyon in miniature?

Nerves. So much was riding on this marriage. Her reputation. Clown-Around. Helene's campaign. Her father's political ambitions. And maybe deep inside, she hoped that saying *I do* would magically shift things between her and her father. It wasn't a crime to hope.

But neither was any shifting likely. So far, he'd stayed on script, expressing nonverbal disapproval in the usual ways while tossing out backhanded comments about getting chummy with Helene. It had soured her lunch dates with Hendrix's mom to the point where she had canceled the last one. It had killed her to lose that one-on-one time with Helene but Hendrix had been so weird about it that Roz figured it was better not to get too attached. Her response was mostly self-preservation at this point.

As she leaned into the mirror to work on her eyeliner, her hand started to shake.

Lora glanced over from her spot next to the bride. "You okay? You've been jumpy since this morning."

Dang it. If Lora had noticed, Hendrix would, too. Maybe she could sneak a glass of white wine from the reception before walking down the aisle. Just to settle things inside. "Brides are allowed to be jumpy."

Her friend eyed her. "But this isn't a real wedding. You've been so calm and collected this whole time. It's kind of a shock to see you having this strong of a reaction."

"It is a real wedding," she corrected, fielding a little shock of her own that Lora had classified it any other way. "And a real marriage. I'm taking his name. We'll be sleeping in the same bed. Can't get much more real than that."

That started tonight. Holy hell. That was a lot of reality, orgasms notwithstanding. She'd be an honest-to-God wife who could legally sign her name Mrs. Harris. It suddenly felt like a huge gamble with no guarantee of a payoff.

Lora shrugged and tossed her long blond hair over her shoulder, leaning into the mirror to apply her own cosmetics. "But you're not in love. It's not like he swept you off your feet with a romantic proposal that you couldn't resist. I'm kind of surprised you're going through with it, actually. You didn't plan one tiny part of the ceremony. I had to force you to pick a dress."

All of that was true. And sad all at once that such a cold recitation of facts so accurately described her wedding day. She tossed her head. "I never dreamed of my wedding or scrawled my future married name on stray pieces of paper growing up. I'm marrying a man with bedroom skills a gigolo would envy. My life will not suck. And when we get tired of each other, I get a no-fault divorce. It's a business arrangement. It's the perfect marriage for me."

She'd keep telling herself that until *she* believed it too, and ignore the huge gap in her chest that she wished was filled with something special.

Grinning, Lora waved her mascara wand in Roz's direction. "When you put it that way... Does he have a friend?"

"Sure. I'll introduce you to Warren. You'll like him." Doubtful. Lora wouldn't look twice at a man who accessorized with his cell phone 24/7. "Hendrix's other friend is married."

Jonas and Viv had come across as one of those couples who were really in love. You could just tell they both firmly believed they'd found their soul mate. Honestly, Roz thought she'd be exactly like that if she ever fell in love, which was why she hoped she never did. Her parents had been mad for each other and watching her father waste away alongside her dying mother had been a huge wake-up call. Love equaled pain. And then when it was gone, she envisioned being alone for the rest of her life, just like her father. Carpenters weren't good at serial marriage.

The one she'd get with Hendrix Harris *was* perfect for her.

Hendrix sent a limo to pick up the bride and bridesmaid. Roz felt a little silly at the size of the vehicle when she spread out her white pearl-encrusted skirt on the spacious leather seat that could have held four people. But the fact of the matter was that she didn't have a lot of friends that she would have asked to be in her wedding party. She had acquaintances. They'd all been invited to the social event of the season, though she didn't fool herself for a moment that they were coming for any other reason than morbid curiosity.

All at once, the door to the chapel loomed and her feet carried her into the church's vestibule without much conscious effort on her part. Her father waited for her inside as arranged, but she couldn't quite shake the feeling of walking through a surreal dream.

"Roz," her father called as he caught sight of her. "You're looking well."

Geez. Exactly what every bride dreams of hearing on her wedding day. "Thanks, Dad."

He wasn't effusive with his praise, never had been. But was it too much to ask for a little affection on a day when she was doing something that would benefit him?

Crooking his elbow in her direction, he stood where the coordinator directed him to and then it was Roz's turn to get in line behind Lora, who was stunning in a pale pink column dress with a long skirt. It would have been more appropriate for an evening wedding, but that was one thing Roz had cared about picking out. She'd gotten the dress that looked good on Lora, not the one societal convention dictated.

She was still Rosalind Carpenter. For about thirty more minutes. Oh, God.

What if this was a huge mistake?

Music swelled from the interior of the chapel that Hendrix had insisted would lend validity to their union. That seemed be the litmus test for pretty much all of his wedding decisions—how legit the thing was. She'd never have pegged him as that much of a traditionalist but she got more than an eyeful of his idea of what a proper wedding looked like as the coordinator flung open the doors to the chapel, signaling their entrance.

Five hundred guests rose dutifully to their feet, heads craned toward Roz for their first glimpse of the bride. An explosion of color greeted her, from the bouquets at the end of each pew to the multiple stands holding baskets of blooms across the front. Hendrix had chosen pinks to complement Lora's dress, but hadn't seemed too inclined to stick with a flower theme. There were stargazer lilies she'd picked out at the florist, but also roses, baby's breath, tulips, daisies, and something that might be a larkspur, but her father started down the aisle before she could verify.

Wow, was it hot in here. Every eye in the house was trained on her. Her spine stiffened and she let her own vision blur so she didn't have to see whether they were quietly judging her or had a measure of compassion reflected on their faces. No way was it the latter. No one in attendance had a clue how difficult today was for the motherless bride.

Then her gaze drifted past all the flowers and landed on the star of the show. Hendrix. She stared into his pale hazel eyes as her father handed her off in the most traditional of exchanges. Her husband-to-be clasped her fingers and the five hundred people behind her vanished as she let Hendrix soak through her to the marrow.

"You're so beautiful it hurts inside when I look at you," he murmured.

Her knees turned to marshmallow and she tightened her grip on his hand.

That was the proper thing to say to a bride on her wedding day and she didn't even try to squelch the bloom of gratitude that had just unfurled in her chest. "I bet you say that to all your brides."

He grinned and faced the minister, guiding her through the ceremony like a pro when nerves erased her memory of the rehearsal from the night before. The space-time continuum bent double on itself and the ceremony wound to a close before she'd barely blinked once.

"You may kiss the bride," the minister intoned and that's when she realized the complete tactical error she'd made.

She had to kiss Hendrix. For real. And the moratorium on that thus far had guaranteed this would become A Moment. The carnal spike through the gut at the thought did not bode well for how the actual experience would go down.

Neither did the answering heat in his expression. He cupped her jaw on both sides, giving her plenty of time to think about it. No need. Her whole body had just incinerated with the mere suggestion of the imminent follow-through.

And then he leaned in to capture her mouth with his. It was a full-on assault to the senses as their lips connected and she couldn't do anything else but fling her arms around his waist, or she'd have ended up on the ground, a charred shell that was burned beyond recognition.

Oh God, yes. With that one hard press of his mouth, Hendrix consumed her. This kiss was but a shadow of the many, many others they'd shared, but it was enough to slide memories along her skin, through her core.

This was so very right, so perfect between them. Everything else faded—the weirdness, the nerves. This heat she understood, craved. If he was burning her alive from the inside out, she didn't have to think about all the reasons this marriage might not work.

He teased the flame in her belly into a full raging fire with little licks of his tongue against hers. Hell, that blaze hadn't ever really been extinguished from the moment he'd lit that match in Vegas. Masterfully, the man kissed her until she'd been scraped raw, panting for more, nearly weeping with want.

This was why she'd thrown down the no-kissing-no-sex rule. She could not resist him, even in a church full of people. Her body went into some kind of Hendrix-induced altered state where nothing but basic need existed. And he wasn't even in full-on seduction mode. Thank God he'd played by her rules or there was no telling what new and more horrific scandals might have cropped up prior to the wedding.

That was enough to get her brain back in gear. She broke off the kiss to the sound of flutes and strings. The recessional music. They were supposed to walk and smile now. Somehow, that's what happened and then she floated through a million photographs, a limo ride to the reception and about a million well-wishers.

All she really wanted was to dive back into Hendrix and never surface.

The crowd at the reception crushed that hope flat. No less than ten people vied for their attention at any given time and she'd lost count of the number of times Hendrix had introduced her to someone from his business world. The reverse wasn't at all true, a sobering fact that brought home the reasons she was wearing a wedding band.

She'd spent the past few years having what she'd staunchly defend as a "good time" but in reality was a panacea for the pain of losing first her mother to cancer and then her father to indifference and grief. The scandals were just the cherry on top of her messy life and ironically, also the reason she couldn't move forward with something respectable like running a charity.

Her new husband would change all of that. Had already started to.

The pièce de résistance of the event came with the first dance between husband and wife. Hendrix, whom she'd scarcely said two words to since that pantie-melting kiss, whisked her out onto the dance floor. He drew her close and when his arms came around her, the strangest sensation floated through her as they began to move to the classical piece that she'd have never picked out but fitted the occasion.

"Hey," he murmured into her ear. "How is Mrs. Harris doing?"

"I don't know. I haven't spoken to your mother." When he laughed, she realized he hadn't meant Helene. "Ha, ha. I'm out of sorts. It's been a long day."

"I know. That's why I asked. You seem distracted."

She pulled back a touch to look at him. "Ask me again."

The smile in his eyes warmed her, but then it slid away to be replaced by something else as their gazes held in a long moment that built on itself with heavy implications. "How are you, Mrs. Harris?"

A name shouldn't have so much color to it. If anything, it should have sounded foreign to her, but it wasn't strange. It felt...good. She took a deep breath and let that reality expand inside her. *Mrs. Harris*. That was her name. Rosalind Harris. Mrs. Roz Harris.

She liked it. Maybe she *should* have practiced writing it out a bajillion times on a piece of scratch paper. Then the concept wouldn't have been such a shock. There was a huge difference between academically knowing that you were changing your name and actually hearing someone address you that way. Especially when the man doing the addressing had the same name and you were married to him.

"I'm better now," she told him.

Understatement. Hendrix was solid and beautiful and he'd pulled off the wedding event of the season. Why hadn't she participated more in the planning?

Sour grapes. Nothing more complicated than that. She'd started getting a little too touchy-feely with the peanut butter and jelly analogy and he'd set her back on the right path with timely reminders of what they were doing here. For his trouble, she'd frozen him out and then used that as an excuse to pull back from a friendship with his mother.

Well, she was over it. They were married now and both of them knew the score. The no-sex rule wasn't in the way any longer. Thank God. They could spend all their time in bed and never have to talk about mothers, peanut butter or anything difficult.

"This was amazing," she said earnestly. "So much more than I was expecting. Thank you."

Surprise filtered through his expression. "I... You're welcome. I'm glad you liked it. The wedding planner did all the work. I just approved everything."

"I should have done it with you." The fact that she hadn't made her feel petty and childish. If nothing else, it was an effort that benefited her, so she could have done half the work. Then maybe she'd feel more like she'd earned the right to be called Mrs. Harris. "I'm sorry I didn't."

For the first time since their disastrous date, Hendrix smiled at her like he had that night in Vegas. As if he'd found the end of the rainbow and the pot of gold there was more valuable than he'd ever dreamed.

She liked it when he looked at her like that.

"It's okay. It wasn't any trouble." He spun her around as the last notes of the waltz ended and something a little darker and more sensual wafted from the string quartet on the dais in the corner. His arms tightened, drawing her deeper into his embrace. The crowd on the dance floor grew thicker as people filled in around them. "I'm enjoying the benefits of it, so it's all good."

His body pressed against hers deliciously. A slow simmer flared up in her core, bubbling outward until her nerve endings were stretched taut with anticipation. "The benefits?"

"Dancing with my bride, for one," he murmured. His hands drifted along her body with sensual intent, pressing her more firmly against him as he stroked her waist, the curve of her hip, lower still, and there was so much wedding dress in the way that she strained against his touch, yearning for the heat of his hand in places that hadn't been *touched* in so very long.

Dancing was a great excuse to let Hendrix put his hands on her in public. "I'm enjoying that part, too."

"It's been a long time," he said gruffly, "since I had free rein to hold you like this."

Yes, and judging by the oh-so-nice hard length buried in her stomach, he was as affected by their close proximity as she was. "You were a trouper about it."

"Wasn't easy. But it's over now. I can kiss you whenever I feel like it." To prove the point, he nuzzled her neck, setting off fireworks beneath her skin as he nibbled at the flesh.

"That's not kissing," she muttered, biting back a gasp as he cruised to her ear, molding it to his lips as he laved at her lobe.

"I'm getting there."

"Get there faster."

He pulled back and swept her with a glance that was equal parts evaluation and equal parts *I'm a second from throwing you down right here, right now.* "Is that your way of saying you're ready to leave?"

"We can't," she reminded him and tried to ignore how desperately disappointed she sounded.

This was a networking event as much as it was a wedding. Helene had a throng of people around her, and the movers and shakers of Raleigh stood at the bar. If the bride and groom dashed for the door fifteen minutes after the reception started, that wouldn't go over well.

"No," he agreed and bit out a vile curse that perfectly mirrored her thoughts. "We need tongues wagging with positive comments about us, preferably with lots of praise about how respectable we are."

Exactly. Especially if they spouted off at the mouth around her father. He needed a whole lot of reassurance that Roz had turned a corner, that her photo ops with naked men were a thing of the past. From here on out, the only scandal associated with her name should be more along the lines of serving the wrong wine at a party she and Hendrix threw for Harris Tobacco Lounge executive staff.

"So maybe we don't leave," she said as a plausible alternative began to form in her mind. Oh God, did she need that alternative. Fast. Her insides were already tight and slick with need.

His expression turned crafty as he considered her comment. "Maybe not. Maybe there's a...closet in the back?"

"With a door. That locks."

His thumb strayed to the place along her bodice where it met the skin of her back and heat flashed as he caressed the seam, dipping inside just enough to drive her insane and then skimming along until he hit the zipper.

"One tug, and this would be history," he said, the hazel in his eyes mesmerizing her with the promise as he toyed with the hook anchoring the zipper to the bodice. "It feels complicated. Challenging."

"Maybe you don't start there," she suggested and swayed a little to give the couples around them the impression the bride and groom were still dancing when in reality, her attention was on the perimeter of the room where two very promising hallways led to the back of the reception venue. "You might have better luck checking out how easily my skirt lifts up."

"Mrs. Harris, I do like the way you think." In a flash, he grabbed her hand and spun to lead her from the dance floor.

Well then. Looked like the honeymoon was starting early. She had no problem with that and she was nothing if not ready to ignore the fact that the bride and groom were still dashing for the door fifteen minutes after the reception started but with this plan, they'd be back in a few minutes. At least ten. Maybe once wouldn't be enough. Was married sex better than one night stand sex? Oh God, she couldn't wait to find out.

Breathlessly, she followed him, ignoring the multitudes of people who called out to them as they scouted for this hypothetical closet with a door that locked. In a true wedding day miracle, off the kitchen there was a linen closet full of spare tablecloths and empty centerpieces. No one saw them duck through the door, or at least no one who counted. They passed a member of the waitstaff who pretended he hadn't noticed their beeline through the back rooms where guests typically didn't tread. Whether it was a testament to his discretion or the fact that Hendrix and Roz were tied to powerful families, she didn't know. Didn't care.

All that mattered was the door had a lock. She shut it behind her with a click and flipped the dead bolt, plunging the room into semidarkness. Maybe there was a light but before she could reach for it, Hendrix pinned her against the door, his mouth on hers in an urgent, no-holds-barred kiss. No time to search for a light. No time to care.

Her knees gave out as the onslaught liquefied her entire body, but he'd wedged one leg so expertly between hers that she didn't melt to the ground in a big hot puddle. She moaned as his tongue invaded her mouth, heated and insistent against hers. He hefted her deeper into his body as he shifted closer.

Too many clothes. She got to work on his buttons, cursing at the intricacy of his tuxedo. Shame she couldn't just rip the little discs from the fabric but they had to reappear in public. Soon. Giving up, she pulled the fabric from his waistband so she could slide her hands under it.

Oh, yes, he was warm and his body was still drool-worthy with ridges and valleys of muscle along his abs that her fingers remembered well. He pressed closer still, trapping her hands between them, which was not going to work, so she shifted to the back as he gathered up her skirts, bunching the fabric at her waist. Instantly, she regretted not making him take the time to pull the dress off. She wanted his hands everywhere on her body, but then she forgot to care because his fingers slid beneath the white lacy thong she'd donned this morning in deference to her wedding day.

"I want to see this thong later," he rumbled in her ear as he fingered the panties instead of the place she needed him most. "It feels sexy and tiny and so good."

"It feels in the way," she corrected and gasped as he yanked the panties off, letting them fall to her ankles. She toed off the fabric and kicked it aside. She needed him back in place *now.* "Touch me. Hurry."

Fast. Hard. Frenzied. These were the things she wanted, not a speech about her undergarments. This was sex in its rawest form and she knew already that it would be good between them. She hoped it would put them on familiar ground. Eliminate confusion about what they were doing here.

"What's your rush, Mrs. Harris?" He teased her with short little caresses of his fingertips across her shoulder, down her cleavage, which ached for his attention, but had far too many seed pearls in the way for that nonsense.

"Besides the hundreds of people waiting for us?"

Her back arched involuntarily as his fingers found their way beneath the tight bodice of her dress to toy with her breasts. Heavenly heat corkscrewed through her core as he fingered her taut, sensitized nipples.

"Besides that."

"You're my rush," she ground out. "I'm about to come apart and I need your hands on me."

She needed oblivion like only he could give her, where all she could do was feel. Then it didn't matter that he was totally on board with a closet quickie for their first time together as husband and wife. Neither of them did intimacy. It was what made their marriage so perfect.

"Like this?" His hand snaked between them to palm her stomach and she wiggled, hoping to get it lower. He complied inch by maddening inch, creeping toward the finish line with a restraint more suited for a choirboy than the bad boy she knew lurked in his heart.

He'd licked her in places that had never been touched by a man. He'd talked so dirty while doing it that she could practically give herself an orgasm thinking about it. They were having sex in a closet with five hundred oblivious people on the other side of the wall and he had every bit of the skill set necessary to make it intoxicating. She needed *that* man.

"Hendrix, please," she begged. "I'm dying here."

"I've been dying for weeks and weeks," he said and she groaned as he wandered around to the back, wedging his hand between her buttocks and the door to play with flesh that certainly appreciated his attention but wasn't the part that needed him most.

Practically panting, she circled her hips, hoping he'd get the hint that the place he should be focusing on was between her thighs. "So this is my punishment for not letting you have your way with me until now?"

"Oh, no, sweetheart. This is my reward," he murmured. "I've dreamed of having you in my arms again so I could feel your amazing body in a hundred different ways. Like this."

Finally, he let his fingers walk through her center, parting the folds to make way, and one slid deep inside. Mewling because that was the only sound she could make, she widened herself for him, desperate for more instantly, and he obliged with another finger, plunging both into her slickness with his own groan.

"I could stay here for an eternity," he whispered. "But I need to—"

He cursed as she eased her way into his pants, too blind with need to bother with the zipper. Oh, yes, there he was. She palmed his hot, hard length through his underwear and it wasn't enough. "I need, too."

Urgently, she fumbled with his clothes and managed to get the buttons of his shirt partially undone, hissing as he withdrew his magic hands from her body to help. But that was a much better plan because his progress far eclipsed hers and he even had the wherewithal to find a condom from somewhere that she distinctly heard him tear open. That was some amazing foresight that she appreciated.

Then her brain ceased to function as he boosted her up against the door with one arm, notched his hard tip at her entrance and pushed. Stars wheeled across her vision as he filled her with his entire glorious length. Greedily, she took him, desperate for more, desperate for all of it, and he gave it to her, letting her slide down until they were nested so deep that she could feel him in her soul.

No.

No, she could not. That was far too fanciful for what was happening here. This was sex. Only. Her body craved friction, heat, a man's hard thrusts. Not poetry.

Wrapping her legs around him, she gripped his shoulders, letting her fingers sink into the fabric covering them because even if it left marks, who cared? They were married and no one else would see his bare shoulders but her.

He growled his approval and it rumbled through her rib cage. Or maybe that was the avalanche of satisfaction cascading through her chest because Hendrix was hers. No other woman got to see him naked. It shouldn't feel so good, so significant. But there was no escaping the fact that they were a unit now whether he liked it or not.

They shared a name. A house. Mutual goals. If he didn't like peanut butter and jelly, he should have come up with another plan to fix the scandal.

Shifting ever so slightly, he hit a spot inside her that felt so good it tore tears from her eyes. The position sensitized her to the point of madness and she urged him on with her hips as he drove them both into the stratosphere, the door biting into her back as she muffled her cries against his suit jacket, praying she wasn't smearing makeup all over his shoulder.

That would be a dead giveaway to anyone who bothered to notice. And she liked the idea of keeping this encounter secret. Their own little wedding party.

Explosion imminent, she rolled her hips until the angle increased the pressure the way she liked it. Hendrix grabbed one thigh, opening her even wider, and that was it. The orgasm ripped through her and she melted against him, going boneless in his arms until his own cry signaled his release.

He gave them both about five seconds of recovery time and then let her legs drift to the floor so they could hold each other up. Which she gladly did because he'd earned it.

"That was great for starters," she muttered against his shoulder because it felt expected that she should reiterate how hot—and not meaningful—this encounter was. "I can definitely report that took the edge off, but I'm nowhere near done."

There was so much more to explore. Best part? She could. Whenever she felt like it, since they'd be sleeping in the same bed. Married sex had a lot to recommend it.

Someone rattled the doorknob, nearly startling out of her skin.

"You have the key?" a muffled voice from the other side of the wall called.

Oh, God. They were about to be discovered.

Seven

Where was her underwear? It was so dark in here. Had she kicked them to the left? Panic drained Roz's mind and she couldn't think.

The doorknob rattled again. Whoever it was probably had no idea that the bride and groom were in the closet. But they were probably packing a cell phone with a camera. They always were.

Stuffing her fist against her mouth, Roz jumped away from the door and knelt to feel around for her panties, dress impeding her progress like a big white straitjacket for legs. Hendrix fumbled with his own clothes. His zipper shushed, sounding like an explosion in the small room. At least he'd gotten that much covered. Any photographs of this tryst would be of the dressed variety. But still not the commemorative moment they'd like captured digitally for eternity.

The door swung open, spilling light into the closet, and Roz had a very nasty flashback to a similar moment when she was twenty, with the obvious difference this time being that she was wearing a wedding dress and the man tucking in his shirt behind her had recently signed a marriage license.

Two white-coated waiters stared at her and Hendrix and she'd like to say her years of practice at being caught in less-than-stellar circumstances had prepared her for it, but it was never as easy as tossing her hair back and letting the chips fall where they may.

Besides, she refused to be embarrassed. Everything was covered. Married people were allowed to be in a locked closet without fear of judgment—or she wouldn't have bothered to go through with all of this. The wait staff was interrupting *her*, not the other way around.

She shot to her feet and it was a testament to her feigned righteous indignation at being disturbed that she didn't break an ankle as one of her stilettos hit the ground at an awkward angle.

"Um, sorry," the one on the left said, and he might as well have hashtagged it #*notsorry*.

His face beamed his prurient delight, like something naughty was showing, and she had half a moment of pure horror over not actually locating her underwear. She tugged on her skirt to make sure it wasn't caught on itself, but then Hendrix came up behind her, snaking an arm around her waist. Claiming her. They were a unit and he had her back.

She leaned into him, more grateful than she had a right to be.

"Can you give us a minute?" he said smoothly to

the interrupters and actually waited for the one waiter's nod before he shut the door in their face. Brilliant. Why hadn't she thought of that?

Hendrix flipped on the overhead light, the white lace scrap on the floor easily identifiable at that point. But instead of letting her fetch her panties, he tipped her chin up and laid a kiss on her lips that had nothing to do with sex. Couldn't. There were people outside who wanted inside this closet and they'd been busted.

"I wasn't finished, either," he murmured against her mouth by way of explanation.

She nodded, letting his warmth bleed through her via their joined lips, mystified why that sweet, unnecessary cap to their closet hookup meant so much. Eventually, he let her go and they got everything situated well enough to mix in polite company again. Hendrix reopened the door and they slipped past the waiters hand in hand.

Her husband's palm burned against hers. She couldn't recall the last time someone had held her hand, like they were boyfriend-girlfriend. Or whatever. They were married. Nothing wrong with holding hands. It was just…unexpected.

"You okay?" Hendrix said softly, pulling her to the side of the short hallway that led to the reception area. His attention was firmly on her, but before she could answer or figure out why his concern had just squished at a place inside, more people interrupted them.

Why couldn't everyone leave them alone so she could spend about a dozen hours exploring why everything with Hendrix felt so different now that she'd signed a piece of paper?

Hendrix's arm went tense under her fingers and she

turned. Her father. And Helene. They stood at the end of the short hall, varying expressions of dismay and relief spreading across their faces.

Oh, God. The very people they were trying to help with this scandal-fixing marriage. Now it was obvious to everyone that she couldn't resist Hendrix, that she had something wrong with her that made it impossible to wait for more appropriate circumstances before getting naked with the man.

"We got a little concerned when we couldn't find you," Helene said with a smile. "But here you are."

Her father didn't smile. He crossed his arms and even though he could look her in the eye when she wore stilettos, she still felt small and admonished even before he opened his mouth. Marrying Hendrix had been a last-ditch effort to do *something* her father approved of. Looked like that had been a vain effort all the way around.

"Glad to see that you're dressed," her father said and it was clear that he was speaking directly to his daughter.

The *for once* was implied and sure enough, flooded her with the embarrassment she'd managed to fight off earlier, after being discovered by wait staff. Thank God their parents hadn't been the ones to fling open that door.

"That's not really your concern any longer," Hendrix said to her father.

She did a double take. Was he sticking up for her?

"It is my concern," her father corrected. "This marriage isn't guaranteed to remove all of the social shame from the photographs. Additional fodder could still be harmful and Roz is quite good at feeding that fire."

"Still not your concern," Hendrix corrected mildly and his hand tightened around hers.

As a warning to let him handle it? She couldn't speak anyway. The knot in her throat had grown big enough to choke a hippopotamus.

"Roz is my wife," Hendrix continued. "And any bad press that comes her way is my responsibility to mitigate. She has my name now. I'll take care of her."

Okay, there might be crying in her immediate future.

"Hendrix," she murmured because she felt like she had to say something, but that was as much as her brain could manufacture.

With that, her husband nodded to his mother and swept Roz past the inquisition that should have ruined her day. Instead, Hendrix had relegated that confrontation to an insignificant incident in the hall.

How had he done that? She snuck a glance at him. "Thank you. You didn't have to do that."

He shot her an enigmatic smile. "I did so have to do that. Your father should be proud of you, not throwing you to the wolves."

"Um, yeah. He's never really appreciated my ability to keep my balance while having sex against a door."

Hendrix laughed at that, which actually made her relax for what felt like the first time all day.

"I appreciate that skill." He waggled his brows and guided her back into the reception where they were swallowed by the crowd, none of whom seemed to notice they'd been gone.

If it was at all possible to receive an indicator that she'd made the right decision in marrying Hendrix Harris, that moment with her father had been it. Half of her reason for agreeing had to do with gaining approval from a man who had demonstrated time and time again that she could not earn his respect no matter what. That possibility had been completely eliminated...only to be replaced with a completely different reality.

Her husband wasn't going to take any crap from her father.

Maybe she didn't have to, either.

And that's when she actually started enjoying her wedding day.

Despite Paul Carpenter's comments to the contrary, the wedding had apparently gone a long way toward smoothing over the scandal. The snide looks Hendrix had witnessed people shooting at Roz when they'd gone to the florist, and even to some degree during their one date, had dwindled. There were lots of smiles, lots of congrats, lots of schmoozers.

And what kind of crap was that?

It was one thing to have an academic understanding that they were getting married so that Helene Harris for Governor didn't take unnecessary hits, but it was another entirely to see it in action. Especially when he was starting to suspect that some of the issue had to do with what society perceived as his "bad taste" to have mixed it up with the wild Carpenter daughter.

He was fixing it for her. Not the other way around. What was just as crazy? He liked being her go-to guy. The dressing-down he'd given her father had felt good. No one deserved to be judged for a healthy sexual appetite when her partner was a consenting adult.

He needed to get the hell out of here and make some

wedding day memories at home, where his wife could do whatever she so desired without anyone knowing about it.

"Let's go," he growled in Roz's ear. "We've been social for like a million hours already. Everyone here can suck it."

"Including me?" Her gaze grew a hungry edge that had all kinds of appealing implications inside it, especially when she dragged it down his body. "Because coincidentally, that's exactly what I had in mind."

"Really?" His groin tightened so fast it made him light-headed.

"True story," she murmured. "Or didn't you get the memo earlier that I wasn't done?"

Wheeling, he waved at his mother and snagged Roz's hand to lead her to the limo that waited patiently for them at the curb of the North Ridge Country Club. He'd paid the wedding coordinator a hefty sum to manage the logistics of the reception; she could handle whatever came after the departure of the bride and groom.

The limo ride took far too long—a whole ten minutes, during which he kept his hands off Roz like a good boy because this time, he didn't want quick.

Slow would be the theme of his wedding night.

Except his wife smelled divine and she cuddled up next to him on the roomy leather seat, letting her fingers do some serious wandering over his lap. Strands of Roz's dark hair had pulled out of the bun-like thing at her crown, dripping down in sexy little tendrils, and all he could think about was how it had gotten that way—his fingers.

He'd like to tug on a few more strands while deep inside her.

By the time the limo pulled up to the house, which his housekeeper had lit up for their arrival, his hard-on could cut glass and his patience had started to unravel.

"Inside," he growled. "Now."

To help her along, he swept her up in his arms to carry her over the threshold because it seemed like a legit thing that people did on their wedding day. She snuggled down into his embrace, looping her arms around his neck, and then got busy testing out his ability to walk while she nibbled on the flesh near his ear. Her tongue flicked out, sending a shower of sparks down his throat, and he stumbled, catching himself immediately. Wouldn't do to drop his new wife.

"Unless you'd like our wedding night to be memorialized with a trip to the ER, I'd suggest waiting five seconds for any more of that," he advised her, which she pretty much ignored. Now that he was on to her and better able to compensate, he walked faster.

They cleared the double front door, barely, as she'd started exploring his collarbone with her lips. There was no way he was doing stairs in his current fully aroused, highly sensitized state, so he let her slide to the ground and hustled her to the second floor.

Roz beat him to the gargantuan master suite that he'd yet to christen properly. He shut the doors to the bedroom behind him. In Vegas, they'd had a strict rule that no surface would go untouched. His bedroom's decor had been pulled together by a professional and contained solid pieces stained with a shade of espresso that was so dark, it looked black. Not one Carpenter piece in the bunch, not even the woman beckoning him with a hooded, enigmatic expression that portrayed her very naughty thoughts.

Good God she was gorgeous in her white dress. She had the fullest lips that needed nothing extra to be lush and inviting. He could write poetry to her mouth for a decade. And her eyes…they did a thing where they were both transparent and mysterious all at the same time.

Would he ever get tired of her face? What if they were the kind of couple who actually stayed married on purpose, affording him the opportunity to watch her age? One day he might wake up and wonder where her looks had gone. But he didn't think so. She'd still be Roz inside and that was the part he wanted with a burning need he scarcely recognized.

And need was supposed to be his wheelhouse. When he couldn't quantify something related to sex, that was a problem. It felt too much like the intimacy that he religiously avoided.

No, the real problem was that they weren't having sex yet. Sex eliminated all of the weirdness with pure mechanics of pleasure. And while he was busy composing sonnets to his wife's beauty, she was standing there staring at him like he'd lost his mind, likely because he hadn't made a move on her yet.

Clearly, he was slightly insane. What was he waiting for?

Striding forward, he did the one thing he hadn't been able to do thus far. He spun his bride to face away from him, undid the catch on her zipper and yanked it down. The strapless dress peeled from her body, baring her back and oh, yeah, that was nice. Her spine beckoned and he bent to fuse his mouth to the ridges, working his way down until he hit the hollow above her buttocks. Laving at it, he adding some lip action until he earned a sharp little gasp from her.

This was what he'd come for. Blinding, carnal pleasure. All of the other internal noise? Not happening. The faster he got to a place where he couldn't think, the faster all of the stuff inside that shouldn't be there would fade.

That spurred him on enough to want more. Easing the dress down her hips, he pushed her gently, encouraging her to step out of it. That sexy little thong that he'd thus far only felt was indeed amazing in the light. It formed a vee down between her cheeks like an arrow pointing the way to paradise and he groaned as he recalled how much time he'd spent pleasuring her in that exact spot while in Vegas. It was worth a repeat for sure.

Falling to his knees, he slid his tongue beneath the lacy bands, following the dip down and back up again. He accompanied that with a leisurely exploration of the backs of her legs, ending with a nice tour of the covered area between her cheeks. That's when her legs started trembling, whether from excitement or exhaustion he couldn't be sure. He'd have to come back later.

Right now, his bride needed to be more comfortable. He had a lot more where that had come from.

He picked her up in his arms again and without the binding dress, it was so much easier. And more rewarding as her bare breasts were *right there* for his viewing pleasure. That was a much better place to focus his attention.

Laying her on the bed, he looked his fill as he stripped out of his own clothes, impressed that he'd found the stamina to take the time. The last sock hit the floor and the appreciation in Roz's gaze as she watched his show thoroughly stirred him.

The closet gymnastics had done nothing to take the edge off. Roz was dead wrong about that. He wanted her all over again with a fierce urgency that demanded absolute surrender.

Crawling across the mattress and up her body, he took the liberty of kissing his way to the perfect globes of her breasts, licking one bright, hard tip into his mouth. Her flesh rolled across his tongue. Divine. He sucked harder and she arched up off the bed with a tiny gasp. Not enough. Teeth against the tip, he scraped at it while plucking at the other one with his fingertips.

She felt exquisite in his hand. Silky. Excited. She pushed against his mouth, shoving her breast deeper, and he took it all, sucking her nipple against the roof of his mouth. That had driven her wild once before.

It did again. That simple movement got her thrashing under him, driving her hips against his painfully hard erection. The contact lit him up and felt so good, he ground into her stomach with tight circles. *Inside. Now.* His body was screaming for release, shooting instructions to his muscles to tilt her hips and drive to completion.

Not on the agenda. Not yet. He had to slow it down.

Grabbing her hips, he peeled away from her luscious body and kissed down the length of her stomach until he hit her thighs. That lacy thong covered her and as much as he hated to see it go, it went.

He pushed her legs open and kept going. Gorgeous. The faster he sated her, the slower he could go because she was making him insane with hip rolls that pushed her closer to him, obviously seeking relief from the fire that was licking through her veins.

Or maybe that was just him.

Her secrets spread wide, he paused just a moment to enjoy the visual, but she was having none of that.

"Put your mouth on me," she instructed throatily. "I've dreamed about your wicked hard tongue for weeks and weeks."

Oh yeah? That was enough of a compliment to spur him into action. The first lick exploded across his taste buds, earthy and so thick with her desire. For him. This was his wife, who was wet and slick *for him*. It was nearly spiritual. Why didn't they tell you the mere act of signing a piece of paper had so much significance?

That was a discovery best explored further through hands-on experience. Her juices flowed over his tongue as he drove deeper, added a finger to the party, swirled along her crease until she started bucking against his face and still she seemed to crave more.

He gave it to her, sliding a wet finger between her cheeks to toy with her while simultaneously working the nub at her pleasure center with his teeth. Her thighs clenched, and she rocked against his fingers, pushing them deeper, and then she came with a cry that vibrated through his gut.

That was not something he could possibly hear enough.

She sat up far before he would have said she'd had time to recover, pushed him free of her body and rolled him until she was on top. Looked like they were moving on. Noted. But he couldn't find a thing to complain about as she straddled his hips. She'd never taken off her white strappy stilettos and she parked one on each side of his thighs, easing her center into a place just south of where he really wanted it, but that fit with his need to go slow, so he let her.

He'd teased up a flush along her cheeks and her beautiful peaked nipples rode high on her breasts. As she stared down at him from her perch, she was the most gorgeous thing he'd ever seen, with those pursed lips and a sated sheen in her eyes that he'd been personally responsible for putting there.

He wanted to do it again. And again.

And finally, he could. He reached for her, but she shook her head, clamping her thighs tight against him as she laced his fingers with hers to draw his hands away from her body. She weighed practically nothing and it would be an easy matter to break free, but he was kind of curious what she had in mind that required him to stay still.

He found out when she released his fingers to trail her own down his torso until she reached his groin. All the breath whooshed from his lungs as she palmed him to stroke downward with one hard thrust.

Fire tore through his body in a maelstrom of need.

His eyelids flew shut as he struggled to breathe, to hold it together, to keep from exploding right there in her hand. She wasn't in a merciful mood obviously because she crawled backward to kneel over him, captured his gaze in her hot one, and licked him.

The sight of her pink tongue laving across his flesh nearly undid him. Then she sucked him fully into her mouth and he pulsed against her tongue and it was almost too much to hold back. He clawed back the release with some kind of superpower he had no idea he possessed.

Anti-Orgasm Man. He should get a T-shirt for his effort.

Except his wife had some powers of her own and worked him back into a frenzy in under a minute flat. This was going to be a very short honeymoon indeed if she didn't stop *this instant*.

"Whoa, sweetheart," he bit out hoarsely and tried to ease out from her mouth without catching his sensitized flesh on her teeth. She pushed him deeper into her throat in response, melting his bones in the process so it was really difficult to get his arms to work.

"Please," he begged as she swirled her tongue counterclockwise so fast that he felt the answering lick of heat explode outward clear to his toes. His head fell backward against the bed as his legs tensed and he genuinely had no clue what he was begging her to do— stop or keep going.

She took the decision out of his hands by purring with him deep in her mouth and the vibration was the tipping point. The release rushed through his veins, gathered at the base of his spine and pushed from his body like a tsunami, eating everything in its path. She took it all and more, massaging him to a brilliant finish that wrung him out. Spent, he collapsed back on the mattress, too drained to move.

"That was for following the rules," she told him with a smug laugh. "You deserve about ten more."

If he'd known that was the prize for proving to himself and everyone else that he could go without sex, it might have made the whole moratorium a lot easier. Without opening his eyes, he nodded. "You have my permission to proceed."

"Ha, I didn't mean right this minute."

She fell silent and the pause was so heavy that he opened his eyes. Roz was lounging on the bed between his thighs, decked out like a naked offering with one leg draped over his calf and an elbow crooked on the far side of his hip. It was the most erotic pose he'd ever seen in his life. And that was saying something considering the sizzle factor of the photograph she'd starred in.

"Thank you," she said. "For what you said to my father."

Her expression was so enigmatic, he couldn't do anything but let his own gaze travel over it in search of clues for what he should say next. *You're welcome* seemed highly lacking in weight given the catch he'd noted in her voice. Neither was this a conversation he wanted to have while in bed with a naked woman.

Except she wasn't any garden-variety naked woman that he had no plans to see again.

It was Roz. And he most definitely would be waking up with her in the morning. So many mornings that he was at a loss how to avoid the significant overtones of this kind of sex, where they were apparently going to talk about stuff between rounds of pleasure.

Maybe that was the key. He just had to move them along until they were back in a place where there was nothing but heat between them. Clearly he hadn't gotten her hot enough yet if she could still think about things outside of this room.

"Let's talk about that later, shall we?" he murmured.

The tendrils of hair around her face had increased exponentially and he itched to pull the entire mass free of its confines. So he indulged himself. Leaning up, he plucked pins from her dark hair. Slowly, he let chunks of hair fall to her shoulders, and the enigmatic, slightly guarded expression melted away.

Better. She deserved about ten more orgasms, too. Enough that she could only focus on how good he could make her feel and not the crappy stuff about her life that he had an inexplicable drive to fix for her.

"Tonight is about making up for lost time," he told her as the last pin fell free. "I thought I'd never see you again after Vegas. I can't lie. I wanted to."

Why had he blurted that out? They were supposed to be reeling back the true confessions, not throwing down more.

She blinked and let the tiniest lift of her lips register. "I'd like to say I forgot about you. I tried. Never happened."

And here they were. Married. It was something he was having difficulty reconciling in his mind when Roz fit so easily into the "hot fling" box in his head. Surely there had been a woman at some point in the past whom he'd seen more than once, but he couldn't recall the face of anyone but this one. She'd filled his thoughts so much over the past month or so that he suddenly feared he'd have a hard time getting her out when they divorced.

More sex needed, stat. Obviously. They were doing far too much chitchatting.

Reaching for her, he snagged her shoulders and hauled her up the length of his body, which went a long way toward reviving him for round two. She met him in a fiery kiss that shot sensation down his throat. Roz spread her legs to straddle him, this time hitting the exact spot he wanted her to be in, apparently on board with no more talking.

The heat built on itself instantly, putting urgency into their kisses, and the thrust of her tongue against his had sweet fire laced through it that he welcomed. This time, there was no need to go slow and he didn't waste the opportunity. Taking a half second to pull out the box of condoms he'd stashed in his bedside table in anticipation of their wedding night, he dove back onto her, rolling to put her under him so he could focus.

She needed oblivion. He could give her that. Taking her mouth in a fierce kiss, he let his hands roam over her amazing body, caressing whatever he could reach until she was moaning deep in her chest. Her blistering fingers closed around his erection, priming it, and then she reached for the condoms before he could. In what might be the hottest thing she'd done thus far, she rolled it on him, squeezing and teasing as she went, then notching him at her entrance.

He caught her gaze as he paused, savoring this moment before he plunged because it was his favorite. The anticipation built and she flexed her hips, eager for him but not taking the initiative, apparently content to let him go at his own pace.

Roz was his match in every way. The reality seeped through him as they stared at each other, their chests heaving with the exertion of holding back. And then he pushed inside and not even the feel of her mouth could match the exquisiteness of the way her silk caressed every millimeter. He sucked in a breath as she took him deeper, wrapping her legs around him to hold him inside.

The pressure and tension climbed until he had to move, to feel. Gasping, she arched against him, grazing her breasts against his torso, and that felt unbelievable, too. Sensation swirled, driving him faster and faster and she closed around him again and again, squeezing until she was crying out her pleasure. His second release built and she was still watching him, her eyes dark and sensual and so open that he fell into them, hopefully never to surface.

They exploded together and it was only as they came down, wrapped in each other's arms, that he realized that they'd done it missionary style, like a real couple. A first. He'd have said he hated that position but it had felt so right with Roz. Something warm lingered in his chest as he pushed hair out of her face. She kissed his temple and snuggled deeper into his embrace.

This was maybe the most sated he'd ever been in his life. And they hadn't even had sex that many times. Quantity had always been his goal in the past, but apparently quality trumped that. Because they'd gotten married? Because he knew they had tomorrow night and the next and the next, so he didn't have to cram all his appetites into a few hours?

Whatever it was, it felt different. He liked it. Who knew?

This was uncharted territory and he didn't quite know what to do with it. Sex hadn't decreased the intimacy quotient after all. But he'd always shied away from that because rejection wasn't something he dealt with well, or rather, more to the point, he'd never felt like finding out how well he'd deal with it.

His father had done such a thorough job of rejecting him that he'd lived most of his life with total hatred of a man he'd never met. That was what had made the pact with Jonas and Warren so easy. He had no interest in learning how much more it would hurt to be rejected by someone he'd fallen in love with. Obviously it had driven Marcus to a permanent solution. What made Hendrix so much more capable of handling the same?

The rational part of his brain kicked in. Honestly, he'd have to give a woman a chance to reject him in order to fully test that.

Had he been given an opportunity to do exactly that? Roz had been great so far in their relationship. Maybe she was the exception to the rule. Maybe he could test out having a little more with her...

He settled her a little closer, letting her warm him thoroughly, and snagged the sheet to cover them. They hadn't slept at all that night in Vegas, so this would be a first, too. Waking up with a woman had also been something he studiously avoided, but waking up with Roz held enormous appeal.

If "more" didn't work out, then they could get a divorce like they'd always planned. It was practically a foolproof experiment in something that he'd never have said he'd want but couldn't seem to stop himself from exploring.

Eight

Hendrix and Roz had opted not to go away for their honeymoon, largely because that was something real couples did. But also because Helene had already scheduled a splashy fundraiser, the biggest one of the summer, for four days after the wedding. The event was supposed to generate the majority of the money needed to push her campaign through to the election. In other words, it was a big deal.

Helene had specifically asked them to make an appearance so it didn't seem like they were hiding. *Go big or go home,* she'd said with a smile and Roz hadn't really been able to find a good argument against attending. Though she'd racked her brain for one because a big social event with plenty of opportunity for her to feel like she still wasn't good enough to be associated with the Harris name didn't sound like fun.

The afternoon of, Hendrix came home from work

early carrying a bag emblazoned with the name of an exclusive store that Roz knew only carried women's clothing. Intrigued, she eyed the bag.

"You entering a drag queen revue that I don't know about?" she asked from her perch on the lounger near the window of their bedroom. It was an enormous room in an even more enormous house that felt genuinely empty when her husband wasn't in it. Probably because it was his, not hers.

Or at least that was the excuse she kept telling herself so she didn't have to think about what it meant that she sometimes missed him. That she thought about him all day long and only some of it was sexual.

"Maybe." He waggled his brows. "Let's see if it fits."

He pulled the dress from a layer of tissue paper and held it up to his chest as she giggled over his antics. But then the dress fully unfurled, revealing what he'd picked out. Oh, God, it was gorgeous. Red, with a gold clasp at the waist that gathered the material close.

"I think it would fit me better than you," she said wryly. "Is this your subtle way of getting me excited about the idea of hanging out with North Carolina's movers and shakers?"

"Depends." He shot her an adorable smile that made her pulse beat a little strangely as the dress became the second-most-beautiful thing in the room. "Did it work?"

Oh, it worked all right, but not even close to the way he meant.

"Only if it goes with the gold shoes I have in my closet." She held out a hand for the gown because the whole thing felt inevitable. "I'll try it on. But I'm only wearing it because you picked it out."

The silk slid through her hands like water as she laid it on the couch, then stood to wiggle out of her pants and shirt. The dress was strapless on one side and came up into an elegant over-the-shoulder style on the other. It settled against her curves like it had been made for her and fell to the ground in a waterfall of red. A high slit revealed enough leg to raise some eyebrows, which she sincerely hoped Hendrix would use as a convenient way to get his hands on her during dinner.

"You look amazing," he said quietly and when she glanced at him, pride glinted from his eyes.

"You have good taste," she shot back, mystified why the compliment pleased her so much. The gift as a whole pleased her in ways she'd never have expected. No man had ever bought her clothes before. She'd never had a need for one to, nor would she have accepted such a gift from anyone else.

Sure, there was an agenda buried in the middle of his gesture. He needed her by his side at his mother's thing and now she couldn't use *I have nothing to wear* as an excuse to weasel out of it. But she didn't care. The dress fit like a dream, clearly indicating her husband paid attention to details, and the way he was looking at her made her feel desired more sharply than anything he'd done in their entire history. That was saying something.

She half expected him to reach for her, but he started chattering about something that had happened at work earlier as he stripped out of his suit, then went to take a shower. Too bad. She'd be happy to show up late but he wasn't on board with that.

The limo ride was uneventful and she started to get antsy. The wedding hadn't been too bad in terms of dirty looks and noses in the air. But she'd been the bride and it was practically a requirement that people treat her nicely on her wedding day. This fundraiser was a whole different ball game and she didn't often do this kind of society thing. For a reason.

Only for Helene would she brave it. And because Hendrix had done something so unexpected as buy her a dress.

"Nervous?" Hendrix murmured as they exited the limo. "I'll hold your hand."

"You're supposed to," she reminded him blithely. "Because we're married and making sure people are fully aware of that fact."

When he clasped her fingers in his, though, it didn't feel utilitarian. Especially when he glanced down at her and smiled like they shared a secret. "I'm also doing it because I want to."

That warmed her enormously. For about two minutes. Because that's when she saw her father. Whom she had not realized would be in attendance. Of course he'd wrangled an invitation to the premiere Helene Harris for Governor event of the season. Maybe Helene had even invited him of her own free will.

Roz's chest turned to ice.

"I wonder if there's a closet in this place," she said into Hendrix's ear with a little nuzzle. If she could entice him into a back hall, they could spend an hour there before anyone even noticed they'd arrived. Then there wouldn't be a big to-do about them disappearing, and she could get good and relaxed before braving the hypercritical looks and comments.

Hendrix smiled at a few people and snaked an arm around Roz, pulling her close. But instead of copping a feel, like she'd have laid odds on, he held her waist in a perfectly respectable fashion. "Maybe we'll look later."

"Maybe we should look now." She slid her own arm around his waist in kind, but let her hand drift south with a caress designed to remind him they were at their best when they were burning up with need for each other. Though why she had to be the aggressor in this situation, she wasn't quite sure.

Instead of shooting her a salacious grin that communicated all the naughty thoughts in his mind, he pulled her into a shadowy alcove away from the crush. Oh, this had possibilities. The area wasn't enclosed, but could be considered private. Emboldened, she slipped the button free on his tux jacket, gauging exactly how much cover it might provide if he had a mind to get handsy.

That got her a smile, but without much carnal heat laced through it. No worries. She could get him hot and bothered pretty quickly and let her fingers do some walking. But he just laced his fingers with hers and pulled them free of his body.

"Roz, come on."

That didn't sound like the precursor to a hot round of mutual orgasmic delight. "I'm trying to, but you're not helping any."

"Why do we always have to have sex in public?"

Agape, she stared at him. "I must not be doing it right if you have to ask that question."

"I'm being serious." Their fingers were still entwined and he brought one to his mouth to kiss the back of her hand tenderly. "There's no one on earth who gets me more excited than you. We're not talking about whether or not you have the ability to get me off, but why you're trying to do it in the middle of my mother's fundraiser."

Guilt put her back up. "I guess the thrill is gone. And so early in our marriage, too. I thought that didn't wear off until at least after the first year."

He rolled his eyes. "I literally just told you this is not a conversation about how much I desire you. I'm trying to figure out why you have a seemingly self-destructive need to have sex in public. That's what got us into this marriage in the first place."

So now all this was her fault? "There were two people in that hot tub, Hendrix."

"Willingly," he threw in far too fast and that pissed her off, too. "I'm not pushing blame onto you. I wasn't saying no as you pulled me into that closet at the wedding. But I am right now. Wait."

He tightened his grip on her fingers as he correctly guessed she was about to storm off to…somewhere that she hadn't quite worked out yet.

"Sweetheart, listen to me."

And she was so out of sorts that she did, despite knowing in her marrow she wasn't going to like what he had to say.

"You want me so badly that you can't wait?" he asked. "That's great. I want you like that, too. The problem is that we both use that heat as a distraction. From life, from…I don't know. Crap going on inside. Whatever it is, I don't want to do that anymore."

The earnestness in his expression, his tone, in the very stroke of his fingers over hers bled through her, catching on something so deep inside that it hurt. "I don't do that."

He didn't even have the grace to go along with the

lie. "You do. We're cut from the same cloth. Why do you think we were both so willing to go through with this marriage? We understand each other."

Oh, God. That was so true it nearly wrenched her heart from its mooring. If he made her cry, she was never going to forgive him. She'd spent *thirty minutes* on her makeup. "What are you saying?"

His smile did nothing to fix the stuff raging through her chest. "I'm saying let's take our sex life behind closed doors. Permanently. Let's make it about us. About discovering what we can be to each other besides a distraction."

"So there's no more chance of public humiliation, you mean?"

He shook his head, dashing the out she'd handed him. "No. Well, I mean, yes, of course that is a very good side benefit. But I'm talking about removing the reasons why we're both so good at creating scandals. Stop avoiding intimacy and get real with me. At home."

That was the worst idea she'd ever heard in her life. "You first."

He nodded. "I'm at the head of the line, sweetheart. Get in the queue behind me and let's do this ride the way it was intended."

Her lungs hitched. "You're not just talking about laying down a new no-sex-in-public rule. Are you?"

"I don't know what I'm talking about." He laughed self-consciously, finally releasing her fingers to run a hand through his hair. "All I know is that my mom asked me to get married so her campaign wouldn't take a hit and all I could think about was getting you into bed again. Then we made a mutual decision that sex was off the table until after the ceremony. It really made me think about who I want to be when I grow up. An oversexed player who can't control himself? I don't want to be that guy. Not with you."

Stunned, she blinked up at him but his expression didn't waver. He was serious about making changes and somehow, she was wrapped in the middle of all of it. Like maybe he wanted to be a better person because of her. That was… She didn't know what that was, had no experience with this kind of truth.

"So where does that leave us?" she whispered.

He tilted his head until their foreheads touched. "A married couple who's expected at a fundraiser. Can we get through that and then we'll talk?"

She nodded and the motion brought his head up just at the right angle to join their lips. The kiss had nothing to do with sex, nothing to do with heat. It was a sweet encapsulation of the entire conversation. A little tender, a little confused and so much better than she'd have ever dreamed.

Somehow, she floated along behind him as he led her back into the fray and the fact that they hadn't gotten naked meant something significant. Hell if she knew what. Later tonight, maybe she'd get a chance to find out.

Turned out that Roz hadn't actually needed the orgasm to relax after all. Hendrix held her hand like he'd promised and generally stuck by her side through the whole of the fundraiser. The evening wound to a close without one snide comment being wafted in her direction. Whether that was because Hendrix had studiously kept her far away from her father—a fact she couldn't help but notice and appreciate—or because the marriage had really worked to soften society's opinion toward them, she couldn't say.

Ultimately, the only thing that mattered was that she ended the evening on a high she hadn't felt in a long time. Not even sex could compete with the burst of pure gratitude racing through her veins as the limo wheeled them toward Hendrix's house. Their house. It was technically theirs, for now, as he was sharing it with her. No harm in claiming it as such, right?

"I think that was a success, don't you, Mr. Harris?" she commented as he held the door open for her to precede him.

He shut it with a resounding click. "I'm sorry, I missed everything you just said outside of 'Mr. Harris,'" he murmured and propelled her up the stairs with insistent hands on her hips.

She let him because it suited her to get to a place where they could pick up their discussion from earlier. "You like it when I call you Mr. Harris? I can do that a whole bunch more."

"I insist that you do."

Once in the bedroom he sat her down on the bed, knelt at her feet and took enormous care with removing her shoes, unbuckling the straps with painstakingly slow pulls, watching her as he did it. His gaze flickered as he finally slipped off one shoe and then the other. He lifted her arch to his mouth, kissing it sensuously.

It was such an unexpected move that something akin to nerves popped up, brewing inside until she had to say something to break the weird tension.

"We got through the fundraiser," she said. "Is this the part where we're going to talk?"

"Uh-huh," he purred against her foot and dragged his lips up her leg.

It happened to the be the one revealed by the slit that opened almost all the way to her hipbone, so he had a lot of real estate to cover. Her flesh heated under his mouth, sending an arrow of desire through her core.

"First," he said. "I'm going to tell you how absolutely wild you drive me. Are you listening?"

He nibbled at the skin of her thigh and slid a hand up the inside of her dress, exactly as she'd imagined he would—at the table while they were eating dinner. She'd envisioned it being a huge turn-on to have his hands under her dress while they were sitting there with members of high society, especially given how sanctimonious they'd all been about the photograph. And Hendrix had taken that possibility off the table and opened up a whole different world at the same time.

This wasn't a turn-on because she was putting one over on the high and mighty. It was a turn-on because of the man doing the caressing. Exactly as he'd suggested, taking their sex life behind closed doors put a sheen on the encounter that she couldn't recall ever having felt before.

"I hear you," she whispered. "Tell me more."

His fingers slid higher, slowly working their way toward the edge of her panties and then dipping underneath the hem to knuckle across her sex. She gasped as the contact sang through her, automatically widening her legs to give him plenty of access.

"Wild." He gathered her dress in one hand as he slid up the other leg to bunch the red silk at her thighs. "Do you have any concept of how difficult it was to tell you no at the fundraiser?"

"Seemed pretty easy to me," she mumbled and immediately felt like a selfish shrew. "But I'm sure it wasn't."

"No," he agreed far too graciously instead of calling her on her cattiness like he should have. "I carried around a boner for at least half the time. This dress…" He heaved a lusty sigh as he trailed a finger from the fabric gathered over her shoulder down over her breasts, which tightened deliciously from no more than that light touch. "I'm going to have to do this the right way."

"Because you have such a habit of doing it wrong?" she suggested sarcastically.

"I mean, I can't take it off. Not yet." He speared her with a glance so laden with heat and implications that her core went slick and achy instantly, even before he put his hands under the skirt and hooked her underwear, drawing off the damp scrap to toss it over his shoulder.

Pulling her to the edge of the bed, he spread her thighs and treated her to the deepest, wettest French kiss imaginable. A moan escaped her throat as he lit her up from the inside out, heat exploding along her skin as Hendrix set fire to every inch of her body. He closed his eyes as he pleasured her and she could scarcely look away from the raw need plastered all over his face.

It should be the other way around. He had his mouth on her in the most intimate of kisses, and she felt herself coming apart as she watched his tongue swirl through her folds. His fingers twined through the silk of her dress, the one he'd given her as a sweet, unexpected gift, and that gave everything a significance she scarcely understood.

The release rolled through her, made so much more powerful by the fact that he was letting her see how much she affected him. He was still telling her how wild he was over her, and she was still listening. When she came, she cried out his name, hands to his jaw because she couldn't stand not touching him as her flesh separated from her bones, breaking her into a million unrecoverable pieces.

His eyes blinked open, allowing him to witness it as she slid into oblivion and it was a horrible shame that he wasn't right there with her. She wanted that, wanted to watch him come apart with abandon.

"Make love to me," she murmured and guided his lips to hers for a kiss that tasted like earth and fire. It was elemental in all its glory and she wanted more.

He got out of his clothes fast enough to communicate how much he liked that suggestion but when he reached for her, she pulled him onto the bed in the same position she'd just been in and straddled him, still wearing the dress.

"I might never take it off again," she informed him as she settled against his groin, teasing him with her still-damp core. Hard, thick flesh met hers and she wanted him with a fierceness she could hardly contain.

He groaned as she arched her back, thrusting her covered breasts against his chest. "It feels divine."

And that was enough of a recommendation for her to keep going, exactly like this. She pulled a condom from the gathered place at her waist, which she'd stashed there earlier in hopes of finding a closet at the fundraiser, but this was far better.

His gaze reflected his agreement, going hot with understanding as he spied the package in her fingers.

"I see you attended the fundraiser fully prepared to go the distance."

"Yeah. But it's okay. This is exactly the way our evening was supposed to go." How he'd converted her, she still didn't know. But it sure felt like how this ride should be experienced. If it wasn't, she didn't want to know about it.

Condom in place, she slid down until they were joined and he was so deep inside that there was no room for anything else. He captured her gaze and held it for an eternity, even as he slid his arms around her to hold her tight. It was the most intimate position she'd ever been in with another human being and it was so beautiful her heart ached.

And then it got even better as they moved in tandem in a sensuous rolling rhythm unlike anything she'd ever felt. Her head tipped back as she rode the wave of sensation and Hendrix fused his mouth to her throat, suckling at her skin. He murmured things against it, telling her how much he liked the way she felt, how sexy she was. The pretty words infused her blood, heightening the experience.

The release split through her body almost before she'd realized it was imminent. It was quieter, deeper than the first one. More encompassing. She let it expand, grabbing on to the sensation because it was something she wanted to savor. Hendrix's expression went tense with his own release and he drew it out with a long kiss, perfectly in sync with her in a way she knew in her bones would never have happened if they'd banged each other in a closet.

This was something else, taking their relationship to the next level.

He picked her up and set her on her feet so he could finally remove the dress and then gathered her into his arms to lay spoon style under the covers. She didn't resist, couldn't have. She wanted all of this to be as real as it felt, but as she lay there in the dark listening to her husband breathe, her eyes refused to stay closed.

None of this was going to last. She'd forgotten that in the midst of letting Hendrix prove they could have a closed-door relationship. She'd forgotten that their marriage had become intimate long before they'd signed any papers and she'd let herself get swept away in the beauty he'd shown her.

She did use sex as a distraction, as an avoidance tactic. Because she hadn't wanted to be in this position. Ever. But she'd let him change the dynamic between them.

They were still getting a divorce. She *couldn't* forget that part because it was the theme of her life.

She lost everything important to her eventually and Hendrix fell into that category just as much as anything else. This wasn't the start of a new trend. Just the continuation of an old one that was destined to break her heart.

Nine

Helene made a rare appearance at the office, bringing a huge catered lunch with her that the employees all appreciated. Hendrix let her have her fun as the company still had her name on it even though she'd transitioned the CEO job to him long ago. As the last of the potato salad disappeared from the break room and the employees drifted back to their desks, Hendrix crossed his arms and leaned back on the counter to contemplate his mom.

"What gives?" he asked with a chin jerk at the mostly decimated spread. "You get a large donation or something?"

Her lips curved into the smile that never failed to make him feel like they were a team. At last, it seemed like they were back on solid ground again.

Sure, she smiled at everyone, because she had the sunniest personality of anyone he'd ever known, but she was still his mom no matter what and he valued their bond more than he could explain.

"Paul Carpenter dumped five million in my lap. You didn't have anything to do with that, did you?"

He shrugged, wishing he could say it was an act of generosity and that she shouldn't read anything into it, but odds were good the donation came with strings. Carpenter had another think coming, if so. Having the billionaire as a father-in-law hadn't checked out like he'd expected. It chafed something fierce to have his hopes realized of being aligned with a powerful old money family, only to find out the patriarch was an ass.

"Not even close. I don't like how he treats Roz. If you recall, I might have given him that impression the last time we spoke at the wedding."

"Well, he's not the only one with a giving soul. The fundraiser was a huge success. I came by to thank you for hanging out with us old people."

Hendrix snorted. The day Helene could be described as old had yet to come. She had boundless energy, a magnanimous spirit and could still give women half her age a run for their money. "You're only seventeen years older than me, so you can stop with the old business. And you're welcome."

"You know what this means, right?" Helene eyed him curiously. "Your marriage to Roz worked to smooth over the scandal. My approval ratings are high. Seems like you did it. I don't know how to say thank you for this enormous sacrifice you made for me."

He grinned to cover the slight pulse bobble at what his mother was really saying—he and Roz had

reached their goal much faster than originally anticipated. Her speech had all the hallmarks of what you
said as something was winding down. And he did not
want to think of his marriage that way. "It was really
my pleasure."

His mom stuck her fingers in her ears in mock ex-
asperation. "I don't want to know. This time, keep your
sex life to yourself."

"I'm trying." And it was working well. So well, he
could scarcely believe how easily he'd slid deeper into
his relationship with Roz. They fit together seamlessly
and it was nearly too good to be true. Far too good to
be talking about ending it already. "I really like her."

God, was he fourteen again? He was an adult who
could surely find a better way to describe how his insides got a little brighter at the mere thought of his wife.
But what was he supposed to say about the woman he
woke up to every morning? Or about how he hadn't
yet figured out why his marriage *wasn't* making him
run screaming for the hills?

"I can tell," his mom said lightly. "I'm headed to see
her next. You wanna come with me?"

His eyebrows shot up automatically. "You're going
to see Roz?"

Helene and his wife weren't having lunch any longer
even though he'd told Roz repeatedly that it was fine
if she built a friendship with Helene. He still felt like
he'd nipped that relationship in the bud prematurely.
It didn't sit well and if they were mending the fences
he'd knocked down, he definitely didn't want to get
between them again.

"I am," she confirmed. "I can't put off my promise

to her any longer and still sleep at night. So I'm doing the clown thing. Full makeup and all."

"The press will eat it up," he promised and she nodded her agreement.

"Yes, I'm counting on it. It should be quite a circus, no pun intended."

He laughed, glad that despite the many other changes that had been forced on them over the years, they could still hang out and crack jokes with each other. He'd never censored one word to his mother and she was the one person he could be completely real with.

Well, not the only one. He could be real with Roz. He'd never censored anything he'd said to her either, a first. Usually he watched what he said to women because who wanted to give false expectations? But his relationship with Roz required absolute honesty from the get-go and it was a facet of their relationship he hadn't fully appreciated until now.

Tomorrow if he woke up and knew with certainty that he was done, he just had to announce it was time to file for divorce and she'd say okay. It was freeing to know he never had to pull punches with the woman he was sleeping with.

Not so freeing to be contemplating the fact that he'd practically been handed permission to bring up that divorce. He wasn't ready to think about that. They hadn't been married that long and surely Helene would want them to see this thing through a little while longer. Just to be absolutely certain that a divorce wouldn't undo all the good they'd done already.

"I have to admit, I'm intrigued by the whole clown idea," he told her. "But I have that presentation on restructuring the supply chain and I need to do a thorough sweep of the warehouse like I've been threatening to do for weeks."

Helene wrinkled her nose. "That sounds boring."

"Because it is. Being the CEO isn't all curly wigs and water-squirting flowers." Neither was being a political candidate, but she knew he was kidding.

"That's the benefit of being the boss," she reminded him and pushed him ahead of her out of the break room where his admin had started cleaning up the leftover boxes. "You can leave the boring stuff for another day and come watch me be a clown. It's for a good cause. And it's an opportunity to be seen with your lovely bride in a stellar photo op where everyone will not only be dressed but overdressed."

Seeing Roz in the middle of the day for no other reason than because he wanted to held enormous appeal that he chose not to examine too closely. And it was coupled with an opportunity to see what she did on a daily basis unobtrusively. He did have a certain curiosity about her charity. Because...*clowns*. It was such a strange thing to be passionate about.

"Sold." He buttoned his suit jacket. "Let me—"

"Not one foot in your office or you'll never emerge." Helene looped an arm through the crook of his elbow and tugged. "Ride with me in my car. We'll drop you off back here to get your car later."

And that was how he found himself at Carolina Presbyterian Hospital with his mother in clown makeup. The children's ward was a lively place, if not a little depressing. Easy to see why clowns might make the whole thing a tiny bit less awful. God willing, he'd never have to personally empathize with what these families were going through. He made a mental note to write Roz a check, which he should have done a long time ago.

He snuck a glance at Roz from the corner of his eye as he lounged in the spot he'd reserved for himself, which was well out of the way, yet afforded him a front-row seat for the show. His wife was gorgeous, focused and quite possibly the tensest he'd ever seen her, including the time they'd braved the florist, their wedding reception and, his least favorite, the encounter with her father in the hall after nearly being caught with their pants down.

Either she didn't like that he'd accompanied his mother or she was worried that something was going to go wrong with this once-in-a-lifetime opportunity to get buzz for her charity.

While Helene entertained the kids with stuffed animals she'd carried into the hospital in a big bag, Hendrix edged toward Roz, who had yet to acknowledge his existence. Not that he was nursing a teeny bit of hurt over that or anything.

"Hey," he murmured, mindful of the two separate news crews that were covering the gubernatorial candidate's foray into the world of therapy clowning, a thing he'd had no idea had a name, but apparently did.

"Hey." Her mouth pinched back into a straight line that he immediately wanted to kiss away.

Definitely tense and dang it if it wasn't on the tip of his tongue to suggest they find a closet somewhere because she was wound tight. But they weren't *that couple* any longer. For a reason. So he'd have to handle his wife's tension verbally. "You have a problem with me being here?"

"What?" She glanced at him and then immediately flicked her gaze back to Helene. "No. I don't care. It's a free country."

Which was the kind of thing you said when you *did* care but hadn't planned on letting anyone else in on the secret.

"Your shoes are too tight?" he guessed but she didn't smile at the joke.

"This is a big deal, Hendrix. I'm allowed to be nervous."

The sarcasm lacing the edge of her words was pure Roz, but he'd spent far too much time in her company to accept her comment as pure truth. She wasn't nervous. Tense, yes. But it wasn't nerves.

And like what had happened at their engagement party, he was nothing if not painfully aware that he could read her so easily because he was paying attention to *her*, not how best to get under that severe suit she'd donned like armor.

"She's doing fine," he told her with a nod toward his mom. "Come get some coffee with me."

Roz shot him another side-eyed glance, as if afraid to take her gaze off Helene for one second. "I can't leave. This is my charity on the line."

"On the line?" he repeated. "Like if Mom does the wrong thing, it's all going to collapse? You know no one is going to stop letting you do clowns just because she fails to make one of the kids smile, right?"

Her shoulders rolled back a couple of times as if she couldn't find a comfortable stance. "Maybe not. But maybe it's all going to collapse for other reasons."

That wasn't the fierce Rosalind Carpenter he knew. "If it does, that's not on you."

"It is," she hissed back under her breath. "Why do you think I needed your mother in the first place? Not because I thought kids would like to meet the woman who may be the governor by January."

"Will be," he corrected automatically because there was no way Helene was going to fail to reach her goal, not if he had anything to say about it. After all, he'd signed a marriage license to ensure that his mom got to move into the Governor's Mansion. The fact that his marriage had become so much more still wasn't something he had a handle on. "Why don't you clue me in on why Helene is really here if it's not to bring joy to some sick kids?"

Roz's eyes snapped shut and her chest heaved a couple of times through some deep breaths. "Actually, coffee would be good."

Despite being certain she'd found yet another avoidance tactic since she couldn't use sex, he nodded once and put a hand to her waist to guide her out of the room. After all, coffee had been his suggestion, but not because he'd intended to give her an out. It was a little uncomfortable to realize that while he might not be censoring his words with her, that didn't mean she was returning the favor.

And he wanted to know what was swirling beneath her skin. He wanted to know *her*. They might be on the downslide, but he couldn't contemplate letting her go, not right now. There was still too much to explore here.

Instead of taking her to the cafeteria where the coffee would be weak and tepid, he texted his driver to hit the Starbucks on the corner, then found the most private corner in the surprisingly busy children's ward.

He let Roz choose her seat and then took the opposite one.

She stared out the window, and he stared at her. The severe hairstyle she'd chosen pulled at her lush features, but nothing could change the radiance that gave her such a traffic-stopping face. When he'd left her this morning, she'd still been in bed, her long dark hair tumbling over her shoulders the way he liked it.

But he didn't think she'd appreciate it if he pulled the pins free right here in the middle of the hospital. "Coffee's on its way."

She nodded. "Thanks. I need it."

"This is the conversation you want to have?"

Her mouth tightened. "I didn't want to have a conversation at all."

"But you needed the air," he guessed and her wince said he'd called it in one. "Roz, I'm not going to bite. If you want to talk to me, I'm not going anywhere. But if you don't, then let's sit here while you collect yourself. Then we'll go back and do clowns with no one the wiser that you had an anxiety attack or whatever."

Her double take was so sharp, it should have knocked her off the chair. "Anxiety attack? Is that what it looked like? Could you tell I was mid-freak-out? Oh, God. Did any of the cameras pick it up? They did. Of course they did. They're all over the place and—"

"Sweetheart, you need to breathe now." He gathered up both her hands in his and held them in his lap, rubbing at her wrists as he racked his brain for information about what he'd accidently triggered with his random comment. "Breathe. Again. Roz. Look at me."

She did and no, he hadn't imagined the wild flare of her irises a moment ago. Something had her spooked.

But she was breathing as instructed, though the death grip she had on his hands would leave a mark, particularly where her wedding rings bit into his index finger. Didn't matter. He didn't have any intention of letting her go.

His driver appeared with two lattes, set them on the table and vanished quickly. Hendrix ignored the white-and-green cups in favor of his alternately white-and-green wife, who, if he didn't miss his guess, might actually be about to lose her lunch.

"Um…" How did you go about delicately asking your wife if she had a positive test result to discuss? "Are you feeling faint? Do I need to call a doctor?"

What if she *was* pregnant? A thousand different things flashed through his head in an instant. But only some of them were of the panicked variety. Some weren't that unpleasant. Some were maybe even a little bit awed and hopeful.

"Oh, God, no!" she burst out. "Please don't bother anyone. I'm fine."

"Of course you are," he murmured and rubbed at her wrists again. "But maybe you could give me a little more to go on as to why we're sitting here in the corner not drinking the hot coffee that I got for us?"

She slipped a hand from his before he was ready to lose the contact and palmed her cup, sipped at the contents and shot him a fake smile. "See? Drinking."

"See?" He waved a hand in front of his face. "Still sitting here in the dark about what's going on with you. Roz, we're married. I've touched you in the most intimate places. I've done more illicit, dirty, sinful things with you than with anyone else in my life. You fell asleep in my arms last night. What is all of that but a demonstration of trust? There is nothing you can say to me that would change—"

"I'm afraid of clowns."

Oh, God. Now it was out there and Roz had nowhere to hide. She'd blurted out her deepest secret and even worse, she'd done it in the middle of Helene's shot in the arm for Clown-Around.

Hendrix wasn't laughing. He should be. There was nothing scary about clowns. Especially not when it was her mother-in-law underneath the makeup. Geez, she'd half thought seeing Helene all dressed up would be the magic bullet to fix all of the crazy going on inside that had only gotten worse the more Roz forced herself to be around the source of her fear.

"Okay." Hendrix's beautiful eyes flashed as he removed the coffee from her grip and recaptured her hand. As if he knew that holding her in place was something she desperately needed but didn't know how to ask for. "That's not what I thought you were going to say."

"No, probably not." Her mouth twisted into a wry smile designed to disguise the fact that she wished she could cry. "I wasn't expecting me to say it, either. It's dumb, I know."

He shook his head fiercely. "No. What's dumb is that you're holding all of it inside when I'm here. Tell me what I can do, sweetheart."

That's when her heart fluttered so hard that there was no way it could possibly stay behind her rib cage. *Now* she was feeling light-headed and like she might need a doctor to fix whatever he'd just broken inside her.

"Hold my hand," she mumbled because what else was she supposed to say when his impassioned statements might loosen her tear ducts after all?

"I am. I'm not going to stop."

He wouldn't, either. Because he was Hendrix Harris, the hero of her story, who stood up to her father and had such a good relationship with his mother that he'd willingly marry the wild Carpenter daughter with seemingly nothing to personally gain from it. In bed, he worshipped Roz. Out of it, he talked her down. He was everything she'd never have said she wanted—but did—and that was pushing buttons inside that weren't meshing well with clowns.

But at least she didn't feel like she was standing on the edge of a mile-high cliff any longer, legs about to give out as the darkness yawned at her feet. She could breathe. Thanks to Hendrix.

"I started Clown-Around because I needed to stop being afraid." He didn't blink as she blurted out her second-biggest secret, and he didn't interrupt with a bunch of advice on how to fix it. "I really thought it was going to work."

"Facing your fears is a good step," he agreed and shut his mouth expectantly, as if to indicate this was still a conversation and it was her turn again. He was good at that and she didn't mistake it as anything other than a skill.

That or he was just good at being with *her*, and she might appreciate that even more.

It was the thing she clung to as she spilled out the story of her eight-year-old self missing an entire semester of school because no one could figure out how to tell her she wasn't allowed to sit at the bedside of her dying mother.

At first, they'd tried. Her nanny would drive her to school, only to get a call from the headmistress that Roz had snuck out again. Fortunately, her father had found her at the hospital before the police had gotten involved, but his mandate that she not try that trick again had only fueled her need to both defy him and spend time with her mother. Sneaking out of school became great practice for later, when she did it to hang out with boys nearly twice her age.

As she recalled all of it for Hendrix, she didn't leave any of it out, especially not the ugly parts because he deserved to know what was going on with her, as he'd asked to.

"She was so sick," Roz recalled, not bothering to wipe the stream of tears that finally flowed. They'd just be followed by more. "The chemo was almost worse than the cancer and they'd come to get her for the treatments. I wouldn't let her go. There were these clowns."

She shuddered involuntarily, but Hendrix didn't say anything, just kept rubbing a thumb over the pulse point of her wrist, which was oddly comforting.

"Every day, I imagined that I was helping draw all the poison from her body when I sat by her bedside and held her hand. But they wouldn't let me go with her to the treatments and when she came back, it was like they'd sucked a little more of her life away."

Verbalizing all of this was not helping. If anything, the absolute terror of it became that much fresher as she relived how the two clowns wrenched her hand out of her mother's, with their big fake smiles and balloon animal distractions. They'd been employed by the hospital administration to keep her out of the way as the staff tried to care for her mother. She knew that as a rational adult. But the associations in her head with clowns and the way her mother slipped away more and more each day—that association wasn't fading like the psychologists had said it would.

"And now you know the worst about me," she informed him blithely.

Instead of responding, he dashed away the tears from her cheeks with one thumb, still clinging to her other hand as promised. His strength was amazing, and definitely not a quality she'd have put on her top twenty when it came to men. It was a bonus, particularly since he had twenty out of twenty on the list of what she'd have said would embody her perfect man.

What was she going to do with him?

Divorce him, most likely. Her heart lurched as she forced herself to accept the reality that all of his solid, quiet strength, the strength that was currently holding her together, wasn't permanent. She didn't get to keep things. The clowns were a great big reminder of that, one she needed to heed well.

"So what you're telling me is," he drawled, "that the worst thing about you is that you went through an incredibly traumatic series of events as a child and clowns were in the middle of it. And now they freak you out. Stop me when I get to the part where I'm supposed to cast the first stone."

She rolled her eyes. Miraculously, the fact that he was cracking jokes allowed her to reel back the emotion and take a deep breath. "Yeah, okay. It's not on the same level as adultery. But it's still real and scary and—"

"Something we need to deal with," he cut in, his

gaze heavy on her with sympathy and tenderness. "And we will. You know what most people do with fears? They run really fast in the other direction. You started an extremely worthwhile charity while trying to deal with *your* fear. I don't think I've ever been more impressed with a human being in my life than I am with you right now."

Okay, not so much with reeling back the emotions then. The tears started up again as she stared at him. "It's not working, though, in case you missed that part."

He shook his head. "Doesn't matter. We'll try something else. What matters is that you're amazing and you can't erase that by throwing down your failures."

She hadn't done anything special. But he had. She felt hollowed out and refilled all at the same time, and Hendrix was the reason. That scared her more than anything else that had happened today. "I don't think I can go back in there."

Which wasn't the biggest issue but the only one that she could reasonably be expected to address at this point. It was also the most critical.

Nodding, he squeezed her hand. "That makes sense. The problem is that you want to."

How did he see the things inside her so clearly? It was as frustrating as it was extraordinary. It meant that she needed to watch herself around him. If she wasn't careful, he'd pick up on the way her insides were going mushy as he sat with her in the corner of the children's ward holding her hand when he had a multimillion-dollar business to run.

"The problem is that I need to," she corrected. "This is my charity. Your mother is helping me enormously by bringing credibility to my organization."

And it was doubtful she needed to explain that her credibility was lacking. He understood how scandals affected everything—regardless of whether you deserved it—far better than anyone else in her life.

"Here's an idea," he said casually. "Why don't you be a clown?"

"Say what?" But she'd heard him and the concept filtered through all the angst and fear and found a small snippet of reason, latching onto it with teeth. "You mean with makeup and everything?"

"Sure." He shrugged. "Maybe you haven't been able to fix your fear because you're too far away. You can't just get near your fears. You need to be inside them, ripping the things to shreds, blasting them apart internally."

"Oh, sure, because that's what you do?"

The sarcasm didn't even faze him. He cocked his head and stared straight down into her soul. "Married you, didn't I?"

Before she could get the first of many questions out around the lump in her throat, one of Helene's staffers interrupted them, shattering the intensely intimate moment. Good. They'd gotten way too deep when what she should be doing is creating distance. The last thing she wanted to hear was how freaked he'd been to lose his independence and how great it was that he had an imminent divorce to keep his fears of commitment at bay. It wasn't hard to imagine a player like Hendrix Harris with a little calendar in his head where he ticked off the days until he could shed his marriage.

It was *very* hard, however, to imagine how she'd handle it when that day came. Because losing him was a given and the longer this dragged on, the harder it was going to be to keep pretending she wasn't falling for him—which meant she should do herself a favor and cauterize the wound now.

Ten

Hendrix didn't get a chance to finish his conversation with Roz. Helene's stint as a clown ended faster than anyone would have liked when one of the patients took a scary turn for the worse. Hospital personnel cleared the area and a calm but firm nurse assured Helene that someone would update her on the little boy's status as soon as they knew something.

A somber note to end the day. Hendrix couldn't stop thinking about how short life was, the revelations Roz had made about her childhood and how to pick up their conversation without seeming insensitive. But his own fears that he'd mentioned were as relevant now as they had been before he'd agreed to this marriage.

Even so, he wanted to take a chance. With Roz. And he wanted to talk about how rejection wasn't something he handled well, air his fears the same way she had.

But she insisted that he go back to the office with his mom so she could take her car to Clown-Around's tiny storefront and finish some paperwork. He wasn't dense. He'd given her a lot to think about and she wanted to be alone. What kind of potential start to a real marriage would it give them if he pushed her into a discussion before she was ready?

Distracted, he went back to work but he couldn't concentrate, so he drove home early. The expressway was a mess. Bumper-to-bumper traffic greeted him with nothing but red taillights. Of course. Probably because he wasn't supposed to go home.

It didn't matter anyway. By the time he got there, Roz wasn't home yet. He prowled around at loose ends, wondering when the hell his house had turned into such a mausoleum that he couldn't be there by himself. He'd lived here alone for years and years. In fact, it was extremely rare for him to bring a woman home in the first place. Roz had been unique in more ways than one.

By the time Roz finally graced him with her presence, he'd eaten a bowl of cereal standing up in the kitchen, chewed the head off of his housekeeper because she'd dared suggest that he should sit at the empty dining room table, and rearranged the furniture in the living room that he'd used one time in the past year—at his engagement party.

In other words, nothing constructive. He had it bad and he wasn't happy about it.

Her key rattled in the lock and he pounced, swinging the door wide before she could get it open herself. Cleary startled, she stood on the doorstep clutching the key, hand still extended.

"I was waiting for you," he explained. Likely she'd

figured that out given his obvious eagerness. "You didn't say you'd be late."

A wariness snapped over her expression that wasn't typically part of her demeanor. "Was I supposed to?"

"No. I mean, we don't have that kind of deal, where you have to check in." Frustrated all at once for no reason, he stepped back to let her into the house. "You weren't late because of me, were you?"

She shook her head. "You mean because of our earlier conversation? No. You gave me advice that I appreciated. I appreciate a lot of things about you."

Well, if that didn't sound like a good segue, he didn't know what would. "I appreciate a lot of things about you, too. On that note, my mother told me earlier today that things are looking really good for her campaign. She thinks the marriage did exactly what it was supposed to."

Roz swept past him to head for the stairs, scarcely even pausing as she called over her shoulder, "That's great."

A prickle of unease moved down his spine as he followed her, even though he probably shouldn't. She'd come home late and didn't seem to be in a chatty mood. He needed to back off, but he couldn't help himself. This conversation was too important to wait.

"It is. It means that everything we hoped this marriage would do is happening. Has happened. Her donations are pouring in. She helped your charity, and while I guess we don't know the results of that yet—"

"It was amazing," she said flatly and blew through the door of the bedroom to sink onto the bed, where she removed her shoes with a completely blank expression on her face. "I had calls from three different hospitals looking to form long-term partnerships. Helene's already agreed to do a couple more go-rounds for me."

"Wow, that sounds...good?" Her tone had all the inflection of a wet noodle, so he was flying blind.

"Yeah, it's good." She shut her eyes for a beat, pointedly not looking at him. "Things are going well for her. She told me that too when I called her. So we should probably talk about our exit strategy. It may be a little premature, but it's coming faster than I'd assumed and I'd really like to get started on it."

Exit strategy? "You mean the divorce?"

The word tasted nasty in his mouth as he spit it out. It reverberated through his chest, and he didn't like the feeling of emptiness that it caused. A divorce was not what he wanted. Not yet. Not before he'd figured out how to step through the minefield his marriage had become. He couldn't fathom giving up Roz but neither did he want to come right out and say that. For a lot of reasons.

The pact being first and foremost. It weighed so heavy on his mind that it was a wonder his brain wasn't sliding out through his nose.

She glanced up at him for the first time since walking through the door. "I was thinking it might be safe for me to move back to my loft. I miss it. This house is nice but it's not mine, you know?"

He nodded even though he didn't know. Hell, if she'd wanted to live at her loft while they were married, he would have accommodated that. They'd chosen his house for their marital experiment because it had historical significance and there was a possibility they'd do a lot of entertaining.

That possibility still existed. This conversation was

extremely premature, in fact. They couldn't get a divorce tonight.

But all at once, he wasn't sure that was his biggest problem. The divorce was merely symbolic of what was happening faster than he could wrap his hands around—the end of his marriage. "You're thinking of moving back to your loft soon?"

She shrugged. "Maybe tomorrow. No one is really paying attention to us anymore now that we're a respectable married couple. It would hardly raise eyebrows if anyone realized I didn't live here anymore."

"It might." The first tendrils of panic started winding through his chest. Roz was already halfway out the door and he hadn't had one second to sort through what he hoped to say in order to get her to stay. "I think it would be a mistake to split up too early. We might still be called on to attend one of my mother's functions. It would look weird if we weren't there as a couple."

"I don't know." Roz rubbed at her forehead again as if this whole conversation was giving her a headache. "I got the impression from your mother everything was fine. Maybe I don't need to be there."

Maybe I need you there.

But he couldn't force his tongue to form the words. What if she said too bad or laughed? If she really cared about him the way he cared about her, she wouldn't have even brought up the divorce. She'd have left that conspicuously out of the conversation. For the first time, she wasn't so easy to read and he was definitely paying attention to *her*, not her panties.

He'd had enough practice at it over the course of their engagement and marriage that it was second nature now to shove any physical needs to the back-

ground while he focused on what was happening between them. He didn't need the ache in his chest to
remind him that what was happening had all the hallmarks of the end.

Because he'd taken public sex off the menu of their
marriage? Surely not. The ache in his chest intensified
as he contemplated her. What a not-so-funny paradox
that would be if he'd ruined their relationship by attempting to remove all possibility of scandal. Actually,
that was irony at its finest if so. They had a marriage
built on sex. Only. Just like he would have sworn up
and down was perfect for him. Who wouldn't want
that? He was married to a hot woman that he got to
sleep with at night. But apparently that wasn't enough
for her to stick around.

What would be? The continued irony was that he
wasn't even talking to her about that. Couldn't even
open his mouth and say *I'm falling for you*.

If he didn't use the word *love* in that sentence, he
wasn't breaking the pact, right?

He was skating a fine line between a mutual agreement to end an amicable fixer marriage and laying his
heart on the line for her to stomp all over it—and the
way this was going, the latter felt like more and more
of a possibility.

That couldn't happen if he didn't let on how this
conversation had the potential to rip him to shreds.

"We don't have to get divorced right away. What's
the hurry? Why not let it ride for a while longer," he
said casually as if his entire body wasn't frozen.

She blinked at him. "What would be the point?"

What indeed? All at once, the ache in his chest grew
way too strong to bear. Wasn't she the slightest bit sad

at the thought of losing what was great about them? The parts that were great were really great. The parts that were bad were…what? There *were* no bad parts. So what was her hurry?

"Because we enjoy each other's company and like the idea of being married?"

She recoiled. "You mean sex."

"Well, sure." Too late, he realized that was probably not the smartest thing to say as her expression closed in. "Not solely that."

But of course she knew as well as he did that sex was what they were both good at. What they'd started their relationship with. What else was there?

The black swirl in his gut answered that statement. There was a lot more here—on his side. But she didn't seem overly interested in hearing about that, nor did she jump up in a big hurry to reciprocate with declarations of her own about what elements of their marriage she might wish could continue.

"I can't, Hendrix," she said simply.

And without any elaboration on her part, his world fell apart.

It was every bit the rejection he'd been so careful to guard against. The only saving grace being that she didn't know how much those three words had sliced through all of his internal organs.

It wasn't Roz's fault that he'd hoped for something legit to come out of this marriage and ended up disillusioned. It was his. And he had to step into the role she'd cast for him whether he liked the idea of being Rosalind Carpenter's ex-husband or not.

It was fine. He still had a decade-long friendship with Jonas and Warren that wasn't in any danger. That was the place he truly belonged and it was enough. His ridiculous need for something real and legitimate with Roz was nothing but a pipe dream.

They didn't talk about it again, and neither did they settle back into the relationship they'd had for that brief period after the wedding. Hendrix hated the distance, he hated that he was such a chicken, hated that Roz didn't seem overly upset about any of it. He moped around until the weekend, when it all got very real.

While Roz packed up her clothes and personal items, Hendrix elected to be somewhere other than the house. He drove around Raleigh aimlessly and somehow ended up at his mother's curb on Cowper Drive, where she lived in a gorgeous house that he'd helped her select. It was Saturday, so odds were good that she was at some event cutting a ribbon or kissing some babies as she rallied the voters. But he texted her just in case and for the first time in what felt like a long while, fate smiled on him. She was home.

He rang the doorbell. Brookes, the head of his mother's security, answered the door. Hendrix nodded at the man whom he'd personally vetted before allowing him anywhere near Helene. Brookes had checked out in every way. On more than one occasion, Hendrix had wondered if there was something a little more than security going on between Brookes and his mom, but she'd denied it.

Given his reaction when Helene and Roz had lunch, he wouldn't have handled sharing his mother in that respect very well, either. He made a mental note to mention to his mother that he'd recently become aware that he was a selfish crybaby when it came to anyone intruding on his territory, and that maybe she should think about dating anyway despite her son's shortcomings.

"Hey, you," his mother called as she came out of her study wearing a crisp summer suit that had no wrinkles, a feat only someone as stylish as Helene could pull off. "I've got thirty minutes before I have to leave for brunch. Unless you want to be my plus one?"

He shrugged. What else did have to do besides watch the best thing that had ever happened to him walk out of his life? "I could do worse."

Her brows drew together as she contemplated him. "What's wrong, sweetie?"

"Why does something have to be wrong?"

She flicked a subtle hand at Brookes, who vanished into the other room. "Not that I don't enjoy seeing you, but when you come by on a Saturday and start talking about a date with your mother like it's a good thing, I'm concerned. Spill it. Did you have a fight with Roz?"

"No fight." There would have to be a difference of opinion for there to be a fight and he'd agreed with every word she'd said. There was no point to continuing this farce of a marriage. "You said yourself that things were fine with your campaign. You even went out of your way to tell us both that. So what else would be the natural conclusion to a fixer marriage but a fast, no-fault divorce once the problem is fixed?"

Besides, he was pretty sure the black swirl in his gut that wouldn't ease meant he'd been right all along to never have a woman in his bed twice. Better all the way around not to fight Roz on her insistence that it was over. What was he supposed to do, open himself up for exactly the same kind of rejection that had devastated Marcus?

His friends wouldn't have an ounce of sympathy for him either, not after he'd violated the pact. Jonas at least might have had some understanding if Hendrix had managed to find someone who loved him back like Jonas had. Warren wouldn't even let him get the first sentence out and would get started on his own brand of rejection. Hendrix would be dealing with Roz's evisceration *and* lose his friends.

Thankfully, he hadn't even tried.

His mother cocked her head. "So, what? You're done with Roz and thought you'd hang out with your mom for the rest of your life?"

"Sure. What's wrong with that?"

He and his mother were a unit. The real kind. Maybe not peanut butter and jelly, but better because they'd been there for each other over the years when neither of them had anyone else. His mom would never reject him.

Nor did she have a life of her own with someone great who took care of her. Guilt swamped him as he wondered if he had something to do with that.

"For a Harris, you're being a moron," she said coolly. "I told you and Roz that my campaign was fine because I wanted to take that out of the equation."

"Well, congrats. You did and now we have no reason to be married. What else would you have expected to be the outcome of that?"

"A marriage, Hendrix. A real one. I didn't come up with the idea of you marrying Roz *solely* to save my campaign. It was a great benefit and I genuinely appreciate it. But I want to see you happy. She's it for you, honey. I could see it in the photograph."

"What you saw was chemistry," he countered flatly before the hopeful part inside could latch onto the idea that he'd missed something crucial in this whole messy scenario. "We have it. In spades. But there's nothing else there."

"That's ridiculous. You might have figured out a way to lie to yourself, but I have thirty years of practice in reading you. I saw you two together. I listened to Roz talk about you. There's more."

On *his* side. Sure. Not hers.

"Doesn't matter," he growled. "She's out. She told me straight to my face that it was over. Unless you're suggesting that I should resort to chaining her up in the basement, I have to accept that it's indeed over. I wasn't given a choice."

Clearly exasperated, Helene fisted her hands on her hips and despite the fact that he'd been taller than her since he'd turned seventeen, she managed to tower over him. "So, let me get this straight. You told her that you were in love with her and that you might have married her to fix the scandal, but now you'd like to see what it looks like if you stay married because you want to. And she said 'forget it, I'm out'?"

He shifted uncomfortably. How had his mother conjured up the perfect speech to describe the things in his heart when he couldn't have spit out those words at gunpoint? "Yeah. Basically. Except not quite like that."

Or at all like that. He hadn't given her the opportunity to hear those things because it was better not to lay it all out. Saying that stuff out loud meant Roz could counter it easily. Who wanted that kind of out-right rejection?

"You didn't tell her, did you?" His mother's gentle tone still had plenty of censure in it.

"I don't deal well with rejection," he mumbled.

"Call Channel Five. There's a newsflash for you."

Her sarcasm wasn't lost on him. The fact that he hadn't told Roz meant he *never* had to deal with it. Instead, he was hiding at his mother's house.

He didn't deal well with relationships, either. He'd spent the whole of his life yearning to belong and holding on with a death grip where he did eke out a place. Neither had led to a healthy balance.

"You don't deal well with it because you have no experience with it. Plus it sucks," she told him. "No one wants to stand in line to let another person hand out pain and misery. But sweetie, Roz makes you happy, not miserable. Why don't you want to fight for that?"

"My father…" He swallowed. He hadn't mentioned the bastard in probably fifteen years and he didn't like doing it now, especially as his mother's mouth tightened. "He didn't even know me and he rejected me. How much worse would it be if I told Roz that I wanted to stay married and she said no anyway?"

"Let me ask you this. How bad does it hurt now?"

Horrifically bad. Worse than he'd allowed himself to admit. Talking about it wasn't helping. "Pretty much like a constant stomach ache."

She rubbed at his arm in that comforting way that only moms knew how to do. "That's also what it will feel like if she says no. So you'd be no worse off. But if you tell her and she says yes, how much better will that feel? Also, you should remember that your father didn't reject you. He rejected me. You didn't even exist yet, not as a real live person he could look in the face and then say he didn't want. You can't let someone else's mistakes cause you to make mistakes of your own."

"You think letting Roz go is a mistake?" His gut was screaming *yes* at a million and five decibels, drowning out the very excellent points his mother was making.

"The important question is whether you think that. But I wouldn't have encouraged you to marry her if I didn't think she could be much more than a mechanism to fix a problem. I'm shocked you didn't realize that already." His mother's voice broke unexpectedly and he glanced at her to see tears gathering in the corners of her eyes. "Just when you think your kid can't surprise you… You really were doing this whole thing for me, weren't you?"

He scowled. "Of course. Well, at first. You're the only mom I have and you're the greatest. Why wouldn't I do anything you needed from me?"

It hadn't hurt that marrying Roz on a temporary basis gave him the perfect excuse to avoid rejection. Too bad it hadn't worked out that way.

"Good answer." She grinned through her tears and then turned him toward the door with a little push. "Now I need you to go home and tell Roz to stop packing because you have important stuff to tell her. Do that for me and at some point in the future we'll laugh about how you almost really screwed this up."

His spirit lightened so fast that it made his head spin. She made something hard sound so easy. Hendrix took two steps toward the door and then stopped. "What if—"

"What-ifs are for losers who can't carry the name

Harris, sweetie. In other words, not you." She hustled him toward the door in an almost comical one-two shuffle. "I didn't raise a coward and I'm not going to be satisfied until I have grandbabies. So just keep that in mind."

Babies. The same emotions reappeared that had flooded him back at the hospital when he'd had a small suspicion Roz might be sick for reasons that had nothing to do with clowns. That might have been the clincher. He was too far gone to do anything other than take his mother's advice. "More favors? Marriage wasn't enough for you?"

"That's right. And more important, it's not enough for you, either. Chop, chop. I have a brunch to get to."

His mother closed the door behind him and he got all the way to his car before letting loose with the smile he'd been fighting. Helene Harris was one-of-a-kind. And so was his wife. He had to take a chance and tell her how he felt about her, or he'd never forgive himself. This was his best shot at being a part of something that made him happy and he'd given it a pass instead of fighting for it.

Hopefully, Roz was still at home so he could convince her to stay for reasons that had nothing to do with sex and everything to do with a promise of forever.

The moving company Roz had called made short work of transporting the boxes of clothes, shoes and other personal items she'd taken to Hendrix's house. Good thing. She wasn't in any mood to handle logistics right now.

Hendrix had left earlier, probably to go celebrate his forthcoming independence, and the fact that he was gone was good, too. She could leave without an extended goodbye that would likely yank more tears from her depths that she didn't want to lose. The first and second crying jags of the morning had already depleted what small amount of energy she still had after packing the boxes.

What was wrong with her? There had never been a scenario where she wasn't going to lose this marriage. Why was it hitting her so hard? Because she hadn't prepared properly for it to end? Maybe because it had ended so quickly, with almost no protest from the man she'd married, never mind that she'd stupidly begun to hope things might turn out differently.

That was the problem. She'd fallen into this bit of wonderful she'd found with Hendrix and forgotten it would soon vanish like so many other things in her life.

The moving truck pulled away from the front of Hendrix's Oakwood home and there was nothing left for Roz to do except follow it to her loft. Except she couldn't force herself to pull into the parking garage. She kept driving. The moving company had preauthorization with her building security and they were professionals who didn't need a neurotic, weepy woman supervising them.

Clown-Around could always use more attention. The boost Helene had given the organization surpassed Roz's wildest dreams. Becoming a Harris had launched her into a place that being a Carpenter had never touched. In more ways than one. The thought of how often she'd been *touched* as a Harris depressed her thoroughly.

The paperwork on her desk held zero appeal. She scouted around her tiny office for something else to do, finally landing in the supply closet. It could use organizing. All of the clown makeup and props had fallen into disarray after Helene had stopped by, and frankly, the last thing Roz had wanted to do was surround herself with the trappings that still held so many horrible memories.

But she was already so out of sorts that for once, the wigs lining overhead shelves and the multicolored outfits on hangers at her back didn't bother her. They were just costumes. Easily donned and easily taken off. She grabbed one of the wigs and stuck it on her head.

See? Easy. Not scary. Just some fake curly hair in an outrageous color.

All at once, she sank to the ground and put her face in her hands as the sheer weight of everything overwhelmed her.

Clowns hadn't taken her mother from her. Cancer had. For that matter, no one in a red nose had forced her father to stop caring about her—unless she was doing something he disapproved of, which he cared about plenty. Floppy shoes had done nothing to get her in trouble or bring down society's censure over a racy photograph. She'd done all of that on her own.

Clowns weren't the problem. She was. She'd assigned so much blame to the crappy hand fate had dealt her as a child that she'd practically let it ruin her life. It was only because luck had handed her Hendrix Harris on a silver platter that anything good had happened.

She didn't want that to be over. She didn't want to live each day scared to death to assign importance to the man she'd married. Most of all, she wanted to know what it felt like to know she could wake up each day next to someone who got her. Someone who loved her.

She'd been so busy looking for the hammer about to drop on her happiness that she hadn't considered the possibility that there was no hammer. Hendrix had even said they could put off the divorce, yet she'd let herself become convinced it was better to get it over with rather than see what might happen if she stopped assuming the worst. Maybe they could have tried being married for a few more weeks and let things develop. Go a little deeper.

If only Hendrix was here, she'd tell him that's what she wanted before she lost her nerve.

A chime sounded at the front door as someone pushed it open. Great. She'd forgotten to lock it again. She had to get better at remembering that or else move her offices to a more secure location. Anyone could wander in off the street.

But when she popped out of the closet, cell phone in hand in case she needed to dial 911, the nerves in her fingers went completely numb. The phone slipped from her grip and clattered to the parquet flooring.

As if she'd conjured him, Hendrix stood just inside the door, as gorgeous in a pair of jeans and a T-shirt as he was out of them. Because he had the same smile on his face regardless, the one that he was aiming at her now. The same one that had flushed through her on that dance floor at the Calypso Room a million years ago when she'd first caught sight of him.

"Hendrix Harris," she'd murmured then. And now apparently, as she realized she'd spoken out loud.

"Rosalind Harris," he returned easily, which was not even close to what he'd said to her that night in Vegas but almost made her swoon in a similar fashion. "I like what you've done with your hair."

Her fingers flew to her head and met the clown wig. Oh, God. She started to pull it off and then defiantly dropped her hand. "I'm practicing."

"To be a clown?"

She shook her head. "Facing down my shortcomings. How did you know I was here?"

Which was only the first of a whole slew of other questions, ones that she couldn't seem to get out around the lump in her throat. Hendrix was so close that she could reach out and touch him. She almost did. But she'd given up that right because she was an idiot, clearly.

"I didn't. I went to your loft first but the moving guys said they hadn't seen you. So it was worth a shot to come here. I saw your car outside."

"You were looking for me? That's funny. I…" *Need to tell you some things.* But she had no idea how to take the first step. When she'd wished he was here so she could say what was in her heart, she hadn't actually thought that would happen. He was so beautiful and smelled so delicious and familiar that her muscles had frozen. "You could have called."

"I wasn't sure what I was going to say. I, um, drove around a lot so I could practice." His smile reappeared. "I guess we're both doing that today."

Oddly, the fact that he seemed nervous and unable to figure out how to navigate either melted her heart. And gave her the slimmest glimmer of insight that maybe she'd been completely wrong about everything. "Were you practicing something like, 'watching my mom at the hospital made me realize I have a lifelong dream to be a clown'? Because that can be arranged."

Instead of laughing or throwing out a joke of his

own, he feathered a thumb across her cheek. "More like I messed up and let you pack all your stuff so you could leave me, when that's not what I want."

Her whole body froze. Except for her heart. That was beating a mile a minute as something bright fluttered through it. "It's not?"

He shook his head once, never letting go of her gaze. "You're my peanut butter *and* my jelly. Without you, I've got two useless pieces of bread that taste like sawdust. I want a chance to see what kind of marriage we can have without all the extra baggage. I mean, not to put too much pressure on you all at once." He hesitated, looking so miserable that she feared he would stop saying these beautiful things. "I'm trying to say that I want—"

"I love you," she blurted out. Oh, God. What was wrong with her that she couldn't stop behaving like a dimwit when it came to this man? "Not that *I'm* trying to put pressure on *you*—"

"I love you, too," he broke in and she was pretty sure the dazed look on his face was reflected on her own. "I'm changing my answer."

"Because you're a dimwit, too?" Maybe she should stop talking. "I mean, I'm a dimwit. Not you. I was scared that I was going to lose you—"

"No, you're right," he agreed readily. "I'm a complete and total dimwit. I have a problem with rejection so I try really hard to avoid it."

"I wasn't— I mean, I would never reject…" Except for when she'd told him she couldn't stay. She should have stayed. What if he'd never come looking for her? She would have missed out on the best thing that had ever happened to her. "I messed up, too. A lot. I should have told you I was falling for you and that I didn't want a divorce."

Something tender filtered through his gaze. "Funny, that's exactly what I practiced saying to you in the car as I drove around the whole of Raleigh. You stole my line."

"So that's it then? I don't want a divorce, you don't want a divorce. We love each other and we're staying married?" It sounded too good to be true, like a situation ripe for being ripped from her hands. Her pulse wobbled. This was the part where she had to calm down and face her fears like an adult who could handle her life. "I have a hard time trusting that all good things aren't about to come to an instant end."

She swallowed the rest, wishing he'd run true to form and interrupt her with his own revelations. But that didn't happen. He did hold out his hand and when she clasped it, the way he squeezed back was better than any time he'd ever touched her, bar none. Because it was encouraging, accepting. A show of solidarity. *I'm here and I'm not going anywhere*, he said without saying a word.

That loosened her tongue fast. A multitude of emotions poured out as she explained how clowns and cancer and rebellion and marriage had all tumbled together in her head. How she wasn't afraid any longer. She wrapped it up by pointing to the wig. "I'm inside my fears. Blasting them apart where they live. You gave me that. That, along with about a million other reasons, is why I can tell you I love you."

Sure, she still didn't want to lose him but she had absolute faith that if that ever did happen—regardless of the reason—she'd find a way to be okay.

"My turn." Hendrix reached up and plucked the wig off of her head, then plopped it onto his own. "This is the approved method to work through all this stuff, right?"

She nodded as the tears spilled over. "You look like a dork."

He just grinned and patted his red curly hair. "I look like a man who has finally figured out the key to dealing with the idiotic crap running through his head. I almost gave you up without a fight because I was convinced you were going to say thanks but no thanks if I brought up the things I was feeling. Color me shocked that you beat me to it."

"Not sorry."

"I'm just going to insist that you let me say 'I love you' first from now on."

"That's a much better marriage deal than the first one you offered me. I accept." Roz fished her wedding rings from her pocket and handed them to him solemnly. "As long as we both shall live?"

He better. She wasn't a serial wife. This was forever and she knew beyond a shadow of a doubt that she'd love him until the day she died.

He slid the cool bands onto her third finger and it was a thousand times more meaningful than the actual wedding ceremony. "I do."

Epilogue

Jonas and Warren were already seated in the corner booth when Hendrix arrived—late, because his wife had been very unwilling to let him out of the shower.

"This seems familiar," he joked as he slid into the seat next to Jonas and raised his brows at Warren. "Down to you being buried in your phone."

Warren glanced up from the lit screen and then immediately back down. "I like my job. I won't apologize for it."

"I like my job too but I like conversing with real people, as well," Hendrix shot back mildly, well aware that he was stalling. "Maybe you could try it?"

With a sigh, Warren laid his precious link to Flying Squirrel, his energy drink company, facedown on the table. "I'm dealing with a crap-ton of issues that have no solution, but okay. Let's talk about the Blue Devils why don't we? Or maybe the Hornets? What's the topic du jour, guys?"

Hendrix picked up his beer and set it back down again. There was no easy way to do this, so he just ripped the Band-Aid off. "I'm not divorcing Roz."

A thundercloud drifted over Warren's face as Jonas started laughing.

"I knew it." Warren put his head in his hands with a moan. "You fell in love with her, didn't you?"

"It's not that big of a deal." Hendrix scowled at his friend, knowing full well that it was a big deal to him. "Jonas did it, too."

Warren drained his beer, his mouth tight against the glass as his throat worked. He put the glass down with a *thunk*. "And both of you are really stretching my forgiveness gene."

"It was a shock to me too, if that helps."

"It doesn't."

Jonas put a comforting hand on Warren's arm. "It's okay, you'll find yourself in this same situation and see how hard it is to fight what you're feeling."

"I'll never go against the pact," Warren countered fiercely, his voice rising above the thumping music and happy hour crowd. "There were—are—reasons we made that pact. You guys are completely dishonoring Marcus's memory."

Marcus had been a coward. Hendrix had only recently begun to reframe his thoughts on the matter, but after seeing a coward's face in the mirror for the length of time it had taken for him to figure out that love wasn't the problem, he knew a little better what cowardice looked like. "Maybe we should talk about those reasons."

Instead of agreeing like a rational person might, Warren slid from the booth and dropped his phone into his pocket. "I can't do this now."

Hendrix and Jonas watched him stride from the bar like the hounds of hell were nipping at his heels. Dealing with rejection did suck, no two ways about it. But he was getting better at it because he wasn't a coward, not any longer. He was a Harris through and through, every bit his mother's child. Helene had raised him with her own special blend of Southern grit and he'd turned out okay despite never knowing his father. He was done letting that disappointment drive him to make mistakes.

"Welcome to the club." Solemnly, Jonas clinked his glass to Hendrix's and they drank to their respective marriages that had both turned out to be love matches in spite of their bone-headedness.

"Thanks. I hate to say it, but being a member of that club means I really don't want to sit around in a bar with you when I could be at home with my wife."

Jonas grinned. "As I agree with the sentiment, you can say it twice."

Hendrix made it to his house in Oakwood in record time. Their house. His and Roz's. She'd moved back in and put her loft up for sale even though he'd told her at least four times that he'd move in with her. His Oakwood place was a legitimate house but wherever Roz was made it home.

He found her in the bedroom, spread across the bed. Naked.

"Thought you'd never get here," she murmured throatily. "I was about to send you a selfie to hurry you along."

"So our next scandal can be a phone-hack leak of our personal photo album?" His clothes hit the floor in under thirty seconds.

"No more scandals. We're a respectable married couple, remember?" Roz squealed as he flipped her over on the bed and crawled up the length of her back.

"Only in public. Behind closed doors, all bets are off."

She shuddered under his tongue and arched in pleasure. "See what you've done to me? I'm a total sex addict, thanks to you. Before we got married, I was in the running for most pious fiancée alive."

"Not sorry." As much as he enjoyed Roz's back, he liked her front a lot better. That's where her eyes were and he'd discovered a wealth of intimacy in them when they made love, an act which he planned to repeat a million more times. He rolled her in his arms and sank into her.

She was his favorite part of being married.

* * * * *

CONTRACT
BRIDE

KAT CANTRELL

One

Women must have some kind of manual they passed around to each other, opened to the section labeled "How to Dump a Man."

If so, it would explain why for a record fourth time in a row, Warren Garinger had received the same text message: You're the world's worst workaholic. I hope you and your company will be very happy together.

He didn't think the women meant it as a compliment. Nor did they understand what it took to run a billion-dollar conglomerate. The Garinger family bottled and sold nearly half the world's pick-me-ups. You couldn't escape the logo for Flying Squirrel, the number one energy drink, no matter where you looked.

Women did not appreciate the effort that had gone into that kind of success.

Tilda popped her head into his office. "Got a minute?"

Except that one. He nodded instantly.

Tilda Barrett was the one woman he always had time for. Partly because he liked her Australian accent more than he should. "Sure. Come on in."

But mostly Warren liked Tilda because, as his marketing consultant, she'd exceeded his expectations. And that was saying something. His expectations were always sky-high, for himself and for everyone in his orbit. Flying Squirrel wasn't performing as well in the Australian market as he'd like, and Tilda was changing that. Slowly but surely.

"I saw the numbers on the new campaign. They're promising," he said, as Tilda strode into his bright corner office overlooking downtown Raleigh. Of course, he rarely glanced out the window unless he needed to gauge the weather in advance of a sporting event Flying Squirrel had sponsored.

Today was no exception. Tilda commanded his attention easily, both because of her professional role and because of the one she played in his head. Yeah, he'd had a fantasy or two starring Tilda Barrett, and he refused to be ashamed that he'd noticed she was very feminine beneath her buttoned-up exterior.

Not one strand of swept-up hair dared escape her severe hairstyle and, not for the first time, he wondered what would happen if it did. Most likely, her sheer will would tame it back into submission. She was the most hard-core professional woman he'd ever met. They got on famously.

"The numbers could be better," she countered. Nothing ever satisfied her save absolute domination, and the fact that she was on his team made him downright gleeful.

Tilda took the straight-backed chair to the right of his desk, as was her custom when they had briefings. The company's main competitor, Down Under Thunder, owned the Australian market, and Tilda's strategic expertise filled a gap in Warren's roster that he'd been thus far unable to bridge any other way.

"But that's not why I'm here," she said—and hesitated.

Tilda never hesitated.

Something was up. The dynamic between them had shifted. Normally they worked so well together that he scarcely had to speak before she'd already read his thoughts, and vice versa. But he couldn't get a bead on her blank face.

Warren leaned forward to steeple his hands on the desk that had nothing more on it than his laptop and cell phone. Paperwork was for other people to handle, a hallmark of the CEO philosophy that had allowed him to focus on ideas and game plans instead of minutiae. Thomas had taken to the role of chief operating officer like a duck to water, and Warren had never questioned letting his younger brother assume the reins of daily control while Warren got to have all the fun in the corner office.

"Please speak freely," Warren said, a little concerned he'd had to clarify that when Tilda had spent hours in his company during this project. Normally, he preferred people respect the distance and reserve he deliberately injected into all of his professional relationships. But he hadn't insisted on being so formal with her. There'd been no reason to. Tilda had always struck him as the female version of himself—dedicated, professional and, above all, never overtly familiar.

In this moment, however, things felt different, and he didn't like it.

"Right-o. The thing is, I'm not sure how free I am to speak about this issue," she began cautiously, her accent rolling through him accompanied by inappropriate heat, especially given the gravity of her expression. "At this point, all I can say is that I'm being pulled from this project."

"What?" Warren shot half out of his seat before catching himself. He sat back in his chair with deliberate care. "You cannot be pulled from this project. The contract I have with your firm is for a full year and we've barely covered a quarter of that."

She nodded once. "The contract doesn't specify that I will be the consultant for the full year, and unfortunately, there's an issue with my visa that they've chosen not to address. I'm being chucked back to Australia and they'll provide you with an American replacement."

Outrageous. Warren clamped down against the flow of obscene words on the tip of his tongue. He'd hired the best consulting firm on the planet precisely so that "issues" with visas did not impede his progress. "That's a breach of contract. I need an Australian expert who has been immersed in the culture for the whole of her life, not an American who's read some things on the internet."

"I'm afraid I can't speak to the specifics," she intoned, as if the entire project wasn't now in complete jeopardy. "My superiors seem to believe replacing me is well within their contractual rights. I do apologize for the short notice."

Warren ran a hand through his hair as he contemplated contingencies that didn't exist. This project needed Tilda. Period. "How short?"

"I'm to wrap up with you today and be on a plane by Friday."

"Friday? As in the day after tomorrow?"

This was a disaster. And only in being presented with a looming deadline could Warren admit that *he* needed Tilda, as well. He couldn't work with another consultant who didn't get his style the way she did. He could be gruff, short and to the point, and she took it all with grace.

Plus, he liked listening to her talk. Sometimes, when they worked through dinner, she relaxed enough to laugh and he could indulge in a very harmless fantasy about what her chestnut hair might look like when it was down around her shoulders. He'd undone enough hairstyles in his day to know that hers likely hit her midback and would be shiny and smooth under his fingers.

Warren was as adept with a well-shaped fantasy as he was with running Flying Squirrel.

Harmless fantasies fueled a man who was still at the office during the hours other men might indulge in all things female. Harmless fantasies worked for him on so many levels because he'd never act on them. Tilda's expertise on this project was too important to add her to the list of women who would eventually gift him with an unoriginal text message.

Tilda folded her hands together in that no-nonsense way he'd always secretly appreciated. Her slender fingers locked in place with strength of purpose. No stray movements, as if she never accidentally got into an uncomfortable position worth correcting. Lack of mistakes was as much a part of her personality as her incredible efficiency.

"Yes, this Friday," she said. "I have about four hours to get my things in order. My replacement should be here in the morning to pick up where I left off."

"That's not happening." As if Tilda could be replaced. It was ridiculous to assume even for a moment that this was a done deal. "Who do I need to speak with at your firm about this? If nothing else, I'll sponsor your visa."

Surely that was doable. Tilda gave him the name and number of her superior and strode from the room to update the project plan in the event his call didn't go as planned.

It didn't. The contact at the consulting firm cited a mix-up in renewing Tilda's visa and then informed Warren that Tilda had to leave the country before her immigration papers expired on Saturday, or she wouldn't be permitted to return once the renewal had been sorted out. He cited several clauses in immigration law that the firm couldn't in good conscience violate, which was entirely too much legal jargon for one o'clock in the afternoon.

Warren ended the call and immediately consulted an immigration lawyer. What was the point of having a lot of money if you couldn't spend it where you needed to most? Two hours later, he was out of time and out of options. Save one. A green-card marriage.

The lawyer cautioned Warren about the dangers of fake marriages for residency but allowed that the immigration department was overrun with work, so likely wouldn't be examining things too closely.

Warren was just desperate enough to pitch the option to Tilda. Odds were good she'd say no so fast his head would spin. But he had to try.

She had an all-business persona that lent itself to an in-name-only relationship. She'd definitely welcome the continued distance and reserve he would insist upon. He didn't do deep dives beneath the surface. Not anymore. He worked like a fiend for a reason—his relationship skills left a lot to be desired. The more he worked, the easier it was to forget he'd been responsible for his college roommate's death.

Marriage was the last thing he should be contemplating. Not given the pact he'd made after Marcus died; Warren had sworn to never fall in love. Jonas and Hendrix, who'd also been friends with Marcus, had vowed, too, but they'd broken the pact by falling for their wives. Warren refused to dishonor Marcus's memory that way.

But surely, with a woman as professional as Tilda, if she said yes, he'd have no problem keeping their relationship one hundred percent business. A green-card marriage was the only solution he could pull together before it was too late.

He had to try this last-ditch alternative. Down Under Thunder had a large piece of Warren's pie and he wanted to crush the competition. Tilda was his magic bullet. He would convince her to stay, no matter what it took.

When Warren called Tilda back into his office later that day, she had to do a serious gut check to see if she'd gotten the wild swing of emotions under control. Thank God she hadn't *actually* burst into tears in Warren's office earlier.

That would have been highly unprofessional. Tilda relied on the aloof front she'd erected to prevent anyone from getting too close. Displaying the slightest vulnerability felt squicky.

Of course, it wasn't any more professional to have a minibreakdown in her own office, either. Telling herself that hadn't stopped the panic that had welled up right after her boss, Craig, had called to drop the news. Not only was her visa expiring, the firm had decided against getting it renewed. Too difficult a climate right now, too expensive, he'd said. Sorry about the mix-up, but she could have a job in Australia, no problem.

Except there was a problem...named Bryan McDermott, her ex-boyfriend who was evil personified, a man with police force clearance, friends in all the right places and zero conscience. He didn't technically have the powers of God, but he sure put on a good enough show to make her believe he did. That's why she'd left Melbourne. Why she could never go back.

This time, he might make good on his threat to kill her with his bare hands if he caught her with another man, never mind that they'd been broken up for over a year.

Okay, not doing so hot on getting her emotions under control. Warren was waiting on her to reappear in his office. There was no way he'd sorted out the procedure for renewing her visa in a couple of hours, though if anyone could do the impossible, it was Warren Garinger. He took no prisoners, left no stone unturned and put whip-wielding oxen drivers to shame in the motivation department. In other words, he was every inch the chief executive officer the plaque on his door claimed him to be.

She might have a little crush on him. Who could blame her? He was gorgeous, never hit on her and could buy and sell a man like Bryan before lunch. She was pretty sure Warren could clock her ex and easily be the one to walk away from the fight with nary a scratch.

What was wrong with her, that the ability of a man to cause bodily harm to another man turned her on?

Deep breath.

She stuck her head into his office. "You rang?"

Warren waved her in, clicking his laptop shut the moment she crossed the threshold. That was one quality that set him apart. He never multitasked, except in his head. His brain worked in fascinating ways she could scarcely comprehend, describing the big picture as easily as he did the details many people overlooked.

She was going to miss him more than she'd let herself admit.

"Sit, please," Warren said. "We have much to discuss."

As was his custom, Warren stayed behind his desk, keeping them separated by glass and wood. He never breached that space between them, never let his gaze stray to her nondescript suit, which displayed none of her assets by design.

That was another of his qualities she admired. Other men never seemed to understand that familiarity wasn't easy for her. That she didn't want a man anywhere close to her, not after Bryan. He'd been so successful at sucking away her confidence that the first time he'd smacked her across the face, he'd somehow spun it as being her fault.

The worst part wasn't having abuse in her past. The

worst part was when she woke up at 2:00 a.m. in a cold sweat because a small part of her might believe it *was* her fault Bryan had hit her. And she couldn't exorcise that small part, no matter what she did.

She squared the tablet computer in her hands. "I've taken copious notes for my successor—"

"Not necessary." Warren waved that off. "You're not going anywhere."

The wildest bloom of hope sprouted in her chest before she could stomp it flat. "You got Craig to agree to fix their screwup?"

Warren could sell hay to a farmer. Getting Tilda's boss to admit he'd made a mistake had probably been child's play.

But Warren waved that off, too. "No, of course not. You were right. Your boss is an ass who can't be trusted with a box of animal crackers, let alone my campaign to expand in Australia. So I fired him and threatened to sic my lawyers on him if he so much as breathed the phrase *cancellation clause*."

"Oh." She'd have paid good money to be a fly on the wall during that conversation. "So, I'm at a loss on what to say next. Dare I hope you found a way to get my visa renewed in two days?"

If by some miracle he had, she wouldn't have to go back to Melbourne. She could stay here and work, burying herself in this job that had come to mean so much to her—

"Not exactly."

Of course not. Warren wasn't here to make all of her dreams come true, especially not the ones where she imagined him riding to her rescue like a modern-day knight in a shining Tom Ford suit.

Deflated, she fought to keep her face blank. Wouldn't do to communicate an iota of her emotional state. That was how men got the ammunition they needed to hurt you. "Please elaborate."

Warren leaned into his steepled hands, a move he made often, which she'd come to recognize as his game stance. It meant he was ready to get serious.

"I spoke to an immigration lawyer. He assures me the best option here is to immediately file for an extension and renewal. But, as you may be aware, that can take months and you would have to travel to the nearest consulate to get the renewal, which would be either Canada or Mexico, depending on your preference, but that means—"

"I would be out of status when I went." The reality of the legal ramifications swamped her and her shoulders slumped. Ruthlessly, she straightened them. "They wouldn't let me back in the country if the extension wasn't in place yet."

"You see the problem, then." Warren nodded once. "The project would be on hold again and you'd be stuck in whichever country you traveled to. It might as well be Australia, at that point. The key is that you can't be out of status when you go to the consulate."

She felt like Warren was leading her somewhere, but she couldn't for the life of her figure out where.

"Then I would have to go before Saturday, and the renewal paperwork isn't even filed yet." Thanks to her employer's snafu, she would be in a lot of trouble if she stayed long enough to let her paperwork expire. "That would be a wasted trip."

As he'd said, she might as well go back to Australia. Maybe she could sweet-talk the firm into assigning her a job in Queensland instead of Victoria. Brisbane might be far enough away to escape Bryan's insidious reach. Of course, if he had friends on the police force there, her precautions wouldn't matter. He'd set up surveillance on her phone and house, like he had last time, and she'd have no recourse because he was too slippery to get caught.

She shuddered. The problem was that she didn't *want* to go back to Australia. She felt safe here. Valued. As if her contributions mattered for the first time since she'd escaped a relationship where she constantly was made to feel *less than*. This job had saved her and giving it up was unfathomable.

But what other choice did she have? Warren wasn't presenting any alternatives that justified his hope-inducing opening comment that she wasn't going anywhere.

"Yes. Completely wasted. *If* you were out of status." His gaze locked onto hers. "The lawyer suggested the easiest way to ensure you're not out of status at that indeterminate point is if you already had a green card."

"Green cards are even harder to get than visa renewals," she blurted out. The rules were inconsistently applied, pending which way the immigration office interpreted them. And Warren was talking about a green card, the Holy Grail for someone in her circumstances. "I would never be able to file for a green card so quickly."

Warren held up a finger. "There's one way. If you marry a US citizen. It would be easy enough for us to go to the courthouse Friday morning and get this taken care of. The marriage would be in name only, of course. Our professional relationship would continue as is."

The sound in her ears increased to a dull roar as she processed his meaning. He was offering to *marry* her in the most unromantic proposal she could have imagined. They'd be lawfully wed with no hope of any sort of physical relationship. Warren would be her husband, yet never even try to touch her.

Something was definitely wrong with her, because it sounded so perfect she feared the tears pricking the backs of her eyelids might actually fall.

But she'd fallen prey to the illusion of perfection in the past. The only way to ensure there were no repeats was to spell out every possible contingency she could think of.

"We'd be married in name only. That means no intimacy," she said briskly. "None. Forgive me if I find it hard to believe a man of your stature would accept such a thing."

At that, Warren actually smiled, a tilting of his lips that lanced her through the stomach as sharply as if he'd actually touched her.

"That sounds vaguely like it should be a compliment. Don't worry about me. I can handle a few months of no intimacy."

The way he caressed the term with his American accent did not settle the swirl still heating her core after being treated to his smile. One minute into their business discussion about resolving the issue with her visa her body had already betrayed her. She cleared her throat. "And when my visa is renewed, we will dissolve the marriage."

He nodded. "An annulment. My lawyers will take

care of everything. I've already laid out the pertinent points to them in an email. I just need your agreement before I hit Send."

This was moving far too fast. She could feel the threads of control slipping from her fingers. If she married Warren, he could easily change his mind about the no-intimacy clause. They'd be legally married and she hadn't a clue what kind of recourse she might have if he decided they would consummate the marriage whether she liked it or not.

If he knew she wore racy lingerie beneath her staid suits, would he change his mind?

She shook off those thoughts. Warren wasn't offering this solution so he could take advantage of her. They'd worked together late into the night many times, long after the last of his employees had gone home. He'd never been anything but the soul of propriety, which was why she loved this job. He listened to her, valued her opinion. Otherwise, he wouldn't have gone to these lengths to keep her on the project.

That alone went a long way. Her knees might be weak at the thought of putting herself at his mercy. But she was also continuing in a positive environment that was good for her battered psyche.

There wasn't really a choice. She could never accept her employer's mistake and take the offered job in Melbourne. She'd have to agree to become Warren's bride by contract.

The thought unleashed a shiver she couldn't control. They'd be living together. Wouldn't they? How could they convince the authorities they were married unless she moved into his house? But that would make it so much harder to keep her normally vivacious personality under wraps, lest she accidentally give Warren the impression she welcomed his advances.

The complications rose up in her throat like a big black rock, cutting off her air.

"Tell me what you're thinking, Tilda." Warren's quiet voice cut through her angst easily. "Do you want to keep this job or go back to Australia? If it's the former, let's work through this from the top and mitigate all of the potential landmines."

As frequently as they'd been on the same wavelength over the course of this project, it shouldn't be such a shock that he'd picked up on her reservations. Could he see the panic, too? Surely not.

She'd tried hard to hide what was really going on beneath the surface for the entire length of their acquaintance, adopting the granite-hard professionalism that she'd been convinced no one could crack.

Warren Garinger managed to crack it without breaking a sweat. Likely without even realizing it. This was her opportunity to retake control.

"All right." *Deep breath.* "I want to keep this job."

That meant she had to take the issue of her visa seriously and consider his offer. *Marriage.* It was a dizzying proposition, rife with pitfalls, both legal and personal.

But still viable, nonetheless.

"Good. I want you to keep it. What else concerns you about this plan?"

Oh, God, *everything* about this plan concerned her. One hurdle at a time. "No issues with your wife working for you?"

"None. This is a family company through and through. Thomas's wife is head of accounting and all of the shareholders are named Garinger." Warren flashed her another brief smile. "If you like, I would be happy to give you a block of shares as a wedding present."

She swallowed as the black rock grew in her throat. The gesture had probably been an act of good faith, but no one had ever offered to make her a part of a family with such decisiveness. It felt…nice. She got to belong for no other reason than because Warren said so. She nodded, since speaking wasn't possible.

"What else?" he prodded gently. "I have a master suite at my house that connects to a smaller bedroom via the bathroom. The door locks from the other side. You may have that one or one on the first floor if you like. My staff is paid well to exercise discretion, so we don't need to worry about them tattling to the immigration bureau that the marriage is fake. Of course, we will need to put on some appearances as if we're happily married."

"I'm not sure I can do that." She cut in before thinking better of it. How could she explain that she didn't think she could let a man touch her without jumping out of her skin? She didn't have to. Warren didn't miss a beat.

"I don't mean with public displays of affection." His smile turned wry. "No one who knows me would be shocked if I never touched my wife in public. What would be shocking is if I put my cell phone down long enough to do so."

That did it. Her lungs loosened, allowing her to breathe. Finally. Sweet air rushed into her system and she went a little lightheaded from relief. She found herself matching his smile without fully realizing he'd affected her enough for that. "I see your point. They would probably call the authorities much faster if you showered me with attention. Perhaps we'll let them think of us as having an affair of the mind."

They shared a moment of understanding that grew sharper the longer they stared at each other. The man was brilliant, sexy without being in your face about it and respectful of her boundaries. How much closer could they become if she lowered a few?

Warren cleared his throat first and looked away. "What I meant was that you might have to accompany me to family functions so as not to raise eyebrows. The last thing we need is immigration questioning whether we married strictly for the green card. The attorney I consulted said they do investigate red flags."

She nodded. "I got you."

"Also, you should know that I'm not warm and fuzzy in a relationship. Acting like I'm in love is frankly outside my skill set. I wouldn't know what that looks like, nor do I intend to learn."

"That's fine with me." Perfect, actually. She didn't know what love looked like, either, and trying to fake it would only bring up issues she'd rather leave in the dark. Boundaries were her friends. Always. "In that case, I accept your proposal."

"Great. I'll have some papers for you to sign tomorrow, a standard prenuptial agreement and the marriage license application. We'll go to the justice of the peace on Friday, as mentioned, and then it will be done."

Warren reached out a hand and she clasped it. A handshake to seal the deal. Should have been innocuous enough and seemed appropriate under the circumstances.

But the moment their flesh connected, a jolt of electricity shot up her arm and her awareness of him as a man settled deep inside. Not just a man. One who would be her husband.

Her little crush might be wholly inadvisable, but as Warren held her hand, she didn't for a moment believe she had the will to stop finding him inconveniently and enormously attractive.

Two

Jonas Kim and Hendrix Harris met Warren at the courthouse on Friday. Predictably, his best friends since college didn't miss the opportunity to give him a hard time about his impending marriage. Warren had fully expected it after the equally hard time he'd given both of them when they'd gotten married.

The difference here was that Warren wasn't breaking the pact the three of them had made their senior year at Duke University. Jonas and Hendrix had. They'd broken the pact seven ways to Sunday and without shame, no less. After Marcus had committed suicide over his irreparably broken heart, the three surviving friends had shaken hands and vowed to never fall in love.

Warren would stick to that until the day he died. His friends might have found ways to excuse their faithlessness to themselves, but Warren was still working on forgiving them for putting their hearts at risk in their own marriages.

"Well, well, well." Jonas crossed his arms and gave Warren a once-over that held a wealth of meaning as his two friends cleared the metal detector at the entrance to the Wake County Courthouse in downtown Raleigh. "I do believe this is what eating crow looks like. Don't you agree, Hendrix?"

"I do." His other friend shot Warren a grin that sharpened his already ridiculous cheekbones. "It also looks like I should have put money on whether Warren would eventually get that mouth full of feathers when I had a chance."

"Ha, ha. It's not like that," Warren growled.

It wasn't. His marriage did not compare to his friends' situations; both of them had married women they already had relationships with. Jonas had married his friend Viv to avoid an arranged marriage with a stranger, and Hendrix had married Roz to end a scandal caused by risqué photographs of the two of them. They'd both sworn they weren't going to cross any lines, but it had only been a matter of time before things started getting mushy.

Mushy was not even remotely in the realm of possibility for Warren.

"What's it like, then?" Jonas asked. "Tell us how it's even possible that you're getting married after being so high and mighty about it when me and Hendrix came to you with our plans."

"I'm marrying Tilda because I can't trash Down Under Thunder without her. This is a Hail Mary designed to keep her in the country. No other reason. End of story."

"Oh, so she's a hag you would never look at twice on the street. I get it," Jonas said with a smart-ass nod.

Hendrix shook his head. "That's just sad, if so."

"Shut up. She's not a hag. Tilda is gorgeous." The headache brewing between Warren's eyes stabbed a little harder as his friends gave each other knowing glances laden with a side of I told you so. "This marriage is strictly business. I would never be anything less than professional with an employee."

"Except you are," Jonas countered. "You're moving her into your house tomorrow. Trust me when I say that leads to all sorts of things you might swear on your mother's life you would never contemplate, but it happens, man. First you're having a drink together after work and next thing you know, you're giving your in-name-only bride diamonds and orgasms in the foyer."

"Or in the linen closet at your wedding reception," Hendrix threw in helpfully with a gleam in his eye. He and his new wife had pulled just such a disappearing at the social event of the season.

"There are no linen closets here," Warren pointed out unnecessarily, not that he had to explain himself to his friends. But he was going to anyway, because they needed to be clear that he was the lone holdout in their pact.

Marcus's suicide was not something Warren had ever taken lightly, and neither was the vow he'd made to honor his roommate's death. Love had stolen a young man's life. Warren would never let that be his fate. "I've never done anything more than shake Tilda's hand as a form of sealing our arrangement. She's working on my project, not working her way into my bed. This is not about my sex life. Period."

"We'll see about that." Hendrix jerked his chin over Warren's shoulder. "Would that lovely lady be your intended bride? She looks like your type."

Warren turned to see Tilda striding toward him, her sensible heels clacking on the marble floor of the courthouse, hair swept up in the no-nonsense bun he'd dreamed about again last night and a serene expression on her face that didn't change when she caught his gaze.

Good. She'd been edgy in his office the other day and he'd half expected her to back out at some point. After all, he hadn't really had to sell her on the idea of a marriage to keep her in the country. It had been remarkably easy to talk her into it, and for some reason, he'd become convinced that she'd change her mind after she had a chance to think about it. Marriage was a big thing to some women and maybe she'd dreamed of falling in love with a capital L.

But she was here. His shoulders relaxed a bit, releasing tension he'd been carrying since Wednesday. This was going to work. Down Under Thunder was toast. And if he had the opportunity to develop a few more harmless fantasies starring his wife, no one had to know.

Tilda halted in front of him smelling fresh and citrusy. Funny, he'd never noticed her scent before and his imagination galloped toward the conclusion that she'd wanted to do something special for the occasion.

"We have a conference call at one o'clock with Wheatner and Ross," she said by way of greeting.

A timely reminder. That's why she was worth every dime of her paycheck. But he couldn't seem to stop looking at the thin strand of hair that fell from her forehead down across her temple.

It wasn't more than a millimeter wide, but it followed the line of her face to hit just under her jaw, and he had the strongest urge to slide it along his fingertips as he tucked it behind her ear. What madness was this, that she'd missed that miniscule bit of hair when she'd gotten dressed this morning?

New perfume. Defiant hair. Was it possible she was affected by the gravity of what they were about to do? Because he was. He'd lain awake last night, unable to close his eyes as he thought about the realities of having Tilda under his roof, how he'd see her in the morning before they left for work, have a cup of coffee together, even. Maybe he'd give her a ride. It only made sense that they'd go to the office together since they were coming from the same place. They could talk about things and—

Jonas might have a point about the inherent lack of professionalism that would come with having an easily accessible woman in his house. Too late now. He'd have to bank on the fact that he and Tilda had already discussed the necessary lack of intimacy.

Warren cleared his throat. "Then we should get on with it."

She nodded with a slight smile. "It helps when we're on the same wavelength."

They always were. They were cut from the same cloth, which was what made her so easy to work with. Conversely, it also made it easier to imagine slipping in deeper with her, loosening her up, finding ways to make her laugh more. They'd be good together, if he ever did find himself unable to resist crossing that line.

No.

There would be no line crossing. The project was

too important to take those kinds of risks. His vows were too important. He gestured to Jonas and Hendrix as he doled out the introductions.

"Mr. Kim." Tilda shook Jonas's hand briskly. "I worked on the campaign for your hybrid printer during the global rollout two years ago."

Jonas's brows lifted as he nodded. "That was a great product launch for Kim Electronics. I didn't realize you were on that team. It was very impressive."

Crossing his arms, Warren tried not to smile too smugly, failed—and then decided there was no shame in letting it be known that he only hired the best. Which shouldn't be a surprise to anyone.

Hendrix slid right into the space Jonas had vacated, charm in full force as he shook Tilda's hand for about fifteen beats too long, which *wasn't* a surprise to anyone. The man would probably flirt with a nun, given the chance. Regardless, Warren did not like the way Tilda smiled back, never mind that Hendrix was happily married to a woman who could command a cover spot on a men's magazine.

"We have a marriage to conduct," Warren reminded everyone briskly before he had to punch his friend for taking liberties with his wife-to-be.

Employee. Wife was secondary. Which shouldn't be such a difficult thing to remember.

The strand of hair across her temple settled into place, drawing his gaze again. He couldn't take his mind off it, even as they navigated the courthouse maze to find the justice of the peace who performed marriages.

They stood in line waiting for their turn, an oddity in and of itself. Warren had never given much thought to what should constitute a proper wedding ceremony, especially since he'd started the week with zero expectations of ending it married. Not to mention the fact that his marriage had strict business connotations. But these other couples in line surely had more romantic reasons for tying the knot. In fact, they were probably all in love, as evidenced by their goo-goo eyes and the way they held hands as they waited. A courthouse seemed like an inauspicious start to a marriage that was supposed to be till death did them part.

He shrugged it off. Who was he to judge? It wasn't like he knew the proper ingredients for a happy marriage, if such a thing even existed. Divorce rates would indicate otherwise. So maybe Warren and Tilda were the only couple in the Wake County courthouse today who had the right idea when it came to wedded bliss: no emotional component, a carefully worded prenuptial agreement, a date on the calendar for follow-ups with proper government agencies so the annulment could be filed and mutual agreement to part ways in the future. No surprises.

Tilda engaged him in a short conversation about the campaign she'd been working through. He fell into the rhythm of their work relationship easily, despite the weirdness of doing it while waiting for the justice's inner chamber doors to open. They'd enter single and emerge married.

It wouldn't change things between them. Would it?

All of these other couples surely had some expectations of things changing or they wouldn't do it. They'd just stay an unmarried couple until the day they died, but instead, they'd done exactly what Warren and Tilda had. Applied for a marriage license and come down to the courthouse on an otherwise unremarkable Friday to enter into a legal contract that said they could file their taxes differently. Why? Because they'd fallen prey to some nebulous feeling they labeled *love*?

"Warren."

He blinked. Tilda was watching him with a puzzled expression on her face, clearly because she'd asked him something that he'd completely ignored. God, what was wrong with him? "Sorry, I was distracted."

Why couldn't he just talk to Tilda about the project and stop thinking about marriage with a capital M, as if it was a bigger deal than it really was? Like he'd told his friends—business only. Nothing to see here.

Wedded bliss wasn't a thing. And if it was, Warren Garinger didn't deserve it. Marcus's death was his fault and a lifetime of happiness with a woman wasn't the proper atonement for his crimes.

Flying Squirrel was Warren's focus, the only thing he could realistically manage. For a reason. A company didn't have deep emotional scars. A company didn't waste away while you looked on helplessly, unable to figure out how to stop the pain. A company didn't choose to end its pain with an overdose after you thoughtlessly said, "Get over it, Marcus."

That was the real reason Warren would never break the pact. It was his due punishment to be alone the rest of his life.

The county clerk gestured Tilda and Warren into the justice's chamber. Her pulse fell off a cliff, skipping beats randomly as her stomach churned. The effort she'd made to talk shop with Warren, strictly to calm her nerves while they'd waited in the hall, had evaporated, if it had even done any good at all.

They were really doing this. What if they got caught in a green-card marriage? Was it like the movies, with instant deportation? She'd be forced back to Melbourne, and after Warren's unceremonious threat to Craig and the firm she'd worked for over the last eight years, she had no illusions that a job waited for her. She'd be lucky to get a reference. Which mattered not at all if Bryan figured out she'd returned. Finding a job would be the least of her concerns.

Warren had stipulated several contingencies in their agreement that meant she'd be well compensated in the event the marriage didn't resolve her residency issues. But that wasn't the point. She didn't want money; she wanted to feel safe and she wanted to do this project with Warren, in that order. This job gave her a sense of purpose that she'd never fully had before. When she'd worked on other projects, she'd never been the lead. The Flying Squirrel campaign was her baby, one hundred percent, especially now that she'd cut ties with Craig.

That went a long way toward getting her pulse under control. She had this. The wedding ceremony wasn't a big deal. A formality. Warren wasn't flipping out. He shot her a small smile that she returned because the last thing she wanted was for him to clue in that she wasn't handling this as professionally as she'd like.

But then, marrying her boss hadn't really been in the job description. Maybe she was allowed to have minor cracks in the hard outer shell she'd built around herself with severe hairstyles and monochrome suits that hung on her figure like potato sacks.

She just had to make sure any potential cracks didn't reveal things underneath that she wasn't ready to share, like the fact that she *hated* monochrome suits. The lacy red underwear and bra set she'd chosen in honor of her wedding day was for her and her only.

The ceremony began and she somehow managed not to flinch as Warren took her hand with a solemnity she hadn't expected. Fortunately, the exchange of words was short. Simple. She relaxed. Until the justice said, "You may kiss the bride."

At which point her pulse jackhammered back up into the red. They weren't really going to do that part, were they? But Warren was already leaning toward her, his fingers firm against hers, and she automatically turned her face to accept his lips.

The brush of them came far too fast. Sensation sparked across her mouth and she flinched like she always did when something happened near her face that she wasn't expecting. Not because the feeling of his lips was unwelcome. Kissing Warren was nothing like kissing Bryan. Or any other man, for that matter, not that she had a lot of experiences to compare it to. He wasn't demanding or obtrusive. Just…nice. Gentle. And then gone.

That brief burst of heat faded. Good. It was over. Back to normal. But she couldn't look at Warren as they left the courthouse.

She'd walked over from the Flying Squirrel building on Blount Street, but Warren insisted on taking her back via his limo, citing a need to go over some notes for the meeting with Wheatner and Ross. He said goodbye to his friends and then she and Warren were swallowed by leather and luxury as they settled into his limo.

"So," Warren said brightly. "That went well."

"Yes. Quite well."

God, everything was weird. This was supposed to be where they relaxed back into the dynamic they'd had from day one, where it was all business—the way they both liked it. But as she turned to him, a little desperate to find that easiness, her knee grazed his. The awareness of their proximity shot through her and she couldn't stop staring at his mouth as a wholly inappropriate lick of desire flamed through her core.

Where had *that* come from?

Well, she knew where. Warren had kissed her. So what? It shouldn't be such a big deal. She shouldn't be making it a big deal. But the part she couldn't figure out was *why*? There was no law that said they'd be any less married if they skipped the kiss. Had he done it strictly for show or because he'd been curious what it would be like?

She'd had absolutely zero curiosity. None. Not an iota. Or, at least, none that she'd admit to, and now that it was out there, she couldn't stop thinking about what he'd kiss like behind closed doors.

Ugh. She had to get back into her professional head space already.

"Um, so the senior partners themselves are attending the meeting today," she threw out, mortified to note her voice had taken on a husky quality. "We should press them on the social media presence they've presented. I don't like the ratio of ad placements between the various platforms."

Warren didn't seem to notice her vocal quirks and nodded. "I was thinking that, as well. Tell me what you'd do instead."

Tilda reeled off the changes she'd prepared and then memorized last night at midnight after she'd given up on sleep. The familiarity of talking numbers with the man who was now her legally wedded husband somehow soothed her to the point where her tone evened out.

Until she realized Warren's gaze had strayed to the side of her face. She faltered. "What?"

"Oh, nothing." His gaze snapped back to dead center. And then drifted again. "It's just that you have this loose strand of hair—here, let me."

Her hand flew up defensively at the same moment he reached out to brush her cheek and their hands collided. Oh, God. She'd batted his hand away from her face. Now he'd know she was a freak about people touching her.

Everything shifted back into awkward again as they said "Sorry" simultaneously, and there was no way she could ignore how her skin tingled where he'd touched her. The errant strand of hair he'd made her so very aware of lay across the spot, sensitizing it.

"I'll fix it when we get back to the office," she murmured, at a loss for why her stupid hair had generated such interest that he couldn't keep his focus where it belonged—on her stats.

"Don't fix it," he said instantly. "I like it."

Not what she'd expected him to say.

Heat prickled over her face and not all of it was in her cheeks. Unlike what would have been a becoming blush on anyone else, her whole face got red when she was embarrassed. Like now.

He liked her hair.

It was the most personal comment he'd ever made and she turned it over in her mind, examining it from all angles.

"Oh," Warren continued. "I forgot that Jonas and Hendrix asked if we could join them for dinner. To celebrate. It'll be low-key, just them and their wives. Is that okay?"

She nodded, though she'd rather have said no. But refusing would have felt petty when clearly he meant they were supposed to be celebrating their wedding. Social events were a part of the deal, whether she wanted to avoid opportunities for more weirdness or not.

Get a grip, she scolded herself. The weirdness was all on her. Warren wasn't Bryan and she had to stop cringing as if her new husband was going to morph into someone completely different after lulling her into a false sense of security. Not all men did that.

She hoped.

For the remainder of the afternoon, she forced a smile and slayed the meeting with Wheatner and Ross, earning approving nods from Warren, which shouldn't have meant as much as it did. He'd always approved of her work. That's why she was still in the US and not on a plane at this moment, as she'd fully expected to be when she walked into his office on Wednesday to explain the issue with her visa.

Now she was married, complete with a gold ring on her finger that contained nine emerald-cut diamonds sunk into the band. It was exactly the right ring for her, low-key, not at all flashy. How had Warren known what she would like? Luck? She would have been fine with a plain band from a vending machine. This one had weight. She curled her hand into a fist but she could still feel it on her finger.

Warren herded her back into his car at the end of the day to take her to the restaurant where his friends were waiting for them. He'd made it very clear that they wouldn't have to do any sort of acting like a lovey-dovey couple in public, but she still had a fair amount of trepidation about whether she'd get along with his friends' wives. She knew how things among men worked, and she didn't want to fail this important test of fitting into his world for however long she would be required to do so.

"Is it okay to go straight there?" Warren asked politely as they settled into his car for the second time that day. "If you want to go home first to freshen up, that's fine."

"No, thank you." What would she do, shellac the errant lock of hair to her head that Warren had already said not to fix? Not a chance. And she didn't own any suits that weren't dove gray or brown, nor would she ever change into something like jeans and a T-shirt to meet his friends, so she was as ready as she ever would be. "I appreciate the offer."

He dove into a very long summary of the day's progress, which was fairly typical of how they usually parted for the night. But today they weren't parting. Would it ever *not* be weird to realize they were a couple now?

At the restaurant on Glenwood Avenue, Warren's friends had already arrived, crowding into a round booth with a table in the center that was probably meant for six people but seemed quite cozy given that she'd only met Jonas Kim and Hendrix Harris for the first time earlier today.

The two women at the table slid out from the booth to meet her. Tilda shook the hand of Rosalind Harris, Hendrix's wife, a gorgeous dark-haired woman who could have come straight from a catwalk in Paris. Her friendly smile put Tilda at ease, a rare feat that she appreciated. Viv Kim, Jonas's wife, immediately pulled Tilda into a hug, her bubbly personality matching her name perfectly.

"I'm thrilled to meet you," Viv said and nodded at Rosalind. "We've heard absolutely nothing about you, and when our husbands keep their mouths shut about something, we're instantly curious."

Rosalind scooted a little closer and plunked her martini glass down on the table.

"Tell us everything," Rosalind insisted, leaning in with the scent of something expensive and vaguely sensual wafting from her. "How long do you think you'll have to be married before your immigration issues will be resolved? Are you going to stay in the country even after you annul the marriage?"

"Um…" Tilda's butt hit the table as she backed up, and she briefly considered sliding under it. Warren had apparently told his friends the truth about their marriage, so obviously she could trust them, but still. These were things better left out of polite conversation. You could never be too careful.

Salvation came in the form of her husband, who scowled at the two women, clearly having overheard despite his involvement in his own conversation with

Jonas and Hendrix. "We didn't agree to dinner so you could gang up on my wife."

For some reason, that brought a smile she couldn't quite contain. In one short sentence, Warren had turned them into a unit. They were *together*, an integrated front. She was his new wife just as much as he was her new husband, and it apparently came with benefits she hadn't anticipated. But liked. Very much.

Rosalind scowled back, clearly not cowed in the least. "You have to know that we're curious."

"Darling." Hendrix held out his hand to his wife. "Your curiosity is one of my favorite qualities. Come over here and be curious about the advantages of a round booth when you're sitting next to your husband."

An intense smile that held a wealth of meaning bloomed on Rosalind's face. She clasped his outstretched hand, allowing him to draw her into the booth and over to his side, where he slung an arm around her. He murmured something in her ear and she laughed, snuggling against him with such ease that Tilda got a lump in her throat while watching them. They were so clearly in love, so obviously the kind of lovers that trusted each other implicitly.

The white-hot spurt of emotion in her chest was nothing but pure jealousy. Naming it didn't make it any more acceptable or understandable. Where had that come from? Longing for that kind of intimacy with a man had gotten her into trouble with Bryan, leading her into dangerous water before she fully realized she'd left the shore behind. Tilda swallowed as she tore her gaze from the two.

"Don't mind them," Warren said with a note of disgust in his voice. "They embarrass the rest of us, too. They have no boundaries in polite company."

"That's so not true," Hendrix countered with a smirk, scarcely lifting his gaze from his wife's luminous face. "We've turned over a new leaf. No more public nakedness."

That broke some of the tension, and Jonas slid into the booth with his wife, which left Warren and Tilda. He sat next to Hendrix, leaving Tilda at the edge. Which suited her fantastically. She liked nothing less than being trapped, and luck of the draw meant she wouldn't have to be.

Across from her, Viv settled in close to her husband. Viv and Jonas might not have sensual vibes shooting from them the way the other couple did, but it was clear they were newly married and still in the throes of the honeymoon phase.

Happiness in marriage wasn't a goal of Tilda's. Burying herself in her job was. That was all she could handle at the moment, all she would allow herself to hope for. Intimacy wasn't on the table in her marriage, by design, and that was a good thing. After all, she couldn't trust herself any more than she could trust a man.

Warren had left a solid foot of space between his thigh and Tilda's. Appropriately so. He would never slide his arm around her and nestle her close, turning his head to murmur something wickedly naughty or achingly sweet into her ear.

And it shouldn't have taken the rest of the evening for her to convince herself she didn't want that.

Three

The moving company Warren had hired arrived at his house with Tilda's things around midafternoon on Saturday, meager as they were. She'd apparently not brought very much with her from Australia, just a few paperback books with well-worn covers, several boxes of clothes and shoes, and a set of china teacups.

He was curious about both the teacups and the books. But asking felt like a line they shouldn't cross. Too personal or something. If she wanted to explain, she would. Didn't stop him from thinking it was a strange state of things that he didn't feel comfortable getting personal with his wife.

The lack of boxes meant she didn't need any help unpacking and he had no good reason to be skulking about in his bedroom as she settled into her room on the other side of the connecting door in his bathroom.

He couldn't find a thing to occupy his attention, an unusual phenomenon when he normally spent Saturdays touring the Flying Squirrel warehouses with Thomas.

But his brother was on vacation with his wife—somewhere without cell phone reception, apparently, as he'd not answered his phone in several days. That was unfathomable. Who wanted to be someplace without cell phone reception?

If Warren had been occupied with work—like he should have been—then he wouldn't have heard Tilda rustling around in the bathroom. Nor would he have wandered through the door to appease his sudden interest in what she was doing. She glanced up sharply as he joined her in the cavernous room.

Immediately, she took up all the space and then tried to occupy his, too, sliding under his skin with her presence. He'd been in a small room with her before, lots of times. But not at his house, a stone's throw from the shower where he'd indulged in many, many fantasies starring the woman he'd married.

The problem wasn't the married part. It was the kiss part. He probably shouldn't have done that.

Or, more to the point, he should have done it right. Then he wouldn't be thinking about what it would be like to kiss Tilda properly. He couldn't take his eyes off her mouth. That short, utilitarian peck yesterday had been ill-advised, obviously. But the officiant had said to kiss the bride. Warren hadn't seen any reason not to. It was a custom. He wouldn't have felt married without it, a twist that he hadn't anticipated. So he went with it.

But it hadn't been worth the price of admission if he was going to be constantly on edge around Tilda now.

Constantly thinking about whether it would change their working dynamic if he kissed her as thoroughly as he suddenly burned to.

He cleared his throat. "Settling in all right?"

She nodded. "You have a lovely home."

Which she never would have seen, even one time, if they hadn't gotten married. "It's yours, too, for now. I have to admit, I was a little surprised you picked the adjoining bedroom. It would have been okay to take the one on the first floor."

But she was already shaking her head. There were no loose strands in her hairstyle today. He'd somehow expected that she'd adopt a more casual look on a Saturday, but Tilda had shown up in yet another dove-gray suit that looked practical and professional. But it also generated a fair amount of nosy interest in her habits. Even he wore jeans and T-shirts on Saturday, despite the assurance that he would put in an eight-hour day in the pursuit of all things Flying Squirrel before the sun set. Did she ever relax enough to enjoy a day off?

Well, that didn't matter. What the hell was wrong with him? He didn't take days off, either. Why would having a woman in his house change his ninety-hour workweek? And certainly finding himself in possession of a wife didn't mean they should take a day off together like he'd been half imagining.

"I know you said the staff is very discreet," she said and nodded to the open door behind her that gave him only a glimpse of the room beyond. "But taking this bedroom seemed like less of a problem. Less obvious that we're not, um…sleeping together."

Well, now, that was an interesting blush spreading over Tilda's cheeks, and he didn't miss the opportunity to enjoy it. He crossed his arms and leaned a hip against the nondescript marble vanity, which suddenly seemed a lot more remarkable now that it had several feminine accoutrements strewn across it.

"Yes, that was why I suggested it," he drawled.

But now he was thinking of the reasons it was less obvious they weren't sleeping together—because of the accessibility factor. This was an older home, designed in the style of a hundred years ago when women had their own chambers but understood the expectations of producing heirs. These women needed discreet ways to travel between their bedrooms and their husbands', and vice versa, without disturbing staff members.

He'd never even so much as imagined a woman using that adjoining chamber. And now he couldn't unimagine how easy it would be to steal into Tilda's bed in the middle of the night. She wouldn't be wearing a suit, that was for sure. What *did* she wear to bed? In all of his fantasies, she was naked.

And that was absolutely not the right image to slam into his mind during a conversation with his in-name-only wife while stuck in a netherworld between two beds that were not going to see any action of the sensual variety. A man with his imagination should be putting it to better use dreaming up new ways to sell energy drinks, not undressing his buttoned-up employee with his eyes.

"Did you want to go over the project plan?" she asked, very carefully not looking at him as she pulled open an empty drawer to place her hairbrush inside.

"In a little while. After you're settled. And only if

you want to. I don't expect you to work weekends just because we're together."

The drawer slammed shut, the sound echoing from the mostly bare walls, and she flinched. "Sorry, I'm not used to your house yet. Even the drawer mechanisms are higher end than what I'm accustomed to. Takes hardly any force at all to close."

He eyed her, not liking the way the vibe between them had gotten more stilted. They'd been easy with each other for so long. He yearned to get that back.

"No problem. I don't expect you to automatically know how everything in the house operates. You take some time to get acclimated and we'll have dinner together later. In fact, no work for you today. I insist."

Dinner. That sounded nice. An opportunity to keep things casual, learn some things about each other. Get used to being married and find their way back to the easiness that had marked their working relationship.

But instead of taking the hint and nodding enthusiastically, she froze. The vibe between them grew icicles and he scouted around for the reason she'd suddenly gotten so tense.

"Dinner?" she repeated. "Will it be like a…date?"

Mayday. Obviously she didn't want the icicles between them to melt, and if her tone was any indication, the idea of a date was not welcome.

That needled him. Was he so terrible a companion that she couldn't even fathom having a dinner that wasn't about business? Lots of women enjoyed his company…right up until they realized his cell phone was an extension of his arm.

This conversation was going south in a hurry.

"No, of course it's not a date." Dates came with connotations that he didn't know how to deal with, either. All of his dates consisted of interruptions due to work emergencies and the occasional late-night booty call that left him feeling increasingly lonely. "Would it be so bad if I did mean it that way?"

Wow, he needed to shut his trap, like, yesterday.

"I, um…don't…know."

She looked so miserable that he had to take pity on her. Clearly she didn't know how to respond to that, and technically, he was her boss more than he was her husband.

"It's just dinner," he practically growled. "I want to eat with you. Let's not attach any more meaning to it than that."

She nodded, her eyes a little wide.

There was a reason he didn't have more practice at this. *The pact.* And, frankly, drawing out his wife for the express purpose of getting to know her wasn't a good plan. Where could this possibly go? Granted, she already knew he was a workaholic, so that realization wasn't likely to stall things out before they got started. But in order for that to matter, they'd have to have some type of relationship beyond business.

Now was probably not the right time to figure out that that sounded really great.

Tilda spent about an hour rearranging her clothes in the closet of her new bedroom. If *closet* was even the appropriate term when the thing in question was the size of the entire corporate apartment she'd been living in for the last two months as she worked on the Flying Squirrel campaign. She'd expected to stay in that tiny apartment for the entire year. Funny how things worked out.

Not so funny were the second thoughts she'd been plagued with about selecting the bedroom near Warren's. The reasons she'd given him were sound. The effect of his proximity was not.

Sure, she'd had an academic understanding that the rooms connected via the enormous bathroom. There was an ocean of wide marble tile between the two doors, locks on either side and then a lot of carpet. They never had to see each other except perhaps in passing—she'd presumed.

That hadn't worked out. He'd just wandered in while she was putting away her things, perfectly fine having a chat in the bathroom. Why hadn't she taken the bedroom downstairs? Well, she knew that one. Because she'd had a moment of panic at the idea of being adrift in this huge house. Warren was the only person she knew in this place, the only person who had given her a measure of comfort in the whole of the United States. She shouldn't have to second-guess choosing the bedroom that meant she'd be closer to him. If she liked the fact that he was convenient, no one had to know. Nor would she ever act on that convenience. He was her boss and she owed him a debt of gratitude for keeping her out of Australia.

Plus, he'd backed off in a hurry when she'd tried to put parameters around this nebulous thing he'd called "dinner." Of course, it was crystal clear now that he hadn't defined it as a *date* in any way, shape or form.

Which was good. She was telling herself it was good, even as she tried to figure out what you wore to dinner with your husband who wasn't really a husband. One of her serviceable dove-gray suits felt too… officey, despite the fact that she'd been wearing one all day. Jeans and a T-shirt, like what she wore to the grocery store, seemed too casual. But then, Warren had mentioned they'd be dining at the house, so maybe casual wasn't off base.

In the end, she couldn't do it. She picked the brown suit and hid a peacock-blue silk bra with corded straps and a matching thong under it. Defiantly. It was her favorite set, bought with her first paycheck from the Flying Squirrel campaign. She'd waltzed right into that high-end lingerie store in downtown Raleigh and bought the classiest, most beautiful fabrics in the place. The clerk had folded her purchase into silver tissue paper, then tucked her lingerie into a foil bag the size of a paperback. Nothing she'd bought needed a bigger package, since both scraps were tiny and revealing.

Not that she'd ever reveal any of it to anyone. Her little secret. A kick in the teeth to Bryan's memory, who had never wanted her to wear anything remotely flashy or skimpy. She didn't dress that way on the outside, but that barrier of boring clothing was for her own peace of mind. Better to avoid attention than to seek it.

Dinner was exactly as advertised. At home, low-key and not a date. Warren wore the same T-shirt and jeans he'd had on earlier, but of course he looked like a dream in anything. She so rarely saw him in something besides a suit that she took time to enjoy the way his shoulders filled out the soft cotton, graceful biceps emerging below the cuffs.

Wordlessly, he pulled out a chair at the twelve-seat dining room table off the foyer.

"Do you entertain a lot?" she inquired politely, since she felt like she had to say something, and *heebie-jeebies, are you a good-looking man* didn't seem appropriate.

"Never. This was my mother's idea. Apparently it's the done thing to have a room big enough for a basketball team to dine in."

She smiled at the joke and slid into the chair he offered, careful not to brush him as she sat. But as he helped her push in the chair, it caught on an uneven slat in the hardwood floor and his fingers grazed her shoulders.

The coil of heat low in her belly surprised her with its intensity. The man had barely touched her. What was wrong with her that she had to fight the instinct to lean back against his hands in wordless invitation?

But his heat vanished from behind her as quickly as he'd established his presence. Taking a seat to her left, he eased into his own chair and turned his focus to her.

"Are you unpacked yet? Need any help?" he inquired.

She shook her head. "No, thank you. You've already been so generous with your staff and in allowing me time to get settled. We should really go over the project plan again, now that we've got Wheatner and Ro—"

"No work." Warren broke off as his housekeeper came in with plates of white fish and green beans, serving dinner with precise efficiency. Once he'd nodded his thanks, she disappeared. "We're just eating dinner tonight. As a couple. Not as coworkers."

"But we're not a couple," she countered, wondering how she was supposed to eat with such a thing thrown down between them. And wondering whether that note of panic had sounded as squeaky to him as it did to her. "We agreed. In name only."

A couple. She'd never been part of a couple, or rather, a *normal* one. She turned the term over in her head, trying not to attach any significance to it. Her dating life had been nothing remarkable. She'd longed for the kind of relationship that seemed to come so easily to everyone around her, but nothing had ever clicked for her. Until Bryan, whom she'd met at her university roommate's wedding.

In retrospect, they'd clicked far too easily, largely owing to her desperation to finally have the kind of companionship and intimacy she'd craved.

And over the last year, she'd proven that she could live without either. Being one half of a couple wasn't her goal any longer.

Warren didn't pick up his fork, despite having just laid down the law about the activity they were pursuing. "We did agree to in name only. But I'd like to get to know you. We're going to have some interview rounds for your green card. It would be beneficial if we didn't stumble through basic things like the names of our siblings or where you were born."

"I'm an only child and I was born in Melbourne. Your brother is Thomas. I was thinking that after Wheatner and Ross come back with the revised promotional—"

"Tilda."

Warren's voice snaked through the low light of the dining room to seep through her chest with jagged teeth, freezing her vocal chords.

"Is it that difficult to put work aside for an hour?" He cocked his head. "No judgment on this side of the table, if so. I'm the last person to cast the first stone when it comes to being all about the work. But it's Saturday night and I want to have a nice dinner with my wife, not with a project manager."

He wanted to *what*? "I'm only your project manager. The rest is strictly for show. In order to keep me in the country."

Wasn't it? Something unnamable gripped her shoulders, tightening them as she contemplated the gorgeous face of the man she'd married, who didn't seem all that boss-like as he nodded his agreement.

"Yes. And no. It strikes me as ironic that we're so similar. Here we are, married, and we can barely have dinner together without resorting to work. Maybe it's an opportunity to practice relaxing. For both of us. I like that we're on the same wavelength about nearly everything. It facilitates a good working relationship. I don't want the fact that we now live together to interfere with how we work together, and it feels like there's a potential for that if we can't eliminate the weirdness."

Oh, God, she was going to botch this whole thing up. He could feel her hesitancy, the way she tensed up the moment he looked at her with the slightest bit of warmth. And he was calling her on it. How was she supposed to stop being a freak about a man getting personal with her? "Seems to me like the best way to eliminate the weirdness is to talk about work."

Yes. Work. The one place she felt one hundred percent safe.

He flashed her a smile. "Which is what I'd rather do. I'm asking you to humor me, as this is a difficulty of mine as well."

How could she say no to *that*? He was asking her for help with his own social clumsiness, which she'd never have called a failing in a million years. "I like that you're so business focused. There's a certain confidence required to be the CEO and you carry it well."

It was far sexier than it should be. She'd never admit it out loud, but she could certainly visualize how those skills might extend to the bedroom. She could pretend she might drop a few hints about the nature of her undergarments, just to see where that led.

Now that she was thinking about them, the tiny scraps chafed the intimate places they covered, teasing up a fair amount of unexpected heat. She couldn't seem to ignore the fact that she was wearing the most daring lingerie she owned while having dinner with her husband.

What would he say if he knew?

The bubble of awareness grew until she could hardly stand it.

His gaze caught hers, burning with a strange intensity, as if he'd guessed the direction of her thoughts. "I like that you think that."

What was this conversation they were having? Normally, Warren had the concept of distance down to a science. That was why they worked so well together.

This had nothing to do with feeling pressured and everything to do with the sudden chemistry between her and Warren that she had no idea how to handle. Okay, she had *ideas*. So many ideas…

"But," he continued. "I was being serious about the interviews. No time like the present to get more comfortable about being a couple. Soon enough, we'll have to do it for real in front of government officials."

That popped her bubble in a hurry. She'd been lulled into a false sense of security where she could ignore the marriage part of this marriage and still get her green card. He was right. It simply wasn't going to be that easy. And utilitarian tasks she could handle.

"I like books," she offered warily. "Cozy mysteries."

"I don't think I know what that means." Finally, he picked up his fork, starting to eat as if this really was a casual dinner between a married couple with no expectations. "Tell me."

She launched into a rundown of the difference between cozy mysteries and detective stories. This was an innocuous enough subject that she didn't feel uncomfortable. But she was going to have to figure out how to be a little more open with him or they could be in trouble with her green card. How much trouble, she didn't want to find out.

He asked her a few questions, guiding the conversation well enough that she'd taken the last bite of her green beans without realizing she'd cleaned her plate. Huh. Somewhere along the way, he'd gotten her to relax. Good. She could do this. Being married to Warren wasn't any different than being his employee, and they'd navigated dinner without a lot of hoopla.

"Have a glass of wine with me," he said without preamble as the housekeeper picked up their dishes. Her gaze flew to his and he shrugged with a solid smile. "I have a beautiful terrace overlooking the garden and I never use it. Sit with me and let's continue the conversation."

She shouldn't say no. Not when a lot rode on playing the part of a wife. And maybe, in the grand scheme of things, it was okay to stop being such a sook and admit she didn't want to say no.

And not all of her reasons had to do with green cards.

Four

The terrace was one of Warren's favorite parts of the house. He'd bought this historic home in an exclusive Raleigh neighborhood for many reasons, mostly having to do with boring concepts like asset management, resale value and tax write-offs, but he'd made the decision to sign on the dotted line the moment he'd stepped through the double French doors.

Wrought iron curlicued through the railing like an endless black vine, affording an unobstructed view of the half-acre garden that the groundskeeper kept thriving through some alchemy that baffled Warren. Dollar signs, he understood. Living things, not so much.

Tilda would be one such example. She had turned into a quiet mouse the moment she crossed the threshold of the terrace. She'd been off-kilter all night. He'd been trying to change the dynamic, move them past boss and employee for God knew what reason. She clearly wasn't on board. Gingerly, she took a seat on one of the wicker chairs with bright orange cushions. The thing swallowed her; it was big enough to seat an elephant or two cozy lovers, which they definitely were not.

Which didn't necessarily mean he couldn't slide into the chair next to her and see if he could coax a little more cheer out of the woman he'd married. Funny, he'd never even noticed the size of that chair. Perhaps because he seldom came out here. A shame.

And now that was all he could think about. Giant chair. Pretty woman. Beautiful view. Lots to enjoy.

He cleared his throat and extended the wine bottle dangling from his fingers. "Red okay?"

She nodded, relaxing not an iota as she shifted in the chair. He had the distinct impression she would have agreed in exactly the same manner if he'd casually suggested paint thinner as their after-dinner drink.

It was nearly painful how thick the tension had grown, and that was not going to work come Monday morning when they'd spend hours in each other's company doing the job she'd married him for. That was his excuse and he was sticking to it. Though the miniscule bit of intel he'd gleaned during dinner had only whetted his appetite to draw out this puzzle of a woman from her workaholic shell and see what made her tick.

There was a part of him that wondered if he'd figure out what made *him* tick in the process. The point wasn't lost on him that there were two uncomfortable people on the terrace, neither of whom had a lot of practice at putting work aside. Why couldn't they practice with each other? The fact that they needed to *get* comfortable—for more than one reason—was just a bonus.

He uncorked the wine that his housekeeper had already opened and then poured it, handing Tilda the glass of deep red wine by the stem—deliberately. Their fingers brushed and he wasn't a bit ashamed to enjoy the blush that worked across her cheeks. The setting sun threw all kinds of interesting shadows across the terrace and the atmosphere was far more romantic than he'd fully anticipated. Seriously, he'd just hoped to spend a little more time with Tilda before it was back to all business, but this had turned out better than he could have dreamed.

And he'd done a lot of that. Fantasies were harmless. The problems cropped up when he couldn't figure out how to engage the real woman, especially since he didn't have the possibility of dropping them both into one of his sensually charged imaginary scenes.

Bad thing to be thinking about. And still be thinking about. His lower half had gotten uncomfortably tight in half a second, and she was going to clue in that his groin was stirring if he didn't reel it back.

Not that there was anything wrong with a healthy attraction between two people. They just happened to be the two worst people on the planet to indulge in any kind of attraction, healthy or otherwise. They needed to be relaxed around each other, not hot and heavy. Though he was markedly better at the kind of conversations that he had with her in his head, the imaginary ones where all the words were sexy and led to both of them getting naked very fast.

Get a grip with a capital G right now.

Instead of taking one of the smaller chairs near the railing, he pulled over the footstool that went with Tilda's chair and perched on it, sipping his wine as he contemplated her.

"Tell me more about your life in Melbourne."

Her eyes widened. "Why?"

Yeah, practice definitely needed, stat. Along with an icebreaker, more wine and maybe a nice fire at the Flying Squirrel warehouse that would allow him to escape, because of course it would take hours to untangle.

He bit back a sigh. "Tilda, we're married. We work together. The green-card people will think it's weird that I know nothing about you, your childhood, your hopes, dreams. That's what people who get married talk about as they're falling in love."

Didn't they? He'd never talked about stuff like this with women. Hence the reason he was failing at it. Quite handily, too.

"Right-o." She shut her eyes for a blink and then glugged about a third of her wine in one shot. "I'm not very good at this, either. I don't date."

That was an interesting admission. "Really? Not at all? It seems unlikely that you don't get asked out. You're an attractive woman."

Something bright flared in her eyes and then vanished. "It might not have escaped your notice that I work a lot. Means I don't have much time for dating."

"You might have noticed that's something we have in common." The smile he flashed her was immediately returned and that was so encouraging that his widened involuntarily. "This is good for both of us. Indulge me in something. Relax," he told her as she raised her brows in question. "It's just me, and I solemnly swear not to tattle to the boss that we didn't spend the evening talking about spreadsheets."

That actually got a laugh out of her and it warmed something inside to hear. Because it meant she was taking his point seriously. That he might not be so bad at this, after all. Emboldened, he sipped his own wine and nudged her knee with his. "Melbourne?"

To her credit, she didn't edge away from the physical contact, and he gladly took it as a small victory.

"I lived there with my parents, attended Victoria University on a full academic scholarship."

"That's impressive."

She shrugged that off. "We weren't wealthy by any stretch. If I wanted a degree, that was the only way."

"You went to work for Craig right out of college?"

Nodding, she sipped more wine and the conversation ground to a halt. Okay. They were stuck together and he owed it to her to keep her eyes from glazing over.

"Come on." He stood and held out his hand without thinking better of it.

But then he didn't pull it back to his side. They could touch each other. It wasn't a rule that they couldn't. In fact, he'd say it was expected that a husband and wife touch each other, both in public and at home. How else would they get comfortable with it?

She eyed his hand. "Are we going somewhere?"

"Yes, to the railing so I can show you the garden. The personal conversation was too forced and people can get to know each other by means outside of the third degree."

That got her vote of confidence. She slipped her hand into his and let him help her from the gargantuan chair. Now that she'd done so, he couldn't help but notice that her hand was small and feminine in his. She was so capable and focused. He forgot occasionally that she couldn't, in fact, walk on water, and if she had vulnerabilities, she didn't advertise them.

He liked the reminder that she had softness hidden away, so he didn't release her hand. Instead, he guided her to the edge of the terrace and stood with her at the railing, as promised, wedging in close.

She didn't comment on his proximity, just stared over the circular rows of flowers that radiated outward from the center of the garden like a pinwheel. The sun was in the last throes of setting and the landscape lighting had clicked on sometime back, illuminating the grounds. The brightness was a security measure, but he pretended it was an extension of the romantic atmosphere. Everything in his life felt utilitarian all at once, and he wasn't in the mood to continue in the same vein with his wife.

"This is a very unusual garden," she remarked, pointedly not looking at their joined hands. But she didn't pull away. "Do you spend a lot of time in it?"

He couldn't help but smile, both at the hilariousness of the question and the fact that she'd fallen into personal conversation in a snap, exactly as he'd hoped. "My groundskeeper occasionally consults me on things like whether I'd like to change out the annuals, but no. For the most part, it's just magic that I enjoy occasionally when I remember that it's here."

"If this was my house, I'd be out on this terrace all the time."

And that was as telling a comment as any. "You are aware of the fact that you live here, yes?"

She smiled. "Not permanently. And, yes, I don't seem capable of forgetting the fact that I now live here. With you."

The landscape lighting did her no favors when it came to hiding the blush that sprang up, spreading across her cheeks and into her hairline. It was as becoming as it was intriguing. She clearly didn't like to discuss personal matters, but he couldn't quite put his finger on whether it was because she didn't like to give up details or because she worried that she'd say the wrong thing.

"Yes, that's an important part of the equation. We live here together. Have you not ever lived with a man before?"

She shook her head and, lo and behold, one rebel strand of hair escaped her severe hairstyle, floating down to graze her cheek. And of course that made him wonder why she always shellacked her hair into place when there was at least part of it that didn't want to conform to its mistress's will.

The hank of hair caught his gaze and he couldn't stop thinking about what her hair might look like down. Better yet, what it might look like with his fingers shoved through it.

And that was the tipping point. He wanted to touch.

He reached out to sweep the strand from her cheek. But she jerked backward before his fingers connected, moving out of reach. Her hand slipped from his and the softening vibe between them shattered.

"I'm sorry," he muttered, though he wasn't quite

sure what he was apologizing for. "You had this piece of hair—"

"No, I'm sorry," she cut in, more color rushing into her face. "That was uncalled for."

"It's fine. We're not at the place where we can act like a couple yet. We only got married yesterday."

"But we are married."

She looked so miserable that he almost reached out again, but he caught himself this time. She didn't want him touching her. That much was obvious. "Yes. Are you regretting that?"

"No!" A horrified expression replaced the embarrassment of a moment ago. "I'm just… I told you I don't date, and you surprised me. Not that you can't—I mean, I'm not *that* much of a… Sorry. I'm rambling."

Shutting her eyes, she waited about four beats, as if collecting herself, and then opened them. He gave her that time because he was busy reading her nonverbal signals. Her arms had stolen around her midsection defensively, though he couldn't imagine a scenario in which she'd have to be defensive. Was she afraid of him? Or did she object to him personally in some way?

His first instinct was to blaze through this problem, the way he would any challenge that came across his desk.

But this was not a thorny personnel problem with Flying Squirrel or an accounting discrepancy that someone needed to explain. It was Tilda. He respected her. He'd *married* her. Warren forced his shoulders to relax and bit back the first phrase that had sprung to his lips, which sounded a lot like what he'd said to Marcus. *Get over it.*

Whatever had been going on with Marcus prior to

his suicide was not something he could just get over, no matter how logical a solution that had seemed to Warren at the time. What he'd really meant was *move on*. Forget about it. Focus on something else. Whatever worked.

Marcus had needed compassion, not directives. Warren had missed that. He couldn't make that mistake again, which was why he limited his personal interactions as much as possible. Distance was his friend for a lot of reasons. But he needed Tilda for his project. And maybe to assuage the sudden protective instinct that had sprung up out of nowhere. Tilda was his wife and it was not okay that she was so skittish around him. He had to figure out how to change things between them—without his CEO hat on—or his project would go down in flames.

The terrace had been a bad idea.

Or rather, the terrace was fine. It was Tilda who was the problem. What had she been thinking when she'd agreed to a glass of wine and getting cozy with Warren? Well, that was no mystery. She'd assumed he'd never breach that physical distance between them, that the natural reserve he'd always exhibited would be her saving grace. Big mistake.

The hand-holding had been one thing. That, he'd allowed her to ease into, which was precisely what she hadn't known she'd need. Though it had been entirely unwitting on his part, she suspected. But then he'd lifted his hand toward her face. She hadn't been fully prepared for it and now he was looking at her with a mixture of hesitancy and concern. Because he thought she was slightly crazy, no doubt.

Who flinched just because a man's hand had come toward her face?

Only the victim of previous abuse. And unless she wanted to start explaining that to him—which she'd rather not do—she had to pull it together. A woman who could handle a project the size of Flying Squirrel did not flinch. For any reason.

"I'm sorry," she repeated a little more strongly. "It's a difficult transition from employee to wife."

His expression softened. "I'm not making it any easier, either."

"You absolutely are." Oh, God, now he thought that he was the problem. None of this was his fault. "You've been nothing but kind to me. Extremely patient."

"Really?" he asked with a wry quirk of his lips. "Because from my side of the table, it seemed like I was rushing you."

This was a disaster. She'd thoroughly enjoyed the idea of Warren showing her his garden. It was sweet. Low-key. Exactly the kind of thing she'd have loved if it had been the tail end of a real date. For a moment, she'd let herself pretend that was what was happening. That he'd closed the distance between them because he'd correctly perceived that she needed to practice touching. There wasn't anything threatening about it, yet her instincts had triggered automatically.

That was not who she wanted to be. Not around Warren. Rationally, she knew she could trust him. They'd been acquainted for two months. He'd been more than fair in their agreement. What more incentive did she need to use this opportunity to get over her fear?

"You're not rushing me," she said. "This is important. We have to work together and we have to convince people that we're married for reasons that have nothing to do with green cards. If anything, we're taking it too slow."

Surprise filtered through Warren's expression. "Would you like another glass of wine, then?"

"Yes," she told him decisively and held out her glass. "Let's start over. Tell me a funny story from your childhood."

That was the kind of thing that seemed like a good segue. Finally, she felt a little more in control and her lungs expanded as Warren filled her glass, then his, with the remainder of the wine. This, she could do. If she knew what to expect, could guide the conversation, then she'd be okay.

Warren obliged, recounting a time when his brother had let Warren cut his hair. By the time he got to the part where their mother had caught Warren with the shears and tufts of Thomas's hair under his bed, her smile was genuine. He let one of his own bloom and it did funny things to her stomach. Or perhaps that was the wine.

"It sounds like you were a mischievous little boy," she said.

"No," he corrected with a laugh. "I was always in charge. If I wanted to do something, I did it. That's how I ended up as the CEO. It was the only job I was interested in."

"I didn't think work talk was allowed," she teased and bumped him with her elbow. See, she could initiate contact without freaking out.

"That's not work talk. It's personal. I like getting what I want."

The way he was watching her lent an undertone to the statement that made her shiver. In a good way. It was a little decadent and a lot delicious. What would happen if she stopped being such a weirdo about her boundaries and let her professional veneer drop away? Warren wouldn't fire her. He certainly wasn't going to hurt her.

She was still in control. Which meant she got to guide where things went next.

"Curious," she murmured. "What were you going to do with my hair?"

His gaze shifted to the strand that was still grazing her cheekbone. That errant lock had set them off on the wrong track earlier. Maybe now it could get them on an entirely different track. One that would get them over this hump that caused them to be so cautious with each other.

"Tuck it back," he said simply. "I should have just mentioned it."

The floodlights from the garden played over them as they stood at the railing. A few stars had started to twinkle in the sky but she couldn't seem to take her eyes off his face. They were in the middle of a vibrant city, but here on this terrace, they were insulated from everything else—bad, good or otherwise—and it was easy to pretend they were the only two people in the world.

"You commented on that in the car. After the wedding. Is it bothering you?"

"Yes," he admitted, surprising her. "You're normally so perfectly put together. It's like this little piece of you is begging to be free of the confines you've imposed. It's extremely distracting."

That was a fair assessment of her entire personality. Intrigued that he'd picked up on that, she decided to press it. "I thought you liked it. Remember? You told me not to fix it last time."

"It's distracting because it makes me wonder what you look like with your hair down," he responded huskily.

Somehow, they'd drifted a little closer together. He'd picked up on the shifting vibe and had angled his body toward her. Not too close, because he wasn't an idiot. Her minor freak-out earlier had cost them a degree of ease she wanted to recapture.

"Wearing my hair up is professional," she informed him. "Since we've banned all work talk, maybe that should go, as well."

Before she lost her nerve, she reached up and pulled the clip loose from the twist at the back of her head. As she tucked it in her pocket, her hair cascaded down her back, with a bit of volume for once because it had dried in the chignon.

Warren made a noise low in his chest and it sounded far hungrier than she would have supposed would be appropriate for a simple thing like taking down her hair. She shook it out, her scalp crying in relief. Releasing her hairstyle was one of the highlights of her day, usually, and doing it in front of Warren added a measure of intimacy that she hadn't expected. It was like he was watching her undress at the end of the night, and a hum of expectation started up in her core.

It had been a very long time since a man had looked at her with an edge. The way Warren was looking at her now.

"As your boss, I must insist you continue to wear your hair up at the office." With that odd pronouncement, he plucked her wineglass from her hand and set it, along with his own, on a table behind him then returned to her side. "As your husband, I hereby ban that twisted-up hairstyle from crossing the threshold."

"What are you saying, that the moment I enter the house I should take my hair down?"

"Or I'll do it for you." The temperature of the sultry evening rose a few degrees as Warren's gaze played over her face. "You should really never wear it up. But, selfishly, I want to keep this secret all to myself."

The heat that prickled across her cheeks then should have spread clear down to her neck, but she'd been the one to introduce this new dynamic. Boldly. It was getting a far bigger response than she'd expected. Were they practicing for a green-card interview or was this something else?

More important, what did she want it to be?

"It's not really a secret," she said inanely.

The real secret was beneath her clothes and she couldn't stop imagining what might happen if he'd made a random comment about how distracting her suit was. His expression might heat with something entirely different if she started shedding clothes. The scraps of lingerie left almost nothing of her body covered. And that's why they were hidden.

She had very little practice at flirting and even less practice at taking control in intimate situations—or, at least, not successfully. Bryan had chipped away at her confidence every time he called her those horrible names whenever she was aggressive. Professionally, she knew her strengths, could easily pivot between situations with confidence. This was way out of her depth and she had to stay in control or panic would overwhelm her.

"Oh, yes, it's a huge secret," he countered, his voice low. "With your hair down, you transform from an attractive professional woman into a complete temptress."

That thrilled through her to the core, easily eclipsing the panic. No one had ever said anything like that to her before. "What could I tempt you into doing?"

"Anything."

The moment stretched out to the point of snapping, but still he didn't shift his gaze from her. Boldly, she stared back, hardly recognizing herself in this scenario. A man had invited her to his private terrace and plied her with wine, setting the scene for a seduction that she was actively participating in.

And yet, he was holding back. She could feel it. He didn't want to step over her boundaries, a detail she appreciated far more than he could ever know. They'd mapped out an in-name-only marriage that had seemed simple on the surface. That was before she'd known all this heat would spring up between them. Before she'd known she'd want to see where things might lead.

This was her seduction to move forward. Warren wasn't Bryan. Logically, she knew this was different. He'd flat out said she could do the tempting and he'd follow her into whatever she laid out. It was heady and powerful, and she couldn't stop marveling at the amazing qualities of the man she'd married.

"Warren," she murmured. "I mean this in all sincerity. You're the most patient man I've ever met. Too patient. I feel a distinct need to have my hair tucked back."

His expression slipped, falling into a category more easily defined as carnal. It was delicious as he slowly reached out to slide one hand through the loose strands at her nape, and then she had a whole different problem as his touch electrified her skin, zinging through her core with heat that weakened her knees.

He picked up on that, too, easing his other hand to her waist and pulling her into his body. It was slow and sensuous and exactly what she needed in order to acclimate before things ratcheted up a notch higher.

And that happened quickly. Before she realized it, his arm had stolen around her, engulfing her in an embrace that aligned their bodies. He was hard in all the right places and all those places were teasing hers, particularly the ones covered by shockingly small scraps of silk. The fabric toyed with her breasts in combination with the rub of his body and it was the most turned-on she'd been in a very long while.

Without taking his gaze off her face, he brushed her hair back behind her ear, his thumb lingering far longer than the simple act required. It turned into a caress and her breath caught as she read the intention in his eyes. He wanted to kiss her. But wouldn't unless she gave him the all clear.

"Is this part of the green-card interview?" she asked breathlessly as her lungs caught up with the rest of her body, clueing in that something momentous was going on here.

"No. This is because your hair is driving me mad," he murmured, shoving his hand deeper into the recesses of the mass, his touch sensitizing the back of her head beyond anything she'd ever imagined. "If you like, I can tell the immigration department that."

"That's okay. We'll count it as part of the secret."

And now she and Warren had secrets. That, more than anything, solidified them as a couple. The smile her comment put on his face rushed through her with heat, enlivening her blood.

"As secrets go, I like this one."

"It's pretty tame," she countered with a small wrinkle of her nose. "Perhaps we should add a few more. Just to keep the authenticity factor."

His brows lifted. "I can't find anything wrong with that. Though now I'm insanely curious what might count as a non-tame secret in your world."

"You should kiss me, then, and find out."

To his credit, he didn't blink, just leaned down and laid his lips on hers in a cautious kiss that had none of the heat she'd envisioned when she'd made such a bold statement. Her fault. He was still feeling her out, exhibiting incredible patience that nearly made her weep with gratitude. And that was the sole reason she could twist her fingers into the soft material of his T-shirt and yank.

Their bodies slammed together and, instantly, the kiss intensified. Warren groaned, his fingers nipping into her neck as he angled her head, his tongue sliding into her mouth. The first demanding lick of it between her lips electrified her and she opened automatically, drawing him in, welcoming his mastery over her man-starved senses. But she wasn't capable of letting him have complete control and switched the angle herself, dragging him along as she deepened the contact, sliding her hands up his back to acquaint her fingertips with the spread of muscles.

That galvanized him, her enthusiasm seeming to act as permission for Warren to let go. He spun her, backing her against the railing and shoving a hard thigh between her legs to rub at the tight, sensitized spot that was already enflamed. Heat erupted in her core, shamelessly flinging her into a miasma of sensuality.

His hands roved up and down her body as he kissed her and the railing bit into her back. His erection, so prominently pressing against her pelvis, awoke something primal inside her and her back arched, raising her breasts higher against his torso. He took that as invitation, sliding a hand beneath her suit jacket and blouse to cup her bare waist.

The shock of his fingertips against her flesh tore something open inside, and all of the things she tried to keep under wraps spilled out. Desire, longing, carnal needs—they all welled up, drenching her with a flood of damp heat, engulfing her so fast that in that moment, if he'd stripped her, she would have demanded he take her right there on the terrace, hands gripping the railing as he drilled into her from behind.

That was enough to jolt her into pulling away. The kiss ended abruptly. Warren took one look at her face and stepped back, running a hand through his hair with something akin to confusion. Of course he didn't know what to think—she'd been into it and then she wasn't.

"Did I overstep?" he asked cautiously.

Her lips stung as she stared at him. How was she supposed to explain that she'd forgotten for a moment that she couldn't do normal? She was wanton and shameless, and when she let a man find out how truly wicked she could be, he changed, morphing into something monstrous.

She shook her head. "I'm sorry."

And then she fled before he could ask any questions, or God forbid, kiss her again.

Five

Warren prowled around his bedroom until one in the morning, far longer than he should have before giving up the idea of sleep. Stalking to his study, he logged on to his PC and pretended he had the capacity to focus on Flying Squirrel, when in reality, every bit of his mind was on the woman he'd married.

She was, hands down, the hottest kisser he'd ever met.

Who could have seen that coming? Not him. And he'd imagined her in every dirty scenario his liberal imagination could spin up. But he'd never expected her to *actually* give his fantasies a run for their money.

Ms. Straitlaced Suits knew her way around some tongue action. It was killing him that he'd used that as an excuse to take it up about twelve notches, only to be shut down. And he couldn't quite work out why. She'd been like molten lava in his hands and then *poof.*

Turned into an ice cube instantly. It was almost fascinating how quickly she'd shut herself back behind her reserve, or it would have been if it had happened to someone else.

As it stood, he was the one it had happened to and he was not happy about it. Especially given that he'd seen genuine distress in the depths of her gaze when she backed away from him. There was something going on with her that he was just not getting, and she wasn't planning to be forthcoming about it, either.

Clearly he was going to have to figure it out on his own.

Because he couldn't help himself, he did a quick search on Tilda Barrett and found several mentions of her in relation to campaigns she'd done for her former employers, including the one she'd done for Kim Electronics. Huh. There she was, looking much the same in a staid suit, standing next to a man the picture identified as Craig Von, the same ass who had screwed up Tilda's visa.

Obviously she'd been wearing boring suits since puberty. In his head, she wore red dresses with plunging necklines. After kissing her on the terrace, he was of the opinion that the red dress fit her better. She didn't seem to be of the same mind, nor did she give the impression she had any intention of showing off her hot kissing skills again—not with him, anyway.

His mood went from bad to worse when he couldn't find anything online about Tilda that told him who she was. They'd had two stilted personal conversations and one wet dream of a kiss. And all that had done was whet his appetite to get under those suits and see what else Tilda was hiding.

The next morning, he didn't see Tilda at all. As far as he knew, she'd never left her room. Avoiding him? That was crap. Except, he didn't own her, and as long as she showed up for work on Monday, he had little call to barge into her room demanding to know what was so horrible about kissing him that she felt compelled to turn herself into a prisoner in his home.

Well, clearly the kissing part was the problem. *Oops. Married a man I'm not attracted to and now we're stuck together until I get my visa.*

By midday, he'd started to grow concerned when she still hadn't emerged. What, she wasn't going to eat? He tracked down his housekeeper and learned that Tilda had asked to have meals delivered to her room. Mollified that she at least wasn't going to starve herself on his account, he removed his presence from the house so she could have some peace.

The warehouse staff was not pleased to see him on a Sunday, and without the buffer of Thomas, they got the full brunt of Warren. Usually he visited the distribution center with the chief operating officer because, technically, this part of the business fell under Thomas's umbrella. His brother genuinely liked the people who worked for him and he did a great job managing the daily ins and outs of the minutiae required to get pick-me-ups into the hands of customers. But Thomas reported to Warren, so the staff also technically reported to him. Much to their chagrin. And Thomas was on vacation.

The warehouse manager, a solid Midwesterner named Bob Page, scurried along behind him as Warren barked out questions. "Have you made the changes to the inventory locator software?"

Page nodded. "Last week."

The man wasn't scurrying fast enough; he barely kept pace with Warren as they rounded the corner to the main section of the warehouse where the rows and rows of canned drinks sat waiting to be loaded onto eighteen-wheelers. "Thomas gave you schematics on the new layout of the pallets. Done?"

"Almost."

"Doesn't count. By the end of the day." Surely there was something else he could tear apart. "How are contract negotiations going with Chuahan?"

"I…haven't been updated," Page admitted.

What he meant was, he hadn't bothered to ask anyone in Legal about the incredibly important contracts Flying Squirrel had with their main equipment manufacturer. If they didn't have pallet loaders, forklifts and other various machinery in top shape, distribution would grind to a halt. "Get updated."

"It's Sunday," the beleaguered man pointed out. "Legal isn't in the office."

"We are. They should be, too." Though odds were good no one else working on a Sunday was doing it for the same reason Warren was—to avoid putting undue pressure on the woman he'd married who regretted kissing him on the terrace last night.

Though she had asked him to. That's what was sticking in his craw as he blasted through a few more areas of the distribution center. By the time he left the warehouse, there was little that had escaped his fine-tooth comb and he'd endeared himself to no one.

Fine. People weren't his forte and he'd definitely earned his reputation for being remote with the staff.

If they didn't like it, they could find someplace else to work.

When he got home at seven, the house had an empty quality that he'd never noticed before. It was filled with staff, but they usually stayed invisible, as he preferred. But there was a distinct lack of Tilda.

What the hell was wrong with him? She'd only moved in the day before and already he found himself looking for her, wondering why she wasn't using the solarium to read a book or lounging around the pool.

He ate dinner alone and answered emails on his phone. Same as he did most nights and had for a very long time. It was teeth-numbingly boring all at once.

Was it so bad to be thinking that companionship could be a benefit of having a wife under his roof? Sure, there was the utilitarian purpose. He'd already filed the forms required to petition for a green card for his alien family member, a phrase that still made him smile, and now they were just playing the waiting game until it was approved. Then she'd file for her green card. But, in the meantime, they both lived here, and he was insanely curious about the woman he'd married. Also, he was perhaps still a little crushed about the way she'd backed off last night.

Surely he could do better. Take it a little slower. If she'd just make an appearance.

Nada. At nine o'clock, he was back in his bedroom staring at his Louis Moinet Magistralis. After all, what good was it to have such a precise, gorgeous wristwatch if it wasn't to mark each painful second of the day as it crawled by?

As he stormed through the bathroom door to shower, he found his wife. Tilda whirled. All the blood drained from his head as the sight of her in sheer white lace axed through his gut. Instructions spurted through his consciousness. *Abort. Huge mistake. Get out.* He couldn't move.

Tilda snatched a robe from the counter and slung it over her shoulders, fumbling with the belt, and that's when he slammed his lids closed. Didn't help. The vision of her killer body decked out in *sheer white lace* had been seared into his mind.

And it wasn't the virginal kind, either. The cups of the bra had scarcely covered her nipples, which mattered hardly at all since the lace had been mostly transparent, begging for a man's tongue to taste her through it. Little scraps of lace V'd down between her thighs, held in place by three silken cords over each hip and, yeah, he'd had *plenty* of time to note it was a thong. He'd gotten only a glimpse of one bare butt cheek, but it was enough to know that she had a high, rounded rear that would fit into the hollow of his groin perfectly as he ground into her from behind.

His whole body strained to do exactly that, and he was so hard he couldn't drag enough oxygen into his lungs.

"Sorry," he mumbled, eyes still closed as he felt around for the vanity.

He gripped the marble with one hand, mostly to keep himself off the floor, because his knees were in very real danger of collapsing beneath him. All the blood that should be feeding his muscles was currently coiled up in his groin, poised to strike. Hell, maybe he should just let his knees hit the floor, but it was a toss-up whether he'd end up groveling for forgiveness or begging for her to slide that robe off so he could worship that lingerie set the way it deserved.

"What are you doing?" Tilda squeaked out. "You shouldn't be in here."

"I know. I'm sorry," he muttered again. "The door wasn't locked," he protested weakly. Stupid. That's what he should have led with. *I'm sorry. By the way, what the hell kind of lingerie is that for a woman who wears boring gray suits every day?*

Better question—*who are you wearing it for?*

"I thought I did lock it," Tilda shot back. "You have these fancy tumblers that don't click when they're turned so I thought it had engaged. We've both learned otherwise."

Her accent had deepened with her distress and that was not helping matters because, God, was it sexy. Coupled with the secrets he'd learned about her—*hot kisser* being first and foremost in his mind right after *hot lingerie wearer*—he was about to come apart.

"Are you…covered?" he rasped, terrified that if the answer was no, he'd cop another peek. He squeezed his eyes shut so hard that sparks exploded against the dark of his eyelids. "I'm not sure I can edge out of here blind."

"You can open your eyes."

He did. She'd burrowed so far down into the robe that her face was half covered by the lapels, and somehow she'd managed to get her hair mostly swept up into her trademark twist, but bits of it were falling down into her face, which was nearly as hot as when her hair was down.

Frankly, it wouldn't matter if she cut armholes in a

potato sack and wore a bird's nest as a hat. Everything about her was a turn-on now.

"So, the problem is that I can't unring this bell," he muttered and, no, he should not have spoken aloud. He should have been exiting stage left and ordering diamond earrings that doubled as an apology to his wife. Instead, he was standing there staring at her like an imbecile.

"Sorry?"

Warren shook his head and was a half second from spinning on his heel to flee the torture chamber his bathroom had become when he had a flashback to last night. Tilda had been the one doing the fleeing then—*after* asking him to kiss her. As a result, he'd spent the day in a crappy mood, and there was too much unsaid.

His wife was a fascinating, maddening mix of temptress and puritan, and he wanted to know which one was the real Tilda Barrett.

"We're dancing around some things, you and I. And we need to settle them." Her eyes went wide and, again, there was the flash of distress that he'd noted last night. His pulse stuttered. "Please. I just want to have an honest conversation with you, but not like this. Get dressed and meet me in the solarium."

Then he left.

Tilda spent a solid ten minutes after Warren vacated the bathroom getting her lungs working again. He'd been so close and she'd been so aware of how little she had on under the robe—and so very aware that he *knew*.

Her panic was only matched by the level of wanton heat that the whole scene had generated. If only

she could just stop being such a freak long enough
to have a simple physical reaction to a gorgeous man
who kissed like a dream, life would be a lot easier.
And better. But it wasn't like she could snap her fingers and change or she would have stuck around on
that terrace last night instead of scrabbling away as
fast as her scaredy-cat legs could carry her.

And now Warren wanted to have a little chat, did
he? Because he'd figured out that she wasn't being
on the square about her demure suits, most likely. He
expected her to answer for her deception. Now what
was she going to do? If he was angry enough, he'd fire
her for being a liar and send her back to Melbourne,
wouldn't he?

Nothing to be done about it now. The cat was out
of the bag and, by God, she was wholly sick of sticking her natural personality under wraps. He'd said he
wanted a candid conversation; maybe it was time to
take him at his word, whether he knew what he was
asking for or not.

As such, there was no way she was putting on a
suit to talk about why she wore atrocious suits. Tilda
slipped into a pair of jeans and a T-shirt, one of two
sets she owned, tried not to think too hard about what
a horrifically bad idea it was to have kept on the lacy
white bra and panties under her clothes, then strode
to the solarium before she lost her nerve.

Too late. The second she spied Warren sitting in one
of the wicker chairs, staring out over the pool through
the glass walls, everything inside started quivering. He
held her life in his hands and she'd thoroughly messed
up, first by kissing him and second by not figuring out
the locks to the bathroom better.

When a competent woman had secrets, she didn't screw up. This was all on her and she needed to fix it.

Her bare feet squeaked on the hardwood floor and Warren's gaze flicked to her, darkening with something she could only misinterpret if she'd arrived in the solarium blindfolded. Maybe not even then. The awareness that had permeated the bathroom had followed them to the solarium, not at all lessened by the fact that she'd traded her easily untied robe for jeans and a T-shirt.

"I didn't know you owned any clothes that aren't brown or gray," he commented, his voice deep with a color that had only recently become a thing.

She liked it when he let her see that she affected him. It bolstered her confidence in a way nothing else could have in that moment. "Surprise."

"Yeah, there's a lot of that going around," he said wryly. "Which is why I shouldn't be so shocked that you actually showed up after avoiding me all day and then receiving an unwelcome guest in a place that should have been sacred."

There was a half second when she considered lying, or at least downplaying what he'd already guessed, but in the spirit of the evening's apparent theme, she surprised herself by nodding. "Me, too. I didn't know what to say after leading you on, so it seemed easier to stay away from you."

His brows lifted but he schooled his expression quickly. "You didn't lead me on. I went too far with that kiss and you have every right to call a halt to something that was making you uncomfortable."

That was so much the opposite of what she'd expected him to say that she blinked.

"But I asked you to kiss me." And oh, God, had she wanted him to.

"I don't care if you asked me to strip you naked and put my tongue between your legs. You're allowed to say stop at any time. I will always honor that."

Her eyelids fluttered shut as she internalized the absurdity of a notion like asking him to *stop* if he was between her legs pleasuring her with that wicked tongue. Uncomfortable and achy all over again, she sank into one of the seats and crossed her arms in hopes that he couldn't, in fact, see how hard and pointy her nipples were through the sheer bra and thin T-shirt.

"Thank you for that," she said and, yes, she meant for both the carnal image he'd put into her head and his promise. What else was she supposed to say at this point? Might as well get this crucifixion over with. "You wanted to talk."

"How are you?" he asked out of the blue, instead diving right into a litany of her sins. His open gaze roved over her face and held nothing of the censure she'd been expecting. "I...missed you today."

"You, um...what?" Her heart tumbled over itself in an effort to beat and swoon at the same time. Except she shouldn't be swooning over pretty, bewildering words.

"Honest conversation," he reminded her somewhat ruefully, which was also unexpected. "I wasn't kidding about being straight with you."

Yeah, apparently not. "I was under the impression the honesty you were after was mine."

"Why would you think that?"

His brows scrunched together in confusion and it was a testament to her utter befuddlement that she was watching his nuances so carefully. This was where things would take an ugly turn, when she wasn't paying attention. When she let her guard down. Which was why she needed to stay in control of the conversation and not let it get away from her into subjects better left out of the mix.

"Because you ordered me to appear straight away after you saw my underwear. You must feel deceived."

"That's…" He shook his head. Hard. "No, I didn't order you. I said please. It was a request. I'm screwing this up."

That's when he did the most surprising thing of all. He knelt by her chair and took one of her hands into his, holding it against his thigh gently as his dark gaze latched onto hers, thoroughly capturing her. It should have been easy to break away if she wanted to. But she didn't want to, all at once. The sheer beauty of so much masculinity at her feet, particularly when the most commanding man she'd ever met was encased inside, overwhelmed her.

Speechless, she stared at him as he swept her into his orbit without moving at all.

"Tilda, the honesty that needs to be happening is on my side. The marriage was one hundred percent conceived with the intent of keeping you in the country. I want you to believe that. But I was…attracted to you before that."

He paused to let that bombshell sink in, and when it had reached optimal depth, that's when he detonated it.

"Now that I've kissed you," he continued, his voice dropping a few smoky degrees, "and seen exactly what I'm missing out on under your clothes, I'm afraid I can't go back to thinking of you as only an employee. It's impossible. I'm sorry."

"You're, um…what? Did you just apologize?"

She was the one who should be apologizing, and he hadn't even gotten to the part where it was disingenuous of her to pretend to be a staid matronly type while hiding centerfold wantonness underneath. Bryan had made it clear how men felt about a woman who wanted to express her sexuality. At odd times, in her head, she still heard the names he'd called her.

"I did. And I'll do it as many more times as I need to in order to get you comfortable with the idea that I can't unsee you in that lingerie you were wearing earlier. If I'm being completely honest, which is the goal here, I don't want to forget. You're an amazingly beautiful woman," he murmured, and his grip on her hand tightened. "I can't help the fact that I want to kiss you again, but I totally understand that you don't feel quite the same way about it. I'm telling you it's okay. I'll back off."

Speechless—again—she worked her throat, somehow managing to swallow several times in a row, a minor miracle since her mouth had turned into a desert. What a patient, saintly man she'd married, speaking of deceptions. He'd sold himself as remote, a banger of a professional. A CEO who brooked no nonsense—look how quickly he'd dispatched Craig and solved her problem in one shot.

This sweetness she had no idea what to do with. Other than return a bit of the honesty that seemed to be what he was looking for.

"Warren, I—" Wow, this was not the conversation she'd prepped for, and when she wasn't in her element, the words weren't so forthcoming. The fact that he wasn't pressing her about her suits was throwing her off. "Trust me when I say my hesitation is not you, it's me."

"That's what they all say," he said with a bit of a smile that coaxed one from her, as well. "It's fine if you're not attracted to me in return. This is supposed to be a green-card marriage and I will keep it that way despite my earlier statements."

"Not attra—" She choked on that so hard that she coughed, sputtering around the rest of the syllables until her throat cleared. "That's patently ridiculous. Please, sit in your chair."

She couldn't think with him crouched at her feet like Romeo come to court her. Romance wasn't a part of her world, nor could it be, no matter how much she yearned to have that between her and Warren.

It wasn't happening. And he needed to understand why.

When he'd taken his seat, she dragged air into her lungs and watched him as she launched into the short version of how she'd met Bryan. To his credit, he listened without interrupting or asking what in the blazes any of this had to do with him.

She'd get there. "Our relationship was fantastic, at first. He showered me with gifts and compliments. I was so in love. After two months of dating, he asked me to move in with him because he couldn't stand the thought of being apart. It was too soon, but I walked into that willingly."

That was the part she couldn't forgive herself for. She'd had reservations but swept them aside for the romance of a man being so caught up in her that he couldn't live without her.

The changes had been small, at first. He'd murmured that he loved her so much that a thing like passwords shouldn't come between them and given her his. Of course she'd reciprocated, and then at odd times her phone wasn't where she'd left it. Once she'd gone into her laptop's browser history to find the website where she'd seen a pair of shoes she'd liked and noted several visits to her favorite links that had occurred the day before, when she'd been out to lunch with her mother.

Bryan had been checking up on her, she explained to Warren, and when she confronted him about it, he got angry. Demanded to know what she was accusing him of and then got upset that she didn't trust him. That was the beginning of the downward spiral that had gotten uglier, but she'd gone along because he always turned it back on her.

"Everything that happened was my fault in some way," she said quietly. "Even when he hit me."

And that was when her voice broke. She'd gotten through most of it pretty well, reciting the facts by rote as if they'd happened to someone else, and in some ways, they had. She wasn't that naive anymore, nor did she trust so easily. She was taking steps to become a permanent resident of the United States. If she could, she'd give up every bit of her Australian blood and embrace the safety she'd found here.

"He hit you?" Warren's voice had gone tight. "On purpose?"

She nodded and told him the unvarnished truth. "It was in a fit of rage because he'd found out that I went to a party for work that I hadn't told him about. I shouldn't have gone, but Craig strongly encouraged me to make nice with the senior partners if I wanted to get better assignments."

"You should have called the police is what you should have done." Warren's hands had clenched into his lap but he uncurled them and gripped the armrests of his wicker chair. "Please tell me he's in jail."

"No." That would have been too poetic. "Bryan is a police officer. Who would have come to arrest him? His cronies? He bragged to me once that he could have his record completely expunged if I so much as made a single complaint to the police force. I moved out of the house we shared after the second time he hit me and hid out at my mother's house. That's when he got really bad. He was so angry, he used detective grade equipment to stalk me. Threatened me. Followed me around and scared my mother."

"No wonder you're so skittish sometimes," Warren muttered. "I owe you a whole lot more apologies, then. I'm sorry if I pressured you in any way. Please don't take what I told you earlier as any sort of demand on you. I need you at Flying Squirrel. If you quit, the campaign will never be the same."

Why in the world would she quit the best job that she'd ever had? "I have no intention of quitting. This is my explanation for why I bolted from the terrace. Why I avoided you all day. I don't do normal interactions with men very well. This is my apology."

"Tilda..." He shut his eyes and sighed. "This is a lot for me to process."

"I know." This marriage of convenience had been so perfect for someone like her who needed to fade into the background. If only she hadn't asked Warren to kiss her, she might have kept up the facade. "I'm sorry if I've disappointed you or led you on or gave you false hope. I'm kind of a mess, so keeping things professional is best."

It was better this way. She'd confessed her shame and it was oddly cathartic. Oddly as if she'd gained a confidante in Warren. He'd go back to treating her with the same reserve he'd exhibited thus far, never barge in on her in the bathroom again and she'd continue to feel safe and in control.

His eyes flew open and the calm, detached CEO had fully vanished. Her breath caught. He was nothing less than fierce and magnificent as he stood, towering over her.

"I'm not disappointed," he said. "I'm a lot of things right now, but that's not one of them. Until I sort out the rest, you bet we're keeping things professional, because if nothing else, we've always worked well together. Nothing that's happened this weekend changes that."

Six

Warren wasn't a jogger. There was something so inane about running for the sake of running. It made so much more sense to have a destination if you were going to tax your body in that manner.

But after learning that he had a desire to murder another human being in cold blood—someone he'd never met and who currently resided half a world away in Australia—running was the only thing that had the slightest chance of keeping him sane. Otherwise, he might get on a plane and make good on the need to see Tilda's ex so Warren could explain a few things to the man. With his fists.

The farther he ran from his house, the easier it was to keep his hands off Tilda, too, which wasn't so much of a given after her incredibly brave recitation of the horrors that she'd left behind in Australia. His first instinct had been to reach for her, to engulf her in his embrace. As a shield, first and foremost. She'd needed protection from her ex and hadn't found it. He was more than willing to step up where the authorities had failed.

First thing tomorrow, he'd hire a fleet of private detectives to find the bastard who had struck Tilda and then Warren would make his life a living hell.

In the meantime, the Australia campaign required his undivided attention and he had about as much chance of working platonically with Tilda as he did of sprouting leaves and bark. But he was going to try because he'd told her he would. They'd both needed space while he spent the night calming down.

The next morning had dawned well before he was ready. He'd subsisted on four hours of sleep before, many times, but never after having erotic dreams starring his wife wearing white lace, a smile and nothing else. He awoke with his body on fire and his mind filled with dirty images that he had no shot at eliminating from his consciousness, not considering he'd be closeted in a small space with Tilda for a good long while.

Of course, the fates had a field day with his beleaguered senses. Tilda emerged from her bedroom at the same time he came from his and they met in the hall.

"I thought we could ride together," she said with a small smile that was but a shadow of the one she'd worn in his dream. It didn't seem to matter to his already primed body. "If that's okay."

"Sure," he croaked. "We're going to the same place."

A total and complete lie. She was going to Flying Squirrel. He was going insane. As she slid into his limo and perched on the seat next to him, he got a whiff of something fruity, but he couldn't put a name to what she smelled like. Because it couldn't be something simple like apple or cherry. Whatever it was had coupled with her natural scent to become wholly exotic and slightly spicy. Delicious. He had the wildest urge to unbutton her blouse and bury his nose in her cleavage on a mission to discover the source of the fragrance.

While he was there, he could satisfy his burning curiosity for what she had hidden under the suit today. They never had circled back around to that after she'd thrown him totally off track with the story about her ex.

Today was a new day. Plenty of opportunity to nose around, so to speak.

The torturous car ride mercifully ended a few minutes before eight when Warren's driver dropped them off near the entrance to Flying Squirrel. Warren's father had built the corporate office complex about fifteen years ago and then left his sons in charge when he retired. Invisible hands kept the grounds meticulously groomed, and a cheerful fountain gurgled in the central pool in the middle of a courtyard area shadowed by a large arch spanning the entrance. Typically, Warren didn't register much of it because he always had his phone out as he swept through the courtyard, but it seemed rude to be face down in his email with Tilda by his side, so the phone stayed in his pocket.

He should keep his phone in his pocket more often. A quiet sense of pride sneaked over him as he soaked in the landscape of the company he ran with his brother. This was his legacy, the continuation of the drinks his father had started making in his mother's kitchen during the seventies. That's why Warren worked as much as he did. He truly loved what he was doing here, contributing to the vision on his way to global domination.

Tilda was a big part of that. For now. Eventually the campaign to smear Down Under Thunder off the map would be successful and his need for Tilda's marketing expertise and project management skills would be at an end. Then what? She no longer worked for Craig. She'd have a green card, so she could stay in the US if she wanted to, but that didn't necessarily mean she'd choose to stay in Raleigh or even continue her association with Warren once their marriage was dissolved. They'd have no reason to see each other again.

Unsettled Warren shrugged that off, nodding to the people who worked for him as he and Tilda navigated the building to the executive office suite on the top floor.

"Get some coffee and meet me in my office," he told her brusquely, and she scurried to do as requested.

God, did he always sound like that? He'd never really paid attention to how he talked to his staff other than to notice whether they did as he'd directed. It was his job to run the company, not to make friends, and the more distance he employed, the easier it was to avoid complications that came with his drive to run other people's lives in much the same way he did Flying Squirrel.

That's what ultimately had happened with Marcus.

But Tilda wasn't a run-of-the-mill employee. She never had been. And when he'd admitted that he'd been attracted to her prior to the marriage, he was also acknowledging it to himself. Her response? *I'm skittish because the man in my past is an ass.*

When she bustled into his office with coffee in one hand and her tablet in the other, she wore her game face and what he'd noted earlier was the world's ugliest suit. He had the strangest urge to take her shopping. She was his wife. Wasn't it normal to want to buy her pretty dresses? She'd look spectacular in green. One of those soft fabrics that draped at the hip, a wrap-around maybe, with a neckline that crossed over her breasts into an X that marked the spot Warren could not stop obsessing over.

"I was thinking we should start with the Wheatner and Ross proposal," she said and took her typical seat on the other side of his desk.

Too far away. That was not where he wanted her, but somehow he didn't think she'd appreciate the suggestion to hop up on his desk so he could get to work stripping her out of that horrific suit. It was criminal that she hid such an amazing body behind the boxiest, most unattractive outfit imaginable.

"That's a great place to start," he told her as he rose from his seat and rounded the glass desk to sit in the matching chair next to hers.

Her slightly widened eyes tracked his progress as he settled in. "What are you doing? You always sit behind your desk."

"The view is better from here."

As he let his gaze trail down her legs, the only part of her she hadn't hidden, her cheeks pinked up. "You can't say things like that. We're at the office. We agreed to keep things professional between us."

"I agreed to no such thing. We work together. Ergo, our relationship is defined as professional by default. But that's not the extent of it and you know it. I can't unsee you in that white lace." He pointed to his temple. "It's all right here."

"It shouldn't be," she countered under her breath and shot a glance at the shut door, like the lingerie police might burst in at any moment to arrest her for daring to wear something racy under her utilitarian suit.

All at once, it dawned on him, and *wow*—he wasn't normally that slow. The only excuse he had for not realizing the source of her ups and downs was that she'd fried his brain from second one. "You like wearing things that show off your body. But he didn't like it at all, did he?"

That son of a bitch.

Fiercely, she shook her head and she might as well have had *denial* stamped all over her. "My style is my own and I'll thank you to stop questioning me about it."

"Come on, Tilda. I thought we agreed to be honest last night. I was honest with you and I thought you were reciprocating. But you only told me half the story, didn't you?" Guilt crowded into her gaze and he pounced on it. "That's why you were worried I felt deceived. Because you're lying to everyone. Every day."

"It's not lying," she whispered.

He bit back a curse, feeling as if his heart had been wrenched out of his chest to land somewhere on the floor, still beating.

Her ass of an ex had done a number on her, obviously. She'd flinched when Warren raised his hand, hid her sexuality beneath a layer of boring and then plainly told him not to bother with her because she was messed up.

To hell with that.

"Tilda, I'm sorry," he murmured, but it wasn't enough.

Last night, he'd let the conversation go because he'd genuinely feared he might put his fist through the wall since he couldn't unleash it on Tilda's ex. But she needed something else from him.

So he did what he should have done yesterday. He stood, set the computer tablet in her hands aside and pulled her into his embrace. For a half second, she hesitated, her body vibrating with a million unspoken emotions, and then, holy God...she melted into him, conforming to his contours as if she'd been fashioned from a mold with his exact dimensions.

"I'm sorry," he murmured, not even sure why he felt compelled to repeat what had become a common phrase between them, but he wanted her to know he *was* sorry—for Bryan's behavior and his own. "I don't mean to keep upsetting you."

What else would be the result of a cross-examination? He knew how to get results, not how to comfort. Look what had happened when he tried to comfort Marcus. He'd truly hated to see Marcus in so much pain, had truly wanted to help. But he'd ultimately failed.

"You're not the problem," she said, her voice muffled against his lapel because she hadn't bothered to move her face from where she'd snuggled into his shoulder, which felt a lot nicer than it should. "I am. I tried to tell you that."

"Stop. Your ex is the problem. And I'm not him."

Her amazing, sexy body unpeeled from his. "You think I don't know that?"

She stared at him, composed and blank faced. It was nearly miraculous how she morphed so easily back into the formal woman he'd first met a few months ago when she'd started on this project. Obviously she'd had a lot of practice at hiding behind her reserve.

That made two of them. And this was not one of those times when he could retreat.

"No. You don't know that. Maybe rationally, you can repeat it to yourself. But it's not sticking where it counts."

"Now you're an expert on me?"

He cocked his head. "That wasn't a denial."

"I'm here to do a job, Warren. Can we just focus on that and forget about the personal side of things?" The desperation in her tone hurt nearly as much as the tears.

He nodded, but not because he agreed that the conversation was over. His problem in a nutshell: he was as much of a liar as she was. He didn't maintain distance with people because he liked being that way. It was how he protected himself from failure.

Yes, he was pushing her. Because she was free to be as sexy as she liked around him and he'd treat it like the gift that it was. She needed to *feel* sexy and have a bone-deep understanding that it was okay to be as demonstrative with it as she wished. She needed to know that she was desired, but at the same time, that she could kiss a man and back off without retaliation. Bottom line, she needed Warren to undo all the damage the bastard had done to her.

He'd failed Marcus, but he couldn't fail Tilda. She was his wife. Not in all the ways that counted, but that didn't seem to matter to his bleeding heart, which was still somewhere on the ground.

Tilda was his do-over.

Warren had shut up about her sexy underwear, thank God, but the overwhelming vibe of awareness in the room never faded. By lunchtime, Tilda was a wreck.

This was so far from the professional veneer she'd worked hard to maintain. What had possessed her to spill all her secrets to Warren? She could have left it alone, appeared before him last night in the solarium with some made-up explanation about her lingerie set and gone on. But no. She'd had to blab about Bryan and give Warren enough ammunition to figure out that her ex had stripped away her confidence when it came to her interactions with men.

Easier to not engage. Which she'd tried to do by avoiding him, only for him to yank her back into his presence with a flick of his wrist. She should hate how dictatorial he was about everything, but of course, she didn't. Apparently all he had to do to fix that was hug her in what should have been an awkward show of comfort and support.

Not awkward. A total turn-on. Warren was an authoritative man with a kind streak who was keeping her away from Melbourne. Her little crush on him had exploded into something she had no idea what to do with.

Warren, on the other hand, had plenty of ideas.

"Let's go to lunch," he announced at ten till noon.

"We're in the middle of crunching these numbers from Wheatner and Ross's revised proposal," she reminded him—unnecessarily, since they'd been doing it for hours. But hey—at least her voice hadn't squeaked.

The very last thing she wanted to do was go somewhere with Warren. The less he clued in that she was a quivering mass of nerves and emotion, and had been ever since he'd touched her, the better.

"They're crunched. We both knew the revisions were on target the moment we looked at them. Now we've both appeased our obsessive tendency to overanalyze and we can move on. The only thing that makes me hungrier than overanalyzing is being obsessive. Indulge me."

Against her will, she had to smile at his perfect assessment of why they'd spent an entire morning buried in a proposal she'd known by nine o'clock that they'd accept. "Fine. You pick."

Dumb, ridiculous idea. She should be spending her lunch hour getting herself under control, not having lunch with her boss in the middle of downtown Raleigh where everyone would see them.

Clearly she needed to redefine her parameters, because the moment they left the building, Warren ceased to be her boss. He held doors for her, helped her into the limo and settled into the creamy leather so close to her that it would have been awkward if he didn't sling his arm around her, so, of course, that was exactly what he did.

She braced for more discussion about stuff she'd rather not talk about, but it never came. Warren sat in the car with her as if they always cruised around town in a pseudo embrace as he pointed out various landmarks like her own personal tour guide. In all the weeks she'd been in Raleigh, she'd never once done any sightseeing. There'd never been time—one of the symptoms of being a workaholic.

When she actually relaxed, she noticed that Warren's body was warm and she didn't hate the little hum in her core that seemed her constant companion lately. How could she help it? He seemed to know by some kind of osmosis exactly what she needed and when she needed it most. It was unsettling. And wonderful.

When the car rolled to a stop—at home—she glanced at him. "I thought we were having lunch."

"We are." He pulled her from the car by the hand, but instead of guiding her inside, he took the stone walkway leading around through a wrought-iron gate and they emerged in the circular garden she'd seen from the terrace Saturday night.

Her breath caught.

Warren had obviously called ahead. A lavish picnic had been painstakingly spread out in the center of the blooms in the grassy section of the garden. "What is all this?"

"A circus," he shot back wryly. "What does it look like?"

It looked like the perfect place for Warren to pick up where he'd left off this morning, poking into things that he shouldn't while hiding her away from prying eyes. It was far more brilliant and devious than taking her to a restaurant, where they couldn't have any sort of frank conversation. Instead, he'd gone for romance. Seduction.

"It looks like a man who's playing dirty."

His eyebrows lifted. "Then my work here is done. Come. Have a glass of champagne."

At lunch? On a Monday? Baffled, she watched the CEO of a multibillion-dollar corporation pull a bottle from a bed of ice and pop the cork. He handed her a glass flute that had been blown into the shape of a delicate tulip, the stalk of the flower forming the stem.

When in Rome. She sipped the champagne because she had a feeling she'd need it. Warren clinked his glass to hers, watching her over the rim as he drank his own. And then, when her attention was fully occupied, he reached up and pulled the clip from her hair.

As it fell out of the twist and down around her shoulders, he stuck the clip in his pocket. "I'll put it back later. Still my secret."

"Warren," she squawked and choked on the word as she registered the rising electricity arcing between them.

"Shh. I'm only looking at you."

She should protest. Or something. But they were hidden from the street, encased in their own private sanctuary. Her hair brushed her nape and it was incredibly freeing. What was the harm in letting her scalp breathe for a while?

When Warren led her to the heavy canvas spread across the grass, she found out.

Instead of focusing on drinking his champagne, he took off his shoes and reclined on the ground, gesturing for her to join him. She followed his example and stretched out. It took less than a second for his gaze to grow heavy with dark, delicious intent.

"I love your hair," he murmured. He didn't move, but she felt his voice curling through her midsection like a dense fog. "It's such a rich color, and with that slight wave, it looks like it's alive."

"It's just hair." But there was no harm in being secretly pleased with the compliment.

"I beg to differ. 'Just hair' wouldn't do this." Before she could protest, he pressed her hand to his chest. His heartbeat galloped along at a breakneck pace, and if she didn't know better, she'd think he was as swept up in the romance of this garden lunch date as she was.

"Maybe you should lay off the caffeine," she advised. "You always drink at least two test items from the research lab every morning."

"Tilda. Don't be dense." His thumb stroked down her palm as he set aside first his champagne flute, then hers. "My out-of-control pulse is not because I had an energy drink. It's all you. You're so sexy, I can't process it sometimes."

Heat prickled through her cheeks, flooding along her hairline. Might as well sport a big neon sign that announced he'd flustered her. "Not in this outfit."

"In that outfit," he corrected and trailed a fingertip along the buttons of her tailored shirt. "Because I know what's under it. Secrets. Here, let me show you." When she started to pull away, he clamped down on her palm, holding it in place against his thundering heart. "Stay with me. Trust me. I'm just going to show you how sexy you are."

That statement was so intriguing that she didn't move. Couldn't. He fingered the top button of her shirt and slipped it free, then slid to the next one. She couldn't breathe as the intensity of the moment pushed down on her chest while his touch simultaneously lit up her center.

It was a horrible, magnificent paradox. She'd long given up feeling safe enough to be with a man again, but Warren had patiently sorted through all her barriers. Still was. But she was still half turned-on and half anxious.

The next button popped from its slot and he peeled back her blouse into a V that revealed the slightest bit of cleavage. His hum of approval vibrated against her palm and it loosened something inside her.

Without a word, he leaned over and replaced his fingers with his mouth, kissing the slice of breast he'd uncovered but going no farther than the line he'd created with her blouse. She let her fingertips nip into his chest, registering his heartbeats as a barometer of his excitement—it was nearly as good as having a mindreading device. How great a concept was *that*?

It got even better as he mouthed his way up the column of her throat and wandered along her jawline. If she moved her head a fraction, they'd be kissing. The anticipation coiled through her belly, releasing as he settled his lips at the corner of her mouth in a light, exploratory nibble that rushed through her center.

One taste wouldn't kill anyone.

She turned her head to catch him just right. The kiss brewed for a half second before becoming a reality, mouths aligned and so very hot. She moaned as his hands slid down her back, and he rolled her half beneath him. The kiss turned carnal and heavy in a flash as his leg notched between hers, riding against her skirt, which he quickly gathered up at her thigh, exposing more of her secrets than she'd expected for a Monday afternoon.

But his thigh was so delicious against her burning core as he chafed it, feeding the flames as he shifted even further, covering her with a full-body press. He was big and firm, and the feel of him should be thrilling through her. But it wasn't. Instead, it was too much.

She gasped for air as her throat closed and she couldn't speak to save her life. Her nerves frayed, sending her into a panic attack. She pushed at him weakly, knowing she had absolutely no chance of moving him unless he chose to remove himself.

Warren froze and pulled back, his gaze roving over her face. He swore and sat up, running a hand through his hair.

"I got carried away again," he mumbled, his eyes shut. "I have no excuse for not checking in with you sooner. Please forgive me."

God, this was a never-ending nightmare of a merry-go-round that she desperately wanted to exit.

"No, Warren." She crawled to him and pulled his jaw into her hands to force him to look at her. "Don't apologize. I'm the one botching this."

She couldn't stand that he thought this was in any way his fault. Couldn't stand that she had no idea how to fix the way her insides got too tight when she felt threatened. Why did she feel threatened? Who knew? It was a mystery to her; otherwise, she'd figure out how to shut it off for good.

"Do we need a…code word or something?" he asked cautiously. "Or have I already ruined things so much that you're through with all of this?"

"Nothing is ruined. You're so incredibly patient with me and I feel like a sook. But facts are facts, and I've got some issues. You shouldn't pin any hopes on this marriage becoming anything more than a way to keep me in America."

The lovely vibe between them dissolved and vanished like so much smoke from a chimney. Great. Leave it to her to be the one ruining things with her angst and back-and-forth, as if she couldn't make up her mind whether to be hot or cold. It wasn't fair to him.

Slowly, he reached out, his gaze on his fingers as he rebuttoned her shirt to the very top.

"Who said I had any hopes for our marriage? What's happening between us has nothing to do with that and everything to do with giving you a safe environment to express your sexuality. You're so much the opposite of who you pretend to be. If you get to a place where you feel free to be yourself while you're with me, then that's all I could hope for."

Oh. She blinked, but the seriousness in his expression didn't fade. He wasn't suffering from the effects of an unrequited love, which was a relief. Or, at least, it would be a relief as soon as she convinced herself of it, which was practically the same thing.

She obviously couldn't handle a relationship right now and he'd realized that. Because he was paying better attention to her emotional landmines than she was.

But that didn't stop the twist of disappointment that he wasn't falling at her feet, spouting poetry about his poor broken heart that could only be healed by her love. Silly. She didn't want that. It was just that she'd thought the surprise picnic meant something that it didn't. So it wasn't quite the romantic gesture that she'd believed, but it was, in fact, something better. A safe place. Not a magic fixer-upper love potion that wouldn't have worked anyway.

She was still the one with the biggest stake in working through her problems, and he'd given her permission to skip the guilt if she failed because Warren wasn't emotionally invested.

"I'm having a very nice time at lunch," she told Warren solemnly, which made him smile, so she considered the outing a victory all the way around.

Despite the slight hollow feeling in her stomach where the warmth of Warren had been a few moments ago.

Seven

The way things had gone down at the picnic bothered Warren for two solid days. The date had ended on exactly the right note, with zero pressure on either of them. Tilda had learned that she could be and act however she wanted around him. Wear sexy lingerie. Let her hair down. What else could he have expected out of the afternoon?

He had some work to do in the pay-attention-to-her-subtle-cues department, but mostly he'd passed the test of proving he could back off when she needed him to. He had a feeling he'd be proving that one over and over again, but that was okay. It had to be. Tilda needed slow. It wasn't the end of the world.

So, why was he still on edge?

Maybe because he wasn't sure what the next step was. He was flying a little blind here, especially given that his usual go-to mode was distance. *Out of his element* didn't begin to describe it. Where he normally buried himself in work to cope with feeling ineffective on the people side of things, the source of his frustration was front and center in his professional life—by design.

Everything was tied together, and the more time he spent with Tilda, the more she dazzled him. She assassinated items on the project's to-do list like an Australian ninja, shining at whatever task she picked up. Sometimes it was dizzying when she really got going, but that's why he'd fought for her to stay.

He needed her. Or rather, Flying Squirrel needed her. But they were slowly becoming one and the same. And, near the end of the week, he started to question whether it hadn't always been that way.

On Friday, she emerged from her bedroom with chunky strands of hair falling to her temples on each side. Deliberately. He smiled and met her in the hall, as had become their habit. One he would never have said would become so entrenched in his routine so fast. But he enjoyed riding to work with her and then riding home again afterward as they recapped the day. So far, they'd eaten dinner together every night, too.

"That might be the sexiest hairstyle I've seen on you yet," he murmured, then he indulged himself by first holding his hand up as a notice that he was about to touch her, and then doing it, sliding a finger along her jaw to turn her face to the side as he evaluated. "I like it when you experiment with ways to drive me mad."

"Is that what I'm doing?" she volleyed back saucily. "Then you probably don't want to know what color my underwear is."

He groaned, which only made her laugh. She'd been experimenting with her flirting, too, and—not for the first time—it had taken a naughtier bent, which he fully deserved for creating this monster. "You're so wrong. I absolutely want to know."

She leaned into his touch, another jerky step forward in this dance. His reward for learning that he had to tread carefully with her.

"Ice-blue silk."

"My favorite," he murmured, his gaze tight on her as they stared at each other.

If she'd been any other woman, he'd have segued this serendipitous moment into a kiss, but he'd blown it twice now by getting too frisky too fast. And, of course, ice blue could be any number of shades, and he'd be hard-pressed to not slip a few buttons free as he kissed her so he could see this color for himself. Which was probably a bad idea.

This was a delicate balance of push and pull, and when she stepped back, letting his hand drop from her face, he knew he'd made the right call. Biting back his disappointment, he let her go ahead of him down the stairs and spent the day imagining the hell out of Tilda spread out on his desk in her ice-blue bra and panties.

To say that the day ended up a waste of time on his part was an understatement. Tilda did all the work while his brain stayed stuck in her cleavage. Which he could not actually see.

Clinical insanity might be a blessing at this point.

Things did not improve at dinner as Tilda launched

into a discussion about a study she'd read in a trade publication about energy drinks and their positive effects on college students' ability to concentrate. Animated, Tilda talked with her hands, and every time she gestured, the collar of her shirt wrinkled an iota. His gaze strayed to it over and over, but like all his other frustrations, nothing good popped out.

Interrupting the one-sided conversation, which she seemed not to notice he'd yet to participate in, he put his fork down. "Tilda."

She paused midstream, mouth open. "I'm talking too much."

"You're not talking enough," he corrected. "About the right subjects. Why did you tell me about the color of your underwear earlier? Just so we can be clear. Was it strictly to drive me over the edge or were you inviting me to see it? Because I don't want to upset you, but I don't want to miss a signal, either."

She blinked and blinked again. "I…didn't have an agenda."

"The hell you didn't."

He reeled back his temper, which, rationally, he knew was only due to old-fashioned sexual frustration. But naming the source didn't ease it any. Only a good long session between his wife's thighs would take care of that, and at this point, he wasn't particular about the nature of the activity, only that he was about to bust something inside if they didn't move past this nebulous in-between place where they'd gotten stuck.

"Warren, I—" She rubbed at her temples. "I don't know either. I like flirting with you. I think about letting you see my underwear all the time."

"Really?" That piqued his interest in a big way. "Like you wish I'd burst in on you as you're undressing again? Because that can be arranged."

He'd clear his schedule for a week straight. All he needed was a green light.

That got a small smile. "Maybe not that. But I need…something to move the needle. I don't know what."

So she was feeling a little stuck, too. That was news, and as headlines went, he was a fan of this one. It meant she was equally frustrated. Neither was she telling him to back off. More like, "come and get me." But that hadn't worked so well for them before, which put them right back where they started—dancing around each other.

It was killing him.

And not just because he genuinely cared about getting Tilda to a better place. She was slowly coming out of her uptight shell, and the woman who was emerging could tie a man in knots.

One who would let a woman do that to him, of course. Not Warren.

"Tell me what happens. In your fantasy where I see your underwear," he prompted.

A guard snapped over her expression and Warren nearly cursed, but he kept his mouth shut because they had to do something different. Also, he was wildly curious about what she'd say.

"I wouldn't call it a fantasy—"

"I would." And he was definitely an expert at them. "If you're thinking about it, some scenario came to mind. Where are we? What's happening? Don't pull punches with me. I'm not judge and jury in the trial of Tilda's imagination. I'm just the poor guy you're teasing."

A tinge of pink swept along her skin and he really shouldn't be so pleased to see it, but odds were high the images in her head were very, very naughty given the sheer volume of color in her face, and he desperately wanted to hear what she fantasized about.

"Tell me, Tilda," he murmured, dinner completely forgotten. "You're safe with me."

"I think about coming to your room. With my robe on," she said, her voice growing steadier as she spun out the scene. "You're on the bed. Watching me. And I take off the robe, then climb—"

"Whoa. You're going way too fast." He held up a hand, thrilled his muscles still worked as the erotic images spilled through his own mind's eye. "Give me a moment to catch up."

"What, are you fantasizing about that now?" she whispered, glancing around as if someone might overhear them in the cavernous dining room that could fit a basketball team or the erection she'd given him, but not both. No way.

Holy crap. How hot was the thought of her climbing *anything* while wearing skimpy lingerie? Very.

"You bet." He hummed a little in his throat as he let that last bit play out in his imagination as she climbed *him* and straddled him with her thighs wide—wait. *She* comes to his room, *she* takes off the robe, *she* climbs onto the bed, *she's on top*.

It was all so bafflingly simple. How the hell could he have missed that she needed to be in control?

The only excuse he had was that all the blood in

his body pooled in his lap anytime he was around Tilda lately.

"Here's what we're going to do," he growled, so incredibly peeved with himself at having wasted all this time that he couldn't find the wherewithal to be civil. "You go to your room, put on the most daring thing you own under your robe and come find me. I'll be the one on the bed."

Oh, God. She was really doing this.

But not in this outfit. Tilda stripped off the black lace mesh bralette that left little to the imagination and the thong that left absolutely nothing to the imagination. It was too…dirty, or something.

Sunshine yellow satin bra and panties. Total antithesis of black naughtiness. She posed in front of the full-length mirror that comprised half a wall in the walk-in closet. Nope. Too…yellow.

Tilda changed her outfit five more times, only to end up back in the rose-colored baby doll with matching thong that she'd first selected and then discarded in favor of the black outfit. It was the only thing she owned that she'd ever imagined wearing for a man. It wasn't the slightest bit utilitarian, like a bra and panties. Those she wore every day, could reasonably argue that she was wearing them for herself.

But this outfit…the baby doll bisected her breasts, revealing a healthy slice that almost—but didn't quite—let her nipples peek over the edge. The thong dipped so low that it looked like she was naked under the flirty, floaty fabric of the top. There was no way a man could see her in this and not know she'd worn it for him.

Which was why she wasn't doing this.

What was she thinking? She *worked* with Warren. Getting this personal was a very bad idea.

Stripping off the baby doll, she threw it in the drawer and leaned on it so she couldn't open it again. She couldn't follow through. It was too big a thing, with too many pitfalls.

Except... Warren was also her husband. Not in the traditional sense, but they had a relationship beyond work. She liked him. Was attracted to him. There was nothing wrong with that. And she shouldn't have to spend so much time justifying it to herself, either.

Also, he wasn't asking her to do something hard. Just giving her the opportunity to play out her fantasy. If she didn't feel comfortable doing anything other than dropping her robe and letting him look at her, he'd be fine with that. If she asked him to have drinks on the terrace while she wore the robe and never took it off, that's exactly what would happen.

But none of that was what she *wanted*. What she wanted was to explore the things she felt when Warren looked at her like she was his next meal. *All* the things. She wanted *sex* in all its glory, with more orgasms than she could count, a man who could keep up and free rein to do whatever she wished without fear of being called names.

Maybe that's what *would* happen. She pulled the drawer open. Shut it.

Maybe that's not what would happen. Maybe Warren would be shocked by the positions she'd envisioned them in, horrified by the filth coming out of her mouth, or at best, dismayed that she wasn't the straitlaced woman she'd presented herself as.

Excuses. He already knew she was a big liar. Had called her on it. She pulled open the drawer so hard it came free from the runners and landed on the carpet. Lingerie spilled over the edge in an explosion of colorful silk and lace. As metaphors went, that one was a little too perfect. The drawer couldn't contain her secrets any better than she could.

Her phone vibrated. Warren had texted her a message: Just checking in.

He knew she was waffling. Of course he did. The man missed no tricks.

Warren: If you're not ready for this, it's okay. Remember, you're in control of everything that happens.

A sharp tug in her core filled her with something powerful. She could be in control. Warren was telling her so.

How much control? Would he do things that she asked him to?

Warren: You call the shots.

Yes was apparently the answer. It was like the man had gained the ability to read her mind in the span of an hour. Intrigued against her will, she scooped up the puddle of rose silk and slipped it over her head before she could chicken out again. She had a written guarantee that she could let this evening play out precisely the way she directed. Warren would never go back on his word. She trusted him, and that alone was huge enough to warrant forgetting about everything else for a few hours.

The robe skimmed over her bare skin as she slipped it on and belted it. The fabric was nothing special as she hadn't bought it with the intent of using it in a seduction scene. Oh, God. Was that what she was walking into?

It was if she wanted it to be. She was in charge. The tug in her core transformed into long liquid strings that yanked pieces of her free that she hadn't realized were so deeply buried.

She was really doing this.

Instead of going to Warren's room through the hallway, she ducked into the bathroom. The hallway was where she met him in the mornings to go to work. The bathroom connection between their rooms was more secret. She liked that they had secrets. Liked that they had an easy way to keep their personal and professional lives separate. It was almost poetic.

When she opened the door to Warren's bedroom, she had to pause a moment to fully appreciate the scene he'd set up for her. He was, indeed, lying on the bed, wearing nothing but a pair of boxer briefs that hugged his hips. Wow. So he was just going to be lying there mostly naked, then. As visual gifts went, that one took the cake. He was a beautifully built man, not that she'd expected anything less, but reality brought her up short with a sense of wonder.

"I see you dressed for the occasion," she said wryly to cover the fact that her pulse had just tripled.

"Why beat around the bush?" he asked with smile that did not help her pulse. At all. "Figured it was easier."

Oddly, it was perfect. She was more dressed than he was, and she suspected that the imbalance wasn't an accident. Hot did not begin to describe it. And he'd single-handedly eliminated whatever nervous tension might have sprung up.

But just the nervous tension. The rest of the tension was purely sexual as the atmosphere grew more charged the longer she drank in the nearly naked form reclining on the bed. It was nothing like the fantasy she'd had. In those, he'd always been a little shadowy because she didn't really know what he looked like under his power suits.

Now she was worried that she wouldn't be able to think of him clothed. He was sublime—still powerful, but in a much different way than he was at the office. Mouthwatering, even, strong, muscular.

He could do whatever he wanted to her and she could do nothing to stop him. Her pulse sped up and it had not been slow in the first place. Rationally, she knew she wasn't in danger, but still...

"I'm not moving from the bed unless you tell me to," he advised her. "Think of me as a marionette, if you like. Pull my strings and I do as you command."

His voice rang with the same authority it always had, creating the strangest paradox. Only Warren could pull off maintaining his masculinity while simultaneously telling her she controlled him. The liquid threads of her desire elongated as she traversed the ocean of carpet toward the bed.

"Then I want you to stay there. I'm going to take this robe off," she told him. "And when I do, I want to see how much you like what's underneath."

If it went the way she hoped, she could gauge his reactions. He couldn't surprise her.

"I'm fairly certain that was going to happen anyway." He jerked his chin at his lower half. "Goes with the territory of wearing something that has no shot of disguising how much you turn me on."

That was such a delicious point that she couldn't resist testing it out. Slowly, she untied the robe but didn't open it. Instead, she slipped off one shoulder, and then the other, holding the robe closed as she let the fabric ride her breasts.

"That's a gorgeous color on you," he said huskily as he noted the straps of her outfit. "I can't wait to see the rest of it."

She let the robe fall, unveiling the baby doll all at once. The noise he made in his throat warmed her, and he sat up but made no move to leave the bed, as promised. His gaze hungrily drifted over her, catching at all the right places as he drank in the details. His shorts gained a prominent bulge, the outline of which drew her gaze.

"This is more difficult than I thought." His voice had gone thin and hoarse. "I want to touch you so badly."

But he wasn't going to. Unless she gave him permission. His expression burned with longing—a desire he was denying himself because he'd told her he would. The control was so heady that a smile bloomed, and it was wicked.

"It so happens that I want you to touch me."

His gaze zeroed in on hers, hot, hungry, edgy. But he didn't so much as flex a muscle in her direction, exercising extreme patience and mastery of himself. She couldn't help but appreciate both.

"Give me more parameters, Tilda. Here? There? Touch you how?"

All of the above. She was still in control and he was proving it to her moment by moment. The last of her anxiety dissolved and she waltzed to the bed, pushing him back onto the mattress. She crawled up the length of his body and straddled him, settling against that bulge until it nested into her core exactly the way she wanted it.

"Put your hands on my breasts," she instructed, and when he reached up, her insides went slick with need. But not panic. There was a huge difference. Of course he could easily flip their positions, but she trusted he wasn't going to do that.

The first firm contact of his palms on the underside of her breasts felt better than anything she'd imagined. Then his thumbs flicked across her taut nipples, tugging her core so hard that she gasped. "More."

He stroked again and then reversed the position of his hands, sliding his thumbs under the fabric to touch her bare skin. "What else would you like, Tilda? My mouth?"

She nodded because speaking didn't seem to work too well as he leaned up to flick his tongue across her covered nipple, wetting the silk.

"Pull down the fabric," she murmured, and cool air kissed her aching breasts a moment later. "Suck on me."

His lips closed around one nipple and the swirl of his tongue lit her up inside. Fortunately, she had the perfect hard length to grind against, and he was right there, circling his hips to create greater friction at her core. She fell into the fire, eyes closed, sensation exploding through her body.

This was nothing like she'd expected. Having a man do exactly as she directed was far more thrilling than she would have guessed.

Warren switched to the other breast without being told, laving at her flesh so expertly that she couldn't argue that she hadn't wanted it. She did. She wanted it all. Gasping out his name, she tangled her fingers in his hair, arching her back to give him better access. His teeth scraped across her nipple so exquisitely that she felt it all the way to her toes.

Wrapping her legs around him, she urged him closer with her heels, wishing she'd had the foresight to skip the underwear. But wasn't that the benefit of having a man at her full command?

"Strip me," she told him and couldn't find a shred of embarrassment at how easily she fell into this role.

He didn't hesitate. In one second, the baby doll top hit the floor and then he eased her back onto the mattress between his legs. He watched her as he hooked the waistband of her thong and pulled it free from one leg, then the other.

"Please tell me the next thing you want me to do is spend a lot of time pleasuring you," he said, and the look on his face...pure heat and carnal intent. "Because I can't see you like this without wanting to taste you."

"Yes. That. I want that."

"I need to move you. Is that okay?"

She nodded and he slid his hands under her buttocks to maneuver her to the edge of the bed. Then he dropped to the floor on his knees between her legs, kissing her quivering thighs. Why she couldn't control the shakes, she didn't know.

"Shh. Relax," he murmured. "I'm just going to touch you."

He did exactly and only that, running his hands up her legs to her stomach. But he never tried to hold her down, never made any quick movements. It was costing him, though. She could see the restraint in the lines around his eyes. He was holding back *for her*. The effort he'd undertaken, the patience, the sheer magnitude of what he'd done—continued to do—overwhelmed her.

After an eternity of bliss that nearly made her weep, he spread her legs, opening her up. "Stop me if I do anything that bothers you."

He waited until she nodded again. And then his tongue circled her fevered center and she could do nothing but mewl. The harder he licked, the better it got, until her body was bucking against his mouth, silently begging for more. He gave it to her, somehow sensing that she didn't have the words. It was too big, too amazing, too much, too little. His fingers stroked her in places she didn't know were erogenous zones, and his tongue hit spots over and over that made her body sing.

Frenzied and feeling like her skin was going to incinerate, she babbled something but had no clue what she'd told him to do. Whatever it was must have done the trick, though, because he lapped harder and twisted his fingers through her center, splitting her apart. The orgasm tensed her whole body and she came in a rush of a release, crying out his name.

So *that's* what all the fuss was about.

He let her come down, backing off immediately to lie next to her on the bed, not touching her at all. She stared at him, her chest heaving, and wished she had something to give him. A medal. A plaque maybe.

"I've never had an orgasm that way before," she said, instead of the gush of things in her heart that sounded mushy and blubbery and not at all the kind of thing a woman said to a man she'd married for a green card.

His brows raised. "Seems like you're a natural at it, then."

She laughed. "That was all you."

"I had good instructions."

Yes. She had a knack for it. Who knew? "Am I still calling the shots?"

"Of course. If you're done, you say so and get up and leave. Or stay here and sleep in my bed, and I'll go someplace else. This is your fantasy."

None of this added up and she was insanely curious about the million-dollar question that she should have asked a long time ago. "Why? Why on earth would you do all of this?"

"What, let a gorgeous, sexy woman do a strip tease for me and then indulge myself in the extreme pleasure of watching her in the throes of an orgasm I gave her? Yeah, that is a mystery. I must be crazy to have signed up for that."

"Stop. You did it for me, not you."

"That's the secret, Tilda. It was good for both of us."

More secrets, and that one was her favorite so far. The distance between them was too much, and she inched closer, linking their hands together, which was nice. "But you're still...you know. Not done."

"Oh, no. Far from it. I can go for hours and hours still, but as discussed, this is your show to run. I'm just here for the party favors."

"Then I'm not done, either. But here's the thing." She hesitated, because how was she supposed to tell him that, while she appreciated having ultimate control, she was nowhere near experienced enough to know how to please him? And she wanted to. So much. He deserved to be treated like a king. "Can we be co-hosts of this party?"

Eight

Cohosts. The phrase shouldn't make him smile, not when everything inside ached with so much unrequited need that Warren couldn't stand to be in his own skin. Her thumb stroked over his knuckles and he'd never have said that would be a turn-on, but pretty much anything Tilda did got him hotter than July, so it shouldn't have been such a shock.

"You're going to have to help me out with what that means," he said when he thought he could speak. "Cohosts might have a totally different connotation in Australia than it does here."

"I'm doing okay," she murmured. "With you. Here. Naked. It's good. You don't have to be so…careful with me. This should be about you, too, not just me."

Understanding filtered through the sexual haze that had saturated his brain. "You mean, you're okay with it if I do some things that you didn't verbalize. That I have permission to be creative."

She nodded and something bright filled his chest. He'd done what he'd set out to do—get her comfortable with him. How fantastic. And brave. There'd been no guarantee that they'd ever get to this point, no matter what he did, and even less of a guarantee that she'd tell him so.

All at once, his throat closed as he internalized the magnitude of the gift Tilda had just handed him. Instead of telling her, it seemed appropriate to show her. It worked out well that he wanted to dive back into her, anyway, and talking wasn't high on his list of bedroom activities.

Warren took a moment to shed his briefs and Tilda watched him, her eyes bright, rewarding that decision with a sound low in her throat.

"I don't know why you ever get dressed," she muttered. "It's almost sinful to cover all that up."

The grin spreading across his face might have been a little sloppy. "I take it I meet with your approval."

"And then some. I used to think I liked you in suits. Now I'm wondering what I was thinking."

"You were thinking we had a professional relationship?" That was a dumb thing to bring up. The last thing either of them needed were reminders that they still had to work together tomorrow. But on the flip side, they did work together, so maybe it was okay to be real about the situation. "That doesn't have anything to do with what's happened here at home. We can keep them separate, right?"

"No. Absolutely not."

His heart ground to a painful halt for a half second until she continued.

"I like it when you use your boardroom voice. It's sexy."

He had to laugh at that. "You mean my boss voice?"

She wasn't the first woman to express a similar sentiment. But she was definitely the first one who had needed to be in full control.

Once again, he was flying blind. The only thing he could do was pay attention to her cues. Easier said than done. But he was doing okay so far tonight. Much better than he'd expected when he'd suggested the idea of her coming to his room in her robe.

He wouldn't apologize for the bone-deep desire to erase *prim* and *proper* from Tilda's vocabulary.

"Maybe talking isn't the right approach to take here," he murmured. Distance was the only way he could guarantee no one would get hurt, and all the conversation wasn't helping.

He rolled closer and resettled her into his arms. She came willingly and all her gorgeous skin snugged next to his. The heat dialed up a notch, not that it had cooled all that much in the first place.

Naked Tilda eclipsed all his fantasies and he still couldn't quite believe she was here, in his arms. The sexy lingerie had been nothing more than a precursor to the main event, and he was not sad that she'd asked him to remove it. Catching her mouth in his, he dropped them both into a kiss that quickly grew intense.

His first inclination was to touch more of her, but even though she'd said she was okay with creativity, he'd prefer some guidelines.

He lifted his mouth and murmured, "Did I mention how thoroughly hot it was when you told me the things you wanted me to do to you?"

She shook her head. "It was a turn-on for me, too. Surprisingly."

"You've never—" He bit that back. Of course she'd never had a man clue in that she'd needed that or they wouldn't be here right now. She'd needed him to pull it out of her, just like she'd needed him to come up with the idea of playing out her fantasies.

What else did she need that he hadn't discovered yet? His curiosity exploded.

"We're not finished letting you explore that," he advised her and shut up in favor of kissing her.

Her sweet mouth opened under his and he groaned. So trusting. It was beautiful how responsive she was after almost no time. Tentatively, he set himself into exploration mode, swirling his tongue forward, but she met him halfway, thrusting into his mouth with no fear. She arched against him and he had to check his urge to roll her under him in order to increase the contact.

So he rolled her on top of him. Her thighs fell between his and her stomach ground against his erection, which was so good, his brain melted. No downside to this position that he could find. From this angle, the kiss got deeper still, and as a bonus, his hands were free to thread through her hair. The silkiness flowed over his fingers and he felt it in his blood. He couldn't help circling his hips against her, automatically seeking more.

She moaned and shifted, igniting him with friction,

and there was little chance he was going to be able to hold off much longer if she kept that up.

"Tilda, I need to be inside you. Is that—"

"It's okay. I want that, too."

There was literally no way to misinterpret that, so he went for broke and sheathed himself with a condom in what had to be the land speed record. She'd barely moved enough for his hands to have room to work, which meant a lot of touching of hot, wet parts. In an instant, she sank down on him, drawing him into the most bliss-filled joining imaginable—and he'd imagined this moment a *lot*.

It was far better than anything he'd conjured up in his suddenly feeble fantasies. She felt amazing, tight and, best of all, *enthusiastic* as she rolled her hips to find a rhythm she liked. This position had just shot to the top of his list. He groaned as she took him deeper, and let the sensations break over him.

"That's it, sweetheart," he murmured. "You work me exactly the way you want."

She blinked down at him, registering his words. Slowly, she changed the angle, experimenting with a new speed as her hair fell into her face in the sexiest of manes, and he nearly went blind as heat exploded through his midsection.

"You're so gorgeous," he told her, almost before realizing he'd spoken. What was going on with him tonight? Tilda had turned him into a talker in bed. Insanity. Only people who were intimate with each other talked, because it meant they had stuff to talk about. This was just sex, solely designed to give her some confidence.

"You think so?" she asked, but it wasn't the coy

question of a woman fishing for compliments. She was almost…shy. Asking for confirmation, even.

"Oh, yes." He nudged his hips higher, doing some angle changing of his own to see what spots he could hit to get that expression of bliss on her face that he'd only glimpsed earlier. "When your hair is down around your face, you're ethereal. Amazing. I love you being on top. The view from here is like staring into the face of heaven."

Geez, next he'd be spouting poetry. But he couldn't take it back, not when a smile bloomed on her face that was every bit the opposite of the angel he'd just likened her to.

"I like it, too. The view is pretty good from here for me, as well." She put her hands on his chest and used him for leverage to increase her speed yet again, her eyelids drifting to half-mast as she gasped out his name.

When Tilda was in control of her pleasure, it was breathtaking. He wanted more and ground his thumb into her center. That was the magic button, apparently, because she threw her head back and rode him faster, hollowing him out with her sexy moans. After he'd spent what felt like an eternity clawing back his own release through sheer will, she finally closed around him with a strong pulsing ripple.

He let go with a cry, emptying himself in a release that eclipsed anything he'd ever known.

Tilda collapsed to his chest and his arms locked around her automatically. To keep her in place. That was his story, but in reality, he was holding on—because if he didn't, he feared he'd float away in a haze of bliss.

And he didn't miss the fact that she let him. She was amazing, putting herself out there despite her fears and blazing through to a brilliant finish.

She murmured nonsense phrases against his skin, or rather, his brain was too mushy to interpret something so complex as language, not when she'd just rearranged every one of his molecules into something different. Something he didn't fully understand yet.

But he did know one thing. He'd lied to her earlier.

What was happening between them had everything to do with their marriage because they'd just consummated it. Brilliantly, no less. And he wasn't done.

He cultivated distance to keep people from being hurt by his tendencies to be blunt and abrupt, but even that was a shield against his genuine desire to help when someone was hurting.

He'd dropped all his careful barriers to get Tilda to this point, which he didn't regret, but it was going to be hell to put them back together.

But necessary.

That feeling in his chest? It was happiness. And he didn't deserve that.

When Tilda woke up, there were arms around her and she had a moment of panic. She half pulled away and turned, but it was dark. She couldn't see, and the panic escalated, pounding through her veins. The arms were holding her down. Forcing her to do something she didn't want to.

Then it came to her in a flood. *Warren*. He'd taken her to bed last night and she'd fallen asleep with him. His face floated through her consciousness, so precious, and it centered her.

She was okay. She was in Warren's bed. He was holding her because he was extending their intimacy, not trying to keep her someplace she didn't want to be. That didn't seem to matter to her pulse. Snuggling back against his chest was a lot harder than she'd have guessed. What was wrong with her? If nothing else, Warren had always been about safety.

Lying in the dark, she stared at the ceiling she couldn't see and tried to get her automatic reactions back under control.

"Hey." Warren's soft voice whispered across her shoulder. "You okay?"

She nodded. A lie. He was so wonderful, and this was all about her being damaged beyond repair. But she couldn't breathe. The air wasn't getting into her lungs somehow and dizziness overwhelmed her.

"Do you need to go back to your own room?" he asked.

Yes. That was exactly what she needed. Nearly sobbing with gratitude, she took the out and rolled to kiss his forehead. Then she snatched her robe and fled.

Back in her own room, she snapped on the light and threw on a pair of flannel pajamas, crawling into the bed she'd been sleeping in for the last week, ever since she and Warren had gotten married. It hadn't taken too long to end up in his bed, though. She'd moved way too fast, caught up in the fantasy he'd pushed her to enact. Okay, he hadn't had to push her very hard.

She couldn't deny that she'd wanted to be with him. He hadn't forced her in any way. Quite the opposite. If any tactic would have worked to get her out of the dungeon Bryan had put her in, letting her have at least the illusion of control was it. She wasn't at all fooled, though. Warren could just as easily flip and start controlling all aspects of her life if he so chose. They were married, after all.

The light stayed on. It burned into her retinas as sleep evaded her. She'd screwed up by taking things with Warren so far. She was his employee and she needed to start acting like one. This job was all she had, and she'd started out intending to dazzle him with her skills. Instead, she'd let herself be seduced by things that weren't available to her, like happiness and fulfillment.

Bryan had stolen that dream from her. Sex was one thing, and she didn't even handle that very well. But anything else was completely off the table.

In the morning, she took a long shower and washed away all thoughts of the man who had so expertly made love to her the night before. Then she dressed in the dullest suit she owned and set up shop in the library, which was adjacent to Warren's study. Last Saturday had been wasted on moving and getting settled. Today she had a long agenda of things to accomplish that wouldn't get done if she sat around and daydreamed about the reasons her muscles ached so badly.

The reason popped his head into the library a little before eight o'clock. "Good morning."

Warren's long, delicious gaze wouldn't let hers go, or maybe that was her fault because he was so gorgeous and so dressed and she shouldn't be thinking about beckoning him into the library so she could strip him out of the jeans and T-shirt he'd donned in deference to the weekend.

"Good morning," she squeaked and cleared her

throat. "We have a lot to do before Monday. I've got meetings scheduled with the major entertainment venues—"

"Have you had breakfast?" he cut in. "Work will be there later. Come have some pancakes with me."

"I, um…no, I haven't." Pancakes were her favorite. She had to spend all day in his company, anyway. Might as well get pancakes out of the deal while she tried to figure out how their dynamic had changed.

Because it had. The fact that he hadn't readily jumped into her work discussion told that tale. He'd been hot to have these meetings for weeks because Down Under Thunder had deals with all the music festivals and such. Warren and Tilda had been planning to upend his competition's foothold with the concert crowd.

"The dining room is too formal," Warren announced and led her out to the terrace where more invisible hands had set up a white bistro table inlaid with shiny bits of glass that caught the morning sunlight.

Charmed against her will, she let him pull out one of the chairs for her and settled into it. Then there was nothing left to do but focus all of her attention on the man across from her.

"The meetings will be a great first step toward choking off Down Under Thunder," she said in a rush, mostly to keep her mind centered on the important things instead of letting her gaze wander across his broad shoulders.

She might have used them as a handhold more than once last night, and for some odd reason, she could not stop wondering if she'd left nail marks in his skin. Heat climbed through her core as she recalled the exact position, his body under hers, joined so very intimately. She'd ridden him with abandon. It had been glorious.

"Sure that's what you want to talk about this morning?" he asked lightly as the cook served plates with stacks of fluffy pancakes, a platter of bacon and syrup warmed in a small white urn, then vanished. "There's not something else on your mind?"

The heat in her core intensified as she stared at him. What was she supposed to say to that?

Yes, you rocked my world and I want you again right now?

Because that would be both true and a horrible idea.

She ate pancakes, instead. They melted in her mouth too fast to be a good diversion from the conversation because he just kept watching her as he forked up his own bits of fluffy goodness.

"Nothing is more important to me than getting this project completed," she said firmly, because she had to say something. And then she shook her head. "I mean, not that I'm in a rush to be finished. I want to do a good job and it's very important that each detail—"

"Tilda." Warren reached out and laced his fingers with hers, no hesitation, which told her that he was already far more comfortable with her than she was with him. "You'll ace this project, no doubt. We're having breakfast on the terrace on Saturday after we took our relationship someplace unexpected. If you don't want to talk about what happened last night, fine. Pick another subject. But not work."

Agape, she stared at him. "Work is all there is between us."

"No." His fingers tightened, and his thumb found a sensitive spot on her hand to caress. "Not when you can't even sleep in the same bed with me all night long, it's not. We have an impending interview with the green-card people and the subject of sleeping arrangements may come up. Wouldn't it be better to be prepared for that?"

Something with a dark edge flared through her stomach and she didn't like the direction of the conversation. "What are you saying?"

He let her hand go and ran his fingers through his hair as he sat back in his chair. "I thought…it's just that last night was amazing. Wasn't it?"

Remembering last night, her heart went a little bonkers, flipping over on itself in time with a bird's chirp in the garden below. "It was. So amazing. So unexpected." But she'd made a resolution while lying in bed unable to sleep, and she would stick to it. "I don't want to talk about last night. It was a onetime thing, a fantasy. We're not a couple. We work together. The marriage part of our relationship is incidental."

A heavy block of something landed on her chest and she couldn't breathe.

Was that all there was for her for the rest of her life? The inability to sleep with a man and barely the ability to have sex with one? What about later, when she didn't have someone as patient and kind as Warren? Who would care enough to tease out her fantasies, pay enough attention to her to know that she would like being on top when she didn't even know that about herself?

It was too much. She couldn't do this intimate breakfast on Warren's terrace the morning after they'd slept together.

Of course, fleeing to her room didn't help. She was

still completely out of sorts. Warren seemed to understand that she needed space and left her alone.

For about fifteen minutes.

The knock on the door had his authoritative ring to it. The housekeeper had a much lighter touch, and besides, what had Tilda expected, that he'd let his project suffer because she was being difficult about having slept with him?

"Tilda," he called through the door. "Talk to me. Please."

And say what? Not talking was much easier and avoidance was her current coping mechanism. She'd sneaked away from Bryan when he'd been on an assignment, she'd left Melbourne the first opportunity Craig had given her and she continually shoved Warren into a box called "work" so she could pretend none of the other stuff was happening.

But that didn't make it right to run.

She opened the door and his beautiful, masculine presence immediately swelled into the room, filling up places she'd only begun to realize were empty. "I'm sorry. I tend to run away from anything that scares me."

"That's part of the problem, Tilda." His voice betrayed none of his emotions. But his eyes told a different, far more interesting story. "I don't want to be one of the things that scares you."

Mute, she stared up at him as a wealth of emotions surfaced in his gaze that she'd have missed if she'd never opened the door. This was difficult for him. She was causing him distress. And maybe some pain? The whole time, she'd had a sort of academic understanding that he was being patient and kind, but had never really acknowledged the cost. She'd seen evidence of it last night. How quickly she'd forgotten the effort he'd made to treat her so well. Selfishly, she'd assumed any cost was physical, but there was a very real possibility that he was paying for it emotionally, as well.

That brought her up short.

"Come in." She held the door open wide and stepped back. Did he understand that such a gesture cost her, as well?

Instead of crossing to the bed or lounging against the door frame, he leaned forward and kissed her on the forehead. "Thank you."

Seemed like the answer was yes—he did understand that certain things didn't come easily to her. This was the part where she had to get over herself and start paying attention to what he needed. "What did you want to talk about?"

That's when he took a seat. Not on the bed but in the lone chair situated in the corner near the reading lamp. Crossing his legs at the ankle, he looked at the ceiling and blew out a breath. "I hated that you couldn't sleep with me last night. I... God, this is hard."

"What, Warren?" She moved across the carpet and knelt by his side. "You can tell me."

"Can I?" He flashed her a brief smile. "While we're discussing the things that you run away from, we should have a chat about my problems in the relationship department. I'm not very good at telling a woman how I feel, apparently."

How he felt? As in *feelings*? As in, what? He was *falling* for her?

Her mouth worked but no sound came out. This was a disaster. He couldn't fall for her. That's when everything had shattered with Bryan, the moment he started talking about how much she meant to him; that's when his controlling tendencies showed up.

But at the same time…oh, how she longed for a bit of normality, where she could tell Warren she was falling for him, too.

"Let's start with the basics," she said shakily. "Is this a conversation about how you've got expectations now about our personal life?"

"What? No! Absolutely not. I…" Warren swallowed and there was the longest pause. "I should tell you about Marcus."

Instead of confessing something she was not ready to hear, Warren spun a tragic story about his college roommate and how the poor guy had gotten a fatal case of broken heart. Somewhere along the way, their fingers intertwined and she listened while holding his hand, though she couldn't have said who reached for whom or which of them needed the comfort more. He had awfulness in his past, and she had a lump in her throat by the time he wrapped it up.

"He died, and I swore I'd never go out that way," he said, his gaze dark with memories and pain. "Love isn't in the cards for me and it's been shockingly easy to avoid that, given that I'm usually accused of being married to Flying Squirrel."

That was…not what she'd expected to hear. But, oddly, it was exactly what she'd needed to hear. It loosened the tight clutch of emotion inside her. "Yet here you are. Married to me."

"By default. It's not supposed to matter."

"But it does." Their gazes caught and the very air shifted as the hugeness of the moment blossomed.

He nodded once without hesitation. "It does. Because I can't go back to just working together, but neither can I promise you anything. I hate that we're at this place—"

"But that's okay," she said in a rush, almost laughing with relief. "I don't want promises. I want to feel like there's no pressure. Like we're going to be okay no matter what. Working together isn't affected, the green card isn't in jeopardy and we can just float along wherever the whims of the moment take us. I'm totally fine with that."

She was. It was freeing in a way. She could have secret feelings and he didn't expect her to share them. Once again, he had some kind of sixth sense about what worked for her and it was awesome in every sense of the word.

"But you left last night," he said quietly. "I convinced myself it was because you were sorry that we'd taken that step."

Her heart fell open and she had to clamp it shut.

There was the emotion she'd seen when she first opened the door. She'd fled from his bed last night, then refused to talk to him about it. Of course he'd misinterpreted her angst.

"Not sorry." She shook her head so hard that several strands fell out of her bun. That thing needed to go. Reaching up, she pulled out the pins and let her hair rain down. "See how far I've come already? This is not something I would do with just anyone. Our secret."

His smile grew a wicked edge. "That's not something I want you to do with anyone else."

Feeling bold, she hiked up her skirt and crawled astride his lap, settling on it with surprising ease, given the hard length jutting into her core. "That's all it takes to get you hot? Me taking my hair down?"

His hands clamped down on her waist, holding her in place, but it was thrilling. Because he wanted her with simple, uncomplicated desire. It was in his gaze, the heat of his expression. This, she understood. He was always so careful with her, so gentle.

"All it takes is you walking into a room," he muttered and flexed his hips in a little friction dance that nearly set her on fire. "And I'm wholly unprepared to have a sexy woman in my lap."

"Feels like you've got all the right equipment to me." She wiggled, pushing him deeper into the thin barrier of her panties. He felt so good, and she loved that they could be honest with each other about what was going on inside, whether it was desire or pain.

In response, he stood, boosted her up with both hands on her bare buttocks and strode toward the bathroom. She wrapped her legs around him and went to work exploring his neck with her mouth, nibbling on anything she came across. Warren tasted delicious, like heat in flesh form.

The cool marble of the vanity stung her thighs as he set her on it and, giving her a quick kiss, he rifled through a drawer until he came up with condoms. Holding them up to show her, he then tossed them on the counter and stepped back between her legs.

"Where were we?" he murmured.

"I was playing out another fantasy of mine," she informed him, saucily. Warren did bring out her vixen side with shocking ease. "Where you come into the bathroom and take me apart."

His mouth curved. "I have that fantasy, too. Let's see how they compare."

Slowly, he raised his fingers to the buttons on her blouse and undid the top one. Then he moved on to the next one, watching her with careful, heated intent.

"Not even close. Try this." She grabbed both sides of her blouse and ripped them apart, revealing the white lace bra she'd been wearing the other night. "Not slow this time. Fast."

His mouth was already on hers, sucking her into him as he kissed her. Their tongues clashed, writhing together in search of more sensation. His hands were everywhere, in her hair, shrugging off her jacket and ruined shirt, sliding along her thigh as he fingered aside her panties.

White lightning forked through her center as he thumbed her. She gasped and let her head fall back, thrusting her breasts against his chest. He bent and took one nipple into his mouth through her bra.

"Now," she commanded hoarsely. "Don't make me wait."

He complied instantly, dropping his pants and shouldering off his shirt. She circled her hips, desperate for him to hurry. An eternity later, he was back in place, pushing aside her panties instead of removing them, and the urgency of it thrilled her. There was nothing slow or easy about the way he pushed into her. It was all raw need and power, and she reveled in it because she'd asked for it.

He groaned as she took him. She urged him on with her heels, hands at his waist as he powered her to a dense, heavy release that broke over her without warning. He drew it out with hard, fast thrusts that built on the sensation until she was gasping and sobbing nonsense. His own release triggered and he held her tight to his chest as he came.

That was her favorite part. He was so dominant everywhere but in her arms; with her, he let himself be vulnerable, pulling back a little to catch her in a long sweet kiss as their torsos heaved with the expulsion of passion.

She kept waiting for him to be something other than perfect, but it hadn't happened. He liked it when she was wanton, liked her sexy underwear, liked her. It was…everything.

"Warren," she murmured against his mouth. "I want to sleep with you."

"Tilda." She felt his lips curve up against hers. "It's ten o'clock in the morning. Hold that thought and we'll pick it up again in about twelve hours. Now, about those meetings next week…"

Nine

That night, after thoroughly pleasuring himself on the sound of Tilda's moans, Warren finally let her go to sleep sometime after midnight. But he couldn't do the same. What if she had a nightmare? Or needed a drink of water? He had to be alert and ready to handle whatever happened.

He didn't want her to leave this time.

Nothing happened. She slept through the night or, at least, that was what he assumed was the case. He'd fallen asleep, after all, only to wake with her watching him, one arm under her head and a smile that could mean a thousand things stretching across her beautiful face.

"Good morning," she said simply.

And he couldn't help but reach for her. She came willingly, eagerly snuggling against his body, and she felt so good that he couldn't do anything but wrap his arms around her. What had started out as a bone-deep need to kiss her melted into something else entirely.

She was still here. In his bed. The enormity of it soaked through his body and he tried really hard to push it away, but he couldn't help the tenderness that filled that moment. They should be celebrating the fact that she'd taken huge steps to overcome difficult emotional landmines. Instead, he was fighting the realization that he'd been missing out on this kind of intimacy for the whole of his life.

He liked her in his bed. He shouldn't. But there was no going back now. The baby steps they'd been taking in deference to her triggers had worked on him, too, but for a far different reason. She'd slowly seeped into his consciousness until he didn't know if he'd be able to untangle her from his arms, let alone from his insides.

Thank God they had already decided on a divorce. Once she got her green card, everything would go back to normal. She could move out and he could…what? Go back to being lonely?

That was crap. He had Flying Squirrel. He didn't need anything else to make his life perfect.

But as they finally dragged themselves from the bed and crossed the finish line by having breakfast together, he couldn't sell that lie, even to himself. Before Tilda, his life had been something, all right—empty. What else could he call it when the word to describe how it felt now was *full*?

Fine. He could roll with it for the time being.

They didn't work at all on Sunday in favor of spending the day together. She'd posed it as a way to practice for the green-card interview but the conversations always veered into something that no one from the immigration department would ever ask because the content was X-rated, at best. It seemed they'd both had a lot of fantasies to work through, which lasted the whole of the week, as it turned out. So far, taking her from behind on his desk in the CEO's office at Flying Squirrel was his favorite with a capital F.

The campaign for increasing Flying Squirrel's market share in Australia was going well. He got some numbers from Thomas on Friday that pleased him so much, he immediately invited Tilda to a lavish dinner in celebration. For some reason, the impending dinner put her in a strange mood. She vanished to her office, a rarity, and stayed there for a couple of hours.

Were they still not at a place where she could tell him honestly what was going on with her?

And then she appeared at four o'clock. And knocked. Which she hadn't done in quite some time.

He did not like the idea that their relationship had seemed to regress. Nor the fact that backing off now was likely a good idea, pending how long the approval took on his petition for her green card application. They might have weeks, but they probably had less.

He didn't want to think about it. So he told her tersely, "You don't have to knock."

"Can I come in?" she asked tentatively.

He sighed. His tone had put her on edge. Because he was an idiot. "Of course."

Tilda's hair was coming loose from her bun-like thing and he was pretty sure his fingers had been the cause. Probably from the stolen kiss in the stairwell that he'd initiated as they'd come back from a meeting with the board earlier today. How had they gotten to the point where she was cautious with him all over again in a matter of hours?

"I have a problem," she said and hesitated, stopping just inside the door. Usually she beelined for the seat near his desk. "I didn't want to bring it up, but I feel like I should."

Bracing, he sat back in his chair. "I'm listening."

"I don't want to wear a suit to dinner. But I don't have anything else to wear."

The laugh of relief that bubbled up made him downright giddy. *That's* what had her tied up in knots? "That's not a problem."

She scowled. "It is to me. You of all people should understand."

Screw the distance between them. He skirted the desk and shut the door behind her so they could speak privately, then he leaned on it with his arms crossed. "I do understand. That's why I know it's not a problem. You wear those suits so you can pretend you're a proper consultant to the rest of the world because that makes you feel safe. On the flip side, the kind of clothes you want to wear make you uncomfortable, so you shy away from them. You're stuck in the middle. How am I doing so far?"

Since her mouth had been agape pretty much the whole time he'd been talking, the question was largely rhetorical.

"I pay attention," he told her. "Because I care."

The phrase had come out of his mouth before he could catch it. But the truth settled into his chest, fitting into the nooks and crannies far better than he would have expected. He did care. There was nothing wrong with that. It wasn't the same thing as love, and besides, he already had his out predefined. There was no forever kind of happiness on his horizon with Tilda, nor did he want that.

Or rather, he didn't deserve it.

Which wasn't the same thing at all. He swallowed the bitter taste in his mouth.

"Since you're so smart, what am I supposed to do about that?" she asked him, hands on her hips.

He shrugged. "Easy. You let me take you shopping. The only caveat is that you have to wear whatever I pick out."

"You'd do that?" Now she just sounded suspicious, like he made a habit of offering to take women shopping for nefarious reasons.

"Make no mistake. I'm picking out what you wear under it, too. None of this is for you. It's all for me."

When her shoulders relaxed, that's when he risked reaching out to pull her into his arms. She melted against him and it was every bit the sweet victory he'd hoped for.

"Okay," she murmured into his jacket. "You win. But only because I can't wait to see what you have in mind."

That made two of them. He'd never shopped for a woman before, unless you counted birthday presents for his mom, and that was so not applicable here that it wasn't funny. But he could not deny that he'd longed to dress her in outfits of his choosing.

"That's a secret I can't share yet. Soon."

He kissed her temple as the last of the tension between them dissolved. Funny how often he found himself doing something that had its basis in comfort or affection. Before Tilda, he would have said a kiss led to sex a hundred percent of the time; otherwise, why bother?

But he liked providing Tilda with comfort and affection. And if it helped her, great.

But as he wrapped up work for the day, his mind was squarely on the question of whether it was helping her—or him.

There was no good answer for that.

He led his wife out to the limo that would whisk them to the exclusive shopping center he'd learned about from Hendrix's wife, Roz, and pushed all his questions to the background. Tilda needed a dress.

Actually, the dress needed Tilda.

On the hanger, lifeless. On the woman? A work of art.

Warren could not take his eyes off his wife as she emerged from the dressing room in the teal midlength dress with sleeves to her elbows. It was both elegant and stylish, showing nothing but a bit of leg, which left the eye of the beholder to notice only Tilda's radiance.

"I like it," she said softly, and he nodded because he didn't trust his voice to work. "I'm going to wear it out."

Warren handed the beaming clerk his credit card without looking because he didn't want to miss a moment of Tilda in that dress. "Don't put your hair up."

"I wasn't going to. Thank you." She settled a hand on his arm and her warmth bled all the way through his suit jacket. "For the dress. And coming with me."

"The pleasure is all mine." Understatement.

Warren took Tilda to the priciest restaurant in Raleigh. Not because he cared about being seen, though there was plenty of that going on. More than one diner had shot a sidelong glance at their table, and there was a discreet photographer making rounds who probably worked for a society column. Since it was all good for Tilda's green card, he didn't mind.

What he did mind was how difficult it was to sit across from his wife in a public place knowing what she had on under the teal dress. Yeah, he'd followed through on that, selecting a matching silk bra and thong. There was nothing daring about the lingerie, either. All in all, the whole ensemble was relatively respectable.

What was driving him nuts was how Tilda had blossomed the moment she'd stepped into the room wearing it. She owned her beauty, her confidence. Wore both fiercely, as if daring anyone to try and take them from her. He'd never been more proud of another person in his life and the lump in his throat could not be washed away with any amount of wine.

In the end, he might as well have taken Tilda to McDonald's for all the attention he'd paid to the food. He honestly couldn't have said what he'd ordered or what color the wine had been that they'd drunk, though he was relatively certain he'd noted the bottle had cost him five hundred dollars when he glanced at the bill.

In the car, he scooted Tilda close to him and murmured all the wicked things he planned to do to her when they got home. She suggested a few of her own, which only intensified the heat that had sprung up the moment she'd walked out of that dressing room. Or, if he was being honest, he'd been hot for her since this morning, when he'd woken up next to her after a night of holding hands while they slept.

When they spilled through the front door, laughing over a joke Tilda had made, he almost swept her up in his arms so he could carry her upstairs. It would be the fastest route to getting her out of that amazing teal concoction so he could lick the gooey center of his treat.

But an envelope on the sideboard caught his eye. That was where the housekeeper put ultraimportant items she'd deemed worthy of his immediate attention, and a sixth sense told him he should heed the recommendation. Clasping Tilda's hand so she couldn't escape, he led her across the foyer. Exactly as he'd hoped, the return address was the immigration bureau.

"Fantastic," he said. "This should be the approval of my petition."

The response had been pretty fast in the grand scheme of things. He picked up the envelope and tore it open, scanning the first line. The envelope fluttered to the floor from his suddenly nerveless fingers as he reread the words over and over.

"Warren. What is it?" Tilda asked, concern crowding her eyebrows together.

"Denied," he said flatly and handed her the paper. "They've had an influx of applicants due to the immigration uncertainties going on right now, and they're not approving any new petitions for the next six months until some of the new regulations can be ironed out."

"What?" All the blood drained from Tilda's face. "What does that mean?"

She had to leave.

"We got married for no reason." Lightheaded all at once, he rubbed at his temples. "With all the illegal immigration talk in the news lately, it never occurred to me that the department would be in such flux."

Denied. His petition had been denied.

Tilda couldn't apply for a green card at this point. They hadn't even gotten that far. None of this mattered, not talking over a glass of wine, not the budding confidence Tilda had gained, not the way she looked at him sometimes, as if he was a hero.

"I don't understand," Tilda whispered as her eyes scanned the page. "We're married. What if I was pregnant? That wouldn't make a difference to them? We'd still be split up?"

"What?" Dumbfounded, he pushed the paper away and grabbed Tilda's hand, his gaze tight on hers as he filtered through her expression seeking more information. "Are you pregnant? You can't know that already. Can you?"

The very foundation of the earth started to spin as he internalized the vast and unforeseen complications that had just been dropped in their laps, if so. The sense of awe and wonder had no place in his gut when there were too many other things to worry about.

Pregnant. Tilda could even now be pregnant with his child and—

"No!" She shook her head. "I'm saying *what if.* God, could you imagine?"

Yeah, he could, and that was part of the problem. All of this was a problem. He shouldn't be this devastated. What were they going to do? They'd only just started discovering all the wonders of their relationship. She'd held his hand all night long—more than once. It was a huge stride and it was so sweet.

"I'm sorry, Warren," she said quietly. "I know how important this project is to you."

Project?

He stared at her for a full minute before it registered that she was apologizing because the petition denial meant the project was in jeopardy. The fact that he hadn't even considered the project swirled through his gut.

He was in trouble. Big time.

For the first time in his life, the vow he'd taken in college felt extremely precarious. Panic swirled through his gut and he couldn't even lie to himself that it was due to the imminent danger of breaking the pact—it was all because he *could not lose her.*

"Yes. That's true." He squeezed his eyes shut, but the project didn't magically become the most important part of this equation. That was not a good thing. "We can do it remotely. It'll be fine."

It would not be fine. It would be horrific. He couldn't touch her through a screen. Tilda would be thousands of miles away where he couldn't kiss her whenever he felt like it. She wouldn't be in his bed. Worst of all, she wouldn't be the author of his stolen moments of happiness. The ones he didn't deserve but had come to want. Fiercely.

"Fine? Are you serious?" She stared at him, a shadow dropping over her expression. "I can't go back to Australia. What can we do to fight this?"

"Nothing." His voice sounded hollow, even to his own ears. "We shouldn't fight it. There's no reason you can't work with the Australian contacts there and the American ones via video calls. People do it all the time."

The faster she left, the better. The sooner he could get her out of the nooks and crannies of his soul, which shouldn't be such a hard task to contemplate...

But it was.

All the more reason to get her gone. This was all on him. He'd pushed her into his bed, never realizing how deep things would ultimately go.

He'd lost sight of her importance to Flying Squirrel. Distance could give that back to him. Maybe this petition denial was a blessing in disguise. Her leaving was the only thing that would work.

"I'm not *people*, Warren," she choked out and he glanced at her, finally pulling himself out of his own head long enough to note that the panic going on wasn't all on his side. Her face was still white and her hands were trembling. "Bryan is in Australia."

Oh, God. He hadn't even considered how terrifying it must be for her to contemplate the idea of facing her ex again. "You're so much stronger now than you used to be. Surely the time we've spent together helped?"

She shook her head, her mouth a firm line. "I can't. I cannot go back to Australia."

So all the strides they'd made—that he'd made with her, denying his own needs and desires until she was ready—none of that mattered.

Of course it didn't. He had no business letting his bleeding heart run this show. "I'm not sure what choice we have."

"That's it?" Baffled, she glanced up at him, her eyes wide and rapidly filling with tears. "You can't call someone, or fly me to Canada or England? Surely there's someplace in the world we can go—"

"*We* can't, Tilda." Before she could spin more fairy

tales that could never come true, he had to cut her off. He was the CEO. Flying Squirrel was his life. "If you want to go someplace that's not Australia, we can look into it. But I can't come with you. You know I have to stay here."

And in that moment, a part of him knew he'd have given it all up for her. Which was why this *could not* be happening.

It was an impossible quandary. He wanted things to be the way they had been, where there were no choices and he'd been forced into this bit of wonderful for reasons beyond his control.

"So, all of this is over?" she whispered. "You're done with me now that your project has taken a hit?"

"All of what is over? Our marriage, definitely. That's all there ever was. Now there's no need for it. What else are you looking for?"

The distance in his voice was perfect. Exactly what he wanted. It matched the numbness and vast empty spaces inside that he'd only recently realized were Tilda shaped.

"I...don't know." She crumpled the paper in her hands and held it tight in her fist. "Some indication that you haven't just been leading me down a path to nowhere. You've been so kind and I thought... Well, it doesn't matter now, does it?"

"You thought what? That I might have feelings for you?" He clamped down on the truth before he blurted out things that wouldn't be good for anyone in this situation and shook his head. "I told you about Marcus. What did you think was going to happen, knowing I took a vow?"

Certainly not that he would fall in love with his wife. If he couldn't have predicted that, how could she?

She nodded. "I get it. Everything is a means to an end for Flying Squirrel. The people involved are just incidental."

And with that, she turned and walked upstairs without a backward glance.

Somehow, Tilda was not shocked that Warren followed her to her bedroom.

"This conversation is not over," he told her as he stood at the door, his arms crossed over his incredibly hard heart.

She had to pack. Blearily, she tried to think about where she'd put her suitcases in the cavernous room, but her brain was as frozen as the rest of her. "What else is there to say?"

"What are you going to do? Let me help you figure it out."

"Because I'm your employee? Or your wife?"

What did it matter? She already knew the answer. He was Warren Garinger, CEO of Flying Squirrel. Despite the fact that he'd told her he cared, anything she'd let herself believe—including that—was a lie.

"You're both," he argued. "That was the deal from the beginning. I couldn't have one without the other."

"Right. If my visa hadn't been messed up, the wife part wouldn't have happened." She'd have missed all the gloriousness of being with Warren: his patience, his selflessness. The terrace. This dress.

Falling for him.

"And I wouldn't have you as my wife unless you'd been my employee first."

He came into the room, treading across the carpet slowly, as he'd done from the first. Even now, he was still patiently working through her triggers, as if he *cared*.

Why would he tell her that he paid attention because he cared and then send her back to Melbourne where the worst nightmare imaginable awaited her?

"Tell me what you're thinking," he prompted again. "You don't have to do this alone."

"Don't I?" She surprised them both by laughing bitterly. "What are you offering me this time?"

Halting well shy of touching her, he took her measure. "To help. I'll put you up in an apartment anywhere you like. Name the country. You can go there as if you're on vacation, and the moment you have to leave due to any immigration issues, you can go someplace else."

If she couldn't stay here—and the letter was frighteningly clear on the fact that she couldn't—it didn't matter where she went. Because Warren wouldn't be there. It was an inescapable fact that he'd become her whole world. Of course, the job was important, too, and yesterday, she'd have said it was more important than anything. But in light of the hole in her gut due to these new circumstances, to say so would be skirting the truth.

She was in love with him. Against her will. If only she hadn't come to him with her need for a new dress, he wouldn't have told her he cared and opened up hopes in her heart that had no place there. She'd been fighting her feelings just fine until that had happened.

"So, I'd be living out of a suitcase at the whims of the country's immigration laws." That sounded like the opposite of what she wanted. Anything that wasn't staying in Raleigh with Warren sounded like hell. "I can't think about this now. I just want to go to bed."

And then, tomorrow, she'd have to leave the US. It wasn't like she had a lot of time to comply with the immigration bureau. Thanks to Warren's petition, they knew who she was, where she lived and who she worked for. And when her visa had expired, which was weeks ago.

"I need to know that you're going to be safe." Warren surged forward to grip both of her arms. The automatic recoil she couldn't control threw a heavy wrench into the works. Instantly, he dropped his hands with a curse. "God, Tilda, I'm sorry. I don't know why I did that."

"It's okay," she whispered and rubbed at her arms where he'd grabbed her, not because it hurt but because it wasn't okay. She wasn't okay.

How many more clues did she need that they'd never work? Inside, where it counted, she didn't trust anyone, obviously. The scars went too deep.

Even if he'd professed his undying love, it wasn't fair to saddle him with a wife who couldn't stop herself from jumping when her husband did something as simple as reach out to express his concern. Leaving suddenly felt like her salvation, not the end of their relationship, as she'd been painting it.

There was nothing to end. There'd have to have been a real relationship between them in order for there to be anything to kill.

"I'll go back to Melbourne," she said dully as her heart sheared neatly in half. "I have family there. I can work remotely until the project is complete, as you've specified. You'll send the divorce papers via courier when you have them drawn up?"

"Are you sure that's best? What about your ex?"

"I'll get over it. I'm nothing if not professional. You'll get your market share in Australia, as promised, so don't worry about the project."

She couldn't let him know that she was breaking down inside. That's when it was the worst. When a man got the information he could use to really hurt you.

His expression didn't change, but the distance between them increased exponentially. The very atmosphere grew icicles as he stared at her. "That's great. I do want to get my money's worth."

Ironic how she'd fallen for two very different men. One clung to her like a cocklebur and the other couldn't hold on to anything outside of his bottom line.

Something must be wrong with her that she couldn't find a man in the middle, who understood that she stood firmly in the middle, too—one foot in each camp between proper and provocative.

Warren had been that man for a far-too-brief blip in time.

No. That had been an illusion. Good thing. She couldn't imagine the conversation if her residency status had gone differently.

Because, in the end, if he'd asked her to stay married after she got her green card, she wouldn't have refused.

Ten

Get over it.

The phrase haunted Warren. Had haunted him for a decade. But it had been fresh on his mind all day, courtesy of Tilda, who was on her way to the airport in his limo.

Without him.

Because he couldn't get his head on straight.

Tilda needed something bigger than he was capable of giving her. Obviously. After everything that he'd done and tried and bled all over, she still flinched when he forgot to be careful with her. And clearly he'd forgotten. His ham-handed qualities had been proven over and over.

Still. He could have gone to the airport with her, if for no other reason than to say goodbye. Right? They had a professional relationship that would extend for the next nine months or so. They'd be speaking by conference call on Tuesday, if not sooner, pending whether her connecting flight from LAX was delayed.

The reason why he didn't accompany her had to do with the burn in his chest, the one that made it impossible to explain he couldn't stand the thought of watching her fly out of his life. He couldn't go with her. He couldn't keep her here. It was a merry-go-round nightmare that had no exit.

How the hell had he gotten here? His nice, simple green-card marriage had exploded in his face, and he couldn't even turn to his friends for comfort because they would laugh. The word *sanctimonious* would likely come up. "I told you so" would be thrown around more than once.

The house echoed with emptiness. Or was that his heart? Both. Neither.

The staff hadn't gone anywhere and there were no fewer than five people within shouting distance. But, as always, they were invisible, keeping their distance because that's what he'd always preferred. His heart had no business feeling anything other than guilt for the sin of bleeding all over Marcus and then Tilda.

Loneliness was his due, and he'd been combating that for eons. Of course, that had been easier when he didn't have a basis for comparison. The ghost of Tilda was everywhere. In his bed, in the bathroom, at the dining table. Behind his eyelids when he closed his eyes. Thankfully, he wasn't in the habit of frequenting the terrace, so he didn't have to see it or the garden below ever again if he didn't want to.

That was a good plan. Just avoid everything that reminded him of how he'd screwed up and gotten in way too deep with the woman he'd married.

So deep that it had actually wrenched his soul from his gut when she'd flinched last night. Just as well. He didn't need it anyway. Souls were for people who didn't have a friend's suicide on their conscience.

That's why it was better for Tilda to go. He wasn't good for her. In fact, he'd let her go for her own safety, because he *did* care.

If he repeated that a thousand more times, it might sink in, too.

Morose and sick of himself, Warren barricaded the door of the study and drowned himself in work. That lasted about an hour. He'd gotten so good at delegating as he focused on the Australia project over the last three months that he had little to do. Blasphemy. There was always something for the CEO to do. He captained the whole ship, for crying out loud.

Digging into some of Thomas's reports put him in slightly better spirits. There were discrepancies in the inventory numbers. Grateful for the distraction, he fired off an email for an explanation and moved on to the next report. Five minutes later, an email popped into his inbox. Thomas's reply: I'm aware. That's why the discrepancy is explained in the quarterly report I sent out three days ago.

Warren rolled his eyes. Fine. He dug around until he found the report in the wrong folder on his desktop, read it and had to agree that the explanation seemed reasonable enough. What was the world coming to, that his brother had a better handle on the operations of the business than he did?

That was a question better left unanswered. And now he was thinking about Tilda all over again.

His phone dinged and greedily he snatched it up,

hoping for a text from Tilda that her flight had been canceled or the airport had been destroyed in a tornado. Australia had fallen off the map. Anything that meant she wouldn't be getting on a plane and going to the other side of the globe.

Jonas: Roz and Viv are doing a girl's thing tonight. They want to pick up Tilda. Okay?

He groaned. Excellent timing. Now what was he supposed to do, tell them everything?

Warren: Tilda is.

What? Sick? Busy. *Tilda is busy.* But, instead, the word gone appeared on the screen and he hit Send in the millisecond before he realized his Freudian mistake. He groaned. No point in recalling it now.

Jones: We'll be there in fifteen minutes.

They made it in ten. When Warren swung the door open after waving off the housekeeper, Jonas and Hendrix both stood on his doorstep.

Jonas held up a six-pack of longnecks. "Figured we'd come fortified. The girls went somewhere that I have absolutely no desire to hear about later, so you're stuck with us until maybe Monday."

Rolling his eyes, Hendrix barged into the house without being asked. "Such a liar. They went to a spa that shows romantic movies while they're doing nails and some such. Viv will talk about Hugh Grant when she gets home and you'll listen to every word."

"That's frighteningly true," Jonas agreed with a nod and followed Hendrix, pulling out a beer to hand to Warren, who was still standing at the door with his hand on the knob.

"Please. Come in," Warren told both interlopers sarcastically. "I insist."

"The Tilda story is a doozy," Hendrix said to Jonas in a loud whisper that deaf people in Timbuktu heard. "I told you to get two six-packs."

"I have my own alcohol." Warren shut the door because the smart-ass duo was already in the house. "Is there any chance you're going to shut up and let me sulk in peace?"

"None," Jonas and Hendrix chorused. "We can do this in the foyer or you can let us spread out in the game room. The Devils are playing."

Basketball sounded like as good a distraction as anything. Warren took the lone leather chair that reclined, leaving Yin and Yang to lounge on his couch as they jabbered about their fantasy basketball brackets.

Beer flowed, and in the middle of his second one, Warren started to relax. The name Tilda hadn't come up yet and he appreciated his friends' glaring omission of it more than he could possibly say.

They'd come right over, no questions asked, to keep him company without fully understanding why he'd needed it. Which was a trick and a half considering that *he* hadn't even known he needed them.

They were his friends through thick and thin. Even when the thickness was his own skull.

"Tilda's green card was denied," Warren muttered.

Jonas and Hendrix both glanced away from the second-half tip-off in progress on the screen, their attention firmly on him instead of the game.

"That's rough, man," Hendrix said sympathetically. "Did they say why?"

Warren nodded and threw out the legalese from the letter. "She left this morning. She'll work remotely until the project is done, and in the meantime, I don't know. Maybe I can fly down there occasionally to attend some in-person meetings. Not really sure there's a point in that, though."

His friends glanced at each other, their expressions laden with meaningful eyebrow gymnastics.

Jonas held up his beer in a pseudo toast. "You're a rock. A total inspiration. You escaped that marriage without falling in love and I have to say, I'm impressed. I'm fifty bucks poorer, but eh. Easy come, easy go."

"You bet on me?" Warren tried to get up enough energy to be mad, but pretending he wasn't thinking about Tilda was exhausting.

"Of course," Hendrix threw in. "We had a pool. Roz won. She said you'd never unbend long enough to see that Tilda is as perfect for you as if we'd ordered her from a catalog. Me, I was, like, no way it could fall apart. If she's perfect for you, she'd figure out how to pull that CEO stick out of your butt long enough for you to get there."

The circular logic made his head hurt. Especially given that he'd always thought the same thing. Tilda was a female version of himself, save one aspect—she deserved happiness. He didn't. "Get there? Where is 'there'?"

"If we have to tell you, you're hopeless." Hendrix sipped his beer and high-fived Jonas as the Devils scored a three-pointer.

They let Warren stew in his own juices for an agonizing five minutes until he muttered, "I don't have a CEO stick in my butt."

"Figure of speech," Jonas answered pleasantly, without looking at him. "And we were wrong to bet on Tilda, obviously. Sorry about the lack of faith in your ability to stick to the pact."

Was it going to feel like a hot iron poker had stabbed him in the gut every time someone mentioned her name? How was he going to manage working with her for the long term? "We can stop talking about this any time now."

"You brought it up," Hendrix reminded him. Also without looking at him, because the game was apparently tight enough to keep their attention riveted on the screen.

Geez. His friends were something else. They were supposed to notice that he was quietly coming apart and, like, care or something. "Because I figured you wanted to know, or you wouldn't be here. Your sympathetic ear leaves a lot to be desired."

As if he'd flipped a switch, Jonas swiveled on the couch, completely turning away from the TV, and Hendrix went so far as to turn it off. They both gazed at him expectantly.

That was way too much attention. His chest started to hurt.

"We were waiting for you to admit there was sympathy needed," Jonas allowed, his dark eyes warm with compassion. "You do too have a stick. You're way too proud of yourself for sticking to that ridiculous pact. I'm guessing that's why Tilda is on a plane and you're not on it with her."

"The pact is not ridiculous," Warren countered and couldn't even celebrate the fact that his temper had started simmering. It just meant that he wasn't numb, after all, and frankly, he'd prefer to continue not feeling. "Just because the two of you broke it and figured out how to justify your faithlessness to yourselves doesn't make—"

"Hey," Jonas cut in quietly. "I get that you're upset Tilda's gone. But we were not faithless to the pact. Maybe the letter of it, but not the spirit. You're missing the point. We're still here, still friends after a terrible tragedy."

"I'm not upset." They didn't even have the grace to accept that lie.

"We haven't forgotten Marcus," Hendrix added, setting his beer down on the coffee table and leaning back into the couch cushions with a contemplative expression. "I like to think that what I have with Roz is a fitting tribute to his memory. I never would have married her if I'd thought there was a chance I'd fall in love, and yet, it grew between us, anyway. Without the pact, I would still be alone and I'd have missed out on the best thing that ever happened to me."

"The key is that you have to understand when to admit defeat." Jonas jerked his head toward the door. "After the woman you've fallen in love with gets on a plane to go to the other side of the world is too late."

"I'm not in—"

Too late. It was too late. He couldn't even finish that sentence because the falsehood wouldn't form. Warren's head started to spin in time with his heart.

The pact was irrevocably broken.

He had fallen in love with Tilda. That's why all of this hurt so much.

"It's okay," Jonas said with every bit of the sympathy Warren had railed at him for not providing. "Give it a minute. You put up a good fight."

"The problem isn't that I can't admit I broke the

pact." Wearily, Warren let his head fall back against the chair. Not a problem. But not easy, either. "It's that I kept the pact for a reason."

"We all did." This from Hendrix. "I didn't want to lose our friendship. It's important to me. So I used it as an excuse to avoid what I was feeling. Jonas had his reasons, too. You're sticking to it because you can't imagine loving something more than work, I imagine."

At that, Warren's head came off the back of the chair and he glared at Hendrix. "Really? You think that's the reason? Because Flying Squirrel is more important to me than Tilda?"

Hendrix shrugged. "Seems like as good an explanation as any."

"Except it's not true. I kept the pact because it's my fault Marcus died." Something broke inside as he verbalized the thought that he'd kept quiet for a decade. He'd never uttered those words out loud.

Sitting up straight, Jonas rubbed at his temples. "Warren, Marcus committed suicide. Unless you put him up to it, it's not your fault."

"I…" *Yes.* It was his fault. What could he say to explain this decade-old crime? "I don't mean I killed him. I mean, I thought he was going to snap out of it. I believed that firmly. So I started talking to him. Looking up bits in psychology books I found in the Duke library. At one point, I read that you should pay attention to the depressed person's cues and counter the messages they're giving themselves."

You were supposed to do it nonverbally. Like the way Tilda startled easily. No big mystery how to handle that—you moved slowly and always showed your hands so she got the message that you weren't a threat.

It had worked more often than it hadn't. It was only when he'd let his temper get the best of him that he screwed up.

Like he had with Marcus.

So, frustrated with the lack of progress, he'd blurted out "Get over it," totally convinced that Marcus could have moved on from his broken heart if he'd just tried. Instead, his roommate had swallowed a bunch of pills while Warren had been at a party. Stumbling over his roommate's lifeless body just inside the door of their condo had sobered him up quickly.

Jonas heaved off the couch and sat on the arm of Warren's chair, breaching the invisible shield that had always been in place, even between friends. It should have been weird. Warren had always maintained that distance. When they went to a bar with bench seats at the table, Jonas and Hendrix shared and Warren sat by himself. As he should. Marcus had been his roommate and the empty seat next to him served as a constant reminder.

But it was nice, to have his remaining friends here at a time when difficult memories were his constant companions.

"Will it surprise you to learn that I talked to him, too?" Jonas asked. "I called his mom twice. There were a lot of people concerned about him, and all of us did what we thought was best. But in the end, the blame has to lie with Marcus. He made that decision, not you."

Intellectually, Warren knew that. But his gut was where things didn't feel right. "How can I go on and be happy when Marcus doesn't get that opportunity? It's not fair."

Hendrix sat forward on the edge of the couch. "What, like you have to punish yourself for the rest of your life for someone else's choices? Trust me when I say you'll end up miserable if you do that. You deserve to have whatever relationships you're willing to work for in life. It's that simple. This is about you, not Marcus."

Warren shook his head. "I'm not good with people. I screwed up with Tilda. She left because I can't be what she needs."

"I thought she left because of her immigration status," Hendrix said blithely. "Do tell."

Walked into that one. "I fell for her, okay? Happy now? Is that what you wanted to hear?"

Jonas made a noise in his throat. "Yeah, but only because you needed to hear it, too. You let her walk away because you're scared to be happy, not because you're not good with people. That's an excuse that won't fly here. You don't have to be good with people. Just Tilda. Are you good with her?"

So good.

And he'd let her go.

It was killing him slowly and would only get worse. "Doesn't matter. She only cares about the project. That was the last thing she said to me. Send me the divorce papers and don't worry about your market share."

"Yeah, I'm sure you jumped right on that and told her that market share meant nothing to you," Hendrix said sarcastically. "What a complete and utter shock that any woman who's spent more than five minutes in your company could possibly be confused about your feelings for her versus Flying Squirrel."

"You don't have to be an ass about it," Warren muttered.

The point wasn't lost on him. Tilda's parting words had been a far more painful variation of *Why don't you marry your company?* Every woman in his life had butted up against his workaholic tendencies. Tilda didn't have any special shield against it just because she was as enthusiastic about work as he was.

"Seems like that's the only way to get through your thick skull," Hendrix said. "And while we're on the subject, here's what you're going to do. Get on a plane, go to Australia and tell Tilda you're in love with her. If she says it back, then you can spend the rest of your life figuring out how to feel like you deserve it. If you don't get on a plane, you'll spend the rest of your life regretting that you didn't. It's really not that hard."

"I can't do that." Oh, he wanted to. His heart rate tripled as he envisioned doing exactly that. But he couldn't. What if he forgot about her triggers and grabbed her again? He might destroy her the same way he had... Marcus.

No. That wasn't his fault. Greedily, he clung to that absolution from his friends.

Except it wasn't sticking. He'd messed up with Tilda, too. Clearly, he wasn't good at this kind of thing.

Groaning, he put his head into his hands. Either he believed the things his friends were telling him or he didn't. Getting past this was as much his decision as it had been Marcus's to take his own life, and all at once, Warren didn't want to take on the responsibility for other peoples' choices. Just his own.

And he was choosing happiness.

No, he hadn't bothered to try with Tilda. He'd just

sent her back to Australia to protect himself from further screwups. But what if they could work through her triggers? If she even wanted that. How would he know her mind unless he talked to her? It didn't have to be hard. Like Hendrix had said.

He'd made a mistake in letting her go. The biggest one of his life. And that was a turning point, as well, considering that, for the longest time, he'd have said failing Marcus was his biggest mistake. No longer. He could fix *this* mistake.

"You guys need to leave," he said to them both as he stood, nearly toppling Jonas from his perch on the armrest. "I have a very long flight ahead of me."

Melbourne welcomed Tilda in much the same manner as it had seen her off—with little fanfare. Of course, she'd sneaked away to the US without telling anyone but her mum and had landed at Tullamarine upon her return as quietly as possible.

No point in stirring the pot. She had enough on her plate, what with nursing a bruised heart and a job that she still had to do alongside a man she was trying to forget. Adding Bryan McDermott into the mix would not make things any better. But if he stayed true to form, he'd find out she was home soon enough.

Oddly, she was too numb to remember what it felt like to be so fearful of him. As the taxi drove down her mum's quiet street, the only thing she could focus on was how much she did not want to be in Melbourne, but for far different reasons than the ones she'd expected.

She missed Warren. She'd fallen in love with his house, his smile, the way he held her hand as they slept because he'd somehow figured out she didn't like waking up with his arm across her chest. But she liked being connected to him and he'd known that, as well. Somehow.

Too bad his sixth sense hadn't extended beyond that. He obviously had no clue she'd fallen for him, and how she'd hidden it, she had no idea. But she'd pulled that off brilliantly, hadn't she? He didn't have to contend with a mess of a wife much longer.

Mum was waiting for her at the door, blubbering about how thin Tilda was, the pastiness of her complexion and a multitude of other sins that needed to be fixed right away, apparently.

"I'm fine, Mum." Tilda dropped her bag in the entryway of the small clapboard house at the end of a neat row of similar houses. "I'm tired. I need to sleep."

She had no idea what time it was or when she next had to be on the phone with Warren. Or how in the world she'd handle that when the time came. Melbourne wasn't nearly far enough away to dull the ache that just thinking about him caused.

Falling into the bed located in the small guest bedroom, Tilda let her eyes drift shut, craving the oblivion. When she came to, it was midafternoon and Mum was nowhere to be found. The note on the dining room table said she'd gone to the market and would be back soon.

A knock came at the front door. For a half second, she hesitated—Warren's staff opened the door, not the lady of the house. But she wasn't the lady of any house anymore, and Warren was thousands of miles away. Blearily, Tilda crossed the small living room to answer it.

"Forget your key, Mum?" Tilda asked with a small smile as she swung open the door.

All the blood drained from her head. *Bryan.* Standing on her mother's doorstep as if he had all the right in the world to be there. Struggling to breathe, she gulped air and tried to get her legs to move. Her arms. Something. *Slam the door*, her brain screamed. *Shut it. Right now.*

"Nice to see you, Tilda," he said in that menacing voice she heard in her nightmares.

No! He couldn't be here. Not so soon. How had he learned she was back so quickly? This was ten times worse than she'd ever imagined. He must have people at the airport. Or listening devices on her mother's phone.

"I can't say the same."

Good. Okay. She could talk. She could breathe.

If she slammed the door in his face, would he break it down? She had to think. Distract him. Call someone.

"I've been waiting for you to come back," he said. "We have unfinished business."

That put her back up. What was unfinished? He'd stripped her of everything, and only because she'd wanted her confidence back had she gone in search of it. Warren had given her that and so much more. He'd given her purpose. Meaning. The freedom to be herself.

Actually, Bryan was right. They did have unfinished business. "So, you've come to apologize?"

He blinked. "I'm here to collect what's mine."

"A black eye? That's the only thing that you'll leave here with."

Had that really just come out of her mouth? A quiet

sense of pride joined the sick fuzzies in her stomach, nearly settling it at the same time.

Confidence. She knew what it felt like now and this was it. Bryan wasn't stealing it from her again.

"Are you threatening me?" Bryan asked as if he couldn't quite believe it. "If you so much as touch me, I'll have you arrested. You know I can make your life miserable."

She crossed her arms and leaned on the doorjamb, letting a small smile play about her mouth. "So, you're saying you'd be willing to testify in a court of law that a woman half your size clocked you?"

That sounded like fun. She might even do it just to see if he'd actually follow through with calling his buddies to do his dirty work.

He blinked again. "No. That's not what I'm saying."

"Too bad. I'd love to see the looks on the faces of the guys on your squad when you tell them you let a girl punch you and wouldn't they please run over to arrest her."

Bryan took a step back and it was every bit a retreat, whether he realized it or not. "You wouldn't punch me."

"Won't I?" She swept him with a scorn-filled glance, seeing him for the coward he was. The power of it roared through her, sweeping away cobwebs she'd long grown accustomed to. "I've been in America, as I'm sure your sources informed you. I learned a lot of things about how to protect myself. I wouldn't be too sure what I would and wouldn't do, if I were you."

And it wasn't even a total lie. She had learned a lot about how to pick up her pieces. No matter what, Warren had renewed her faith in herself. And given her the ability to talk down to her former abuser, apparently.

It was not her fault he'd hit her. Not her fault he'd been jealous and possessive.

And she was not taking his crap ever again.

"This is not over," he warned as he stepped back once again. "We're not over. You're mine and—"

She slammed the door and locked it. Sure, he could probably bust through the wood frame easily, but she didn't think he would. She'd stood up to him with stellar results, the likes of which even she couldn't believe.

Warren had given her back her life in more ways than one.

"Tilda," Bryan called through the door. "I—"

"Go away, you piece of garbage. I have my phone in my hand and I will call the authorities to have you picked up for trespassing." It wasn't an idle threat. Surely there would be someone on the Victoria police force who wasn't in Bryan's pocket and would be willing to uphold the law. She'd keep dialing until she found that person.

It went quiet outside and she peeked through the curtain to see Bryan slinking back to the gutter he'd come from. The victory was a little hollow but it was still a victory.

She ate dinner with her mum and didn't think about Bryan at all. Until the next day, when he knocked on the door again while her mother was getting her hair done.

Marching to the entrance, she flung open the door.

"You can't be here." As she met the gaze of the man on her mother's doorstep, her knees went weak.

Warren. Not Bryan. So not Bryan she couldn't even process it.

"I know." Warren held up his beautiful hands as if to ward her off, and why wouldn't he? She'd practically attacked him before even getting the door open. "I should have called. I'm sorry."

"No. It's fine. I thought you were…someone else." But on that note…she slid a once-over all the way down his body, drinking in his wrinkled slacks and the shirtsleeves rolled to the elbows. "Why are you here? You're really here, right? This is not a figment of my overactive imagination?"

The caution eased from his face as he smiled. "Really here. I flew all night on Roz's father's private jet."

Her mouth might have been hanging open. "Why?"

"Because that was the fastest way to get to Australia. And you," he said simply, and everything else in the world melted away as she stared at him.

Her heart threw itself out of her chest and latched onto him greedily, lapping up every bit of his nearness.

"You told me to get on a plane," she reminded him and pushed back the sudden desire to jump into his arms. Their horrible parting still sat in her stomach like a rock. "Only for you to follow me? You're not making any sense."

Clearly flustered, he ran his fingers through his hair, and that's when she noticed he didn't have his cell phone in either hand. Her well-trained eye didn't locate it in either of his front pockets, either, which meant it must be charging in the long limo behind him. That or the apocalypse were the only two things she could think of that would pry his phone out of his hand.

"Only because I'm exhausted and all I can think

about is how much I want to kiss you," he said, and his small smile shouldn't have warmed her as much as it did.

"Oh, I get it," she said before he could say some more things that would make her forget how hopeless it was to think they could be together. "You came to Melbourne for a few days to micromanage the project. The idea of me handling all of it here at ground zero without you in the middle must have really freaked you out. Nice that you can combine your first love with a little side action, courtesy of your project manager."

"Please, Tilda." Warren shook his head, his eyes warm with some emotion she couldn't fathom. "Listen to me. I shouldn't have started with kissing. I haven't slept because I spent the entire flight working out the details for Thomas to take over as CEO."

"You…what?" Her brain was having trouble processing, obviously. "Does CEO stand for something other than what I think it does? Chief Energy Officer?"

He rubbed at his temple as if she was giving him a headache. "It means I gave him the reins. I walked away from Flying Squirrel. There's no Down Under Thunder project anymore. Well, I mean, I guess Thomas can pick it up if he wants—"

Her lungs seized, and she tried to inhale and exhale at the same time, then choked on it. Coughing, she held up a finger to Warren who had a tinge of panic coloring his expression.

"Hold on," she wheezed. "I swear it sounded like you just said you walked away from your company."

"That is what I said. Tilda…" Warren held up a hand, fingers spread, and then dropped it. "I forget that I don't have the right to touch you anymore. It's automatic now to broadcast every move I make when I'm around you, but my muscles didn't get the message that I screwed up and let you go."

She felt his words in her bones. "I don't understand anything you're telling me right now. You gave Thomas the company and got on a plane to Australia to manage a project that doesn't exist anymore?"

"I got on a plane to follow the woman I love."

And that simple phrase changed everything, including the will to stay so far away from him.

"I think you better come in." She opened the door wider, but as he crossed the threshold, she planted herself in his path so neatly that he almost bowled her over. The only way to keep them both off the ground was for him to throw his arms around her, which— not so coincidentally—was what she'd been going for.

"Price of admission," she told him, and his grip tightened, hefting her closer until she fit into the grooves of his body like a second skin. Perfect.

God, he felt so good. Solid, warm, everything she'd been missing, and here he was, in her arms. She shouldn't be so free with her affections, not when he'd ended everything so easily with scarcely a goodbye wave. But he'd followed her, and that counted for a lot.

"I had a whole apology planned out," he said, his voice rough with emotion. "But I'm having a hard time remembering it."

"This is pretty good as apologies go."

That's when he pulled back to catch her gaze in his and she nearly growled in frustration as his heat left her.

"No. It's not. I was stupid to let you go. I should

have told you that I was falling in love with you the moment I realized it."

That was even better than an apology. "Say it again."

"I love you, Tilda Garinger. Assuming you're okay with taking my name and making this a real marriage. I know we have so many things to work through. I haven't been as understanding about your triggers as I could be. If you'll forgive me, I'll spend the rest of my life standing by your side as we work through whatever we need to. I won't abandon you to deal with this alone. I promise."

"You didn't," she protested weakly, still stuck back on *a real marriage*. "You were always patient with me. More than I deserved."

She hadn't wanted to burden him with her problems. But only by coming home could she have dealt with the last remnants of her nightmares. And she had. The blackness inside had lifted, leaving her wide open to accept the things he was telling her.

"You deserve whatever you need to get to a place where we can be together," he told her fiercely. "I'm all in. We can live wherever you feel the most comfortable. Greece, Italy, Canada. You pick. I'm at your complete mercy."

It dawned on her that, once again, he was giving her complete control over their future, and that broke the last of her barriers. "I don't care. As long as I'm with you, we'll make it work."

That's when he kissed her. Fiercely. Possessively. And she loved the idea of being claimed by a man like Warren.

Happily-ever-after was in her reach this time.

Epilogue

In the end, Tilda couldn't pick just one place to live. When Warren handed her the world, she took it. And he had never been happier that he'd gotten on that plane in search of a permanent do-over.

For two people who couldn't have properly spelled *vacation* a month ago, Tilda and Warren were making up for lost time. The word *work* was never uttered. By either of them. He'd sent Roz's father's plane back to Raleigh and bought his own so they'd never run out of options for travel as they tried to figure out what country they wanted as their permanent residence. Since he'd left his cell phone on the nightstand at his empty house in the States, there was nothing to distract him from doing the thing he'd come to enjoy the most: buying his wife clothes.

The city of Milan as a whole appreciated Warren's

money. He'd spent more of it on custom-made Italian lingerie, dresses and shoes for Tilda than he had on the entire Down Under Thunder campaign. Which was fitting, in his mind. She was worth far more than any success Flying Squirrel had to offer.

As they had dinner on the private terrace of the four-story villa Warren had rented in the center of Piazza Giulio Cesare, an exclusive area of Milan, he couldn't help but take a moment to drink in the sight of her beautiful face. Tilda had twisted her hair up into one of her loose chignons, which she only did with the express intent of having him undo it later.

He always undid it later. And sometimes he couldn't wait. Like tonight. He needed to touch all that hair. Dinner would still be there after.

Automatically, he fanned his fingers to be sure she saw him reaching for her, then pulled the clip free. She shook her head with a smile, letting hair rain down her back.

"It's one of those nights, is it?" she asked—rhetorically, as she'd already slid out of her chair on her way to his.

Boldly, she climbed into his lap, dinner apparently forgotten on both sides. She settled into her favorite position—on top—and framed his face with her hands to hold him still while she kissed him. He let her. There was nothing that turned him on more than when his wife took control of her pleasure.

The house phone rang, enough of a rarity that it distracted him from the warm, sexy woman burrowing through his clothes to get their skins touching as fast as possible. Normally, he'd ignore everything but Tilda, but he'd been expecting a call.

Standing easily with Tilda in his arms, he carried her into the house to set her on the back of the couch, her legs still wrapped around his waist as he answered the phone that was sitting on the end table. As he'd hoped, it was his private detective calling, and he listened to the man with half an ear as Tilda got very intrigued by this new position he'd unwittingly found for her.

Warren barely had two brain cells left to rub together when she started unbuckling his pants, stroking him through his underwear. Finally, he got the chatty detective off the phone and let his wife's busy hands finish the job she'd started, namely to drive him insane.

Quickly, she got him good and primed, and within moments, they were both moaning their way through a spectacular finish against the back of the couch. As he crested in a glorious climax, he pulled her into his arms and held on. She returned the favor, keeping him on earth with her solid, amazing presence alone.

"Let me take you to bed," he told her hoarsely, and she nodded, but once he got her there, all he could do was look at her, touching her face reverently as he worshipped her with his gaze. "I love you."

"I love you, too," she returned sweetly. "Sorry I made you get off the phone."

"You should be. I barely got the information I needed in order to give you the good news."

"I like good news. Tell me."

"McDermott is in jail." Finally. All of his efforts to get the case against her ex buttoned up had worked. Warren could give her closure to that nightmare, once and for all.

Her brows shot up. "I hope he finds a very nice boyfriend in prison. One who treats him as well as he treated me. And I'll thank you to never mention that filth to me again."

He smiled. His wife's strength was amazing, and her confidence was one of her sexiest qualities. "Done. Now that you're free from that terror, what would you like to do next?"

"Sweetheart, I was already free." Tilda kissed him gently and she poured so much emotion into it that the backs of his eyelids pricked. "I wouldn't have agreed to a real marriage with that still hanging over us. I never want the past to overshadow the present. Or our future."

And that was the best endorsement of love with a capital L that Warren had ever heard.

* * * * *

COMING SOON!

We really hope you enjoyed reading this book. If you're looking for more romance, be sure to head to the shops when new books are available on

Thursday 4th April

To see which titles are coming soon, please visit

millsandboon.co.uk/nextmonth

LET'S TALK
Romance

For exclusive extracts, competitions
and special offers, find us online:

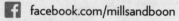 facebook.com/millsandboon

 @MillsandBoon

@MillsandBoonUK

Get in touch on 01413 063232

For all the latest titles coming soon, visit
millsandboon.co.uk/nextmonth